# TO WARM THE
# Earth

# DAVID BELDEN

# TO WARM THE Earth

Book II of the *Gendering* Series

 VIVISPHERE PUBLISHING · NEW YORK

Cover Design by Jay Cookingham

ISBN 1-58776-056-8
Library of Congress catalog number: 2001094474
Printed in the United States of America

**VIVISPHERE PUBLISHING**
A division of NetPub Corporation
2 Neptune Road, Poughkeepsie, NY 12601
www.vivisphere.com    (800) 724-1100

# Acknowledgements to the First Edition, 1988

Some of the books I read while writing this, concerning goddess worship and gender, were so stimulating I wish everyone who enjoys this novel would consider reading them, too. Particularly Starhawk's books, *The Spiral Dance* and *Dreaming the Dark*. Also Marilyn French, *Beyond Power*, Gerda Lerner, *The Creation of Patriarchy*, Barbara Walker, *The Women's Encyclopedia of Myths and Secrets*, Rosemary Reuther, *Sexism and God-Talk*, Karen Armstrong, *The Gospel According to Woman*, and Alain Danielou, *Shiva and Dionysus*.

I learned much too at Sally Abbott's class, The Myths and Legends of the Goddess, at U.C. Berkeley Extension, and first heard Rilke's poem *The Panther* there.

Many people read part or all of the manuscript, and my gratitude for all their comments is heartfelt, even if I was stunned at the time. Thanks to Debi Clifford, Hilary Belden, Jim Breeden, Ed Fourt, Virginia Irvine, Alex Edwards, Sally Abbott, Mary Teetor, Gloria Oberste, Steve Ryals, Michael Grieg, Henry Hitz, Mark Lapin, Naomi Cooper, Melinda Dart, Jo-Anne Rosen, Leslie Holmes, Marta Randall and her short story class on the first chapter, and of course my agent, Virginia Kidd, and editors, John Silbersack and Christopher Schelling. Thanks also to Leslie Holmes, Ed Fourt, and Carol Buchanan for other equally useful help.

*Acknowledgements to the Second Edition, 2002*

I told how this novel and its prequel, *Children of Arable*, were previously published and marketed in my acknowledgments to the Vivisphere edition of that novel. Now both novels have a second chance. Republication offered me a rare opportunity to make the first two novels read and flow better. Scenes were added or changed. This year I am radically rewriting the third (unpublished) novel, and have had to alter various things in the first two to make them conform. I believe both will be understood in a different light when the third is published. So I owe a great debt to Peter Cooper for seeing the value in these books and inspiring me to rework them, and to all at Vivisphere, especially Teal Hutton, Jay Cookingham and Chris Thurtle, for publishing them.

One reviewer questioned why the tense changes in this book. I don't know if he spotted that it is the first chapter of each part that is in the present tense. I saw these moments as images. I would have painted them if I could. So, you are warned.

*For Debi*

# TO WARM THE Earth

# *Part One*

## EARTH

*Earth, Terra Station*
*Years of the Migration 2103 - 2108*

# snow tiger

From the pearly twilight to the owl's first shadow, all in the evening village seems normal. The children are playing in the snow. Hunters and foresters tramp from the steam house to their homes, drawn by the good smells of bread and stew. After the sun's few warming hours, a wind straight off the Himalayan icecap starts to rebuild the icicles at the edge of every dripping shingle roof.

In the poorest home in the village, the mother looks at her eldest daughter with dismay. For once the mother has found the energy to cook, to give her hard-working daughter a rest. But what does the girl do? She works. She sits cross-legged in the corner feathering another arrow. Such an overdeveloped sense of duty. It's deliberate, of course, thinks the mother. It's a reproach. Such concentration for an arrow. It is a way of saying, or of not saying: 'For once Mother is making dinner, but I will not lie around like she always does.'

Almost faint from the stuffy heat of the one-room cabin and from the unaccustomed effort of cooking, the mother stirs the pot on the charcoal stove. Turnips, barley, and salt fish. Winter food.

She knows why her daughter is reproachful. It is because the young are hard-hearted. They know nothing of the misfortunes that can sap a person's energy even though, according to the crones in the forest, she has no specific illness.

Crazy grandmother pokes the fire. But Bilqis, the mother, can see from the wizened old woman's sly looks that she's not too crazy to know what mother and daughter are thinking.

Bilqis turns to her two younger daughters, happily playing jacks by the fire. Their laughter suddenly makes her smile. The prettier one, Romila, aged thirteen, looks up and reflects Bilqis's smile back to her. Romila finds joy even when everything's a mess. Romila loves the boys and they love her, she puts ribbons in her hair and plants flowers round the house, and she doesn't complain about helping her mother. Her smile says she loves her mother. The lift to her heart makes Bilqis taste the stew. It needs a lot of pepping up. She looks along the shelf of herbs and spices and realizes that Anam, her eldest, has put writing on every stoppered clay pot.

Typical. What does a poor forester and mother's helper need with writing? Oh yes, once, long ago there might have been a need of it. Once, before the Goddess withdrew her blessings from Bilqis and her motherline. Before the family's grove of massive oak trees, the greatest in all the villages for three days' walk around, burned. Ever since that day there has been no chance for Anam to become a priestess. But the girl still dreams of it. Whines. Pleads. Puts writing on herb jars. Keeps furious silence while meticulously managing everything, which she does just to show up her mother's inadequacies.

The stew is forgotten. In that one fire twelve years ago Bilqis's status dropped to nothing. She became the woman who could not even look after her family's sacred trees. All her relatives shunned her for shaming them. Three years later the roof of the big old house she grew up in collapsed from rot and beetle. Her husband returned long enough to help her build this pathetic cabin and put another child in her belly, and then left on his wanderings. 'Connection man,' indeed. Big-mouthed tramp. Bringer of news and weaver of pompous philosophical connections through all the forests of Mother Ganga and beyond. A dreamer. That's where his eldest daughter got it from.

Bilqis glares at the young woman who sits cross-legged in the corner, dressed in supple forest leathers, trousers and jerkin sewn from a deer she shot herself, at work on her arrow. The girl is beautiful, but will she pay attention to the young men? No, she's much too grand for that. Wants to go to the Caves and join the priestesses in luxury. Why does she stay and plead and dream? Why doesn't she just go and throw herself on the priestesses' mercy? Because she fears they will reject her, the daughter of the woman who could not look after her trees, and then she will have only her duty and no more dreams. She knows I am accusing her with my stare, but she won't look up at me. She's a coward.

And where's the boy? Her youngest is always out in the snow with his friends. She told him to be in by dusk. She opens the shutter and looks out. Twilight has come and the first stars are out. But it's a normal evening. The women laugh as they bear the last water jars back from the well. As usual, they are teasing the beautiful young man who lives with his parents next door. He answers back pertly, as usual.

Earlier, at the well, everyone was worried. The news was that the crones in the forest had seen the Beast of the Goddess. He was sick, and that can mean danger. Where is that boy? Are people's memories so short? Don't they know the Goddess can bring ruin as easily as wealth? People have been doing too well for too long in this village. She bangs the shutter closed.

A moment later the door crashes open and her boy is here. He rushes in, covered in snow, leaving the door wide open as always. Aglow from his games, he comes straight to kneel and touch her feet.

"The space station's so clear tonight!" He stands up, so eager to tell. "I could almost see the people on it!"

She can't help but smile at his enthusiasm, though he must be rebuked. "Now, now. Don't let your sister hear you say that. She might report it to the teacher."

"I was only joking." He is like Romila, and they are both like she was when she was a girl, carefree with their lovely smiles.

"Some jokes the Goddess doesn't like. If that is a space station, it died when the Ice came. There are no people up there. So no more sky talk from you. Take off your boots and close the door and make amends."

Allowing no time to take off his boots or close the door, he dashes to bow to Shiva Ardhanarishvara, the Goddess Who Is Half Man, who stands proudly in bronze on the right side of the fire. It is right for the boy to bow to Shiva, as it is for the girls to please Gaia-Kali, the Mother of All the World and of all the world's goddesses, whose face is carved in red stone above the fire. These figures came from the old house, and Bilqis watches with sad pride as her boy pays them reverence.

Cold air from the open door has invaded the cabin's stuffy heat. Anam, the eldest daughter, objects. She says Grandma will take a chill. She tells her brother to close it. She ignores her mother, as if she alone has all the authority in this house.

The mother half smiles when she sees that the impulsive boy is already sitting on the floor struggling with one boot half off, disregarding both the authorities in his home other than the Goddess, to whom he has already bowed. And it was his mother's feet, not his sister's, that he touched when he came in. Who cares about a little breeze from the door? The place was too stuffy anyway.

Outside, a brief scream is cut short. The boy is talking so much about his games, he doesn't seem to hear it.

"Hush, boy. Did you hear that?"

The whole village has heard. Silence like a snowfall smothers them. In every house the banter and laughter die. So they were all keeping an ear out after all. On truly normal nights they would not have thought anything of it.

The bubbles of a growl in a broad throat rise in the twilight.

"Oh Mother," the mother whispers. She moves slowly, as if wading upstream, to close the door. "Please, Mother. Not after the trees. Not us again." The crunch of heavy pads lightly placed in the snow outside prevents her. He is here.

Filling the doorframe, white fur haloes bloodshot eyes. Snow Tiger breathes great clouds of stinking steam from the cold into the warm humanity of the cabin. His breath rasps. He is sick. The Beast of the Goddess is sick, and He has come for the easy meat.

A pillar of ice, the mother prays. She prays He will turn. Take the people next door. Take old Grandmother by the fire, but not my boy, not my girls. Take me.

Snow Tiger waits. He breathes heavily. Saliva huffs from His yellowed teeth.

All beasts are of the Goddess. All beasts are the Goddess. This Bilqis knows. But it was only when there were almost no wild beasts left, when the New Clear Winter darkened the world, when the ice sheets wiped clean the north and crushed the Himalayas beneath them, that Snow Tiger came. Snow Tiger came and the rule of the Goddess resumed. Above all the beasts, Snow Tiger is the Goddess. Bilqis is too frozen with fear and dread to pray anymore.

Snow Tiger pads into the hut with massive, careless power. There is muddy snow on His pads; there is old blood on the white of His coat; burrs are tangled in His greasy fur. He is looking at the boy.

The babbling old woman by the fire, scrawny as a senile chicken, gets up and staggers between them. One swing of the paw snaps her backbone with a crack. She dies without a word. The boy has terror in his eyes. He screams. He is smashed to the ground. Blood pours as the sacred incisors rip into his guts.

His mother stands immobile while his screams fade.

The Goddess brought peace and sense and dignity to the world

again. People had nearly destroyed the world, and they needed
Her. An insane world returned to Her hands. But She is to be
obeyed. Even in Her fearful aspects, She is to be obeyed. In two
thousand winters, no one in the North Indian forests has raised a
hand against Snow Tiger. Myths tell of some who tried. In these
forests, no one even says Snow Tiger's name.

In the corner of the room, the seventeen-year-old daughter still
sits on the ground, the half-feathered arrow across her thighs.
Now she rises to her feet with the controlled smoothness of a
hunter. She reaches behind her for her long bow of yew. The
hands that select the arrows are marked with a forester's calluses.
The arms beneath the leather jerkin are strong enough to fell a
tree or to pull a yew bow taller than herself.

For a moment of utter shock, as Bilqis realizes what her
daughter intends, time and bitter suspicion seem suspended and
she sees all clearly. She knows that poor Anam loves the brother
and the sisters she has brought up while her father traveled afar
and her mother wept for the family trees. She loves her senile
grandmother. True, she has been overly dutiful. It is her nature.
True, she has been afraid to go to the Caves to seek admission as
a priestess. But she put it off to the next solstice every time
because of love as much as duty and fear. Because her family
needed her. And now that the Mother of All has finally turned
against these ones she loves she will give herself to save what can
be saved. The boy is gone. The girls may live, though at the cost
of rending the world, of killing the Goddess. Anam is no coward.
But hers is the heroism of those driven beyond sense.

Bilqis tries to call out, "No! It is I who should do it." But she
is frozen still. Is her arm strong enough to pull that bow? Is she
ready to be disowned by Kali, to die alone, her spirit set adrift,
unanchored to the Earth?

Anam lifts the great bow slowly, at arm's length to her left
side. Her feet shuffle silently for the right balance. With her
right hand, she notches an arrow and pulls bowstring and arrow
smoothly to her shoulder. The twang alerts Snow Tiger in His

eating frenzy a thousandth of a second before the arrow slams into His heart. His bloodshot eyes pierce hers. Another arrow is in her hand already. Snow Tiger roars and leaps. The second arrow goes straight down the gaping throat. The young forester disappears beneath half a ton of fanged Goddess.

There is silence in the hut. There is silence in the village.

Snow Tiger is dead.

Anam wakes. She is crushed beneath the world. Weight, black suffocation. Heat and heavy liquid dripping. Is this the Caves already? Is this where Kali takes those who defy her? Her arm is bent at a weird angle, and the lack of pain from it seems reassuring.

She wonders which would be worse, to awake in the shadow world or in the familiar world.

She breathes and her ribs scream pain. No, please, Kali, no. Don't let me be alive.

She hears whimpering. It is her own. She forces herself to be quiet. She has awoken in the real world, and it is far worse.

One eye opens on filthy thick white hairs. The other won't open, sticky with something. She turns her head slightly to try and wipe the muck off against the fur. It is blood.

The blood of the Beast of the Goddess runs thickly on her face, down her neck, into her clothes. His stink is on her. His white fur crushes and stifles her. Her yew bow is caught between her body and His. It feels as if her ribs will snap before the bow does. But to whimper is to deny responsibility. She knows that no one will help her. As surely as if the arrow had pierced her own heart, she is dead to her family and to her village. It is as it should be. She knew that from the moment she saw Grandmother's frail spine break.

If she crawls out from beneath the holy warrior, no one will speak to her. Not her mother, not even her little sisters. Suddenly pain floods her arm and her mouth opens to scream. Instead she bites her tongue. She will not let her mother see her pain. She will not ask her pity. With her good arm she heaves up and convulses her body against the Goddess. The Beast rolls partly off her and she crawls free. Her left arm, which had held the bow out front, is the weirdly bent one, above the elbow. Will it matter? If only she can survive the pain until they leave. Her sisters sit frozen on the floor around their neglected jacks. It is only moments since she killed, then; she thought it was a lifetime.

Her mother gazes at her with the blank eyes of catatonia or trance. It is not she who gets the girls out, but the terrified girls who stagger to their feet and pull her to the door. Anam hears the commotion as her mother collapses outside and is taken away to be cared for by neighbors.

She finds she can stand. She walks slowly to the linen chest, opens the heavy lid, and rips strips from the best sheet. Grandma's stick and her brother's bat will do as splints. It is surprisingly easy to cut her leather sleeve away with her hunting knife. She can't help screaming as she turns her arm straight again. She lays the splints on the kitchen table and eventually, after many false attempts and rests to recover herself, she manages the job of splinting it. It is not good, but it will do. Do for what? Why is she doing this? Because she too is an aspect of the Goddess, even now? Or because something in her already knows that she alone cannot decide what shall be done with a living slayer of Kali in White. She will have to get herself to the Caves, and it is too far for her to travel with an unset arm.

To feel for broken ribs, she undoes the toggles that tie her jerkin down the front. The jerkin comes off and she sees with surprise why she was able to cut the sleeve off so easily. The leather shoulder is ripped to shreds. For the first time she twists her head to look at her shoulder. There are four deep gashes there. She tries to sew them but fails. There will be a massive quadruple scar, the claws of Gaia. They are flowing with blood. She uses another sheet to make an awkward binding.

Her mother and her sisters do not return. One-handed, she starts to skin Snow Tiger with her knife. It would seem to need a superhuman energy to roll the massive beast, but she finds she is still in the power with which she killed Him. No one enters. She barely hears them outside, though occasionally she realizes they are noisy in their wonder and outrage. It is impossible to skin the beast well with one hand, and yet the Goddess demands perfection. Hours go by and she is still working on the legs. She pulls the bloody pelt back with her teeth while her good hand wields the knife.

It takes her two days to skin the beast. She eats nothing, but drinks from the pitcher she had fetched before the home died.

There are no paths to follow. Nowhere is it written what she must do to heal the crack she has opened in the world. The villagers may kill her. Why have they not already? Why have the crones not come at least to chant the prayers for the dead?

She drags on her boots, ties her heavy sheepskin round her shoulders, and walks out. A dozen people stand waiting.

She takes down her snowshoes from their nail under the eaves and rights the wooden sled propped up beneath them. She feels in some kind of trance. She half wonders if it is that that makes the villagers fall back.

She pulls the light sled down the narrow lanes of the village, where mud has mixed with snow to a brown slush. Wood smoke hangs low around the wooden dwellings. At every doorway, silent faces watch her pass. She knows that the multiple aspects of the Goddess in carved and painted oak set over every door and window would rebuke with fierce, wide eyes if she so much as glanced at them. She does not.

She stops before the house of her beloved teacher, the woman who has taught her all she knows of what it would be to be a priestess. There is no reply to her knock, though she can hear people within. She sets off across the fields and into the woods, pulling the wooden sled. It is a long walk. There is smoke from the chimney of the old crones' hut. But they do not reply to her call, either. So it is true. To them, she does not exist. Is this why no tales of the slaying of Snow Tiger have ever been heard, she wonders, because the slayers ceased to exist? Surely once someone else's head burst into madness with blood and pain and made hands do what hers had done?

She collects dead branches as she returns through the snowy woods, trying to choose ones that are not too wet. She feels she must have one from each of the thirteen trees most sacred to her people. She adds each new branch to the sled, until it is as much as she can pull with one good arm. The sun should not be shining nor the birds singing on such a day as this. She tries to ignore both. But it is becoming much more difficult. Their unheeding cheerfulness seems to negate the utter sacrifice she has made of herself. The world ignores her, but it is becoming harder for her to ignore the world.

At the house, she loads the wood inside. She takes all the dry wood for the winter under the eaves and places it inside, log by log. She can tell that while she has been gone from the house, no one has entered. She understands that no one ever will. No one will ever dispose of the bodies in the desecrated house unless she does it herself.

Grandmother is cold and light as she holds her up with her one arm and buries her face in the old woman's sparse hair. She arranges her limbs carefully and brings to her her favorite things – her shawl, Kali figurine, embroidered foot-stool. She covers her brother's body with his blanket, and arranges his child's bow, rocks, and leather lace-up boots by his side.

There are words to be said, libations to be poured, incense and candles to be lit, flowers and herbs to be scattered to ease and sweeten their path back to the Great Mother.

She knows them all.

She has dreamed of being a priestess for many years. Even though the family trees burned and lowered her mother to the lowest ranks of the village, and of many villages around, still she dreamed of becoming worthy to be a priestess.

But now she never will be.

She has killed Snow Tiger. For a moment she wants to scream

out this name that she has never said aloud: what more harm can she do now? But she does not.

She sits for a long time beside the dead. She discovers her period has come. Without thinking, she starts to thank the Maiden and moves to touch first blood to the moonflower stone beside the fire, but her bloody finger hesitates and falls. She sees only the blood of Snow Tiger on her hand. Sinking before the dead fire in the freezing house, she curls up upon herself.

Finally she rises, pulls down her leather trousers and binds herself with dried, absorbent moss and a long, clean strip of cloth, pulls up the trousers again. Then she says the words the teacher and the crones have refused to say. She calls them out in a ringing voice that the Mother cannot but hear. She pours the libations and scatters the herbs and dried flowers, taken from her mother's stocks. These are herbs that she grew and picked and dried herself while her mother complained. She has no regret that her mother will not have the use of them now. She has little regret, either, that her mother will now lose her house to fire as she lost her trees so many years ago. Some people seem born to reap the Goddess's displeasure.

She does not know what to say for Snow Tiger to speed His return. She lays her yew bow and her quiver on His bloody, skinned flesh. She takes outside a few things of her own – her snowshoes, winter traveling gear, the pemmican she dried for her own use, and the heavy hide, already stiff. Back inside, she picks up the stone goddess she was given on her naming day and weighs it in her hand. ANAM, it says, carved upon its back, the name she has had all her life, and has now lost. Then she places it beside her bow on Snow Tiger. When all is done, she lights the pyre. The log cabin blazes up into Gaia's night. As she makes her way through the circling crowd of her people, who have left enough room that she can slip between them without their moving or looking at her, she sees the flames reflected in their faces.

If she tries in this moonless dark to leave for the Caves, wounded as she is, she knows she will die. She would never even

reach the first way-hut in the forest. It is an attractive thought.
To be found when the drifts clear in spring. Will they bury her
or fail to see her? But as she leaves the village and its fields and
reaches the forest edge, she passes the hut where objects for the
mysteries are stored. The door is never locked. She will be safe for
the night there. Duty rules. She must try to reach the Caves alive
with Snow Tiger's hide so that those wise and holy enough to
make amends can do so. And apart from one moment, she has
always followed her duty.

It is cramped but dry inside. She finds a candle and flint. Her
people have no temple or cave or church: the forest, the Earth are
their holy places. This hut houses those things that come alive
outside each on their own day: great wooden goddesses, sacred corn
dolls, painted papier maché snakes and tigers, shields and masks
and puppets. All cast weird shadows on the walls from her gutter-
ing candle. The Goddess Durga on her fierce lion looks down,
luridly colored, eight-armed in her furious warrior energy, ready
to slay the buffalo demon. All the statues seem to start to life in
the dancing light. Many of them are of goddesses taking revenge
on gods and men. Kali dances on Shiva and He does not rise;
Prithvi, in the form of a cow, tramples Prithu; Lakshmi on Snow
Tiger banishes Vishnu; Radha denies Krishna her bed; Hera binds
Zeus; Ceridwen breaks the atomic missiles across her mighty knee.

Her favorite is the life-size statue of Sitala, the village's protectress, who alone has no martial qualities but only love and forest
blessings of health and abundance. She tries to pray to Sitala. But
she has no words beyond "What happened . . . happened." In the
end she turns Sitala's face to the wall and throws a cloth over the
dried branches in her hands, left over from last autumn.

It is bitter cold in the hut. Her splinted arm is too big to go
into her sheepskin jacket. She works for a while cutting the sleeve
until she can pull it on. Her gashed shoulder is stiff and fiery with
pain. How far should duty go? Should she stay here for enough
weeks to cure her arm and back, so that she would certainly reach
the Caves? If she is invisible to the village, she could steal food

from them. She could even take Snow Tiger's skin down to the tanning pits and cure it so it will not be so stiff and heavy. Then she could deliver it to the priestesses for certain.

In the middle of the night she sleeps briefly and wakes terrified. The candle is out, but all the eyes of the wooden goddesses glow red. Beside her the eyes of Snow Tiger glow reddest of all. If only I can get inside, she thinks in her terror, if I can get into Him, I will ward them off. At dawn she wakes again, and finds that she is entirely wrapped in the hide of her kill. The goddesses are lifeless. She staggers upright and the heavy stiff hide stands with her, its head upon her head, dead eyes to the roof and sky. The dried blood and fat stick to her clothes, her hands, her face. She puts on her snowshoes and walks out. The hide does not drag upon the snow behind her, though it is almost twice her length: she had bunched it up around her in the night and its folds have frozen to her shape.

In the summer the trail to the Caves can be done in four days. It takes her four days just to wade through the drifts to the river, barely a third of the way. She thanks her people that they have maintained so many way-huts on the trail. It is as much as she can do to get from one to the next in the course of a day. When she arrives at each hut, there is dry wood, to be used sparingly to warm herself and dry her snow-soaked boots and leggings. There are pemmican and dried fruit. She chews meager amounts, unwilling to make her mark on what is no longer hers. There is fever in her shoulder, and at times in the nights the fever overtakes her. But somehow each day she is able to stagger out. She feels that the strength of Snow Tiger is hers. That He wants her to get Him to the Caves. That He protects her.

As she plows on every day through the drifts, she cannot help being overwhelmed by the life around her. At moments it almost makes her want to laugh, to be alive again. But mostly she takes it as a reproach against her, for she is dead. There are deer in the winter forest, herds of the throwback wild cattle they call aurochs, goatlike bharal down from the hills and occasional elk, prey for

Snow Tiger and wolf. Even lynx and red fox can make a living among the pikas and small rodents that do not sleep all through the cold months. All run from her smell, the smell of the great carnivore.

Marmot and brown bear sleep. But gray langur monkeys poke their black faces out from the branches around the old temple ruins, where the men from the village, in one of those mysteries of their own of which she knows nothing, help them survive the heaviest weeks of winter. The monkeys chatter at her, but their temple is not for her to rest in. The summer birds have gone, but their winter cousins remain: she sees tracks of snow cock and blood pheasant, is irked by laughing thrush, and finds her eye caught against her will by flashes of blue robin and rose finch. Every exhausting day she is assaulted by freezing wet, the tang of winter in the nose, and the brilliance of snow and life. In fierce contra-diction she longs more and more for the depths under the Earth, the cessation of this turmoil of plants and creatures, for the still heart of Gaia.

At last, as if in answer to prayer, the storms come down and wipe out the world of life. She plunges on, blind in whirling whiteness. That night she does not find the hut. She cannot stop. At times, neither can she keep going. She stands frozen for long minutes. But the hide of the Goddess is around her. Every time she finds the strength at last to keep moving. She could tunnel down like a bear and make an insulated cave. But she fears she would never crawl out. It is the Caves or nothing.

The night ends at last and the storm with it. There is a moment when she stands swaying in the early light and all is still, newly covered in snow, and she knows that she is charmed. For she is still on the trail, and the next hut is only half a mile farther on. And indeed she feels as if she were under some kind of charm, for she is numb and all appears to be happening at a distance. Now, when the life of the forest stirs again and the voices of a wolf pack sound nearby, she feels they are a dream, that she will wake in the Caves. Even the connection men, those hardy, perpetual travelers who link the world together when they travel the forests, prefer two companions to one and never go alone. But she has no fear. The skin of Snow Tiger is around her. His head is on her head. Even the wolves leave her alone.

She has lost count of the days when at last one late afternoon she shuffles on her snowshoes into the great clearing where the tower stands guard over the entrance to the Caves.

It is a plain, windowless, round stone tower, battlemented and severe. Two stories show above the snow. In summer it is four stories high, but two are now below the drifts. It is built so tall to give entry however deep the snow. Each story has a massive wooden door. Steps hug the side of the tower for access. Beside each door, carved in stone, tiger heads with ruby eyes and sharpened teeth glare vengefully at her. They are the dvarapalas, the guardians of the tower. She shakes before them and bows her head. Another tiger head, in brass, affixed to the oak door, holds in its teeth a heavy crescent moon with which to strike the oak.

Here the young woman who has plowed unerringly through the winter forest to this point seems to falter. Since the moment she decided to crawl from beneath the slain Goddess, she has lived for this instant. At last it is in the proper hands to decide what to do about the wrong she has done the Goddess. She will pay whatever price so that only she, and not her whole village, suffers. The dvarapalas glare down, judging her in silence. It should be a blessed relief to give up her responsibility and accept judgment. But some weakness makes her take Snow Tiger's pelt from her head and shoulder, and try to stuff it into her pack. The cold has made it entirely rigid, around the form of her body. She cannot hide it. She desperately throws snow over it to cover the head, which sticks up blindly accusing. She takes her linen shirt from her pack and covers the head. She cannot bear to come to them boldly. Let them work out what happened. Then she sinks, shaking, onto the doorstep. It seems that her strength has deserted her. It is an hour or more before she pulls herself up again, reaches up, and smashes the crescent moon in the brass tiger's teeth against the door. It booms hollowly.

There is no reply.

How many years has she longed to stand at this door? But in her dream it would have been high summer. She had hoped to take an elk or a bull aurochs as her petitionary slaying to the Caves. She had longed to be a priestess.

She crashes the moon against the oak once more, and then a desperate strength makes her beat the door repeatedly. However deep the Caves may be, she will wake them. Slowly her crashes diminish, but do not altogether cease. It is an hour or more before the sound of great metal bolts being drawn back can be heard.

"All right, all right, what on Earth is all this racket about?" A severely beautiful older woman stands there in furs. Behind her, two young women peer over her shoulder. The two carry oil lamps with an eager dignity that is a perfect mirror of her dreams. "Who are you who comes in the dead of winter, in the middle of the slow dance?"

"I have no name. I burnt my name." She was surprised how small her own voice had become.

"Such presumption! Why should we take you in? What are the trees of your family?"

"The trees of my family burnt down ten summers ago."

"Then, nameless, why do you come?"

She hangs her head. She seems about to drop from exhaustion, and one of the young priestesses steps forward to support her. But the older checks her with a rigid arm.

"What have you done to come begging our mercy in midwinter?"

At last she turns her back on the priestesses and stoops to the snow and the shirt at her feet. As in a dream, she uncovers her shame and her glory. The mouth, once slack, now seems to snarl. She places her fists inside the snarling head. Suddenly it pours energy and power into her to do this one last thing. As she turns back to them she heaves the head high above her own head. The great white pelt streaked with black falls from the terrifying visage like a stiff robe frozen in folds to the shape of a woman. She calls out in a voice that rings against the battlements and echoes in the depths below the tower:

"I have slain Snow Tiger!"

# One

When dawn woke the forest birds the next morning, the pale light fell on the tower in the clearing but did not pierce its windowless walls. Even the dawn chorus was inaudible inside. In her brief moments of clarity between restless sleep and delirium, the young woman who lay prostrate on the flagstones was thankful for this quiet dark. In a half-dream state she envisioned the Caves below her as a blessed extension of this calm: dark womb of the Mother, holding within it a deep, healing pool of black water, the tombs of the holy, and cessation of the cares and pain of the upper world.

In fact, the hundreds of rooms and tunnels that spread out in a warren southward from the forest tower had been filled all night with tumult. The news had pelted through the Caves. "A slayer of the Goddess in White is at our forest door! Joanna, the novice, threw up when she saw His glaring eyes! Even Amaterasu, the old dragon herself, could hardly find the energy to set spells on the stairway before she rushed down to get help." Pattering feet, bobbing lights, anxious arguments.

After a couple of hours, a dance began to form spontaneously in the hall of Kali Ma. It resembled the winter solstice dance, which begs the Goddess to halt the dying of the days. But suddenly the dancers snaked out into the tunnels to form the dance again before the statue of Amaterasu, Lady of the Easternmost Isles, and thence to the Cave of Ceridwen, She of the Westernmost, and then on as if seeking all the most powerful of the guardians of their realm. Soon more than three hundred dancers were joined in one motion. But still individuals came and went, to favor lesser statues with votive flame or incense.

The walls of every room and many a tunnel were graced with carvings, chiseled by the generations of priestesses who had bored downward from the upper levels with simple tools and complex devotion.

By dawn almost every image of Her had been adorned.

Favorite carvings in the middle levels had received the most attention. Their elaborate surfaces cast ornate shadows of complex symbols on the walls and ceilings, an entire language in filigree stone. But this night the spare abstracts in the deepest southern caves had also been well attended. Even in the damp, abandoned upper rooms, made in rectangles by men before the Ice and lined with dead false stone, the crudest stick figures of Her, unvisited in years, had been warmed with flames and offerings of at least a ribbon, a dried flower, a sprinkle of herbs.

The night's work had bound the countless faces of the Goddess into one. For some novices, it was the first time they had truly felt the Oneness of the Ones they served.

A crone who had felt this Oneness as personally as any living priestess shuffled her slow way along the middle level tunnels shortly after dawn. She was on her way to see for herself the terrible portent that the winter forest had ejected onto their doorstep.

Her face was ebony, her hair white. She had come long ago from Africa, but that was the least of the extraordinary aspects of this old woman. Osen, for that was her name, knew things by personal experience that no one else alive now knew. For example, she knew that people lived on the ancient space station that circled the Goddess Earth. She had not been to the space station in her body, but she had been there in the way that only her motherline could. And of this motherline, she was the last.

In all things Osen took her own unique view. When all the women, young and old, assumed that this demon on their doorstep must foretell unparalleled disaster, when all of them spent the night in feverish attempts to ward off the day, Osen became calmer and cheerier than anyone had seen her in years. She sat outside her room and watched the comings and goings down the corridor with a big smile on her wizened face. She had been foretelling disaster and the resurgence of male power for so long that some people assumed her pleasure was at being proved right. This assumption did nothing to endear her to her Cave sisters, who already saw her as a lovable old nuisance and aggravation. She did not bother to tell them that things in general were often other than they seem, that some things are far more complex and others simpler — she had said this too often before. She certainly did not say that after all her conflicts with her cold-forest sisters, she had sometimes wished she could do something as utterly shocking as shooting one of their precious tigers herself.

She chortled old African songs to herself as she shuffled up the rising tunnels and stairs toward the forest tower. She had wrapped even more garishly bright blankets around her than usual and looked something like a multicolored ball of wool with black face and white hair poking out, a madcap sheep.

She had to rest many times, but at last she reached the chill tower and came off its spiral stair at its third level: the level at which the snow outside had reached. She passed through a stone doorway set with snakeskin and tiger claw, appropriate herbs, sacred spears, and icons of warrior goddesses all set to keep the newcomer at bay. And there lay the object of so much panic, shivering and babbling in fever, wrapped in the hard, uncured skin of the Beast, surely unable to crawl another yard.

Osen clicked her tongue as she pulled off the rancid tiger skin and wiped the face of its slayer. "So young," she murmured as she took blankets from her own shoulders and wrapped them around the killer. She pulled out a skinful of a warm herbal posset she had brewed and dripped it slowly down a straw set through its stopper into the mouth of the semiconscious youngster.

Then she made haste to return to the depths, to warm up and to raise her voice against those who were starting to say the criminal should be treated as invisible and allowed to die in the tower or, better still, on the snow outside, as an example and warning to all.

It was many years since Osen had used the skills of her motherline to sway a whole cave community. She found before she was done that it was indeed far more than her voice that she had to raise to do it. She had to make the bas reliefs on the very walls appear to speak, their stone bodies to glow with vibrant color, before her sisters would consent to give their murderous supplicant the benefit of trial by fury.

"The Goddess alone can decide!" rasped the towering figure of Kali the Destroyer in the great Cave of Kali Ma. The carved skulls that hung from her body appeared to clink and sway, and blood from her fangs ran thick and red down her withered paps to drip in spreading pools upon the floor at the priestesses' feet. Surely all but the youngest present knew that Osen's bizarre mental powers were responsible for the pyrotechnics. All they had to do was turn from the awesome Destroyer to the small, wizened woman in bright shawls who leaned heavily on her staff, her fingers bony and spare around its carved-bird head.

But they did not, because her mental magic spoke the truth to them. Truly the Goddess should decide. Whether from awe or exasperation, from agreement with Osen or from their scenting in the staging of a major trial a relief from the boredom of winter, the sisterhood agreed. It was all that Osen could do, and all she needed to do, for now. She shuffled off to her room at once, leaving them to work out the myriad details and to set the severity of the test. Those who defied the Goddess were occasionally brought for such trial. And all applicants to the Caves were given some such test as initiation. So the sisterhood was well practiced in the required arts.

Only the occasional person died or went mad in a trial by fury. Gaia-Kali was magnanimous and loving, but she guarded her realm jealously. The world had already been almost lost to her once, when a supposedly civilized society had driven innumerable species to extinction and thrown the very weapons of the Sun at each other. The New Clear Winter that had followed had scoured the planet clean of that civilization. The priestesses, the connection men and village militias were vigilant to ensure no aspect of it recurred. To kill Snow Tiger was to strike at the heart of the Gaia-Kali's rule. There was no doubt that this trial would be far more severe than any in living memory.

Osen rather hoped the young woman she had seen would survive it. If she did, there might be work that she could do, if her courage was as strong as it appeared. But Osen put no great store in this hope, for she had lived too long and had been disappointed too many times. Instead she went to her room and slept a peaceful sleep until lunchtime.

The slayer of Snow Tiger knew very little of her first days in the tower. She remembered an old, black, whiskered face that she took to be a hallucination, and later found the bright woolens that had swathed that face wrapped around herself. There was the faintest glow of light from the stairwell, but otherwise it was dark, and she had no idea how long she tossed and turned on the hard stone.

She shivered and burned and felt near to death. Dying

seemed the simplest thing to do. She had only stone to look at, for she could find no strength to get up and try the bolts on the massive door that would give her a view of the white forest. Instead she saw things of her imagining: vines reached up to strangle her; a family of voles gnawed on her foot; the forest itself turned on her and wrapped her in a violent mania of greenness that compressed her at its center until her breath was all squeezed out of her and she collapsed into nothing, void, lost, where she cried "Mother! Mother! Mother!" in hopeless dwindling echoes. Occasionally a girl brought her vegetable stews, tepid after the long journey up from the hearth. The girl was her only finger on reality or sight of sanity. She was a wiry, perky little thing. "My name's Koré," she said. "I've never met someone without a name before. What was your name?"

A softly glowing ball hung from her wrist and lit her sharp face gently. The ball seemed part of a vision, but the face and the voice were too real for a dream.

"Anam," She wanted to say. "I always wanted to be a priestess. If you reverse my name, you get Mana — moon mother. I think that's why my mother named me. She had hopes for me, once." Perhaps she did whisper some of it. It was hard to tell.

"Are you dying?" Koré asked. "My mother thinks you should. Did you really kill Snow Tiger? Can I pet him?" She put out her hand, but couldn't quite touch the great white head. She was a funny little thing.

Next time she came she lugged the nameless newcomer a big warm brick to put under her blankets.

The Tiger Slayer had lost count of the days when they came for her. They were not priestesses who came, but Earth creatures, yoginis of the depths. She thought them another vision at first, with their oiled flesh smeared with dirt and their stinking, ragged furs, until they thrust a foul pelt against her eyes and tied it tightly behind her head, so she could see nothing and all she could smell was their ill-cured skins and the damp bowels of the earth. They were so rough as they dragged her down into the earth that she panicked and struggled against them. Until then she had not realized she had any strength left in her. But her strength was nothing to theirs.

After a long journey, they threw her onto sharp rocks and abandoned her. She worked off her filthy blindfold to find darkness of a thick, suffocating quality that she had never known even in dreams. It was so dark she could barely breathe. There was the sound of dripping water, but no water to drink. No food to eat. No wind or movement of air. She could not walk; her snow boots were back up in the tower, and the rock floor was cuttingly rough. There were rock walls on each side of her, but none before or behind: it felt less like a cave than a crevasse. But she would not scream. She felt sure it was a test; they would come for her.

She slept. Then she woke, her throat burning dry. She felt cautiously over the sharp rocks towards the dripping sound. She didn't have the strength to stop her knees and hands being cut. But she found the drip. There was no pool, just a wet bulge in the rock face moistened by water dripping from above. She pressed her face up against the wet rock and lapped her tongue against it. She felt as if she had passed the first test. She waited for the next.

In the dark she hallucinated gray shapes of the forest, beasts of the depths, women with aurochs heads and men with penises hot enough to freeze the world.

Hours passed, perhaps a day or more.

Then a crack in the darkness turned to mauve smoke. Colors rose through the swirls. The smoking color opened hope in the night-black world. A beckoning canal. A smoking yoni seen from womb side. She tried to rise.

Way down the crevasse there came prancing, in and out of the colored smoke, the two-legged aurochs of her hallucinations, with great horns outspread, bellowing. She shrank from them as they reached her. Their bodies reeked of pungent sweetness. They grabbed her with huge beast hands and half carried, half dragged her down the crevasse to a great cave, its edges lost in darkness. High, smoking torches spouted purple and rose flames. The air was choked with a harsh, ratlike incense.

Drums assaulted her ears after so many days in silence. Incomprehensible dramas appeared from the shadows: aurochs, birds, dragon-lizards, scientists of ancient days with their Destruction of the Large and of the Small, of the Planet and of the Gene. Once a smoke-belching, clanking, roaring engine took her on a ride to see the night sky, and indeed she thought she did see it, and the scientists' space station passing by against the stars, and she felt the wind, though still they were in the cave.

In the end she knew not what was real and what hallucination or madness drew in her mind. At one point she began to scream for an end. Scream after scream after scream against the forcible rape of her mind, until finally, all at once it was gone: not the smoke and visions — they remained — but the terror of madness. Now she was in a new plane, where it mattered not to her whether she was mad or sane, for the Goddess was everything, the sane and the mad, the Anam and the Mana, the world and the sky, the aurochs and birds and the white-coated men. There was no difference. She was in everything, and everything She was, was the Goddess, the real and the unreal, the smoke and the rock. This was an ecstasy such as she had never known before, nor ever dreamed of. The rock was her body and the caves her arms and the sisterhood her mind.

And then the aurochs picked her up as if she weighed nothing and walked a long ways and gave her, warm and stinking of incense, blood and rancid Snow Tiger fat, into the pale cold of a new cave, to Snow Tiger.

Snow Tiger was hungry and She was real. She paced back and forth with all the beauty of the Goddess, for this time there was nothing sick or old about Her. In the cold, unblinking light of strange white lamps, the nameless girl who had just merged with the Goddess leant back for a moment against the door they had closed behind her. She saw the way Snow Tiger's tail flicked. The way She padded fretfully. Her muscles held the condensed power of all the graceful animals She had devoured. She was gorgeous. There was a bleat of terror, and she thought at first it was herself. She was surprised, for she felt no terror. If Snow Tiger wished to incorporate her into Her holiness, what more fitting end or beginning could there be? Already she had lived many days in the skin of the Beast, and now she saw with gratitude that that had been just her dress rehearsal. She raised her arms to her Mother. Come to me. I smell of you. Know that I am yours. I want you. Take me into the black center of your whiteness.

Snow Tiger came up and smelled her, and licked her arm with Her great rough tongue. Then She prowled away and turned back like a hunter, ready to spring and to kill.

Then she heard the terrified bleat again and followed Snow Tiger's eyes and saw the skinny gray goat that was trying to hide behind her. In a beautiful, surging leap of fury, Snow Tiger bounded at them and she lost consciousness. When she came to, it was to feel the great cat's hard furred muscles against her and the sounds of tearing flesh. It took her several moments to realize the flesh was not her own. Snow Tiger was on the goat.

And She pulled the goat away as She worked at it, leaving the tiger slayer cold and alone on the rock.

The Goddess had rejected her.

She was unworthy.

She could not understand it when the first words of the priestesses who came were "Gaia has accepted you. Your crime has been purged. You are free of blemish or blame. Come, Mana, Moon-mother, come, drink and eat." The priestesses drew her back through the door, shut it, and tended her with cool water. They carried her on a stretcher down tunnels to fragrant baths and hot gruel. They threw her leathers on one side and dressed her in a soft linen tunic. They took off her rough splints and made a new one, then bound her arm to it with healing herbs. They were as delicate and cultured as she had ever imagined priestesses could be.

# *Two*

The first night they put her on a bedroll on a dry floor in a small stone room, which they called a cell. She stayed there all the next day and they brought her food and drink. She slept. Koré came and sat with her and held her hand. Osen came and felt her forehead. Words were exchanged. Sometime in the day they brought in a wood frame bed with a lattice of canvas thongs across it. She was asked if she could get up, and she did and staggered to the bed.

"I have to pee," she said.

"There's a pot," said Koré. "Under the bed."

It was a wide pot glazed a deep warm red, as fine as any piece of glazed ware in her village. It was so fine she could hardly bring herself to pee in it. But she squatted and had relief.

Osen came the next day and sang to her. She sat up in bed and asked the old crone, "What is to become of me?"

"To begin with, Mana, you can help me out. I need someone to do little things for me, and to record what happens in the Chronicle of my Motherline. Sarasvati has been doing it, but she needs help. When you're ready. I assume you can write."

"Yes. Yes. I can write," she said. "Is this a prison cell? Can I go out?"

"Of course you can go out. The Goddess in White accepted you. You are free."

"I am going to stay here?" The old black face seemed amused. "Am I truly called Mana?"

"It is all up to you," said the crone, and sat rocking slightly as she hummed a tune that 'Mana' had never heard.

There was a dim light in the room. It came from a glowing ball on a little shelf that stuck out from the rock wall. "Phosphorescent bacteria," Koré said proudly, whatever that meant.

Those first days were about food to eat, water to drink, warmth, and the fact that Koré and Osen both called her 'Mana.' Sounds came to her faintly — chants and voices and bells: Koré explained how the days were constructed, the prayers, meals, work times, and all of them measured by the bells.

Koré said sometime on the second day, "All the home caves are warm all through the year, but some of the caves are damp, lower down. We used to be in a dampish cell and it was bad for my chest so Mama got us moved. You're in one of the best cells. Some people are saying you shouldn't be, but Osen wants you right next door to her."

"I'm right next to Osen?" Mana asked. She still had not left her cell.

All her life she had longed for warmth in winter, not to mention fall and spring or those too frequent rainy days in summer. Getting out of bed at home in her village had been a daily misery. Now it was an unbelievable luxury to throw back her threadbare blanket and slowly swing her feet out onto a sisal mat and rise, stretching until her fingertips touched the rough, curving stone of her cell ceiling.

She could scarcely believe that she slept in a room cut from the living rock of her Mother, a true cave. A frieze around the cell at eye level told the story of Parvati, Lady of the Mountain, who married the dancing beggar bedecked with snakes, Shiva. There he was when she first saw him, smeared with ash, skull in hand, a tiger skin over his shoulder. Here he kisses her feet. Later he comes to their wedding attended by his vagabonds and hideous ghosts, and the bride's mother, Mena, faints from shock at the sight. But then Shiva appears to her in all his shining beauty, crescent moon upon his forehead, jewels on his clear skin. All the women run to see, and Mena herself is dazzled. At the end of the frieze, the New Clear Winter ice cap crushes the Himalayas; Parvati lies asleep beneath it, kept alive by the faint warmth of her sleeping lion.

"It isn't the end," explained Koré. "Lots of the reliefs in the Caves end with blank space, see? When the ice melts and Parvati comes down from the mountains on her lion, hand in hand with her husband, throwing colors on the wind, then the spring festival of Holi can be held again, and the frieze will be completed."

She peed in a red glazed pot and lived inside a storybook?

It was a shock to her that under the portrayal of Shiva, the vagabond with the tiger skin, lay the hide of Snow Tiger. She could not bear to touch it. It lay there, dumped without ceremony or care, to reproach her.

She walked slowly to the heavy colored rug that hung on a

rod across the rock-cut doorway to her room. "Can I visit Osen?" she asked the little girl.

"You can go anywhere. You are one of us now."

But am I? Mana wondered.

She pulled back the curtain, feeling how weak she was all through her body, her legs and arms especially. She stepped through into a tunnel higher than her head, smooth-floored, dimly lit by the same strange glowing balls that lit her own cell. There was no rug over the next doorway and she peered through into another warm and dry room like her own, though many times the size. She asked, "May I come in?"

There was no reply. The room was full of sunshine colors.

"See the story here is Osiris," said Koré eagerly. Mana tore her eyes from the bed and bright cushions to the walls. She quickly recognized the cycles of Osiris, the good shepherd, the resurrected god, but she had never seen anything like this portrayal of them. "See, Osen got them painted in the colors of Egypt and Africa which she remembered." Vivid, primary, sun-drenched colors: yellows, bright blues, pinks, orange.

She wanted to walk round each wall to take in the paintings, but that would mean stepping on bright woven rugs that had been left lying on the floor.

"We can keep carpets in these rooms as long as they are taken out and aired, spring, summer and fall," said the old woman's voice, and Mana jumped. Osen's plump form, wrapped in brightly dyed robes, lay back on the bright cushions. Mana hadn't seen her — she merged into the riot of colors. The cushions' cotton covers had been dyed orange and sun-yellow and sky-blue and crimson, barbaric colors in barbaric patterns, like everything in her room, clashing and shouting with joy.

Mana went and knelt to touch Osen's feet, as once she had touched her mother's. Osen drew back a wool rug so her feet could be touched.

The feet were bare, wrinkled, with cracked soles and splayed toes, dark brown almost to black on top but pink on the soles. Recalling how her mother loved to have her feet rubbed, though it was always Romila who did it and never Anam, Mana took one of Osen's feet in her good hand. The skin was cold. The old woman sighed. Mana settled down on the cushions and massaged each sole, each heel, each splayed toe. She felt energy come into her arm as she did.

After she was done, Osen said, "Thank you, my dear. Now. I want you to write in my Chronicle. See over there on the table? Pen, ink, the bound vellum book with 4 on the cover."

Mana went over to the table. She picked up the book, the quill and the inkbottle, and brought them back to Osen. She sat cross-legged in front of the old woman and opened the book. The first page said: *Chronicle of the WraithDaughters, Osen, Book 4.* Its fine, slightly crackly calfskin pages were covered with exquisite handwriting: neat, small, all the lines leaning backwards in a most elegant fashion. Many of the pages started with beautifully drawn capital letters, embellished with painted leaves, garlands, snakes. "I can't write like this," she said, scared.

"The young tiger slayer passed her trial. The fury of the Goddess was spent upon the goat. The . . ." Osen spoke slowly and deliberately, her eyes closed.

Mana suddenly realized she was dictating.

"But I can't . . ."

"The young tiger slayer . . ." Osen repeated more slowly.

"I . . ." Mana looked around her in panic. Koré pointed at the book encouragingly.

"The." Osen paused. "Young." Pause. "Tiger." Pause. "Slayer." Pause.

Mana picked up the pen, dipped it in the ink, and began to form the words on the page. Embarrassment made her face hot as she saw how her writing, of which her village crones had been so proud, looked like a peasant scrawl next to the other. Her letters were a jumble, sloping any way they fell.

She wrote until her hand was cramped and tired. Mostly she had no time to think about the meaning of what Osen dictated, even though some of it was about herself, and some was about some strange story to do with the space station. Certain words did jump out: "her eager ascetic beauty," "this brave girl" — was that really herself?

Suddenly, in a swish of a sari, a woman was standing next to her, staring at the open book.

"What is this?" she demanded imperiously.

Mana looked up. The woman was not old, perhaps no more than 25, but she looked every inch the priestess of the Goddess. Her deep blue sari was draped elegantly over one shoulder, her long black hair was tied up in an intricate and perfectly woven knot, and the silver bangles on her ankles were worth more than

Mana's family made in a year. She looked down her long nose
with disdain. "You are allowing this barely literate bumpkin to
sully the pages of the Chronicle?" The disbelief in her voice
made Mana's eyes drop to the floor.

Osen said calmly, "Sarasvati, this young woman's name is
Mana. Mana, this is Sarasvati."

Mana could not raise her eyes again. She whispered to
Sarasvati's bangles, "May She be with you."

Sarasvati took the book from Mana's lap without a word of
greeting. "Look at this!" She handed it to Osen.

Osen looked. Mana peeked up at the old woman. There was
something of a rabbit in her face, a twitch to her mouth: was she
trying not to smile?

"Sarasvati, please read to me what Mana has written."

"*The young tiger slayer passed her trial. The fury of the
Goddess* etcetera. Of course I can *read* it . . ."

"Then that is all I require."

"But compare these letters to mine!"

Ah, thought Mana as she contemplated her feet. Now we
know what this is about. Please keep your job, she thought, I
don't want it.

"Sarasvati," Osen said, "you keep telling me what important projects you have, the analysis of ancient texts, the teaching of the graphic arts, the care of ancient carvings, how little
time this leaves you to serve my very humble needs. All I need
is to keep a written record. If you can read it, I am content."

"Huh!" snorted Sarasvati. "I can see I am not appreciated
here! In that case . . ."

"My dear, you have been the greatest support to me and I
do appreciate you in more ways than you know. You are one of
the very few who have been able to conceive that my project
might have its own truth. I need you still. Please be calm and
greet your sister. She will be helping me also."

Sarasvati, slightly mollified, said to Mana, "You have passed
the trial and you are welcome if you decide to stay with us."

If? thought Mana. It is all up to me then, as Osen said. But
clearly, Sarasvati hoped she would not choose to stay.

Over the next days, Mana learned her way around the Caves —
the kitchens, dining halls, worship caves, latrines and washrooms,
fitted amazingly with copper tubes through which clean water

flowed. Whenever possible, Koré was her guide, though the little
girl had a lot of chores to do which she had apparently neglected
when she sat by Mana's bed holding her hand.

Koré made it clear the first day she took her out into the
Caves that Mana should wear her forest leathers, not the sleeping tunic she had been given. Mana had never heard of a piece
of clothing just to sleep in. But she took off the soft, simple and
simply beautiful tunic and pulled on her old leathers again. One
of the first things she realized as Koré led her through the maze
of tunnels and caves was that no one in the Caves wore leathers.

The strangest thing was that in all the bustle and greetings
and talk of several hundred women, none came to speak to her.
She was ignored. The only exception was a fat, jolly woman in
the kitchen window who doled out food to her: Aunty Po. Aunty
Po called her 'love' as she called everyone. The very first day
that Koré led her to get her food herself, Aunty Po said, "Here
you are, love, a nice turnip mush thingy today," as she slopped
a grayish thick soup into a wooden bowl and handed her a couple
of thick chapattis. Aunty Po had a noticeable beard and mous-
tache. She radiated love, and Mana loved her silently in return.
Mana overheard some of the women complaining about this
'mush,' but to her it was delicious. She sat on a bench at a long
table — an odd experience in itself for someone who had always
eaten sitting on an earthen floor, but it was the custom here and
it was a fact that the stone was cold compared to the wooden
bench.

Being ignored was pleasant in one way, since she could just
watch and learn, though disconcerting. What would she have
to do to belong? "It is up to you," Osen had said. But what did
that mean?

That concern was not a great one those first days, though.
She was alive, wasn't she? Snow Tiger had forgiven her, hadn't
She? Gaia-Kali, the Mother of All, had all in hand. All would
be revealed in time.

Every day she averted her eyes from the hide of Snow Tiger,
still bloody, dirty, stiff, on her cell floor.

Every evening she went to a special place she had found, an
alcove in the Morning Cave, to pray. It was a bare place without a single carving, and no one else appeared to use it. She
prayed to Sitala, her village goddess, the one who gave no pun-

ishments, only love and blessings. But nothing changed. What should she be doing — prostrating herself nightly before Kali Ma? One night she went to the great cave of Kali and did just that, all night flat out on her belly on the cold stone. She was so stiff and sore in the morning she felt surely someone would commend her for her piety. No one did.

Still, over these first weeks it became a daily, hourly thrill that Osen seemed to want her to do small services like warm her icy feet and massage her scalp. Osen's lover, it seemed, had died many years before. She had no daughter. Now she had Mana come in to make her herb tea and clean her room. Several more times she dictated and Mana wrote in the Chronicle, strange things about the Space Station that she preferred not to think about as she wrote them. When the splint came off, Osen found out that Mana could play the flute. The old African loved to hear the simple village tunes that were all that Mana knew.

Twice Osen had Mana accompany her to the outside world: a very long walk from the home caves to what they called the Savannah Tower — some miles south of the Forest Tower to which Mana had come with the skin of Snow Tiger. Osen was short, her plumpness exaggerated this time by heavy furs, not garish woolens. When she ventured out onto the savannah, bear and beaver kept the winter from her old bones. She gloried in the knowledge that there were plenty of furred beasts in her day, more than enough to clothe Gaia's people, just as there had been in the ancient days of the fat female figurines that were Osen's greatest treasures. Male rule had come and gone, and Earth had recovered remarkably well, considering.

One day, Osen suggested that Mana tan the hide.

"You can take it to the tanning pits in the local village. Koré will show you the way."

Mana was stunned. The pelt had become huge in her cave, so huge fully half the room was out of bounds to her. She gave it a wider berth almost every day. Osen wanted her to pick it up?

For two days she sweated fear as she tried to approach it, and failed. Then Koré came dancing into the room one early morning before Mana was awake, put her arms around the hide and dragged it over to Mana's bed. Mana screamed. "Come on," said Koré, "Osen wants me to show you the tanning pits. It's going to be an adventure!"

The sparkle and joy in the little girl's face was what broke

Snow Tiger's spell. Mana pulled on her leathers, took the tiger skin from the child, and followed her up through the levels to the Forest Tower. It was just a skin, heavy and smelly.

It was an adventure. Koré held her hand as they walked the woodland path from the Forest Tower and chatted about Caves gossip. But Mana could only look at the trees and the snow and wonder. The village was not far. It was larger and more impressive than her own, but she felt as if she knew the people. She looked at them in wonder also: her former life.

The tanner refused to touch the hide. But when she brushed the snow from the heavy wooden lids on the tanning pits and heaved them aside, he did not stop her. She peered into the dark brown liquor, made from steeping finely ground oak bark according to time-honored ways, the tanner's mystery. Several skins were curing there already. She had seen it done when she was a child running free in her village, poking her nose into everyone's business. She threw in the huge, stiff white fur striped with black: black markings and blackened blood. She pumped it around with the tanner's pole. It seemed as if half the village crowded around to see her do it.

After that, she checked on it every week, and stretched it at last on the tanner's frame, and scraped all the adhering fat from it. Finally, greatly daring, she cut off the head. The hide would be no use to her as a cloak with the head on. At what point in this process she had decided to use it as a cloak, she was not sure. But when she mentioned the idea tentatively to Osen, to see if she would think it an outrageous blasphemy, the old woman said, "Why else did I suggest you tan it, dear?"

Nothing got easier in the Caves those weeks. The Goddess had accepted her in the test, but the priestesses were convinced only in their heads. Their silence amounted to a second test. Mana guessed it was only because Osen wanted her around that she was still there and that really no one could object after so severe a trial. But no one liked it, either.

Yet in the nearby winter village, in those visits to tan the hide, she felt the people's awe and soon their acceptance — they knew her story and felt that she was chosen and holy. Sometimes it helped her feel it herself for a moment.

Some time in the second month, a big change came about. The sisterhood decided that if the tiger slayer was to stay with them, she should pull her weight. Sarasvati announced to her that henceforth she was to do her work shifts like anyone else, and attend the dances and worship like anyone else. It was true that often enough Sarasvati had come into Osen's room and found Mana just doing make-work, or sitting staring into nothing. When Mana told her mentor, Osen said, "More than half of being a priestess is doing the chores."

Sarasvati was everything Mana had dreamed as a child of becoming in the Caves. She was calm and wise, unflappably elegant. Those first months when Mana was just thankful every day to be alive, some niggling part of her longed to look like that. She knew she had the face for it: the old men in the village had been saying that for many a year, "You've got a priestess's face, you have, Bilqis's eldest."

But she was anything but calm. Now she dashed from one part of her day to another. She prayed long into the nights prostrate on the cold stone, seeking union with the Mother, of the kind she had known briefly during her test. When they sang the Deep Fire songs she went hot in the face. She was anything but cool. So why did Osen want her so close all the time? And had distant, elegant Sarasvati done these intimate things for Osen before? It didn't seem likely. She was hardly the type to massage feet.

But nowadays she was too busy to ask. Now every dawn call Mana went down to the morning cave to catch a glimpse of the awakening dance, easing slow and stretching out in union with all the myriad stone images of burgeoning life and tree-form pillars and birthing Shaktis that held up the ceiling and the hill above it, and then she dashed to the kitchens to slave for the cook. After everything was washed up and the place spotlessly clean, she went to clean out the bathrooms, when she grabbed her daily cold shower, an unheard-of luxury in the village. Then it was sweeping the tunnels in the afternoons, when she would glimpse through curtained doorways the priestesses at their magic in scriptorium, herbarium, dance caverns, and music rooms, at the growing of their mushrooms, algae, and crystals, at their carvings in the stone skin of their Mother. In late afternoons it was back to the kitchens again, grabbing a bite as she chopped and wiped and stirred. There were legends about young women like her, she thought grimly or with a smile as the mood took her, over the washing up. At last she could go to Osen's room in the evening; to the mystic in the room of clashing colors; to the contrary African with her bizarre tales of Space. Sometimes she made it to the evening dance, and sometimes she stayed on with the old priestess and listened to her ramble on about the civilization she imagined in Space, and how it might be brought back to life.

Mana still wore her forest leathers. Some time in the third month, she was bold enough to tell Osen she had expected a free day-tunic at least, but Osen said no, the initiation changes the inside; everything then is up to you. That was the first time she had called Mana's test an initiation, as if she were a priestess already. Mana thought, if only the others accepted me as Osen does, then I would be a priestess without more ado.

# *Three*

One day, a good three months after her trial, when Osen asked Mana to accompany her once more to the upside, the young woman wore the supple, headless skin of Snow Tiger for the first time. Osen encouraged her to, though Mana thought it would only alienate the other priestesses more. "Be practical," Osen said. "It'll keep you warm." Osen wore a bearskin, which was twice as warm as Snow Tiger. Her hood was trimmed with white mink.

There was something different about Osen on this day. As they walked the miles underground to the Savannah Tower she moved better than Mana had ever seen her. There was a joy and anticipation in her old lined face that made it beautiful. The priestesses whom they passed looked twice at Osen's face and bearing — they saw it too. But their first look was at Snow Tiger's skin, and not one was pleased to see it.

Finally they were there. Osen climbed the steps of the tower as if she were twenty years younger. There was still deep snow on the ground, and they had to put on snowshoes: there was a supply by the door.

Outside on the open expanse of the savannah, barely twenty paces from the Tower, the old woman stopped. She looked up at Earth's ice-blue skies and said, "And so. A clear day at last. It is fitting."

Her black face peered out from her white fur hood with the same wonder as a mole sniffing at the world above when it breaks through the earth on the first spring day.

"Mana, can you smell the Spring?"

"Not yet. I don't think so, Mother."

"I can't smell much these days. But today, I feel as if the whole crisis of my life is just a natural part of spring."

"What crisis, Mother?" Osen often talked unintelligibly, her mind far away, perhaps in other lands.

"The crisis our naïve sisters have for so long refused to face. I had new hopes when you came. But now that the slayer of

Snow Tiger has been tried, purged, and renamed, they forget again. But today, huh!" she snorted. "It's just life. Even after a hibernation of two millennia comes spring. Rutting stags. Aurochs bulls. Rising sap. Kings and warriors."

"Kings? I don't understand?" The word gave shivers to her spine.

"My motherline always said that warriors and kings would come again. And they did, in my own African homeland, with a vengeance. And they are coming back here, too: raiding parties, fortified villages, stealing cattle and women. But I refuse to feel downcast today."

Osen of the clashing barbaric patterns had never struck Mana as being in the least downcast.

The old black woman raised one foot and then the other, and kept on doing so until her breath started to puff out in white clouds barely visible against the snowy plain. The young woman had to keep from bursting out laughing as she realized the old woman was trying to run in place. The joy of this morning.

"You may smile," said the ancient priestess, who had not looked at the younger one, "but today I become a mother. Today my son is born."

High above the planet, the ancient space station turned.

In the space station's birthing room, the row of fetuses rocked gently in the fluid-filled tanks. They were calmed by motion, music, and recorded conversations played back to them. Dim reddish lights rotated above them. It was the morning of their birthday.

There were no windows or starview holograms in the birthing room. Nor had there been in the gestation room next door, whence a conveyor had brought them in the night. The soft glow of a clock face on the wall said 0815, Standard Galactic Time. Just the slowly moving red lights, the piped sounds, the gentle swish of fluid in the rocking tanks.

At 0830 the gene techs came in and switched on the white lights. They knew the routine well enough in theory, but this day occurred only once a year and their babies were few. So there were plenty of free-floating anxiety and excitement pheromones wafting around them, as if just waiting to pounce on the innocents when they were pulled out of the tanks. The hundred or so different kinds of bacteria that inhabited the gene techs' mouths, not to mention the hundreds more in other niches, were likewise ready to colonize the new, soft territories.

All it would take to start the process would be a few wet kisses.

These, however, the babies would not get. The bacteria would have to find more tortuous routes. For this was Terra Station, a neglected and decaying outpost, but an outpost nonetheless, of the Galactic Collectivity, on whose thousand-plus planets the Space Code ruled. The millions who had fled into space from the Ice that destroyed the old civilizations of Earth had made their own civilization, spread thinly across hundreds of hostile planets and fragile space stations. Their greatest strength, as they saw it, was their discipline.

They had achieved total emotion management.

They were fearless and wholehearted in ridding their society of the old emotions that had led to humanity's fall. In the Space Code there was no love, no partiality, no hate, no madness. There were no families, no couples, no gender. There were no religions, no social movements, no groups beyond the cheery work teams that accomplished everything so smoothly, so safely.

A man stood in a corner out of the gene techs' way, and, remarkably enough, he was thinking about the lack of kisses for babies allowed for in the Space Code. He was not a gene tech, but had arrived especially to see this moment in the gene techs' year. He was the Chairperson of the Committee that ruled this station on behalf of the Galactic Collectivity, and he was worried about many things.

He was worried that the Collectivity had forgotten Terra Station. The station was meant to watch over Earth, but its surveillance equipment had run down over the centuries, and the Center, as they called the ruling planets of the Collectivity, had neglected to send replacements. Everything on the station was out of date and worn out. Right now, for example, he was worrying about the extreme age of the gene tanks. He knew they were obsolete because of a horror feature he had seen in the holie bowl earlier in the year. In full holographic ghastliness it had told of an attack by bacteria-sized intelligent aliens from the Crab Nebula, who had infiltrated the DNA of humans at the gene-splicing stage. Nonsense, of course: in all the Galaxy so far explored, there were no intelligent aliens. But, great exploding nebulae, the gene labs in the holie! They had been beautiful! So massive and gleaming and new. After the holie, the Chairperson had rushed through the multiple levels of his station, for once oblivious to their dirt and decay, to take his first look in forty years at the station's gene lab. "Our children are made in this?" he had shouted, quivering with fright and rage. "These septic tanks? These oxidizing, artery-clogged, metal-fatigued mechanical mothers?"

He was known to be rather odd. It was a sort of tradition on Terra Station. Every third or fourth Chairperson for some reason started to use dirty words like "mother" in public, or to tell his dreams at breakfast. On Terra Station people were disposed to be tolerant. They were used to it. They were rather odd themselves. The people way in at the Galactic Center who monitored their psych reports were of the opinion that Earth's craziness had somehow infected them and made them all just a little bit off.

So the gene techs on that occasion had told him quite kindly what to do. "Go to MAN," they had said. And when in the Space Code one was told, however kindly, to go to MAN, one went. The Mental and Affective Nexus, source of all health and humanity, had counseled the Chairperson, rocked him in its arms, and given him a vent for his frustration.

But still, here he was months later, at the gene tanks again on nervous watch to see if they could still do their stuff. For this batch of babies was particularly close to the Chairperson's heart. This batch had been spliced to be engineers. When they grew up they would cannibalize this rotting hulk, built to house tens of thousands, this patched old spacewheel, and make out of it a nice new station, bright and shining above the skies of Earth. It would be comfortable and no larger than was needed for five hundred people to spy upon their wayward, barbaric, retrogressive parent planet. For the Center had finally authorized Terra Station to rebuild itself. Although *authorization* was cheap. The test would be if they ever sent the new materials and equipment to do it. The Chairperson doubted they ever would. Still, if this batch of baby engineers grew up clever enough, perhaps they could rebuild the station just using what they had.

For the moment, while the Chairperson's thoughts meandered who knows where, the little creatures who were about to be born floated in the rose-colored liquid. They were oblivious to all but the new bright light in which the gene techs worked.

The first fetus in line was labeled: ES12-568345682, GOVIND, 1 MARCH YEAR 2259 OF THE MIGRATION, PEER GROUP G59, DESIGN ENGINEER, FIRST CLASS.

In his tank Govind stirred, waved his arms, and turned himself over even more energetically than he had throughout the last weeks.

"This one's going to be an athlete, for sure," said a gene tech. "Pity hey's not in time to help in the Spin League next week."

"Who cares? We're always bottom of the league," said the other cheerfully, pulling on her plastic gloves with bravado. "There's no helping that. Probably still will be when hey's eighty and ready for the long sleep."

In the corner, the Chairperson frowned involuntarily. He did not always control negative facial expressions, as he had long ago been taught to do by the Code. These days he was increasingly disliking the thought that in twenty years he too would reach eighty, and would have to report for the long sleep. It irked him. It was becoming another of the things he worried about. Damn, he thought, worrying about it means I'll have to go through it all with MAN again.

At 0913 Govind was grabbed by plastic-coated hands. There was a splash and a gurgle as amniotic fluid cascaded away. The burning oxygen assaulted his lungs. Even before the gene tech realized he had breathed in, Govind bawled out his first, surprisingly energetic wail.

"Well done, champ. Hey'll do great things in the Spin League, this one," said the optimist.

They ran the usual tests and handed him on.

"This next one won't even provide hem practice — as limp as a wimp." His optimism only went so far.

The next one's label read ES12-568345683, GAURI, 1 MARCH YEAR 2259 OF THE MIGRATION, PEER GROUP G59, DESIGN ENGINEER, SECOND CLASS, AND ATHLETE.

"Wouldn't you know it," said the cheerful pessimist. "Typical screwup. First one should have been the athlete. If this one makes as good a design engineer as an athlete, we'll be living in a spacewheel that doesn't go around. I think I'd prefer to stick with the station we've got, even if it is falling to bits."

This was over the limit for permissible public negativity. The optimist nudged his colleague, indicating with a nod of his head

the silent form of the Chairperson in the corner. The transgressor
shrugged. No one in his right mind cared about Chair, that shrug said;
he was the slackest person on station for minor Code infringements.

Gauri turned her head in the fluid, as if listening to the un-
spoken words right over her tank.

Chairperson made no attempt to intervene. He knew his
reputation for slackness on the Code, but it was not a priority
among his many worries.

At 0953, in a splash of fluid and air, Gauri joined her peer,
Govind, and her billions of fellow citizens in the thousand worlds
of the Galactic Collectivity, all of them gene-spliced, tank-
gestated, and precisely designed for a particular role in the saving of the human species.

Gauri had to be slapped twice on the back before she would
deign to fill herself with the artificial nitrogen-oxygen atmosphere
of her home.

"Yup, this one's a dodo for sure," said the pessimist as she
weighed her and ran the first brief tests. "May need extra attention, this one, a bit slow," she confided as she handed her through
the hatch to the nursery nurse. What did she care — at least she
had got her to the nursery alive, and it was the department head
who had spliced the genes, nothing to do with her. She moved
at her normal slow but cheery pace to the next tank.

The Chairperson paced next door into the nursery, and solemnly, wetly, unconscionably, kissed the first two babies of the
design team.

Warriors and kings. Osen lifted her face to the sky. Now I have
my warrior, she rejoiced. Look to yourselves, kings.

A great smile split her lined face. As black as a burnt offering, that face, so different from the pale brown of the young
woman who attended her. The old priestess had come from far,
far away to stand on this spot at this moment.

He will not fight with your weapons, warriors, her heart exulted, nor deal in any currency you know. Great and terrible
kings! You will be like statues thrown into the sea! The time it
takes may be counted in generations. But before you rule the
world again, warriors and kings, my son will bring back the Sun.
Earth will be warm again. Earth will be warmed and we will
learn to think of Gaia as the mother of my line did, as did many
of those who worshiped the Goddess with her in the last hours

before the Ice. They did not reject science, or technology, or male energy. But they were not in awe of them, either. They had suffered the worst of them, and knew how to find balance. The world would not listen to them. But when my son comes we will have balance. Shiva and Parvati will dance down from the mountains together, throwing Holi colors on the people. We will leap right over the morphic echoes of ancient kings. Warriors, you will not have your day again. The space people, led by my son, will warm the planet and we of the Goddess will come out of our Caves and our denial.

She felt the sun glow on her face, and she thought of the hot land where she had been born. She thought of the impassive face of the great king who had destroyed the Caves of her motherline, his warriors screaming to keep the dark from their minds as they put the priestesses to the sword.

Always before she had shuddered to recall it: the terror and noise, the warrior white with ashes and streaked with blood who had raped and disemboweled her aunt Dyktynna before her eyes . . . the apology in Dyktynna's eyes that she, the child Osen, should have to watch it, and the fury that this had provoked in her that had enabled her to break away and run, taking secret ways, pulling her broken mother with her.

But now for the first time she thought of it with confidence, for her champion was born. He would find a way to use the great technology of the space people to defeat the kings of Earth, and re-enthrone the Mother. There would be a synthesis of science and Mother, of planetary engineering and respect for the planet, of power and peace, female and male. No need to go through all that wasteful barbarism arising from male insecurities again. That stage could be stepped right over, and Shiva and Parvati rule again, together.

After wiping Chairperson's taboo-breaking kisses from the babies' cheeks and kindly telling him where to go (to the wombroom, to MAN), the first thing the nursery nurses did, even before clothing their new charges, was to take them over to the great starview hologram and hold them up. If there had been no need of a six-foot-thick shield made of moon rock and sand around the entire inhabited surface of the station to guard its inmates against cosmic rays, there could have been windows; if there had been, then the view from the nursery window would have been exactly the same as that displayed now on this starview hologram. It was the real, live view, showing Earth's daily changing weather. The first inhabitants of this station had been from Earth and had insisted that they be allowed to watch the grim struggle of their planet with the Ice.

"There," the first one said to Govind. The view was fuzzy, due to the sandpapering effect of diamond dust on all the exterior equipment during two thousand years of use. Of course, it could have been repaired, but for the expense and the futility of patching a monster station long overdue for replacement. "You'll make us a better one," the nurse said, referring to the station and its starview equipment rather than to the Galaxy still just visible on it. And he sang:

"Space beyond us, Space around us
Cosmic garden fair and free
Let us live amid your bounty
Warm us as we come to Thee."

The stars revolved mercilessly in the blackness. What did the baby see? Streaks of light as the station turned? Pure blur? Govind looked, precociously peering toward the Milky Way and the Center of the Galaxy, the heart of the human species; though perhaps that was only because the nurse held his head in that direction. He gurgled. The stars whisked by. And suddenly the great sphere of blue and white and green sailed into view: Earth. He must have seen that, like a great face: strange, crazy Earth, forever left out of the Galactic Collectivity to which it had given birth, always looking in at the window. The song continued. The nurse had a fine tenor. The gene splicers had factored it in for just such moments as this.

"Worlds collapse and suns go nova
People perish in the din
But upon your myriad planets
Others of us strive and win.

"Space beyond us, Space around us
Give us room that we may be
Never more confined to one world
Never more consigned to one choice.
Warm us as we come to Thee."

The nurse turned to put Govind's warm wraparound on him. Not that the room was anything but cozy warm, but it was important to get him used to constriction from the word go. Swaddled tightly and laid in a gently rocking cot, Govind heard the Hymn of the Migration seven more times as the rest of his peer group were held up to the spinning universe in turn.

The Chairperson, however, could bear to hear the hymn only once, after which he went off to yell at MAN about the shortcomings of the Galactic Collectivity's notions of exactly how to "warm us as we come to Thee." MAN listened, a sensitive nerve ending in the Galactic Collectivity's nervous system, a terminal in the most complex and widespread computer network in history. When the annual starship took MAN's records to the Central planets for analysis, the authorities would be informed. The Collectivity's bureaucracy was sclerotically slow, but unless someone with influence way beyond Chairperson's had reason to make it forget a little something, it suffered no memory loss. Sooner or later, Chairperson would be replaced.

Chairperson knew this. MAN knew this. MAN reminded Chairperson again that they both knew it, and went on to do those other, subtler things MAN could do to work on his client's better nature to bring him into line; the right images, smells, drugs, and martial music. Part of Chairperson was deeply grateful for this. For if he could not trust MAN to save him from himself, who or what could he trust?

Chairperson didn't know whether to laugh or cry. MAN encouraged him to do both.

"You must come in now, Osen," Mana pleaded. She was freezing and hungry despite the bowl of vat algae and barley she had eaten after early worship. "Please, Osen." The edge of the savannah was no place for an old woman to stand in the snow for hours, even on a crisply sunny morning.

Mana was slim and wiry. Unlike Osen, she did not have enough flesh on her to stand out like this, even though she wore the skin of Snow Tiger and, underneath it, a wool smock borrowed from the communal store.

Though how could even bear fur be keeping the old woman warm, after this length of time? Mana knew that was not the reason the old priestess stood so unmoved. Osen simply could not hear Mana's voice, or feel what was happening to her own body as it froze. She was elsewhere. And what was Osen, a priestess of the Earth, doing gazing at the sky, extending into space, anyway? Like so many things about Osen, it was oolta-poolta, topsy-turvy. Wrong. Her savior was still a complete puzzle to her.

Osen's white hair poked out under her fur hood. Her breath froze along the thick white hairs that sprouted from the moles on her chin and along the softer hairs on her upper lip: frost patterns sharp against the deep black of her skin. Black face with white patterns, the reverse of Snow Tiger's white face with black patterns. The young woman wondered: was Osen somehow the reverse of Snow Tiger? Is that why she had fought against all the Caves for the nameless girl who had slain Snow Tiger to be given at least a chance to live? Is that why now she went against the Goddess and stared into space? Almost everyone in the Caves thought Osen was a lovable nuisance, stubborn, contrary, and at times Mana was beginning to feel that way, too. It was confusing and painful to admit it, but if she didn't, the old woman might just freeze here in the snow.

Mana had just decided to be firm and was practicing a line that would go: "Osen, you tell me you have lived all your life for this moment, and your mother before you, and her mother, and all the generations of your line, but if you do not come in and get warm, you may die, and then all that you have gained will be lost."

She did not even think of adding what she actually thought, which was: *It will be lost because you have no daughter with your skills, nor even a son, and neither I nor the others can possibly carry on your cause without you, because we don't really understand what it is, and with all this staring into the sky, we don't like it.* Mana was only seventeen but that is what she would have said if she had thought she could confront the great woman, Osen, WraithDaughter, Earth priestess, African, at all.

But as Mana opened her mouth to speak, Osen came to life. She turned her head and said, "It is well. It has begun. Thirteen minutes past the hour of nine, he was born. He gave a lusty first yell. The first words spoken to him were, 'Well done, champ,' by a technician, who then turned to his companion and said, 'Hey will do great things in the Spin League, this one.'"

"Do I write it in the Chronicle with the genderless pronouns, like 'hey,' or may I write 'he'?" Even with her teeth chattering, Mana wanted to get everything right, even though in her heart she believed the old lady was dreaming the whole thing. Unless it was just relief that Osen had come to life that made her be so trivial at such a moment. This silly business Osen made up about a language where there was no gender — how could there be a society with no "he" and "she"? And how could Mana be silly enough to fuss about it when Osen needed to get indoors, fast, to warm her old bones?

"As you like. I care not. There's no difference between male and female in that poor culture anyway. My Chronicle will be passed to Govind in the end — he will understand it whichever way you write it. But one day, Mana" — it seemed that a new thought had occurred to Osen — "you will tell your story to someone, and he will copy from my Chronicle, too, and he will write it for future generations, and I hope that he will write it with 'he' and 'she,' and not that abominable 'hey.' Because if he doesn't, no one in the future will be able to understand the story. One future day the 'hey-heir-hem' language will be as extinct as . . . oh, I don't know, as extinct as the elephant, or better still, as extinct as Dualism." Mana had no idea what she meant, but she was relieved when she stopped searching for similes. Osen shifted one foot forward and winced, the toe of her rare sealskin boot digging into the snow. "Now help me; I'm all frozen up."

Mana had to use all her strength to get both of them back the twenty yards to the door of the tower that led to their underground home.

The babies spent their first day swaddled in their cots. That, though Mana would have thought it more unbelievable than their society's language, was how they would spend their entire first year. Their arms were bound to their sides, their legs wrapped tight. The cots, tilted at an angle of forty-five degrees, enabled them to see the universe whirling by their starview. After the first month, they would be put in papooses on a frame and wheeled into adult areas — the archaic hydroponics and vats, the sometimes less-than-hygienic food-processing units, the greasy kitchens and dining halls at mealtimes, the absurdly large administrative offices, the Chairperson's office (where he peered at them worriedly, as if there might be something wrong with them, and then kissed each of them on their fat cheeks — that was the last time the nurses took them there), the gym, everywhere and anywhere the nurses wished to take them. Everywhere, that is, except the softroom, since millennia-old experience had proved that adult sex could traumatize them. But everywhere else, in their papooses slung upright on their two quadruple baby frames (on which the pink paint was much scratched and the metal dented) the eight of them would watch, listen, be metaphorically (but not physically) chucked under the chin, and respond as best they could.

Thus they learned the smells and sounds and faces of their whole world. They smelled the rusty fustiness of the decaying space station, oldest in the Galaxy. They were even wheeled briefly into the empty segments, echoing and shivery cold, smelling sharply of metals and ancient brittle plastic. In the kitchens they smelled good food too, soy rissoles on the frying pans and occasional steaming vegetables (the best arrived annually, frozen on distant green planets to release their vivid freshness here. None came from Earth). They heard the clang of pots in the kitchens, the murmuring hum of the design consoles, the hiss and crackle of flares in the asteroid spin games. And everywhere, and above all, they heard the cheery good fellowship of space society, the hearty laughter and verbal back-slapping of asexual teamwork.

And as they were trundled around, strapped in their papooses, they also learned that the human's first role is to be passive and accept the necessary restraints of Space.

But that first day they just lay there while the nurses busied around with bottles and diapers. Automatic feeding and waste removal systems had been tried once, a good two thousand years before, and abandoned. Hands on bottoms, an occasional restrained tickle by experts trained for the task, a bottle received from human hands, had long been judged healthy and not too likely to engender affective or sexual attachments later on in life. If, that is, it was all kept as free of emotion as one would expect.

Besides, it was no matter if children did become emotionally a little attached to their nurses. The nursery nurses were all bred to look like MAN, the friendly hologram who would be lover and confessor to each of these babies all through their lives in that haven of computerized emotion management known as the wombroom. If the nurse did not look enough like MAN — these little genetic mishaps did crop up — plastic surgery was always available. It was no surprise that all the adults on station perked up when the nursery nurses came through with their charges, as if MAN had come to visit.

The one place, other than the softroom, that no one would have thought of taking the babies was to a door in one of the empty quadrants of the station far from human habitation, a door labeled TELEKINETIC PERSONEL ONLY.

Here it was that the station's wraiths lived their segregated lives. They performed their real work down at the station's port at the hub of the wheel, but they did so only once a year. When the annual starship was due to leave, it was the wraiths, sitting in circle on the patterned floor of the glass-domed room at the hub, who looked out at the starship and held it in their minds and flashed it across the light-years instantly to its next destination. It vanished — "pop!" — as they collapsed in exhaustion on the floor. They were the most essential workers in the Galaxy, as they had proved twenty-five years before when their great strike had brought planets to starvation. Since then, these once despised beings had been treated with a new ambivalence: more respect but also more active fear and loathing. No one visited the wraiths.

So it was a great shock when three wraiths were seen one day walking solemnly through the human part of the station. They were skinny brown characters, their sexlessness hidden in white loincloths, so that they looked for all the world like malnourished humans. Their flat chests were bare, as were their arms and legs. In their long, thin hands they bore each a small, brightly colored cloth bundle. They bore their bundles ceremoniously, as if they were bringing them to a visiting member of First Committee from the Galactic Center. They wore no shoes and their toes splayed out. When you looked closer, you saw that their chests lacked nipples.

Within minutes of their arrival, the little car with MAN's helpers in it had appeared. But it didn't intervene. It just followed along behind. Several people dropped what they were doing and followed on behind the car. It was not many minutes before the people figured out where the procession was headed. Soon dozens of people were running to join them. It was rare that anything new happened on Terra Station.

The wraiths reached the nursery door and knocked politely. When the nurse opened the door, they said, "We have come to see the child."

The nurse was shocked, but he saw MAN's helpers there and he let them all in. Then he just stood there while the crowd pressed through the door to watch. The nursery was a large room full of toys, babies, toddlers and children up to five years old. The wraiths made their procession down the room, inspecting every one. The older ones were shy and some of the babies cried. But Govind gurgled and laughed. They knew which one he was without asking. They all touched his head and said some words no one could hear. Then they unwrapped their bundles. Each was a painted cloth aswirl with sun colors of gold and orange and red.

The wraiths shook the painted cloths up in the air and let go. The cloths soared and danced together in the air, swooped down on the children to tickle their faces and behind their ears, and swanned along together near the ceiling. No one had ever seen the like. The cloths were like birds. The people gasped and the children giggled and squealed and jumped up and down.

At the end the cloths stuck themselves flat to the ceiling above Govind's cot where he could see them. For several moments, some onlookers said, the golden colors ran and formed new patterns, flowing like liquid sunshine. But others said nonsense, for how could that be so?

And then the wraiths walked home.

It was the talk of the station for days. But eventually the routine of life took over again.

So the look-alike nurses sang and worked, and the babies were trundled into their untroubled lives. Govind yelled rather a lot, but Gauri slept. Chairperson brooded.

Osen moved with painful slowness down the stairs from the savannah tower. There was a long way to go. The living quarters of the Caves, way north under the forest tower, were about three miles to walk. The tunnel sloped gradually downward, with occasional stairs and twists and upward stretches. At every hazard and at about every hundred yards, the passage was lit by the gentle glow of a phosphorescent bacteria colony. Mana carried a cave lamp, a phosphorescent ball backed by mirrors that shone a faint beam forward into the blackness. The dark was not frightening; it was the dark of their Mother, of home and the depths. It smelled of rock, mice, earth and old incense. The dim light cast shadows on the rock-cut bas reliefs of the old tales.

By the time they reached the bottom of the savannah tower stairs, Mana felt that for once Osen was not going to make the walk home on her own. Right below the savannah tower there was a small living space where the tower guardians stayed. It was a popular job to take for a retreat, and the priestesses took it in turns.

"I'll get the guardians to help," Mana said. "We can carry you on a chair or a stretcher; they must have one."

"No, no, don't bother them. I can manage. I always have before."

"It's no trouble." She moved toward the guardians' door.

"Mana! I said 'no.'" Osen walked slowly on toward home. Mana hurried to catch up and support her arm.

But less than half a mile down the tunnel, Osen stopped for at least the tenth time and leaned against the rock wall with her hand to her chest. Mana laid her Snow Tiger cloak on the ground beneath the old priestess.

"Sit down for a while. I'll go back for help. Are you going to be all right?" She helped Osen to sit.

"I'm so cold." A stone Artemis on the wall forever drew her bow at a snow pheasant.

Mana took off her wool smock and put it around Osen's shoulders. She took off Osen's mittens and rubbed her hands, but her own hands were really no warmer. She put Osen's mittens back on. Then she ran back to the guardians for help.

"I need a stretcher, and a hot drink, soup, or whatever you can get ready right away," she said as she burst in on two middle-aged women who were sitting in lotus on their trance mats in the guardians' cave. "I — I'm sorry. I didn't mean to be so abrupt. Osen is down in the tunnel, collapsed. She stayed out too long. She's in a bad way. We'll have to carry her back."

The two women looked at her only by moving their eyeballs. Mana marveled at them. She looked around for a stove. There was nothing. The heat of Gaia herself warmed the main caves, which were deeper, but this place was chilly. "I'm sorry," she said. They were certainly dressed warmly enough in heavy wool robes. "Please, can you help me?"

"No." The woman's voice shocked her. It was a voice she remembered. Now she recognized the face. It was the priestess who had first opened the door of the forest tower to her three months back. She had not seen her since. But she had learned her name. Some of the younger ones in the kitchens called her the dragon.

"What do you mean, Amaterasu? Are you all right? Is there something wrong?"

"Yes, something is very wrong." The words burst through the tightness of Amaterasu's lips. "Something is very wrong indeed. An old woman goes sky gazing. A young woman kills the Goddess. The old one saves the young one. The young one helps the old one stand in the snow and project into the heavens. These are evil times. I am here to try to see where we went wrong, what we must do for healing, and what do I get but the slayer herself bursting in asking for help for the sky gazer? No, I say. No and No and NO."

"But what if she dies? What if . . . don't you care?"

"Does she? Do you care — about *this* world? Would you bring on us all again the neglect of the Earth, our Mother? Kali had orgy enough two thousand years ago. Osen's way would fill Her blood troughs to overflowing again. Get out of here, and may the Goddess transform you as only She is able before I set eyes on you again."

"But I didn't ask to be chosen to stay. I asked for judgment and Gaia judged."

"It takes more than surviving a rigged trial to become a priestess of Gaia. Now leave!"

Mana ran. Rigged? On the first flight of stairs she missed her footing and fell the last three steps. She threw out her hands and landed heavily on her right wrist. She swore at herself and got up, limping a little on a half-turned ankle. Out loud she said, "It wasn't rigged! I didn't ask to be chosen. I didn't ask. All I ever wanted was to sing to the Earth in the Caves, to be a priestess!"

As an afterthought she added, "And I certainly didn't ask to stargaze!"

But if there was one human being in all the Caves that she would do anything for, it was the old woman who was sinking into the cold down the tunnel. She hobbled on until she could run again.

Osen seemed asleep. "Wake up, Osen, wake up. You mustn't sleep." She held the old face in her hands and pressed her face against it. Now she was at least warm from the running, and she tried to rub life into Osen's hands again. When the old woman came to, she said, "Get up! Can you get up?"

Osen put out her hands and Mana dragged her to her feet. Then she turned her back to her, squatted down, put Osen's arms around her neck, grabbed her legs and hoisted her onto her back. She set off down the long tunnel as fast as she could go.

The tunnel went on and on. She had left both their cave lamps back where Osen had collapsed, but the floor was smooth and the flow of cool air seemed to carry her down the center of the darkness. Phosphorescent bowls loomed up ahead and fell behind, and she never stumbled. The old woman had seemed fairly light at first, but she became heavier and heavier. Mana summoned up all the times she had hauled logs or venison back through the woods to give her strength. The winter weeks in the Caves had done nothing to sustain her muscles.

At last she saw light ahead. At the same moment came the first hints of that lovely mélange of fresh incense, cooking, people smells, and methane fumes that marked the home caves. She grunted beneath her burden in relief. And then she suddenly thought: would everyone refuse her help like Amaterasu? Would she have to stumble all through the caves alone?

The first person she passed gasped with surprise. But Mana refused to meet her eye and struggled on. She went by two more, staring doggedly at the ground rather than risk another rejection.

"Don't be foolish," said a quiet voice. "Let me help you." Mana looked up to see a young woman with a lovely face, soft and dark, whom she had often seen going unobtrusively about her business. She tried to let Osen down gently, but she felt that her hands were locked around the old woman's legs, that if she slackened her grip she would drop her. Her right wrist, which had taken her fall on the stairs, and her left arm, broken by Snow Tiger, both throbbed unbearably. She could not let go gently.

"Help me," she said.

"Here, Dawn," called the young woman, "Help us out. Osen's done in, and so is Mana." It was the first time anyone other than Osen and Koré had spoken her name. The second woman appeared from one of the nearby doors. They lifted Osen down and laid her on the floor. "Get a stretcher," Mana's rescuer said. "Not you, silly," she added as Mana looked bewildered as to where to go. "You take a rest."

Mana wanted to ask her name, but the young woman was

competently attending to Osen, and it was a relief to lean back against the cool rock.

Dawn returned with a stretcher. "Shall we take her to the sick room . . . Sitala, is she all right?"

"Oh," Mana exclaimed.

"Is something wrong?"

"Your name. I didn't know. It's so funny, our village goddess is Sitala . . . you're the first person to help me."

"You're overwrought," Sitala said brusquely. "No, we won't take her to the sick room. She'll be fine. Anyway, even if she was *dying*, Osen wouldn't want to leave her sanctuary and muck in with us cavewomen, would you, dear?" She saw Osen's eyes open, and she kissed her on the cheek. Mana heard the sarcasm, but she also saw the warmth behind the kiss. She stood for a moment bereft as Sitala gathered up the old African priestess and laid her, with Dawn's help, on the stretcher.

Then she kicked herself for the self-pity of wishing that that kiss had been for herself, and followed them through the tunnels to Osen's room.

Mana massaged Osen's old feet back to painful, tingling life. The warm oil she used felt good. Her hands had never been so smooth and clean before. The calluses from the axes and bows to which she had seemed welded from early childhood were already vanishing.

The bluish cold of Osen's feet was the only clue at that moment that another world existed, a land of frost. The caves at this level were warm. Sitala had brought Osen a warm posset of spiced wine and all was well.

All that Mana wanted right now was that the young woman who had helped her would stay in the room. Amaterasu's outburst had made all the cold glances of the previous three months come together in a frightening pattern. The villagers' awe of her when she went to tan the hide and Osen's sponsorship had sometimes made her begin to feel that one day, in spite of everything, she would be a priestess. It was strange how little she had thought of her family, how totally the trial had wiped away her past, how she could not imagine any future now that did not take place in these Caves. Yet Amaterasu's bitter words had fractured any frail confidence she may have had. It didn't take much. If only Sitala would stay awhile.

Sitala left.

"Thank you, Mana," Osen spoke at last.

"Thanks be! You're going to be all right, Mother."

"Mana, Mana, Mana. Who else but the slayer of Snow Tiger would have been able to carry me back all that way? We get flaccid here. I did you a good turn. Now you've done me one. We're quits. You may leave me, if you want."

"What do you mean? I love you. And there is nothing flaccid about Sitala. Or you. I think we're finally getting some warmth back into these feet."

"Is that so?" Osen ruminated and sighed. "Nothing flaccid about Sitala, eh?"

Mana blushed.

Incense curling from a seashell helped Mana concentrate on the simple joy of tending to her mentor's feet. Time went by and then left altogether. What did Amaterasu matter? The Mother of All had a purpose for her, and this was it. Osen's breathing grew long and regular, but her occasional sighs of appreciation let Mana know she was not asleep.

Suddenly the curtain at the door moved, and Sarasvati in an exquisite sari flowed into the room. Her entrance was a perfect mix of humility and self-advertisement.

"Where is my copy of *The Dance of The Dark*?" she demanded imperiously.

"I — I'm sorry, Sarasvati, I don't know. I haven't seen it. Let me help you look." Mana got up. She knelt to look under the bed, under the cushions on the floor, behind the bookshelves where it might have fallen down. Sarasvati made much of the extreme rarity of her ancient copy of the manuscript.

"Oh! This is too trying. Well, thank you so much, my dear, for being so sweet to help me look." The voice was cold.

So, still, were Osen's poor feet. The old woman said nothing during the search, though her beady eyes followed both her helpers around the room, and watched Sarasvati sweep out the door. As Mana's hands returned to her feet, Osen closed her eyes and relaxed again. Mana tried to get back into the moment. But it was gone.

"What will his name be?" she asked, as she reached for more warm, scented oil.

"I don't know. There are many things I do not read. When someone calls him by his name and I am with him, I will learn."

"How did you do it?" Mana humored her. She had to pretend to believe in Osen's sky world, if she were to stay with her.

"That is not a question I can answer to you, my dear."

"I am sorry." Mana bowed her head low over Osen's feet.

Osen smiled. "I remember how it is to join the Caves. Not
on my own account. I was born in caves, like all my motherline
before me. Caves a continent away. But I remember my lover
Chloe's experience. She arrived fresh from a forest village. Chloe
used to tell me of the awe she felt for the old women. Not knowing that in the Caves any questions could be asked, or not trust-
ing the knowledge as it came. Not understanding that the goal
was not to turn the newcomers into somebody else, but to allow
them to be themselves. Just as long as they performed their tasks,
tended the vats, the wells, the fish, the shrines, the methane
plant, the fungi, the air. Chloe didn't realize she could do it
worshipfully or not, sing and joke or not. She didn't know she
could find a lover outside, maybe a man from the village, or a
lover from within the sisterhood. It took her so long to approach
me! She didn't know we were free to bear children or not. I
recall her saying, 'I didn't know we could wear our hair up or
down, plait it or frizz it or shave it off.' She was so busy trying to
be what people wanted her to be, she couldn't be herself at all!
Which is what people really did want her to be." It was by far
the most Osen had ever told Mana of her past.

"No, my dear, you were not wrong to ask how I conceived
Govind," she said after a moment's silence. "You can ask anything you like, anything. I simply mean that those of my line,
the WraithDaughters, we — oh, that feels good, on the heel
there, your hands are so strong and clear, my dear — we can,
sometimes, when all is right, put ourselves elsewhere and even
make things happen, but I have never found out how to explain
it." Osen sighed and slumped on her cushions, drifting into an
exhausted doze. She woke after a while and said, "Will you play
for me tonight, before evening worship?" She lay for some time,
staring up at the arched rock overhead, before she closed her
eyes once more. But she was not asleep yet.

Osen had said that before, about asking questions, though
not at such length. It was one of her themes. So much so that
Mana had felt she needed to make up some questions to make
the old woman happy. But she had felt so blessed to be here,
she had no questions that had to be asked; she just looked and

learned. Now suddenly this evening questions thronged in her mind. Why do you stare at the sky, Osen? Why do they hate you so, and love you so, here? How could Amaterasu refuse to help you — did she know I would make it back with you all right? Why won't they accept that the Goddess chose me at the trial, that it was an initiation? She did, didn't She? What did you mean by Dualism? Why did you leave Africa?

But looking long at the old black wrinkled face before her, the arthritic hand on the chair arm, she held her words. She didn't want to be a pest. Besides, she feared receiving one of those looks when Osen's eyes would pierce straight into her inner being. Her readiness to learn and her face — what Osen had actually called her "eager, ascetic beauty" — had always satisfied her teacher and the forest crones, before Snow Tiger. It had never been enough for her mother, of course, but she had learnt to live with that. But it was not enough for Osen in quite another way that she could not yet understand. Osen found Mana's humility and good looks almost comical. But then, she found Sarasvati's haughtiness and elegance almost comical as well. It was hard to know what would truly please Osen.

Later at dinner, Mana dared to ask Sarasvati, that wise and wonderful twenty-seven-year-old, the Big Question. Someone (she wondered if it had been Sitala) had put in a word for her after her exertions with Osen, and head cook had let her off kitchen duty early to go and eat. For some reason, Sarasvati had condescended to stand beside Mana in the line for dinner. While the lovely fat cook with the beard, Aunty Po, served them dollops of barley stew with goat chunks, Mana had plucked up her courage and said, "Sarasvati, can I ask you something?"

She tried to keep her voice down, because sound was capricious in the Caves and sometimes traveled farther than she thought.

"All right," said Sarasvati, condescendingly. She led Mana to sit on rich cushions embroidered by priestesses long gone in an alcove of the old morning room, the cave where they had held the morning and birthing dances before the present one was carved. It was a meandering cave with many stories told on pillars and alcoves. Mana felt that anyone might be just around the corner.

Sarasvati's look was a little disconcerting, perhaps a hint of kindness, of amusement. Sarasvati smelled so perfect, of rose water, Mana thought. How do you get rose water in winter? Mana sniffed surreptitiously at her old forest leathers as she sat on the rich cushions, and wondered if it wasn't time to start staying up nights sewing a linen tunic instead of praying. But first she had questions to ask. Sarasvati was looking quizzically expectant.

"I don't know where to start. My trial. Did it qualify as an Initiation? Can I be a priestess?"

Then, in case Sarasvati should say just what Amaterasu had said — that it takes more than passing a trial to become a priestess (forget the 'rigged,' which must have just been bitterness in the dragon's mouth) — she went on, and as she did, she realized that it was not really whether she could be a priestess that was the most important question. It was Osen.

"Well, I shouldn't ask that. I'm confused about what I am here, but maybe it will come clear. The Mother of All must have some purpose for me. The thing I really want to ask is: when I dreamed of being a priestess I imagined it would all be so calm, so given to singing the songs of Earth, without dissension . . . I thought it was only my little brother and the men who asked questions about the olden days when men ruled, and about the old space station. But here, Osen is obsessed with it, and because of her, everyone is talking about it." She realized she was talking rather loud, and looked around to see who might be hearing.

"Why, Sarasvati?" she asked in an intense whisper. "Why all this . . . Space stuff?"

In his papoose, Govind had a hard job focusing on the hard, unpleasant outside world.

He cried, of course, when he was hungry. In fact, he could outcry the rest of his peer group put together. He cried often when they unwrapped him to change his diaper.

But that wasn't so much the shock of the air cooling his wet skin. It was more likely because their invading hands tore him away from the real world into this outside world of hunger and wetness and things. In the real, inside world there was his mother who loved him. As often as not, anything they did in the outside world, like changing him, feeding him, or pinching his cheek, interrupted his mother talking to him. It was annoying, and whenever his hands were free of the papoose, he would wave them feebly and irksomely, trying to wipe out the world and let him get back to the black, crinkly, loving smiles of his mother, and to all the pictures she showed him.

Besides, nothing strange came out of his mother's mouth when she talked to him. But when in the unreal world the empty, pale brown face of the nurse bent over him and said, "Here, Govind, have some lovely porridge, you'll love this," a cloud of sand and dust blew into his face out of her mouth. Not real dust and sand, but bad enough.

When the male nurse said, "All right, Govind, you little monster, time to hook you on the trolley — we're going to say hello to all the lovely folks at hydroponics today, you'll love that," flies and beetles flew out of his mouth in a swarm. They were gray and dusty brown-colored beetles, too, not electric blue and green ones like his mother showed him in the real world.

When the other babies burbled and cried, that was fun, because clouds of little colored shapes flew out, dots and dashes and stars in pale greens and violets and pinks. Govind would burble in response.

Gauri was the neatest. She had more shapes: triangles, circles, squares, pentagons. Not that Govind knew their geometry, but he liked them, and they came out of her mouth in brighter colors, too. Gauri was fun.

But that was about all the outside world had to offer. He preferred the real world: the trees and the deer, the white mountains and the taste of snow, the occasional vivid smell she managed to send him, the birds singing on a summer day, his mother's smile, the young woman with the tiger pelt on her back.

# *Four*

"All this Space stuff . . ." Sarasvati repeated slowly in answer to Mana's question. She smiled. "What did you think, Mana, that we in the Caves would not be interested in the universe? It is all One, you know." Sarasvati looked at her with the slightly sad and burdensome wisdom of her extra years.

"But the Goddess has not wanted us to worry about what may have happened to the rest of humanity through these centuries," Mana quoted her teacher from the forest school. "They, out there, if any of them survive, escaped. They abandoned the Earth. We are the ones who have had to recover the Earth and love it. We have no energy for them, too. If they exist."

"If? *If?* Do you mean to tell me you've been with Osen every spare minute for weeks, and you understand nothing about what she's doing? Tell me, when you write the Chronicle, do you think?"

"We are the Earth," Mana retorted. "It's the Earth that needs us. *They,* if they survive, don't care about us." She had a sense of the centuries stretching back behind her, through forests of cold, when the warming songs were always sung in these Caves, right back to the years after the Ice Time, when starvation and disease and the Migration had emptied the world.

"There are *billions* of people out there." Sarasvati swept her hand vehemently up toward the sky, as if there were not thousands of tons of rock above their heads. "'If they survive,' indeed! Don't you see the space station up there, nights? Don't you read the stories you write, about Osen's child? Didn't Osen tell you they sent a spaceship down and took up an African child within her mother's memory? Her mother actually saw it!"

"People are always saying they saw spaceships." Mana surprised herself that she could contradict the exquisite Sarasvati. "And even if Osen is right and some people do live on the space station, how do you know there are billions more of them farther out? And why does Osen want to have a child in space — because she can't have one in reality? And how could she do it anyway. There's such a thing as senility, you know!" Mana was crying as she glared at Sarasvati. Then she hid her face in her hands.

"You believe in the Goddess the way they do in the villages," Sarasvati said. "But those of us who understand Osen's tradition know there's more to the Mother of All than just Gaia. Whatever She, or He, or Hey, or It is, is something that has gone through everything since the universe began. The universe patterns itself, and that is Goddess."

"Old men's tales," said a rough, contemptuous voice. "Sky talk." Mana looked up. It was Koré's mother, Raita. "Mana's right. It's senility. You're too young for that, Sarasvati." Raita was important in the Caves, Mana knew, though the lack of official positions made it unclear to her just how important. Maybe it was for Koré's sake, but she did know that she liked Raita. Her rough edged voice matched her peasant blouse and trousers. She could really laugh, and slap her thighs, and stir the algae vats with gusto. It was odd. She was the sort of person Mana had longed to get away from in the forest, to the learned women of the Caves. But already she missed the energy in those village women. She felt drawn to Raita, even though she had never spoken with her before.

"Giving Osen's line to our lovely newcomer here, are you?" Raita said. Lovely? Mana thought. Since when had anyone here apart from Osen thought her that? Sarasvati stared down at her slippers with a pinched look to her mouth and eyes.

"Fact is, Mana," Raita addressed her as if she were an equal, as if she had spoken to her by name many times before, "some of us agree with you: it's none of our business what goes on Up There."

"Osen's business is our business," said Sarasvati.

"Osen can't help it," said Raita. "She has Wraith genes in her. You know what Wraiths were, Mana? Thought not. Products of the gene monasteries, gene monsters, the ultimate sky men — they have no sex but they can move things by mind power alone: magic carpets, chariots in the sky. An old power. When the Ice came, and billions dying, the scientists got hold of them. Bred them up to magnify their powers. Used them to take off the people in spaceships. Wraiths flashed the spaceships through the void, if you believe the old tales. Where to, Zeus knows. But there's some of their genes in Osen. And if you ask me, that was a mistake to start with

— there was nothing natural about the way *that* was done."
Sarasvati looked at her in horror, but Raita continued. "Well that's
by the by, but the point is, that's the way Osen's made, and it's a
blessing, if you ask me, that there's no more of her line. She'll try
and wrap us up in that space station. Mind you, I love Osen. Who
doesn't? She's got a generous heart. But we have to keep our heads
clear. And our hearts."

"That's right, Raita. It's time it was said." It was a soft, confident voice Mana had longed to hear again. Sitala had joined
them with her usual quietness. Mana suddenly saw that half a
dozen women, young and old, had drifted up.

Sarasvati realized this at the same moment and rose abruptly
to her feet. "'Time it was said,' indeed! You've been saying nothing else ever since our brave tiger slayer appeared on our doorstep!"

Mana could hardly believe her ears. Since when did Sarasvati
think well of her?

"You've never supported Osen, any of you!" scolded Sarasvati.
"And now that her work has found its fruit, you've been trying
to use this silly issue of Snow Tiger to distract her. What did
that matter? A lucky arrow from a premenstrual peasant."

Ah, thought Mana, that's more like the Sarasvati I know.

"A tiger who jumped on a sweet-smelling goat," continued
Sarasvati, "instead of on a filthy peasant who reeked of rancid
tiger fat. Did the Goddess choose true or not in this little case?
That's what obsesses you, while Osen is making history. Well,
grow up! Leave her alone. And about Mana, let me say this:
Osen alone saw that this poor girl might be acceptable to Gaia,
and Gaia accepted her. That's it. That's all there is to it. It's
unimportant. Now leave Osen alone!" Sarasvati drew her elegant sari around her shoulders and swept out, her dinner un-
eaten.

"Raita is right, Mana dear, all the same." Sitala finally broke
the silence in her gentle voice, placing a soft hand over Mana's.
"We are priestesses of Gaia. It's the start of the men's religion
to look at the heavens; it's Brahma and Zeus and Jehovah all
over again."

"But Osen. I love Osen." And please don't take your hand
away from mine, ever.

"We do, too. We all do. And we know that she argued for
you. She saved you." Sitala took her hand away.

"Thing you have to know about Osen," said Raita, leaning forward, elbow on knee, laying it out fair and even like a wood-cutter explaining the awkwardness of elm, "is why she came here. Slaughter. A king killed half the women of her Caves. Her mother was raped. Osen was ten years old. She got her mother out, somehow. A strange lot, her motherline. Very strange. More than a little weird. It's a fact. I'm not against her, but you have to face facts. She dreams of revenge. It's natural. But it's not Gaia's way. It's the old way that brought the world down before. We mustn't deal in their coin."

"But we don't expect you to go against her," Sitala said, her kind eyes seeking out Mana's. "You never wanted to come here. You were driven here and she saved you."

"Of course, I wanted to come here. All my life I dreamed of coming here. All I ever wanted to do was to sing the warming songs. Osen's fantasies have worried me sick ever since I started serving her."

There was an astonished silence.

"You serious?" asked Raita bluntly.

"We didn't know, Mana. Honestly, we didn't know," Sitala put her slim hand on Mana's shoulder.

"Plenty of other things to do here, girl," said Raita.

"Come do the dawn dance with us tomorrow? I've watched you rush in and out," asked another woman.

"My chores — I'm on breakfast duty."

"Are you a healer? Do you want to crystal the wells with me? I do it twice a year. Start in a couple of days." This from the short, stocky priestess who tended the wave structure.

"What you need is fresh air," said another. "Get Sitala to take you. The spring has come and you've almost missed it."

Suddenly Mana was surrounded by warm and intense women who seemed to have decided that they were her friends. It was wonderful. She let Sitala take her hand.

They talked right through to evening worship. Suddenly Mana remembered that Osen had asked her to play her flute for her. She leapt up, and with hurried excuses dashed along the cat's cradle of tunnels and stairs and passages to Osen's room. She drew back the curtain gently, lest the old woman be dozing. Osen was lying on her back on her bed, and Sarasvati was tenderly holding her head, the last stage of a massage. Mana caught Sarasvati's eyes full on, and the controlled hint of triumph she saw there made her stop in the doorway. Keep away, Sarasvati's look seemed to say, I have regained my territory. Mana found herself stepping backward, and the curtain fell across the doorway again, blocking her off. She stood there, hearing her heart beat from the running for several minutes, before she turned away.

There was evening worship to go to. But Mana went down to Kali's Cave, the deepest cave she knew. She lit a candle and stepped from statue to statue. Kali is Beauty. Kali is insane mother who beheads her children as they are born. Kali is wild energy who creates the world. Kali makes Shiva's lingam rise. Kali devours the missiles with her yoni. Kali is Love.

Kali eats the dead of the world. Kali extinguishes the firestorms of the cities with her menstrual blood. Her blood flows from her cavernous dark yoni in a river across the cave and disappears into farther depths. Mana can only see darkness on the other side. Across this river the dead are taken to be laid in their mother. Kali's death is good. She opens her arms to you. She will renew you.

Mana went straight back to her cell. Sitala found her there later, lying face down on the rocky floor, the Snow Tiger cloak scuffed up in a heap to one side. Mana's arms seemed to be trying to embrace the Earth.

Sitala gently touched Mana on the shoulder. There was no response. She shook her shoulder a little. Mana made a small objecting kind of noise and turned her head so that her cheek could rest on the stone. She was fast asleep. Sitala smiled and shook her awake enough to get her to stumble into bed. The bed was a low wooden frame with two-inch-wide strips of canvas woven across and tacked to the frame. There was just room for two, though the one blanket did not cover both. Sitala had brought her own blanket, in case.

In the morning Mana woke to see the lovely dark face awake beside her, and the serious black eyes for once mischievous and laughing. She buried her face in Sitala's neck, unable to look at so much that she had wanted so badly.

At that moment they became lovers; but there was no time to make love that morning, for the lower caves were calling them to worship in a more formal fashion. Before the dance of the dawn next morning, they had remedied that lack. Sitala's skin was as smooth as the silky fur of the mouse. She was as kind and full of laughter as a waterfall in spring. She had been without a lover for a while, but she knew all about love. In the following week Mana got less sleep than even in the week after she slew Snow Tiger, when she had stared at the leaping shadows on the walls of the way huts and at the icons of the Goddess Sitala bearing the blessings of the forest. This week she laughed with joy and garlanded the statues of Radha and Aphrodite with the first crocuses of spring, in thanks for turning the image into the person. "I prefer the person!" she sang to Radha, and placed a snowdrop in each of her eight beautiful hands.

So Mana was woven into the dominant group of the Caves, those around Raita who kept the traditional ways with the most fun and vigor. They made jokes at work, played harmless tricks, sang and danced at the daily ceremonies with more energy than anyone else, and gave little time to study or theological discussion. Mana no longer had the energy left at the end of a day to throw herself on the floor and embrace her Mother Earth. And this was so even though her load of chores was mysteriously lessened. Best of all, she went topside to explore the world again.

In her first months, Mana had abjured the world above. The womb of the Earth, her Mother, was all she had ever wanted. But Sitala went up at least twice a week. And then, well, Mana had to admit that her legs had started to long for running, her lungs for the sharpness of dawn, her eyes for greenness and the sudden dartings of squirrels. So she trod silently with Sitala through the hilly woods to discover the roof of her home and celebrate its beauties. It was a shock to eyes and nose and ears. She discovered that a priestess of the Caves could not help but see Gaia's living mantle with fresh intensity every time. The light alone was blinding.

The Caves were in the old crystalline rock of the hills above the great River Maya. The valley was a vast expanse of forest green through the warm half of the year. There was always the choice of whether to leave by the Forest Tower, which opened into the hill woods above the valley, or the Savannah Tower three miles south, which opened onto the grasslands of the plateau. Mana never liked the savannah, with its vast skies. She and Sitala stuck to the woods.

Aboveground, the priestesses traveled armed with spear and bow, for defense against wild animals and the occasional raiding party that in recent years the plainsmen had sent into the

forest villages. There were warriors in the world again, and although they worshipped Kali, when the bloodlust was on them
they were beyond respecting her servants, if such were young
and female and unarmed.

Mana and Sitala did not use their weapons to hunt, skilled
though Mana was in hunting, from her previous life. The villages for many days around them supplied their meat and grains
and fruits. To be a priestess of Gaia was to hold life sacred,
including the natural balance of carnivore and prey, of wise
omnivore and all its food. To kill to keep their archers' eyes in,
when the villagers provided them enough, would be wrong. They
shot at fir cones instead, or at the woolly catkins of spring, the
hanging acorns, a rotting log. They gloried in the smells of pine
and moss, in the high scrapes of bear claws on bark, in the jay's
and langur's warnings. They sneaked up on civet cubs, and saw
an aurochs calf born in the dusk.

One day they came out onto a wooded hill above a plains
village, at the crossing over from forest to prairie. The village
had a new stockade around it, a line of stakes taller than a man's
head. Instead of the usual brushwood and branches, the stakes
were solid young tree trunks. Instead of a moveable pile of brushwood to block the entrance, there was a heavy gate on hinges.
The gate was open and people and cattle streamed in.

Mana's spine went chill, as if she could barely move.

"This is more than you need to keep out tigers," said Sitala.

Without discussion they sat down in the shadow of an oak
to watch the village below, as before they had watched the civet
cubs play or the aurochs calf born. There were men with long
spears running, a lowing of cattle being moved; women scurried
with supplies on their heads.

Suddenly three young men stood beside them under the
oak. Mana put her hand on Sitala's arm to alert her — neither of them had seen the men coming. The shocking thing
was the painted designs on their faces and chests, as fierce as
dvarapalas, and the shine on their newly polished and oiled
spearpoints.

One was clearly the leader. He stood slightly in front of the
others and his eyes were arrogant, as if he thought priestesses of
the Goddess nothing. His muscles were just as arrogant, as if he
used them differently from other men. His skin glistened with
oil, and the painted lines around his eyes and mouth made her

think of something . . . Then she smiled — the black eyes on a butterfly's wings, whereby it tried to scare predators away by looking fifty times larger that it really is.

Her smile clearly angered him. "This is nothing to do with you. Leave!" he ordered.

Sitala seemed abashed but Mana rose smoothly to her feet, interested that here she seemed more confident than her lover.

"The Goddess is indeed terrified," she said. "The butterfly has raised its wings and we run screaming into the dark."

"Don't . . ." whispered Sitala.

Mana locked eyes with the young man disdainfully. She held out her hand to Sitala. "Come!" she said to her. Sitala rose and took her hand and Mana walked straight at the young men. "We have more important things to do," she said, "than watch wars."

The leader stepped aside and the two women walked between the other two and onto the path back into the forest. They were not followed.

"That thing you did with your eyes," Sitala asked, when they were well out of hearing.

"You weren't brought up in a village with posturing boys," said Mana.

After a good day out, they would return to the coziness of the communal living rooms, the brighter methane and softer bacteria lamps glowing steadily, as they retold the beauties of their Earth to Sitala's friends. Koré would often sit on Mana's lap. Then stories would be told of yetis and satyrs, of sorcerers and *dhole* men. But Koré and Mana agreed their favorite stories were those of the catching of the aurochs bull for the annual initiation drama. The hunters had to get close enough to the huge and dangerous animal to blow the drug dart from the blowtube, and that was a great deal closer than was needed for an arrow notched to a good yew bow.

In her second year, Mana herself went on the aurochs hunt, but the Goddess did not give her the privilege of blowing the dart. She helped to lead the somnolent beast to the savannah tower and down the ramps that led to the depths. She was chosen also to lead it back out after the ceremonies, set it in its forest, and watch to see that it came to life again. She realized what skill and courage had been needed to bring in Snow Tiger

for her trial. She wondered what sort of new consciousness Snow
Tiger itself had been initiated into by its days under the earth.

At solstice they held the great summer carnival out on the
savannah. All the villages for many days' walk around helped
to organize it. People came on pilgrimage from all over the
world, from the deep South and from the holy city and from all
parts of Mother Ganga's thousand-mile journey from the ice
cap to the sea. The summer flowers grew thickest in a circular
dip in the plain, a holy place where certain sacred ley lines con-
verged: the Omphalos of Veshya. There the priestesses lit the
fire and there throughout the seven days they dispensed the
grace of the Goddess to all comers. Mana had had sex with a
village boy or two back home, but now she learned the variety
of men and women, old and young. It was said that the priestess
as Veshya could cure many ills and diseases.

In her second summer, a thin young man from a nearby village came to Mana in the Omphalos. He stooped, his cheeks
hollow with sickness. There was a bad smell around him. Sores
on his neck and forearm wept open pus. She was revolted at the
thought of making love to this man. She had drunk the medici-
nal herbs. All the Sisters of Veshya had done the protective
spells and prayers together. But this! She asked him to sit down
on the turf outside her wattle and grass hut, and said she had to
go and get some water. She went straight to the hut where Sitala
was on duty. A woman was just paying her final respects to Sitala-
as-Goddess. Mana waited until she had left and went in. She
said, "I can't. This man is ill. He disgusts me!"

"I know, love. You just have to pretend. At least he wants
healing. The ones I can't stand are the young men who come in
for a quick fuck. They're disgusting. This one you could be Sitala
to, the bringer of blessings. No woman will lie with him, only
the Goddess."

Mana breathed deep. She summoned up every memory she
could of Sitala the protector of her village, who did not punish
but just gave the fruits of the earth. She picked up a gourd of
water and a slice of fresh mango from the food tent and returned
to the young man.

"I am Sitala. I give to you," she said as she handed him the
fruit and the water. Then she raised him to his feet and led him
into the hut. She let her robe drop and brought his face down
gently to kiss her breasts. When she tried to remove his clothes

he resisted. She saw enough to understand that the evil smell came from sores that he wanted to keep covered. "I am Sitala, I love you," she said, as she gently and firmly overcame his resistance and removed his filthy smock and leggings, stained with blood and pus. He could not gain an erection. She made him lie down on his back on her grass bed and stroked him all over. Eventually he relaxed. She kissed him on his mouth. She took the stink of his breath into herself and breathed out the healing of the good earth. At every stage she pretended to be the Goddess, and at every stage she was given the power to go on. Eventually his lingam rose and she straddled him and took him into herself. He cried out in wonder and thanks and praised the name of Sitala.

Then she dressed him and herself again and sent him on his way. She went down to the stream and washed herself inside and out, and her clothes, giving her own prayers and thanks to Sitala, and dressed in a clean robe. Later she took out the soaked sponge that guarded her against pregnancy in the Omphalos.

The next week it was told through the villages and the Caves that the young man had been cured of his sickness by the Goddess Sitala.

A month after that, he appeared at the Forest Tower and asked for the one who had been Sitala to him. Mana eventually was found and came to see him. He was waiting patiently. His smile was beautiful. He lifted his clean smock to show his chest and arms free of the sores. He smelled of some scent made from flower petals. He asked her to have his child and to visit his hearth regularly. He said all his relatives could tell her he was a fine woodsman and it would be no trial to love him in future. He knew that some of the Priestesses had such relations with men.

"You are the most beautiful and kind woman in the world," he said, "and I love you." He unfolded a beautiful dress embroidered with the leaves of the forest, the sort of dress that had taken some woman years to make. "It was my mother's. It is for you," he said, handing it to her.

But she thought of Sitala, and had no desire to change in any way the joy between them. "I was the most beautiful and kind woman in the world in the Omphalos because I was Sitala," she said, as kindly as she could. "But here in the Caves, I am not, I am just Mana. My heart is given to another."

He was crestfallen but, she thought, not very surprised. "Accept my mother's dress then, and wear it, for I would be dead without you."

"I cannot accept it. Give your thanks to Sitala, and not to me, for it was truly She who cured you."

"You do me wrong to reject my gift."

"Then I accept it. I will wear it. And when you marry, let me know, and it shall be my wedding gift to your wife."

She took the dress, and closed the door on his rueful smile.

Mana still went to Osen as often as she could. But ever since that evening when Raita's group had accepted her, the special quality of their connection had been lost. Now the old woman never seemed to miss her or ask for her to do things anymore. She seemed reluctant to talk so much with Mana about her space fantasies. But she was more single-mindedly obsessed by them than ever. She seemed to have no interest in what was going on in the Caves, the songs and dances that Mana was learning, her joy in discovering that she too could paint with blue fire the ancient symbols of the Goddess in the space between, that she too could work with the energy flow around the circle. It was clear Osen no longer relaxed so well under Mana's massages as she did.

"You don't have to do this," she said to Mana once, with that gentle sharpness that Mana found hard to read.

"But I love to," said Mana, continuing to work the old woman's feet. She had decided that disbelieving in the old African priestess's space scheme would make no difference to her love for her.

But Sarasvati, cool, kind, and superior, did more and more. Her prose was more elegant, and she went back to keeping the Chronicle of Osen's project. Mana heard less and less about it. Osen spent much time topside these days, wrapped up warmly sitting in the savannah snow or on the short grass in summer, when she would take off the straw hat Sarasvati insisted on and lift her face to the sun. She would sit there for hours in trance, oblivious to the herds of bison and aurochs, the wolf packs and summer tigers, who left her perfectly alone.

Once in Mana's first summer when she had promised to help Sarasvati spring-clean Osen's room, she discovered that it was a day of rehearsal for the initiation mysteries.

"I have to go, Sarasvati. I am to be an ancient scientist. It takes practice."

"Well, go then. Be a little scientist. Don't bother with Osen. Don't bother with the fact that she's a real scientist, a gene engineer. And don't bother to come back here, either. Sing the warming songs. Lose yourself in them like you did in your trial. Learn to trance. Dance! Go on. Dance. Spend the next decade learning to dance the energy cone into the air, manifest the pentacle of blue fire — you can do miracles like that, sure you can. I believe in you. Meanwhile we will be doing the real magic, the real transformation. There's a galaxy out there, Mana, and we are going to change it, and we'll warm the Earth about twenty thousand years before you will. But you keep at it, 'scientist.' You know what you're doing."

Sarasvati could go on like this forever, Mana realized. She left. Osen didn't care whether she was there or not anyway.

That night in Sitala's arms she said, "I feel so guilty. I can't believe in Osen's work. I feel like I have disappointed her so. It's almost like the way I disappointed my mother, back in the village." Not back at home, for Sitala and the Caves were home now.

"Sweetness, let me tell you something about Osen. She loves people, yes, she is generous, yes, and she can often see what the rest of us cannot see — such as that you deserved a trial. But she is a Schemer."

"What do you mean? Aren't the Caves full of schemers?"

"Not to her level. Her motherline has been planning this project of hers for *generations*. She thinks it's bigger than any-thing else, that it's worth any sacrifice. Schemers use people — they can't help it, even when they have the best of intentions. You're not a schemer. You're a lover. You loved your brother and grandmother — that's why you killed Kali in White — and Kail recognized that. You work from the heart. Osen works from the head."

"I wish it was as easy as that."

"Follow your heart, my love." She ran her hand up over Mana's breast, and Mana almost swooned with the pleasure of it. After so many years of hardship and loneliness at home, she could never have enough of Sitala's touch.

Mana delved instead into the Earth warming songs. She de-cided to learn the sitar, a project of many years, and to sink herself into the long and complex ragas that wove around the warming chants. She had some aptitude, and so, without knowing that she did so, she turned all that fierce determination that Sitala had diverted from Osen and nightly prostrations before Kali, into music.

So the woods above turned through their seasons of white and green and gold, and years went by, of love and friendship, worship and song. Mana's playing was at last applauded at the concerts that lasted all night and all day, and she was judged ready to be initiated further into the mysteries.

She went to an old woman named Leto, who taught her the meaning of the ancient words "chemistry" and "physics," "atom" and "oxygen" and "carbon dioxide." She learned the mysteries of "albedo effect" and "greenhouse effect." She learned that the fierce, hot words of the Deep Fire saga reflected real places, where real men and women tended coal and oil shale fires under the earth, using clever techniques to filter out the smoke and let the carbon dioxide out into the sky. The warming songs, she learned, were sung to build a greenhouse over the planet, which would begin to melt the icecap on the Himalayas and set Parvati free, as well as to warm the heart of Gaia and the souls of the faithful. Thus were her faith and zeal rewarded, and she began to hope in a new and more enlightened way for Gaia's future.

Leto also taught her a little of history, of things that had happened since the Ice Time that her village teacher had not told: for example, she learned why the Deep Fires had to be kept secret, for simple folk did not realize what they could do for Gaia and resented the lives and resources that went to keep them going. There was little surplus food or clothing to spare in the villages. Better that they thought their tithes had a purely sacred use, something they could understand. And indeed, the fires were sacred.

"Have you seen the fires, Leto?"

"For seven years I led the singing at the Queen's Fire. Our Caves have a long connection with Queen's Fire. I daresay . . ."

"Could I go one day?"

"If the Goddess wills it, and you obey her and work hard. There's nothing special about your voice, but your musical sense is up to it. And they do like an energetic young person sometimes, as a change. In fact, I have already suggested it."

"Oh, Leto! It's what I want to do most in all the world."

"Then I will take over as your sitar teacher, my dear. You must have the best."

She was a priestess at last.

# Five

At Mana's third summer carnival, the talk was all of a young plains warrior called Atlatl, son of a village chief, who that spring had led war parties to conquer several surrounding villages. Atlatl's father now ruled seven plains villages, and the women for miles around were besieging the Caves with prayers for intervention. Amaterasu led a delegation in full regalia to the chief, and he made all the right promises and did all the right obeisances to the Earth Mother. And the next week Atlatl raided a forest village and took ten young women back as slaves. The women of Atlatl's own village let half of them escape, but five were still there, and no one knew if they were coerced or free to go. Amaterasu was even now visiting all the surrounding villages to weave together an alliance of peacekeepers, that is to say, of men and women who could fight if need be. But many in the Caves thought that raising an army against an army was the wrong approach. Osen was suddenly in demand, for she knew more of warriors than did anyone else in the Caves.

The thing that no one expected was what actually happened on the first day of the Omphalos. On this day every year the priestesses danced the Goddess into the navel of the world. They concentrated Her presence in the wildflower-strewn bowl of Veshya, so that for seven days She would be present in all her glorious energy to all comers. This was the time of healing, unity, and joy.

Crowds of villagers always ringed the Omphalos of Veshya to watch the priestesses dance. But this year the crowd was split in late afternoon by a phalanx of brazen young men painted in warrior splendor. They carried their weapons in hand, battle ready. No such thing had ever been seen at the Omphalos.

Especially for those who had listened to the stories of Osen, it was a heart-freezing moment. The dance faltered as half the dancers imagined that they were to be cut down as Osen's Cave sisters had been cut down. And then of course they drew on the power of the Earth and danced as if She was ever and always now. They wore cotton robes that swirled and billowed in the wind of their dance, and flowers in their hair and around their waists and wrists and ankles, and their bare feet stamped and caressed the earth.

The people circling the Omphalos shrank from the phalanx of young men. Everyone's eyes strayed from the dancers to the young men's leader. No one had any doubt as to who he was. On his chest were painted the huge eyes of the butterfly that the Plains people called the Fright. This must be Atlatl. He looked different from other men, as smooth as a hardwood tree stripped of its bark, as arrogant as Brahma. Many women knelt and then lay face down to embrace the Earth, and many men did also, praying to Gaia. Then a young village woman stood up and grabbed the hand of the person beside her and pulled others to their feet and started to walk down into the bowl, between the warriors on the rim and the priestesses circling in the center. Soon all the people streamed together to form a wall between the painted phalanx and the dancing circle.

In the center, Mana danced herself to exhaustion. The bowl of the Omphalos was a good hundred paces across and in the blur of her own motion she could not see clearly the face of the warrior with the painted eyes on his chest. But she felt in her heart that it was the young man she had taunted as a butterfly — what was it, two summers ago? — and she guessed why he might have chosen that design to wear today. She also guessed that he had not come to do murder, though why he should come in such force to taunt the Goddess in her very center, she could not tell.

The dance was at an end. Tomorrow the grass huts would be built, in which the priestesses would be the Earth for all comers. Tonight was the ritual coupling in view of all, of the Corn God with the Summer Queen. They appeared now, elaborately decorated and costumed — so elaborately, in fact, that when after the ritual dance they ritually coupled it was hard to tell exactly what was going on. Still the people sighed and moaned, happy to know that their crops would be full at harvest time.

By their inaction the warriors had lost the crowd's attention. Perhaps everything was going to be all right, and the young men would split up, mingle with the crowd, eat the Veshya cakes, drink the honey beer in moderation, and sing and dance into the moonlight.

But as the Corn God rose from his Queen, the butterfly painted warrior strode alone through the crowd to the center of the navel of the world. His confidence was complete. Even the older priestesses, even Amaterasu, who had been in the circle of dancers much of the day, held back from intervening. This was not someone you could take by the arm and lead out of the circle with a few motherly words. His eyes swept the robed dancers and Mana was not in the least surprised, though surely everyone else was, that they stopped on her. He beckoned to her to come to him.

She recalled how confident she had felt of herself when they had met before. Since that day he had achieved a mysterious transformation. Everything about him was hard. This was no boy but a man, a man who had killed many times, a man who led other killers, a man who wanted to rule over women and children and men way beyond his home ground. But he was here. For a purpose. She held his eyes and very minimally shook her head.

He stared at her and his chest seemed to swell with power contained. His fist clenched on his spear shaft and he raised it high over his head, pointing at her.

"Stop!" cried Amaterasu. She tried to come off as a woman of authority. But she sounded more like a sheep.

Mana remembered the way Snow Tiger turned to her from her brother's body, before He leapt. But there was no such murderous intent in this young man's eyes. He wanted her to grovel, not to die. He wanted to pay her back in front of the other young men, who had seen her best him before.

Mana raised her hand towards the old dragon, Amaterasu. "Let him throw!" she said clearly.

He threw. The spear thudded into the ground at her feet. As the shaft quivered and sang the crowd moaned, and he beckoned her again. Again she minimally shook her head.

He unsheathed his sword. But to threaten her with that he must close the space between them. She could see him realize that he had not planned this well. He strode towards her furiously, raising the sword to strike. She stood perfectly at ease. She raised her hand to stop Amaterasu and the others from coming to her aid. Even while she focused on him, she thought that it was not cowardice, in Amaterasu, but awareness that she, Mana, was in control, that held them back, and this increased her sense of calm.

Close to, she could see the oil and sweat on his skin. He was surely the same age as herself, no more than nineteen or twenty. With the sword raised above her head he hesitated, and now at last she took a step towards him. She raised her hand and touched his face. She spoke softly, in the hope that no one else could hear. "If you would lie with the Maiden, wash off all this paint. Leave your weapons behind. Come to me tomorrow." Her body remembered how it had been to love the diseased young man last summer. Now she would do it again. Without that, she could not have attempted this. But this was different, very different, for she felt her own power rising in response to his. She knew that for him and for the whole crowd his spectacle was matched by her own, for she was twenty and beautiful and filled with the Goddess. If he wanted a power greater than his own to curb his evil, he had chosen right.

He whammed his sword down into the earth, and prostrated himself to kiss her feet. In the mural carved on her cell wall deep in the Caves, Shiva kissed Parvati's feet. Mana had seen that kiss every day for three years now. In the carving Parvati is not embarrassed, as a twenty-year-old village girl would be to have a powerful warrior treat her as Summer Queen. Instead she holds her arms and hands in a classic royal pose. As Atlatl raised his head from her feet to look up at her, Mana realized she had assumed that pose.

That night, the priestesses who had danced the Maiden into the Omphalos all day, and who would give out her blessings over the next six days, were agog with the day's event. Most were suddenly shy of Mana herself. This was even true of the older ones, women in their thirties and forties. There was talking behind hands and sudden silences when she walked into a group of her sisters. She could imagine some would now resent her. Sitala was not here this year, nor Raita. She had no close friend to talk with.

But Amaterasu was full of political advice. "You played that brilliantly. I take back all I have ever said about you. The Goddess was upon you. Now you have an extraordinary chance. You must bind this young man to us. Think what could happen! You must build the kind of relationship that my foremother Kuan Yin had with that terrible man, whatever his name was. There are certainly precedents! Perhaps this Atlatl was even seeking that! Coition can be a tool by which the Mother binds these men to Herself. You must try for a permanent relationship. You must bear his children . . ."

"Please, Amaterasu, I am tired. I need some sleep if I am to build my hut tomorrow and be ready for him."

In the night, the villagers brought piles of ash branches and twigs from which to weave the frame for a simple hut, and more piles of heavy long grasses to cover it in. Each priestess rose early and built her own. As she constructed her hut through the morning, Mana schooled herself to be the Goddess to Atlatl. She knew that, as Mana, she would see in his erect penis the warrior missiles that had near destroyed the world before, and shudder at it. But as the Maiden, the Goddess Herself, she had to take that missile into her wet and warm center, consume its power, and expel it shriveled. She could not imagine it clearly. Amaterasu's words had blown her off center. The power of yesterday was gone from her. Bear his child? Inconceivable. Sitala, she yearned, I need you, now, to hold me.

As soon as Mana's hut was complete, shortly before the sun reached its zenith, he was there. He was washed clean, without weapons or followers. He seemed younger.

Inside the hut, he was reverent. She shed her robe. He knelt and kissed her feet again. Really, it was an anti-climax. Some men come erect and bold to the Maiden at midsummer, some hesitant and fumbling. Atlatl acted surprisingly simply, shrugging off his clothes, his penis limp, until he raised a hand to her breast and his lingam began slowly to rise. It was no missile, no warrior. It was easy in her hand. She could even imagine he was relieved to be shorn of his warrior persona. Outside, he had been the great warrior and she the true Queen of Summer. Had it all been for the crowd? Had he actually longed for once not to have to show off, to just meet an equal, a girl who would not cringe or flatter?

Or had he truly come to pay homage to the All that Is? She put her other hand on his chest and pushed him down on the sweet-smelling pile of grass. He tripped and laughed at his own clumsiness, at ease. She laughed with him. She reached for a garland of flowers she had hung on a twig, and put it over her hair. He stroked her face with a finger. There was no great charge between them, as there had been yesterday, outside. She lowered her hips over his and guided him into the center of the world.

She was Goddess to many more that summer carnival. By the end of the seven days she was sore and exhausted. Back home, Sitala gently rubbed fragrant oils into her aching back and limbs, and they refrained from lovemaking for many days.

It was only two weeks after the end of the seven days, this time, that the young man's request came. Amaterasu brought it, frothing over with excitement and plans. "He wants you! He wants you! Now this is what you have to do . . ."

But this time Mana had talked it over with Sitala and she knew what she wanted.

"Amaterasu, I have served my time in the Omphalos. But I do not love this man. In public, he disgusts me. His cruelty, his terrible insecurity, his need to prove himself."

"No, Mana! You can't let yourself be swayed by your emotions like this. And you said he was different in the hut, gentle."

"He won't treat me as the Maiden for long — and I won't be the Maiden next time. I'll be Mana, the girl whose father deserted her, who disappointed her mother, who is only happy with one lover, Sitala . . ."

"You have to put the needs of society first. This is a critical juncture. You have been put in an extraordinary position. You may save the lives of hundreds of women. If we plan this right . . ."

"Amaterasu. I am not the scheming type. You are political to your finger tips. I am not. I'm a lover, not a schemer. And that's final."

"You are a selfish girl! I always said as much. There's always one bright beautiful girl at the festival — if it hadn't been you it would have been someone else he would have chosen and she would have done the right thing. I knew we shouldn't have let you in!"

Mana knew he would not have chosen someone else. And no one else would have read him as she did or acted as she did. It had happened the way it did because she was who she was. No good would now come out of forcing herself to be something she was not.

At the Savannah Tower door, she found that this one did not bring her a dress lovingly embroidered with green leaves, but a gold neck ring and silver bangles set with jewels. She gravely

declined, and surprised herself by adding: "But they want me
to. They think I can . . . tame you. Bring you back to the ways
of the Mother."

"They? The old bags who run the Caves?"

"They are good women. They fear the rise of warriors and
kings again. You near destroyed the world before."

"Old wives' tales. Look at us. We've been attacked for years.
Too many people all living on the same land. Many more than
in my grandmother's day. You can't stop it. There isn't room
for all."

"You could use words, not swords."

"And did you use words when Kali in White attacked your
home?"

"You know about that?"

"Of course I know about that. Knew you must be that girl
when I first saw you."

"How?"

"Takes one to know one."

"I love another."

"I could bring peace to a hundred villages if I had you by
my side."

"You want the Goddess's protection."

"I want *you.*"

His eyes flashed with the boldness of the moment in the
Omphalos when he threw his spear at her feet. For a moment it
was exciting to her again. To be Queen to his King. To bring
blessings to a hundred villages: protection of sword and Goddess, united.

"It's happening and your cave women can't stop it. There
are too many of us. I want it to happen with the Goddess in
charge."

It was as if he knew her mind. There was a seriousness in his
manner that made her certain for the first time that it was not a
ploy. She believed him. That was why he came to the Omphalos with his warriors. To forge a new union. She had known it
with her body when they met, but she had not been able to
believe it with her mind. Now she did.

She stood frozen on the doorstep of the tower. The world in
front, the world below. Sitala, and music, and the deep fires.
Peace, joy, safety, love. Atlatl, a new creation of male power,
with whom the servant of the All would have to bend and be

supple, invent new ways and rituals, eat insults, fight with every atom of her being, be always in retreat, always a disappointment to Kali, always a slayer of certain sacred tigers in order to save others. A mother of warriors, a mother of queens. Perhaps one priestess among her children, one child with the holy earth in her heart. I am a coward, she thought. I choose below. The proven ways, the old ways of the Goddess. The safe ways. The ways of love. I am owed that, after the mother and father I had.

"No," she said. She felt as hard as a statue in the caves. Harder, for they were filled with love. "It is not Her way. Even if it is," she added honestly — she owed him the hope that someone might be found to mix the magic that he desired, "I cannot do it. It is not in me to create a new world. It is not who I am."

She saw the hope and challenge in his eyes recede as fast as a flower is consumed in a fire. Her hand almost reach out involuntarily to bring it back. But she was not the seventeen-year-old girl who had slain Kali. Now what had been alive in his eyes was carefully covered, as if he had grown an old man's cataracts in a single moment. He stepped back.

There was silence and empty millions, a full crore, of paces between them. She longed to be able to close the door and go below.

He stepped forward and grasped her shoulders with his smooth, hard hands. He tried to kiss her hard on the lips, as a warrior might, but his lips were shaking. She did not respond with anything but her heart, and that in sorrow and loss. Then he picked up his jewels and spear, and leapt down the steps from the Savannah Tower and jogged off into the tawny expanse of grass.

# Six

The eight babies were liberated at last from their papooses. Chairperson breathed easier. Perhaps the nursery nurses did as well. But if so, only MAN heard about it. No person-to-person confidences were exchanged by anyone. All was well with the station.

Able to crawl and wave their arms, the babies nonetheless remained demure and well mannered. As they grew into toddlers, they took their passive, equable place in the cheerful, passionless, error-free life of the station.

At least that is the way it should have been. That is the way it always had been for every single new generation on Earth space station in the previous millennium. But there was something odd about this last lot of babies on Terra Station.

That odd thing was Govind. Govind was hyper. On the other hand, Govind was a lump. Sound and fury, but not at first a lot of motion. He would not crawl. Govind was moody. Govind was clumsy. Govind would not learn to speak. Govind eventually crawled, but would not walk.

But at the same time Govind was in some odd way leader.

There were many curious things about Govind. His hair curled. His skin was very dark, not a nice, soft shade of brown like everyone else's, but dark verging to black. Shades almost of purple could be seen in it. At the same time it was often marred by a surface greyness, almost powdery, that the nursery nurse would try to wash off with a rag. A real mess-up by the genetics crew. He tended to plumpness. Lying alone in his cot, even as a tiny baby, he would gurgle and laugh when no one was near. As a toddler he loved to crawl under the table and gather boxes and cushions around him. Given half a chance he would sit there in solitude and darkness and sing and laugh to himself for ages. When the nurses or the other toddlers pulled his castle to bits, he would get furious and scream and fight and beat his head on the floor.

But he was not always a recluse. He drew pictures on the

walls with crayons, even after being repeatedly told not to, and he had so much fun that others joined him. He threw his food and laughed. He was not in the least abashed when told off. The other children were often drawn to him, the older children too, not just his peers. They copied him, seeming to want the energy and danger that trailed his being.

He pulled off his diaper and peed on his poster paints. The steaming color ran across the floor. Little Garcia, until now the very incarnation of the Space Code, followed suit. Gauri shrieked with joy and brought the others to watch. One of the nursery nurses, provoked beyond the bounds of her experience, went next door and screamed at the gene tech who happened to be plotting the gene chains for the next year's lot. "Don't fuck up this time!" she yelled.

The gene tech had never been screamed at in public in his life before. He had never heard a sexual expression outside of the softroom. He might have survived the experience if it had been just anyone doing the screaming. But to be screamed at by someone who looked rather like MAN, that was what laid him out. The poor man had to be carried on a stretcher to the wombroom, where the real MAN called up two thousand years of computerized therapy to put him back together again. The nursery nurse was afforded similar treatment, with the difference that she walked to the wombroom herself in a daze of shame.

Disaster followed Govind around like an untrained puppy. He was always stubbing a fat toe or upsetting his food on someone else. Withdrawal of love and privileges made no difference to Govind. There was nothing he liked better than to sit chatting to himself in the corner. Cutting down on his food made no difference to him, either: he stayed fat. The nurses suspected the older children of saving bits of their food for him.

The worst thing of all was the way he grew attached to Gauri, his peer who had come out of the tanks right after him. Gauri was unusual herself in some ways. She had a worrisome curiosity — necessary, of course, in a good design engineer and so no doubt bred into her deliberately, but disruptive to the other children, who were also design engineers and weren't curious at all. She was smaller than the rest, smaller-boned and thinner, though she never seemed sickly. On the contrary, there was something dapper about Gauri, well contained and from the start well coordinated. The techs who had found her weak and passive straight out of the tank had mistaken small size and patience for weakness. She was restrained, always, until something caught her interest, but then she homed right in on it. She was the first of the eight to speak, the first to walk, the first to run.

Gauri was the one human being who really seemed to interest Govind. She was just as interested in him, but when he grabbed her she crawled away faster than he could follow, and he bawled. She was always following exciting lines of investigation and chatter beyond his reach.

One thing Gauri excelled at was recognizing people. On the space station this was a greater skill than a person on Earth, like Mana, could have imagined. For throughout the Galactic Collectivity there was neither male nor female (except when naked, and barely then), neither fat nor thin, neither joyous nor depressed. Everyone had straight black hair and smooth brown skin. Ugliness or beauty did exist, for the gene splicers often got it a bit wrong, but there was no beauty that daily make-down could not disguise or plastic surgery correct. Everyone looked the same. Govind never got the hang of it at all, not in his early childhood while Osen still lived. Gauri early on enjoyed laughing at him for never knowing people's names. It did her a world of good to be able to laugh at this dangerous being whom she adored.

"What can we do? We will have to get rid of hem." The head of the space station's genetics department shook his head.

"Why so sad, my dear Genetics?" MAN knew how much this one liked his title.

"Govind is such a delight to watch. I can't help it. It's the truth. I enjoy going to watch hem. I simply can't bear the thought that I will have to terminate hem. Am I very sick?"

MAN looked gravely at the middle-aged male slumped on the couch inside the ovoid therapy cell. MAN could see him simultaneously from every physical angle and electromagnetic wavelength, from skin state, pulse, echolocation, muscle tension, and brain activity. All this was automatic from the moment Genetics stepped into MAN's egg, but if more data should be needed, skin and blood samples could be taken without the citizen even being aware of the loss. This information MAN instantly collated with everything known about his client's personal history, about those of his similar genotype elsewhere in the Galaxy, and in the end with everything known about all human beings back to the beginning of the Migration and even before, though those records of people in humanity's uncontrolled hormonal era were of limited use in these civilized times.

Still MAN groped for extra verbal data, "So what I hear you saying is. . . ?"

"Genetics wants Govind put down," the Chairperson of Station Committee sighed.

"No, I don't believe it," said the nursery nurse. "Hey's always coming around scratching heir head about the child. I think hey likes hem."

"We are, of course, in a unique position here . . ." the Chairperson mused. He was sitting behind his desk in his office, and all was right with, or rather all was right above, the world. He was much less worried than he had been for years, probably because MAN had been working so hard on him. ". . . perched, as we are," he explained, "above a completely uncontrolled genetic pool, and on the most biologically vibrant planet in the Galaxy, into the bargain." The Chairperson was happier partly because he so enjoyed these talks with the nurse concerning Govind. This nurse was particularly sympathetic, and her dimples when she smiled were unusually interesting.

"I suppose you may be right, Chairperson — the normal rules may not apply here, on Terra Station."

"You follow my thoughts exactly," he smiled tenderly at her. "It is our duty to study this planet. The Center thinks we are here merely as jailers, to stop them getting out. But what do we do meanwhile? It'll be hundreds of years, thousands, before they re-invent escape technology."

"You have such a brilliant mind, Chairperson."

"I know. It's the bane of my existence. But this is where I need your mind." He looked deeply into her eyes, which were unusually dilated. "What do you think of this? A minority report from one of the gene techs has gone so far as to suggest that this child, Govind, may represent some kind of genetic contamination from the planet. Hey writes that the boy contains genes that are like throwbacks to the earliest years of the Migration, when there were people with very dark skins and very light skins — if you can believe, hey says, they actually called them 'black' and 'white' people. I know it

sounds bizarre but . . . Do you think you could come back here to
my office tonight after dinner for a really good, long private discussion of this matter, before I have to put Genetics's motion to Station Committee? I wouldn't like to terminate anyone whom we,
you and I, should be studying."

The dimples appeared in gratifyingly exaggerated form, lit
by a certain reddish flush to the warm brown cheeks.

Some deeply unconscious part of Chairperson's psyche must
have been responsible for the fact that just as he was getting on
so well, for once, with MAN, he had to go and set up a private
rendezvous with an attractive nurse. He would never have done
so unconscionable a thing deliberately. One must not forget, of
course, how like MAN the young nurse looked. Nor forget what
strange influence the proximity of Earth seemed to exert.

It was even more bizarre that in the privacy of his office, as
he put a hand on the nurse's back to lead her to his desk, his
other hand somehow came up to her breast. She looked sort of
sleepily shocked and he was overcome by her lips and a certain
scent that rose from inside her clothing, and so he kissed her
lips and then her neck and had to open her fatigues to kiss between her breasts, and pretty soon they were both half out of
their fatigues as well as their minds. By far the worst of it, though,
was not that they achieved sexual intercourse outside of a
softroom. It was that they sat together on his floor and cuddled
and talked afterwards. Of course Chairperson's office was
bugged, but station security was notoriously lax, and it wasn't
until many months after the next annual spaceship left that the
security recordings were analyzed far away at the Center.

"What I am proposing," the Chairperson said, sitting in the Chair
at the round table in the Station Committee room, beneath the
great pane of smoky black glass that would have revealed the
Galaxy spinning by if only the polarization had not got stuck
about two centuries previously, "what I am proposing is that we
give this Govind another few years, until the puberty op at least,
so that we can study hem fully."

"Irregular . . . but interesting," said the head of Food Pro-
duction, a stickler for correct practice. The Chairperson eyed
him with surprise. If even Food Pro was interested, there might
be hope. For some reason, Chair desperately wanted all the little
babies he had kissed to survive.

"With respect, this theory of contamination is surely quite absurd." No surprise here, the accountant responsible for Galactic Connection and Audit was the only foreigner on station, had only been here two years and was counting the days until relocation eight years hence. The day the annual starship came through was the one day in the year when the poor exile looked really happy.

"The idea came from a geneticist, Audit, don't forget that," the head of Health and Welfare said. The Chairperson had expected help from this quarter: Health was always fascinated by things Terran. "It may be absurd to you or me, but our junior geneticists have some pretty strange theories these days. And if you come to think of it, it wouldn't look like an absurd theory to a wraith, would it?" Health laughed hugely at her own joke, and the rest joined in uneasily. Ever since the great wraith strike twenty-five years before, when the once despised, less-than-human beings who made the starships go, had withdrawn their labor and brought three months of stasis to the spaceways and untold suffering to dependent planets, no one had been too sure about making wraith jokes. People half wondered if they might not be listening. Who knew what a wraith could do?

"What do you know of wraiths or of geneticists?" retorted Audit. "I can tell you it's only *Terran* geneticists who have bizarre ideas. *Terrans* of all types seem to have bizarre ideas these days."

The Chairperson was outraged; why, the sneer in the foreigner's voice was almost heavy enough to constitute grounds for sending him straight away to MAN!

"We are not *Terrans*. We are loyal Galactic citizens!" Health defended them all in a shrill voice. "I would have you retract that remark."

"Gladly." Audit smiled with a facility for falsity and irony that the Chairperson was not sure whether he despised or envied. He contented himself with the thought that most of the Station Committee were not intelligent enough to have noticed.

"Do you remember that child Committee brought up, what, about ninety years ago?" Psych and Security changed the subject. "Hey said that the 'priestesses,' as hey called them, could make things happen at a distance — 'wraith daughters,' I believe was what hey termed them. You know, Health, you might be more right than you think about the wraiths. They might not

think there was anything so strange about Terran people con-
taminating us with a genetic mutant. I would vote for our keeping this one alive, to study it."

"Well, you do have a point there," Genetics said. "The child
is certainly quite fascinating."

The Chairperson smiled. Audit might be the only dissent-
ing vote. And how fortuitous that the African child had been
mentioned by someone else. How strange that she lived on in
the space station's memory so vividly. Yes, it was a truly weighty
responsibility. The station dangled over the Earth like a small
magnet over a heap of living, mutating iron filings. Of course, it
would get back to the Center — in the audit, in the MAN records
— but did the Center really care what happened on this decaying piece of driftwood left stranded by the tides of Migration?
He looked up at the blank wall above him. Where there should
have been Earth and constellations, there was nothing. More
than half the starviews on station no longer worked. He wondered whether the Center even remembered the existence of
this old tub. For the first time in his hitherto blameless life, he
found himself hoping they did not. As he thought about it, he
wondered if this subterranean belief of his, that the Center had
forgotten about Terra Station, might be the real reason for his
current, unfamiliar, relative lack of worry. How terrifyingly subversive of him. What a fellow he was! Well, no matter, MAN
would soon put him back in true orbit.

These days Osen seemed very old. She spent such long hours in
the open air, and the rest of the time in her cave, that Mana
barely saw her from one month to the next. Mana's mind was
elsewhere now. Atlatl had laid waste an entire forest village in
the North. To the South, he had added three more captive plains
villages to his father's domain. Amaterasu's contempt for Mana
had grown obvious to all, and was shared by many. But Mana
still refused to do what the majority of her sisters thought she
should do. She buried deeper into Raita's group, who supported
her, and immersed herself in the Deep Fire ragas.

Fortunately, her sitar teacher, Leto, shared her view, and
told her to ignore Amaterasu and the majority. "You follow
your own path," she said. "You only attracted that man because
that is who you are. Go to him out of duty, and you'll lose
him." Amaterasu kept Mana out of the Omphalos mysteries the

next two summers, hoping that another beauty among the priestesses would catch Atlatl's eye. "She's dreaming," was one of Leto's rare comments. She rarely gave her opinion on anything beyond music and the Deep Fires.

But Mana stayed awake those Omphalos nights, in Raita's large sleeping cave to which she had moved to be with friends. She thought of her father, who had abandoned his family to help society. I am like him, she thought, abandoning the villagers I could help, the people who are close to me, for some dream of helping to warm the earth. I can make it sound grand, like father could make his connections work sound grand. But didn't he do it really because he wanted to be away and traveling? Do I just want to bury myself out of sight? She had a reputation now in the Caves, as a tough, wayward, headstrong young woman, when all she wanted was to go deeper into the earth, and into Sitala's arms.

At the end of those Omphalos weeks, Sitala would come back to her bed, and she would start to restore her sense of self. But Sitala would be hurting too, by then, and it would take weeks.

There was one time in deep winter, when Osen gave one of her infrequent reports on her project to all in the Caves who would come, that Mana went. It surprised her to realize that it had been four years since that day when she had helped Osen out into the snow and had been told, "Today my child is born." It was two years since she had heard an official report on the project. Music practice left little time when there was a full schedule of ordinary chores to do as well. She could not have said why, this time, she made the effort to go.

She came in late, slipping through Osen's new orange curtain and squatting on the floor at the back. Osen was seated in a wooden chair, wrapped in violet and green woolens, reminding Mana of the gnarled lilac bush in her village teacher's garden. She held one arm out, her twisted, arthritic hand barely grasping the carved bird head of an ash staff that stood firmly on the floor. For emphasis she would tap the staff on the ground, and it seemed to take all her strength to do it. There were perhaps thirty women crammed into the room, utterly intent. Pine branches had been brought in to freshen the air.

"So this is the point that the WraithDaughters' 'infection'

of Earth station has reached," Osen was saying. "One little boy. Sixty-five generations of infertile WraithDaughters, all descended from one maverick engineer who kept her head in the Ice Chaos and had access to a friendly wraith and a gene lab. Each generation used their psi powers to mock nature and make themselves fertile, and now we are at the end. I have no daughter. I have only a son, and I will surely die before he is old enough to understand my cause. Have we infected the station enough to enable him to grow up? I don't even know that. But I doubt it."

How old was she? She seemed as old as her motherline. She looked so tired. Mana wanted to send everyone away and give her the sort of head rub that used to put her sweetly to sleep. "So," Osen sighed, "any questions?"

"Why a boy?" Mana was surprised to see that it was Raita who had asked the question; she had not recognized the back of her head there in the front. Then she noticed Sitala and several more of their group. They had not told her they were coming.

"Why was the Buddha a boy? Why Christ? If you want to challenge a man's world (and what could be more male than that civilization up there, where even the women are as sterile as the most alienated man down here?), then you do it through a man who is different. They can't ignore an enlightened man. It's a more fundamental contradiction, not to us, but to them. Next?"

"If you could make a son up there, why can't you make a daughter down here?"

"Have you got a gene lab handy?" Osen shouted. The stick shook in her hand until it fell to the floor. Then, more quietly, when Sarasvati had picked up the stick for her; she said, "My body gave out before I could overcome its resistance. Your genes are too different from my line's for me to use one of you. Govind's are closer — he's an engineer, after all, modeled on engineers of the Ice Chaos time, one of whom was my line mother. No, making my own child on Earth was closed to me when I was driven from my homeland.

"But if we have infected that station enough, if their curiosity is piqued enough by Govind, they just might send for one of us to explain how we did it. It is my hope. And if they do, it could be one of you." She shifted in her chair and seemed to sit taller as she enunciated every word slowly for every one of them present: "It could be one of you in this room who would go. Perhaps the Goddess has it in mind for one of you to take this work on to its next stage. Which of you may be Govind's teacher?"

She let her eyes slowly sweep around to take in everyone present. They stopped for a moment on Sarasvati, who returned the look eagerly, as did a couple more young women, this year's initiates, too young to know better. When they reached her, Mana found it hard to meet those eyes, and looked down at her feet. Gradually she felt compelled to look up again. Osen was still looking at her. She felt challenge, incredible daring, in Osen's eyes, focused exactly on her. Those eyes looked through her beautiful priestess's face, through her embroidered priestess's robes into the inner self. She remembered vividly the time she had looked into Snow Tiger's eyes and loosed her arrow. She began to sweat. She suddenly wanted to burst into tears and lay her head on Osen's lap. She held herself rigidly, and her thoughts turned numb. She did not notice that the whole room had turned to look at her.

"Over my dead body!" It was Raita. She rose to her feet, as solid as the rock itself. "This is enough! When it was just your craziness it was one thing, but to infect these young servants of the Goddess with sky dreams . . . it's intolerable! The Caves can not allow it. I declare this meeting at an end."

Everyone looked at Osen. Even Raita herself was compelled to let Osen have the last word, so great was the old woman's aura of assurance.

"And if I succeed," said Osen softly, "and Govind transforms the Galaxy, as he could; and if then the Collectivity, which routinely transforms planets, decides to return the favor by warming this planet, by doing in a hundred years what it will take the Deep Fires unknown thousands or tens of thousands to achieve, who then will say that Raita was the truest friend of Gaia?"

"Senile ramblings! Castles in the sky!" Raita looked truly disgusted. The spell laid by the old black face haloed in white hair was broken.

Sitala and their friends joined in abusing the old priestess's notions:

"If it happened it would be too fast. The ice needs to take its own time."

"The Mother of us All has everything in hand."

"The Deep Fires are Her way. Bringing in planetary engineers from deep space will just resurrect male rule!"

"Assuming that's even possible — which it isn't!"

But Mana sat stunned by the vision. She wondered why on
Earth no one had explained to her properly before that that was
Osen's goal. To warm the earth, to bring the misery of the villages
to an end, to let everyone have as a good a life as the priestesses
themselves had in their warm caves. She wondered how the last
four years of a woman's responsibilities had changed Romila, her
bright younger sister. Mana had felt as if she had grown younger in
the Caves — Romila probably looked older than her now. Yes, of
course, she had heard Osen say that before, but suddenly it all had
a different meaning, as if it might really happen.

The happiest parts of Govind's day were when Osen told him
stories. He liked stories of forests, of priestesses in snow boots,
of cozy woodcutters' cabins and smoke curling from the chimney, of hunters learning the ways of bears, of how the beaver
lives, of animals whose brown fur turns white in winter, of how
Snow Tiger brings down the elk. He heard of would-be priestesses whose quests for worthy prey took them into high mountains, and of how they might be surprised by the beauty of a
young woodsman, and instead of the scimitar horns of an ibex,
bring home a lover, and forget their dream of joining the Caves.
He saw the tundra and the Himalayan ice sheet through Osen's
memory. He saw the rock-hewn temples of Ajanta, which she
had visited in her youth, where the kings of the frescoes worshiped their golden geese, blue gods embraced maidens, and in
the dry cold air the skeletons of bats lay on the Buddha's ancient altars. He loved the lush forests of central Africa and the
great grasslands of the Sahara, with its vast herds of migrating
antelope and attendant lions. He knew the details of Osen's
cell, the story of Osiris in bright African colors. He saw Osen's
long-dead lover, Chloe of the warm eyes. And even at four years
old he worshiped the beautiful young woman who played the
sitar and sang of the Deep Fires. He caught the steely intent
with which Osen regarded her, and knew that she, like himself,
was the special object of Osen's attention.

The stories he dreaded were the ones that had the fear in
them.

"There was a great king, Govind. He was tall as Zeus. He was black as ebony. He was proud as a lion. Warriors came from all over the world just to be near him and do his bidding." And he saw him through the child Osen's eyes, as the old Osen remembered him.

He is seven feet tall, slim and terrible, his long legs bound in bleached whisks of human hair, his ochred skin scarred from war and from unknown royal mysteries. He stands on a dais, a purple cloak clasped at his shoulder. He towers above his people. Around him stand a circle of barbaric warriors from the Caribou Caves of the north. White and pale they are, as things that live in the darkness. He tells one of them to leap the ten-foot-high iron railings into the lion's pit. The warrior runs, leaps, grasps the highest bars, and swings his legs high up above his head until he is flying over. He yells a bloodcurdling yell as he lands, provoking the lioness to attack. The white barbarian's blood is as red as any man's. The king does not smile. But nor do his eyes grow wide, like his people's.

All the stories of the king bore some terrible attendant weight that Govind felt but could not see. He whimpered, but he watched.

Osen said, "Run and play, now. Talk to the other children." But it took him so long to learn to run, to talk. He could hardly concentrate on what was happening in front of his eyes. It was so pale compared to what happened in his head. He sat down in front of the starview and waited for the great blue-white disk to come by. Whatever he did seemed to go wrong. Things had to be bigger than his interior life to get his interest. His energy was wild, he tried to run before he could walk, to write before he could talk. Before he learned to bounce a red rubber ball, he would hold it in his hand, staring at in a trance, until 'pop!' it turned inside out. Without a break in its seamless rubber skin, it was inside out, the rougher pale pink interior now on the outside. And then, as all the kids and nurses watched, 'pop!' it was back again. The other kids hung around waiting for a disaster or for more magic, just because they had nothing big inside them.

Osen spun him closer and closer to herself, fearing the day of her death.

If it had not been for Gauri, Govind might never have learned to relate to a human being of his own kind. Gauri was the only one who could tell Govind off and make him listen. She pulled him to his feet, held him there, and then ran off, until he learned to toddle plumply after. The nurses called her over to help constantly.

Gauri was simultaneously protective of Govind and awed by the intense energy and color within his fat form. But unlike the other children, she did not just gape, she took charge.

When Govind learned to speak at four years old, the first person he told about his universe was Gauri. One day he was uttering only the shrieks and burbles he had got by with from babyhood. The next, he was using whole sentences. "Osen told me to tell you," he said to her. They were his first words. She had long since given up on his ever learning speech. "It's the story of the boy Horus," he said. She listened in astonishment. Then she collected all the children to hear the story over.

The whole station heard the news before the day was out. The fat, dark one could talk. Somehow none of them wanted him terminated. Even if this was the most unruly group of four-year-olds they'd ever had. They liked him. They enjoyed being astonished.

There were others in the Galaxy who were equally interested in Govind, but were less and less sure as time went by that they enjoyed being astonished by him. Pretty soon their enjoyment turned to alarm, and eventually their alarm bordered on panic. These people were the minor psychologists who monitored the Terra Station MAN records in an unimportant office in the massive MAN LABS on Madlarki planet.

They felt important, these people. They liked to use phrases such as "Those of us who direct MAN . . ." and "We at the Center of the Galaxy . . ."

Madlarki was indeed one of the three most important planets of the Collectivity. As far as the Galaxy with its billions of stars was concerned, if it was concerned at all, the Collectivity's thousand-plus planets under tenuous human occupation were insignificant. But to humans, the Collectivity *was* the Galaxy. The Collectivity ruled ninety-nine percent of their species and every one of these ninety-nine percent talked to MAN and was ultimately monitored on Madlarki. And although the Madlarkines were hardly in the actual center of the Galaxy, which was a maelstrom of inconceivable violence, they lived about as near to it as any other humans lived. So they could be forgiven a little self-importance.

Privately, they saw themselves as the puppet-masters of the human race — though the fact that they did not dare to utter such thoughts even among themselves might have suggested to an impartial observer that someone else might be pulling *their* strings.

Madlarki was named after the twenty-third century Huichol Revival God of Good Manners. Every well-mannered Madlarkine had to try to ignore the fact that their planet was essentially a spherical, toxic green swamp, overly well lit by the stars of the Galactic Center, which blazed so bright they outshone Madlarki's sun. Fortunately little of this was visible from within the pressurized mega-habitat in which the humans lived.

At first the three or four minor Madlarkine psychologists who cast an occasional eye over the annual reports from Terra Station were amused to see the agitated fantasies of the gene techs who claimed that this new child, Govind, was a genetic contamination from Earth. It made them feel sophisticated to laugh at these provincial notions. At the same time they found it titillating to speculate about what ghastly barbaric practices might be introduced into civilized society by an "Earthling": speaking one's mind in public, having sex outside of the softroom, fighting with weapons, having families. . . .

Such fun they had with it . . . until those very practices started to appear in the MAN reports from Terra Station.

It was the fifth starship since Govind's birth that brought them some of the first bad news: the four-year-old could talk and was telling uncensored stories of Earth.

"She was only seventeen," he was recorded saying to Gauri. "Her daddy was gone and her mama was feeling bad, so she was the strongest one in her home. So when Snow Tiger killed her grandmother and ate her brother she shot Him! There was blood everywhere and her arm was broken. Then she skinned Him! She wears the skin as a cloak. She's a hero and Osen wants her to come here and be our teacher!"

The words that should have been censored from this story were: she, he, daddy, mama, home, killed, grandmother, brother, blood everywhere, hero; plus of course the idea that such a barbarian might come to 'teach' anyone on a civilized space station.

Tracing back through the previous year's worth of MAN records and security recordings that had all arrived at once on the annual starship, the Madlarki gene techs put together this sequence: Govind had started telling his stories to his little friend, Gauri, and then she had retold them to his whole peer group, and then the other children and nursery nurses had clustered around and he had to tell them the story, and before long the story sessions had to be moved to the dining hall so that everyone could hear.

"The whole station's gone crazy! Have you ever heard of hundreds of people gathered in a big room hearing uncensored stories of violence, worship, mothers, daughters . . . It's disgusting!" said one of the psychs.

"But fun!" said the office iconoclast.

The latest MAN tapes from the year's worth that had just arrived showed that tales of bears, tigers, priestesses and foresters, of love affairs, friends and murder, of giving birth and dying of old age, of jealousy, guilt and yearning desire, were turning up in every MAN encounter of every person on station.

After the initial excitement, it was sobering and instructive for these minor Madlarkine people-watchers.

"I never knew," said one, "how fast a whole society could go downhill."

"It was bad enough with the Chairperson softrooming in heir office. Now everyone will be doing it."

"Worse. It will be mass hysteria next. Nothing like it since 1637 on Salaam Station."

"But they destroyed the station!"

"I know. And *we* are responsible this time."

"Well, not you or I. We're too junior. Ravi's in charge."

They all looked at Ravi.

Ravi's brown face had sunken and paled. Sweat stood out on his upper lip. "But I've warned them! I've warned them every year! If you don't spend more resources on Terra Station, I told them, make them feel the Center has their interests at heart, those people will turn more and more to Earth. It's too enticing! I *told* them, in official reports. I've done everything correctly, everything I could think of to do!" "They" were the executive authorities on nearby Tarcuna planet. As Madlarki planet was the psych center of the Collectivity, so Tarcuna was the administrative center. There was no love lost between the two.

"Ravi! It does not matter one Galactic credit what you told Tarcuna. *You* are still psych in charge of the sector. It is your head will roll."

"What more can I do? You think Tarcuna cares about old stations like Terra?" Ravi looked at them beseechingly.

The drops of sweat that now stood out over his whole face, and which he kept sweeping back off his forehead into his lank black hair, told them as nothing quite had before just how unimportant they all really were. Panic started to rise into their throats as they recalled tales of other disasters in the Collectivity — riots, insanities, accidents. Always they were followed by purges.

"They will deny I ever sent them warnings," Ravi said. "They will wipe me out. But *I* will take each of *you* with me."

"No, *no*. You can prove it." In light of the panic that they were in, it was remarkable that one of them came up with the solution. "What you need is hard copies," the office iconoclast said, "of all your reports on Terra Station. Hard copies stamped 'RECEIVED' by the agency you sent it to. That's the only way to prove you sent them. And I know where you can get them."

"Oh please. Hard copies? I haven't seen one out of a museum. They don't allow people like us to do that. It's private stuff — like having a room of your own." Ravi stared at them and they stared back, trying to pretend they were so sophisticated that they all kept hard copies at the back of their clothes lockers. "How do you get one?" he asked.

"From José, who else?"

"Black Hole, no! Think of someone else." Ravi's eyes darted around the group. "Hey's just more trouble."

"Hey's got influence. Hey knows top people on Tarcuna."

"But how does hey use it?" Someone else got into the exchange. "Hey's an addict. Lives in a greenhouse. A private greenhouse. Probably full of hard copies. I wouldn't go near hem."

"Hey's still a psych. Works on Tarcunan stuff, the tops, doesn't hey?"

"They say hey makes private MAN programs for our great leaders, so they can break the Code and still find solace," said the office iconoclast. Even for them, it was a very daring thing to say. They all looked uncomfortable, and the one who had spoken added, "Not that I believe that, of course."

"One thing is sure: however weird hey is, they have never

seriously disciplined hem. And hey does have Tarcunan connections. I think you had better try hem, Ravi."

"You mean for a hard copy? Or to get heir Tarcunan contacts to move on Terra Station? They should blow that old hulk
right out of the universe. Time to get off their asses and build
that new one they have talked about. They should rotate the
people there too — bring them to other planets — change the
staff there totally every twenty years. It is the only way. Earth is
too seductive. Expensive to do it, but no other way I can guarantee the safety of that station."

"Hey, that is an idea! Good thinking, Ravi. No wonder they
put you in charge of the sector." The group smiled with wan
encouragement. Ravi's hair looked like he'd been in the
shower.

"You see these little fellows here?" José led Ravi down a narrow
path between massive-leaved plants.

Ravi shuddered. It was like being outside! He could actually see the Madlarkine jungle through the transparent walls of
the greenhouse. And inside was a riot of plants and blooms. He
twisted his body to avoid touching leaves that protruded into
the walkway and knocked his head right into a heavy red flower
that dangled from a vine above.

"Aah!" he yelped.

"Don't worry, you didn't hurt it. Comes originally from Earth,
actually, did you know? Your neck of the woods." The old man
chuckled. In his early seventies, the records said, but the man
looked older than that to Ravi: a face more deeply marked by
suffering than MAN's, more gaunt than any he had ever seen.
"These little fellows, now, come from Ah Sung."

Ravi peered into the greenery reluctantly to see what the
old man was pointing to. Then he leaped back. Damn! The old
man had Ah Sung spiders in there, fat purple guys bigger than
any he'd ever seen.

José chuckled again. "Don't worry, they're well fed. They
won't jump at you. Have you ever had one?"

Had he ever? Ravi's mind went a little washy for a moment,
remembering the last spider-bite trip two years ago. He had
saved for months to afford the one bite. And this old weirdo
had . . . "How many?" he asked faintly.

"Three big mommas, one little dad, two babies."

Suffering suns. Must be the wealthiest psych on Madlarki. An addict, they said.

"How much for a bite?" He couldn't help himself.

"Oh, have one on me, dear fellow. Anytime." He reached towards a purple hairiness the size of a large hand.

"No! No. Not now! I came to ask you for something else." Ravi had meant to work up to it gradually, but now he just wanted to get out of this steamy, scented air, the green, the dreams of dreams, the amusement in the old man's eyes.

"What's the problem?"

"Terra Station. It is becoming a major safety risk. There is this child. The whole station is infected."

"They brought up another child from Earth?"

"You know about that? That thing almost a century ago? No. Nothing like that. This is creepier. It is almost, well . . . wraithlike, horrid, abnormal. We have treated it like a bit of a joke, but it is . . . well, no, not a joke, I have given Tarcuna serious warnings every year, but they take no notice . . ."

José watched the poor man babble. Ravi's fear intrigued him. As he gathered the bones of the story, he felt the stirrings of an old excitement. José had spent a lifetime following up every rumor of rebellion, or failing that, just of *difference*. It was the lack of such rumors that had drawn him to the spiders. Now the quickening of his pulse suggested it might be time to put their purple eminences away again and delve into others' lives once more.

No, foolish man, he gently berated himself. He smiled at this ridiculous hopefulness of his that survived every disappointment. Revolutions were for your mother's time, he lectured himself, you'll never see a wraith strike or a people's revolt like the one your mother fomented and died in.

But his heart and pulse belied his wisdom.

"I'll tell you what." José cut through Ravi's jabber about hard copies and Tarcunan influence. "I'll make you an offer. Give me Terra Station. Give me all the records. Tell your friends to forget they ever heard about it. I will take care of it. I will make sure there is no hysteria on the station, and if there should be any, I will take full responsibility."

"You would want to do that? You could make it official? You could remove Terra Station from my sector?" Ravi's eyes were as wide as if a spider had just bitten him.

"Yes," José said confidently. Official enough, he said to himself. "I specialize in cases like this. You'll get authorization from Audit on Tarcuna before the end of the month." He had run up a customized MAN program for a top Audit official on Tarcuna a while back — the woman had certain deeds on her conscience she could not tell regular MAN. She was a traditionalist, dead opposed to reform. But she still needed his services. Although the so-called Reformers had been in power for half a century, there were still plenty of traditionalists like her in the bureaucracy. He found them easier to work for than the Reformers with their secret families and internecine conflicts. Complex, very complex. José was a master at weaving through Tarcunan politics, from his somewhat safe distance on Madlarki. He considered himself the last true reformer. Which was why the disruptive child on Terra Station was irresistible to him.

He closed his eyes. He could already feel the bad-smelling sweat of withdrawal prick out all over his body, the aches in the joints, the silent screams in the skull. It was just the thought of giving up the spiders that did it, just the thought. The actual d.t.'s wouldn't start for a week or more.

"Are you still here?" He glared at the nervous psych. He'd forgotten the man's name already. The fellow was a pathetic product of a safety-first culture. Trying to avoid plants like they were an epidemic. "Here," José said. "Take the spiders." He rummaged around in his pile of flowerpots and came up with a basket he had woven from one of his own vines. He took it over and plopped their big purple majesties unceremoniously into it. A hard copy came to hand, priceless imported paper handmade on Arable. He covered the top of the basket with it, tucked the edges in — they would probably stay in there until they needed their next meal. "Here, for you." He thrust it at the vacillating fellow, whose hands somehow came up to receive it. "To persuade you and your friends that you never ever heard of Terra Station." He turned the man around and guided him back down the greenhouse to the door.

"Thank you, José. Th-thank you."

Exploding supernovae! Ravi thought as he staggered weakly down the corridor away from José's door, one hand under the basket and one holding the paper down on top. Hard copies aren't hard enough for this, he thought as a purple hairy leg explored the gap left between the crinkly paper and basket rim.

But I've been saved, he exulted. There was no doubt in his mind that José had the power to do what he had just done. The man had influence! But for Space sake, if *he* had strings to pull like José had, he wouldn't be piddling around with plants and oddball space stations; he'd be swanning it on First Committee; he'd have a MAN program of his own design that allowed him to do just what he wanted; he'd have lovers and a whole suite of rooms and he'd have Ah Sung spiders every damn weekend of the year.

He practically fainted, realizing that the last item was exactly what he had just got. He wondered in panic, where shall we keep them? In Psych Lab or the dorm? But I've got enough here to pay off anyone with bites. I'll be influential! But what do they eat? Is it just blood? Will I have to supply it all myself? They're big.

And so an active year began for José. It started with the long drawn agonies of withdrawal. Then it entered the ever engaging landscape of a new set of disturbed psyches, as he pondered the MAN records and got into the skins of over five hundred individuals on Terra Station. Then as the months remaining before the departure of the annual starship to Terra Station diminished, he accelerated into the magic land of MAN creation. In a fever, he orchestrated every trick of his multisensual trade to build the moods and subtle shifts in personality that could start a whole community on the road to a reawakening of their humanity. He engaged a team of half a dozen trusted old friends from the psych labs to help roll out the new MAN.

Energized by the deadline, feeling more vital and true to himself than he had at any time since the last time, José made it in time. The starship took his creation away. And so he settled back to wait out the months until it returned: months when their purple majesties would be calling to him. He hoped he would not remember the name of the feeble fellow he had given them to.

# *Seven*

*From The Chronicle of The WraithDaughters — Osen, Book 4:*

Juggling the helix,
and tickling the trout.
Those were the two skills my mother taught me.
Helical juggling
sounds strange and wonderful.
It is.
Psi sci.
The ultimate merger.
I know the meaning of the peptides and the nucleotides,
the neap tides and the spring tides of the insides.
I know the order of the purines and pyrimidines,
the double rings and the single rings,
the chain-mail rings that span the spiral snakes
to form the rungs of the ladder
up which we all will climb to Her.
I know how to scale that chromatic kaleidoscopic melody,
for I know where each gene sings
upon the chromosomes.
I can catch the morphic echoes of health and abnormality,
of psi and rationality.
I can play this sacred game of snakes and ladders.
I can play it with the molecules and I can play it at a distance,
as far away as the Moon if She should require it.
When the double helix halves, I can mutate the rings
to match the patterns in the inherited cabala of my motherline.
Humans were born free,
but everywhere are bound
in sugar-phosphate chains.
When the Goddess moves me,
I can juggle those heavenly helical chains.
I am the last psychokinetic genetic engineer.

   At least, on a good day, in a good year, I can find and alter
a dozen patterns. We're not that ambitious. Not like the gene

techs Up There who think they can create any type of personality. The stars have to be in the right conjunction, of course, the sun, moon, and planets. The rites must be said, and I must be at one with Her. It doesn't happen often.

It never made me fertile. Or most of my line. We were more numerous once. In the end we were unable to overcome that entropic dive to infertility that wraith powers seem to carry with them.

But my psi science did enable me to make those few little changes in the gene splicing of that one little being on Terra Station which opened his mind to me. Govind *is* my child.

But let me tell you this, Sarasvati, and whoever else reads my Chronicle one day:

Tickling the trout is the greater skill.

Psi powers will never be much. Not among fertile sexual beings.

Of course, the whole Galactic economy depends on wraiths flashing the starships through the void. Wraiths are dependable. But wraiths have to be mules. It's the way of things. It's the price the life force pays to entropy for expending too much power. You can't consistently short-circuit the lower laws of physics in the name of the higher laws *and* expect forever to be a participant in the sexual dance.

Ordinary, reproducing, biological beings have got too much vigor, noise, gusto. They can't depend on psi. Psi powers will always flutter like translucent bats in their peripheral vision. The occasional true prophecy, the things flying around a room, the spontaneous healing, the disembodied voices that provide unknowable knowledge: they will always be with you. They will always be the speck of pearl around which saints and charlatans collect the dirty grit of cults: that's the cleverest inversion, cleverer than inverting a seamless rubber ball, and much more to be feared.

You ordinary folk, you can't depend on psi.

Me, I'm halfway between human and wraith. I would be more human than wraith if I could. It is because I can wield some psi powers dependably that I know they are just powers, like muscles, or lasers, or spaceships. Powers are neutral. And we've got plenty enough already to make a decent life. Why search for more? The point is to learn how to use the ones we've got.

That's where trout tickling comes in.

Don't get me wrong. I had the power to make a psi boy up on station, and I used it. The last of the potencies of my line. It was right for me to use it. But can I make good come of it? There's the rub.

Trout tickling. Now, that's a skill. You can move a galaxy if you can tickle the right trout. Without a psi power that you know of in you.

And that's what I will teach Mana to do.

But first I have to tickle her out of the stream she is in. By Gaia, it's proving harder by far than juggling the helix up on station. Harder than catching Govind with stories, which has been a fine piece of trout tickling on its own.

I tried leaving her be. I knew she was drawn to me. It's one of the tools I have to work with in my old age: the fact that I seem to be everyone's favorite grandmother. It certainly wasn't like that when I was middle-aged, I can assure you. Funny how things change. I was too resentful then, I suppose. I can see it now: resentful of being the last one; resentful of my Cave sisters who had lived with knowledge of our line for so long and never shared our vision, never known our broad love of humanity even unto the Galactic Center.

But at that time, I couldn't analyze why people disliked me; I was just itching in my skin. Now that I have given up my resentment in order to enjoy my life (not that it was that easy, or why did I struggle so long? — and yet it was), now, well, everyone loves me. Even if they still hate and fear my cause.

Mana was drawn to me. That was to be expected. But then she got into that girl and that music. I knew from the moment she appeared out of that midwinter storm with Snow Tiger on her back that she was the right one for Govind. Sarasvati was too cool. The other young ones were too ordinary. Only Mana has the heat and steel to match wills with Govind, and I believe, in time, the capacity for subtlety too, to continue my task of tickling him into Gaia's streams.

Above all, she has the originality and courage to survive up there. She killed Snow Tiger, she drew Atlatl to her, she has it. She's a dutiful thing, most of the time. She slaved away bearing all the burdens of her family, unable to turn against her mother until it all exploded in that cataclysm that killed the Tiger. Now in the Caves she's holding out against doing what Amaterasu and the majority think is her duty. She won't do it, because she doesn't want it. I like that stubbornness. But she's avoiding Atlatl in name of another duty, which Raita and Sitala approve of. See how assiduously she practices that sitar. Of course, she's good at it, she enjoys it. But look at how she transformed when Atlatl walked into the Omphalos! She needs a challenge. If only I could catch her imagination for her work of destiny Up There. Her steadfastness will be useful Up There. She'll plug away dutifully for years, and she may have to while Govind is growing up. But then she'll have the fire when he needs it. Oh yes. Trout tickling is only the half of it. At times it takes the sword. The broadsword. The rapier. The tickle. The word. The silence. The laser. Each have their particular role.

I still see her linked with Govind in my trances. But she is far gone from me now. Raita says they will send her to the Deep Fires soon. A long voyage, much of it born on the mercy of Mother Ganga and her daughters, much in the forest.

But still every day I have no sense that I should speak to her. This is the torture of the trout tickler — waiting. Don't grab too soon.

It must come from her. If only she would settle that hatred she has for her mother, which she doesn't even recognize. If only she would go and see her before leaving for the Deep Fires, find forgiveness in her heart. Then she might stop resisting me so.

So now all I can do is pray, many times a day, and light the incense, and cast the spells. All I can do is be right with Her myself. I don't go to the rituals anymore. They fed me once, but I don't need them now — my connection is strong enough. If only I live long enough to see Govind through puberty, to see Mana change her mind.

After Osen had all but named her as the person she wanted to go into space, Mana started to dream badly.

In her dreams she would be in the forest. The great trees bore the snow on their branches, thus sheltering the insects and the little mammals, the snowdrop bulbs in the earth and the patient fir cones. In spring, the life burst forth again. But in summer, a little girl playing house in the family grove lit a bonfire for her corn dollies to watch, and did not put it out well enough. Overnight it ignited the dry oak leaves from the previous fall and the brush pile her mother had not cleared away, and burned the sacred trees all in a raging fire. Hot flames danced like Kali, smoke thick and choking as buffalo demon. She would wake in Sitala's arms and cry out, "I'm sorry! I'm sorry!"

Once she did not wake, but dreamed on. She was on her knees in the burning forest, trying to get below the smoke to breathe. Out of the smoke before her appeared Wolf, her gray coat on fire, her eyes like hot coals, bent on revenge, for she would never escape the fire. Wolf bore down on Anam with fangs that dripped molten fire. Anam huddled down into the roots of a great tree; in panic she tore at the Earth and suddenly found herself traveling down in a tangle of roots and tunnels underground, crawling through a labyrinth of tunnels until there was just one tunnel, and that came to an end. There at the end was an old black crow with accusing beak and cruel eyes. Anam bolted from it and tried to fly away, a panicked, fluttering sparrow, beating her wings against the Earth until she woke.

Mana told the others her dreams, as was the custom in the Caves. It did not exorcise them. She said she had no memory of starting the fire. Sitala said children can feel guilt for things they never did. Raita told her she needed to learn to take control of her dreams, to piss on the flames before they burned the forest. Sarasvati happened to overhear on the occasion over dinner that Mana told Raita and Sitala about her escape under the ground. Unusually, Sarasvati got up, carrying her bowl of cold summer soup and bread, and joined Raita's group. She said she believed the crow might be Mana's mother. She said it might mean that Mana needed to go back to the village and find it in her heart to forgive her mother and ask for her forgiveness. Until she did, she would never be right with the Great Mother. This struck Mana hard, as unexpected truth sometimes does. She thought of her mother and realized how much hardness she felt towards her, how like a harsh crow that woman was in her heart.

Sitala brought her to the deepest healing caves, especially to one where the statue of the Mother held out her arms, and water dripped from the stalactites in a perpetual mantra, washing away hurt. But she remained edgy, unable to forgive, or to be forgiven.

Every day she expected a call to Osen's room. The way Osen had looked at her in that meeting — she wanted her to go into space! She owed her life to Osen; how could she tell her that she was going to go to the Deep Fires?

The call never came.

The dreams continued. She tried to lose herself in her music. But it was hard to concentrate — the quality of her music suffered and there was nothing she could do about it. The joy of it was gone. She longed for the other call she hoped for, the call to go and sing in the Queen's Fire.

And spring turned into summer.

This summer Mana hardly went up above with Sitala at all. After the first year or two, Mana had found the day trips out in the woods with Sitala less easy to arrange. She had chosen the path of the warming songs, and they demanded more and more of her. She and Sitala saw each other alone only at night now. Sitala increasingly found others to go up with. As always, Sitala did this without fuss, calmly accepted the situation and got on with it. Sitala never wasted energy on fretting. If anything needed to be done well, Sitala was a natural choice. But she could not learn the warming songs for her lover. So it was that as spring became the summer of this, her fifth year in the Caves, Mana was very little aware of it.

The solstice was almost on them when Raita came to her one day and told her that in late summer the connection men were going through to meet in the holy city. They would be going from all over the plains and the Ganga Forest, and even from the far South. Some would surely be coming from the Deep Fires, the great ones near the mouth of Mother Ganga, and the lesser ones elsewhere as well, most likely. "If you were to be there," Raita said to her, teasing her with a light tone and face as if she were talking about going to the local village instead of the holy city, "you could talk to them, and find which is most in need of a singer and a sitarist for a few years."

Mana let it sink in for a moment and then gave a great hunting whoop from the village and flung her arms around Raita's neck. Raita hugged her with a great smile on her broad face.

"It's the Queen's Fire I want to go to. Leto told me all about her years there."

"There is one requirement, Mana, that we wish to make of you," Raita replied, disengaging herself. "Queen's Fire or any other, we have a requirement. We are disturbed by your dreams. For once, I think Sarasvati may have something. We have decided you are first to return to your village to take leave of your mother."

"But . . . but she doesn't expect me back. She doesn't want me back."

"She doesn't expect you. But we are sending you."

"But I can't . . . I can't."

They walked in silence most of the first two days. Every now and then Sitala tried to draw Mana out. But all she elicited were snorts, or comments like, "Do they think I'm a child?" The most she said was "This is what will happen: my sisters will babble, to cover their confusion, Mother will keep an accusing silence, and if you try to make nicey nice, I will scream!"

It was turning into a wet, if warm, summer, and their damp leather boots and cloaks did nothing to warm their spirits. They had been lovers for almost five years now and had meshed together well: Mana's intensity and need, Sitala's steadiness. Mana's music had taken from their time together, but it had not caused a rift. Now the years apart in the future stood between them. As did Raita's unwelcome command, which Mana resented and Sitala supported. They spent the first night in a village, the second in a trail shelter, and both times Mana wrapped herself in her cloak on their shared bed and turned her back, needing to be alone.

On the third day, as they came on a diagonal path down the hills, the evergreens and mixed woods gave way to oak and beech. Beech mast, acorns, and dead leaves formed an autumnal carpet in the midst of summer. Lower still, the streams became broader and harder to cross, and then they were down into the great, dense forest that filled the valley of the River Maya. Sitala began to sing a walking song as they entered the deep forest, as a warning to animals. Large, dangerous beasts like water buffalo or tiger would sooner avoid humans than confront them, but if caught unawares would have little choice.

But Mana remained silent.

"Sing!" Sitala commanded. But Mana ignored her. Sitala was pliable and easy most of the time. Lacking Mana's drive to improve, to go deeper into the Earth, she just stuck to the routines of running the Caves and worshiping her planet, and spread her soft warmth and joy around her. But this time she became angry, and her anger made her silent. She stopped singing.

It was two hours that they walked in angry quiet, their presence revealed by the raucous cries of jay and myna and laughing thrush. They ignored the "gorak . . . gorak" of raven, the flashing red tail of bulbul, and even, once, the brilliant crimson coat and blue-black face of pheasant. They pushed through the steamy dankness that hung in the lower levels of the forest even in summer, barely seeing the heavy blooms of orchid, rose, and fungus, or the eyes in the undergrowth. Fear began to seep into Sitala's anger first, and perhaps that is why she reacted in time.

They were coming down the trail toward the river herself, entering a boggy patch in single file, with Mana a pace or two in front, when the undergrowth ahead erupted. There was a smash of bushes and a snort of massive lungs. Afterward Sitala could clearly picture the great curve of those black horns, the power-ful thrust of the shoulders as the infuriated buffalo crashed to-ward them. But at the time it was like her and Mana's anger driving at them, shapeless fury, barely understandable. She threw herself at Mana, and they fell into a thorn bush as the beast crashed by, trampling Sitala's right leg as it went. She screamed and Mana heard the huffing pant of its breath and the thudding of its feet on the trail as it stopped and wheeled around to face them.

Mana held Sitala still with one hand, and stuffed the other into Sitala's mouth to keep her pain quiet. Jays screeched in the trees; the crushed leaves of the bush smelled as sharply as the thorns that drew blood in their flesh. Sitala's teeth bit hard into Mana's hand. So they stayed for minutes. And in the end the buffalo snorted twice and pushed off the trail down toward the water again, snapping branches as it went.

It was some minutes later, when she tried to get Sitala, who had landed on top of her, out of the thorn bush first, that Mana saw Sitala's leg. It was bloody and it was bent at the wrong angle. Mana pulled her knife from her belt sheath and started to cut away the thorn bush around them. It was a long job, with Sitala groaning and whimpering from the pain. Finally Mana was able to slip out sideways, disentangle her bow and arrows from the bush, and let Sitala gently down on a thorny bed. She gathered new bracken nearby and stuffed it underneath her to protect her from the thorns. Then she looked at the leg.

It was snapped just above the ankle. The bone ends pressed at the skin but had not broken through. The blood came from a surface wound. A high, keening voice in Mana's skull accused herself, "I did it. I did it. My fault. My fault. I did this to you."

But she acted calmly, as she had seen adults act in accidents in her childhood. She talked softly and encouragingly, searched the forest for the right leaves to wrap the wound in, the branches that would be long enough and straight enough to splint the leg from foot to thigh. She tore her shirt into strips to bandage the splints, one splint on either side, seven bandages in all. And water for Sitala, and dried pear from their rations, for sweetness to counter shock and the right leaves to chew to dull the pain. None of this could right what her anger had caused, nor still the shrilling accusations in her head. But certainly her guilt wouldn't help Sitala now. She did everything she could think of, and then it was time to decide how to get home.

It was already past midday. She could be in her village by noon tomorrow if she ran during daylight — night was too dangerous; she would have to use a trail shelter. With a couple of village men she could run through the afternoon and night to get back. With Sitala in pain and in danger all the while. Or she could take, what, three days, maybe four, carrying her on her back?

They discussed it and decided to leave Sitala in a hideout made of living and cut thorn bushes. They made it with a space in the middle for a small fire, and Mana spent a good hour scrounging what partially dry wood there was. She left Sitala most of her food and her cloak and kissed her hurriedly, and then was ready to run. Sitala stopped her, "Mana. Don't blame yourself. I am responsible for myself — I kept silent when I knew better."

"Don't be foolish. If I hadn't been such a stupid child, angry and . . ."

"Don't, love. Don't. You always blame yourself. Your dreams. I was going to try to ask you before you got to your mother's, but tell me now . . . I'll never ask again. Is there somewhere deep down in you, some hint of a memory, that the fire that burnt your family trees did really start from you playing house?"

"No!"

Mana ran.

As she ran she yelled. She yelled to keep the animals away, "I did it! I did it! Sitala, Sitala, Sitala. Mother, Mother, Gaia, Goddess, goodness, forgive me forgive me . . ."

She ran into the darkness and all through the night, never seeing the trail shelter, screaming hoarsely into the dark. Before dawn she burst into what had to be her mother's new house, built beside the ashes of the one that was the grave of her grandmother, her brother and Snow Tiger. When someone came to her, she croaked, "It was me, Mother, it was all me, I burned your trees, I've come back, back to stay, I'll help you build back up. Mother, just get the men, get the stretcher, we must get Sitala, I've hurt her . . ."

But it was her father's arms that held her, and his voice that soothed her, and tried to get the sense out of her. He lit a precious oil lamp, gave her last night's tea, cold, to drink, and asked her mother to whip up some food. It was her youngest sister, Devi, the quiet one, who came forward to do that. A tiny child came with her, sleepily holding to her skirts, and a man's voice called from the bed space at the back. So her little sister was married already.

A skilled connection man, her father got the facts out of her quickly, asked Devi to pack up food for the journey, told her husband to roust himself and left to rouse up another helper. Then he was back to pick up his food. He tried to persuade Mana to stay behind, but she insisted on coming.

They led the stretcher party of two young men at a run, the father holding up his oldest child when she stumbled from exhaustion. As the nearest male relative of the one who had been attacked by Buffalo Demon, he carried the small painted icon of Sitala, the village's protectress — it was encouraging to all three men that both protectress and victim bore the same name. They arrived well before dusk.

Sitala was safe, and astonished to see them back so soon. The first thing she did was to persuade Mana to stay and rest. "You'll be no good to me on the walk to your village if you have to be carried yourself," she said. "There aren't enough men to carry us both!" So Mana's father, Rudradaman, stayed with her when Sitala, carrying the icon in her hands, was borne off on the stretcher. Mana collapsed asleep in the thorn hideout. When she woke late in the afternoon, he had a fire going, and they stared into it together while dusk gathered, and afterward into the night.

Rudradaman was a quiet man. To his way of thinking, his work was to pass on the messages of others first. Only then, if at all, did he make his own comments and connections. He walked slowly home with his only unmarried daughter to the great clearing where the villagers kept the forest at bay to plant their grain. He watched as her two sisters and their children clustered around her outside their mother's house, where they had been waiting. The house was a simple log cabin, all that he and she had been able to erect in the lean years after he had come back to find his boy dead and Mana gone. He kept Mana's sisters and their young children out when Mana went in to her mother and Sitala.

Sitala was lying on the bed and her mother sitting on a rug on the floor when Mana entered. She went straight up to her mother, knelt on the floor before her, and kissed her feet. The horny, old red-painted toenails, the cracked skin, the dirt and dust between the toes. She heard her mother's voice of old echo in her head, "If we only had a decent house I would have clean feet for you to kiss . . ." But this time Mana made the greeting with all her heart and refused even to look up until her mother should raise her.

"Forgive me," she whispered to the hard, worn feet, the cheap bangles on the ankle. "Please, Man," she used the respectful ancient word for mother, "please forgive me."

"The healer's been. You're lucky. Your friend's leg will mend." Her mother shifted her feet back under the hem of her old skirt. Surely she had better clothes to wear than this, Mana thought; her sisters outside had been wearing better than this. "But she can't be moved. Who will keep her in this village? Will your sisters keep her? Their hearts are as hard as yours. How can I afford to keep both of you for a month?" The voice was as complaining and shrill as ever.

"I am going to stay, if you want me. I will plant your trees and cut your wood and milk your goat. I will grow your vegetables. I will not go back. I can work to pay you back for Sitala's stay. In time I will build you a new house. We will manage the family forest as it should be managed." Mana said all this to the floor and the hem of her mother's skirt.

"And can you bring the family treasures back? Do they teach you that kind of magic in the Caves? You're a fancy sitar player now. Sitala has been telling me. Can you still milk a goat, can you fell a tree? Can you give me back seventeen years of being the butt of every village joke, the turd under every foot?"

Mana let her forehead touch the dusty floor for one long breath, and then she stood up. "I am sorry to impose. I will go and ask my sisters," she said. "We will stay with them." She sat a moment on the bed. "Are you all right, love? Did they give you anything for the pain?" Sitala nodded. Mana could hardly meet her eyes. She went outside.

When Mana went in to her mother, Rudradaman went to eat at the home of his second daughter, Romila. She was a pretty, bustling young woman not yet twenty, married to a good woodsman and mother of two mischievous toddlers.

"She looks more like a fallen dryad than ever," she said to her father over a glass of her forest wine. "A *shalabhanjika* whose tree has been cut down."

"Yes. She's more beautiful than ever."

"I meant . . ."

"I know what you meant. She was always the tragic one who would never be accepted as priestess because of the fire. But she also brought you up. Don't forget that. She may have felt sorry for herself, but she never let it stop her from doing her duty. She is strong. And then you owe her your life again, that day. She is a chosen one of Gaia. There can be no doubt of that. I fancy if there had been no accident in the forest two days ago, you would have been remarking how happy she seemed, how different."

"Yes, Bapuji. But what is it all about — this running into Mother's house saying she caused the fire?"

"You know her better than I do." Rudradaman stared into his wine.

"How could I? I never knew her. She was always the responsible one — and then it was *that day* and she left. She was never one of us. If she's staying with Uncle Ashwant she'll drive him crazy. He's so straightforward. Perhaps she should stay here and you go to Ashwant's." She sighed. "Funny that Mother insisted on keeping this Sitala with her. A lovely, soft woman. So different from our sister. And it's funny calling our sister 'Mana.' She turned her own name backward."

"Does your mother still have the oiled canvas?"

"It's here." Romila appraised her father. "And yes, the trout are as plentiful as ever in the upper pool. Will you take our sister?" She kissed her father's weathered forehead.

"There's only one way to catch a trout by hand," Rudradaman mused. "And that is to forget everything you ever learned about rod and line. And everything you ever learnt about intention, about manipulation . . . about . . ."

"'I don't have the words for it,'" Mana finished for him.

"How did you know I was going to say that?"

The stream was broad and shallow. Willows and alders crowded the bank, but there was one place where the deer came down to drink and it was easy to wade in. The water rippling over the sandy bottom was warm and clear. Rudradaman had stripped to the buff and put on a genitals pouch he had acquired from some sea people in the far west. He was lean and wiry, and bowlegged from all his riding. Mana smiled to see him easing through the water like a bandy-legged stork.

It was an odd sport. He had spent all the previous afternoon without catching anything. The first few days they were here she had kept saying, "We must go back tomorrow, I promised Mother we wouldn't be long."

"This isn't long," he had said each time.

"I thought you wanted to teach me to catch trout," she had said as many times. But he had said, "When it's time." Now at last he had started to fish, yesterday and today. He was having no success. But he seemed vastly content.

Mana sat in the sun and smelled the wild sage and ruminated on the scrubland around her. Her mother's land, burned almost eighteen years ago and now uncared for, a mess of bushes and young trees of every kind, some of them already quite tall.

The family grove had been growing here for hundreds of years until the fire. Their greatest oak had had a girth of sixty-four feet. Three others had been over fifty feet around. No village for a hundred miles around could boast the like. The massive trunks and heavy, gnarled branches had enclosed Mana's earliest memories. In the lightning-hollowed heart of one of them, the women of her line had kept their family treasures: a brass bowl of ancient design; a terracotta Shakti figure more ancient still, from before the rule of men; a figurine from the men's time, before the Ice, of a flying goddess dressed in red and white stripes, and white stars on blue, made of a strange substance that the teacher called "plastic"; a tooth of Snow Tiger; a carved sandalwood box from the South, and more. All were destroyed.

After the fire, all through her childhood Mana had yelled or sobbed to her mother, "Go to the Caves! Get the priestesses to come and draw the lines for the new grove." But she had never done it.

Almost twenty years lost, and now if they were to plant the

family trees in the sacred order, she would have to cut down the whole area again before she could start. Her mother's stupid bitterness, her own stupid anger. What waste. The scrub was a haven for animals much more than mature forest would be, but her mother didn't even have traps out. She could have traded furs from yellow-throated marten, otter, beaver.

If I hadn't been so angry as an adolescent, she thought, keeping it all in, playing the good girl who does everything in the house, being the precocious would-be priestess, I could have got along with Mother. We could have got the grove started again. The trees would be well established by now, and Mother would be much happier. If I hadn't killed Kali in White and left her these last years . . . If my anger hadn't made us silent in the forest, then Sitala's leg would not have been broken . . . Was it really my fault that the trees burned, as in my dreams? Or am I just temperamentally guilty? Maybe it was a broken piece of glass, or the ashes from someone's pipe. I can't remember.

Why doesn't Father feel guilty? He could have done much more to rebuild than me. She looked miserably at the scrubland that would have to be cleared.

She had asked him the first day up here how the grove burned, and he had only said, "It was the will of Kali Ma."

"Your turn," he called from the stream. She hadn't noticed him catch the trout that was in his hand. She took off her sandals and waded in. She wanted to do her best for him, but it took an eon for a trout to swim close to her. She grabbed. It scattered silver light as it fled.

"Don't grab! Don't try! Don't even want the outcome. If the Goddess wants it, the trout will float into your hand. If not, then you had the joy of dancing as the stream, of swimming as the trout."

"You're so complacent! What if you were dying of hunger? Oh, you catch the damned dinner. I hate this!" She stalked out of the stream, thrust her feet into her sandals, and kept going up toward the scrubland.

It was a hot day; the scrub and emerging woodland lazily abuzz with blooms and bees. Buzzards seemed to doze as they circled. Scents wafted one another out of the way as trees and bushes and flowers fought for space with invisible slow fury. Her forester's and hunter's eye picked up the clues of deer and pika

runs, fox and partridge. She wished she had a bow. She wanted
to kill something.

She walked way beyond the once burnt lands and came back
in the late afternoon, tired but still miserable. She didn't want
another lesson in fishing and philosophy. She wanted her father
to be hunter, not sadhu. Catching fish was just about catching
fish, not about getting right with the world. Of course there
shouldn't be a difference . . . "You're a priestess," he would say
when they ate the trout, "you should know that." But what sort
of priestess was she, consumed with guilt and fury as soon as she
left the sanctuary of the Caves and returned to her family home?
Nothing! She had learned nothing. Her mind was churning so
much she almost missed the sight that was to change the afternoon, and far more than that.

She was walking along a slight ridge bordering a bowl-shaped
dip in the land. The bowl was filled with low bushes and honey-
suckle vines. She caught a glimpse of a bare patch of dusty
ground at the edge of the bowl, by a bank. The sight said, "a
den, a fox's earth where the young have been playing." She
stopped involuntarily. Half a minute later two tiny forms rolled
into view, so bound up in each other she didn't see for a moment that they were wildcat kits. She held her breath and
watched. Two more came scampering after. She was upwind of
them, and it was no surprise when she heard the mother's quiet
but urgent mewing, a sound that froze their tiny forms for an
instant and then galvanized them into dashing back out of sight.

Instead of going on, Mana stopped and sat where she was.
The kits had brought some sudden peace into the afternoon,
and she wanted to stay in it a moment longer before returning
to her father, to whom she would have to apologize. Ten minutes later the wildcat padded into clear view of her and lay down,
watching her. Too astonished to do anything else, Mana stared
back. Slowly the little ones moved to be by their mother, and
then, sensing her content, tumbled into their games again. There
had never been wildcats here before, not in all the history of the
family. Tales would have been told of them. The trees had gone,
but there were wildcats now where the grove had been. The
mother let her watch for half an hour or so before padding back
with the kits as calmly as she had come out. What could account for it? The goddess Sitala had given her a rare gift.

She collected some wild mushrooms to make up for not catching the trout. It was close on dusk when she got back, and Rudradaman had already started a fire and gutted his trout. Instead of greeting him, on an impulse she slipped straight into the stream, sandals and all. It was cool and sweet to her feet. It flowed past her with all a stream's delight and unconcern. She saw the trout at once, a big fat one, nosing into the current under the place where a weeping willow's slim leaves swept the water. It was no problem to move with the stream towards him. It was just hard to see, as the light fell. In the end it was in complete darkness that she felt his scales tickle her fingertips, and then her palm. There was no sense of triumph. She laughed as she gave it to her father to cook, and he laughed back.

They ate the fish and mushrooms fried, with potatoes baked in the ashes, and a wild salad of dandelion leaves and garlic.

Thinking about his bandy legs, she asked, "Why did you become a connection man?"

"I know," he said. "You've been thinking: if only he had stayed after the trees burned, Mother would be well off again by now; no treasures, but at least a decent house. With a hallway where a small boy could take off his boots, and a pulley weight to close the door against intruders."

They watched the flames for a long time.

"I had to get away from her tongue," he said at last. "Like you."

"Didn't you feel guilty?"

"Of course. But no more. It was right for me. I'm a traveler."

They let the fire die down to glowing embers. Finally she threw on another couple of logs.

"Father, I've been asked to go to the Deep Fire places. To play the ragas, to lead the singing. And there's an old priestess, half the time I don't know if she's as crazy as Grandmother was, or saner than all the rest of us put together. She's African. She wants me to go to the space station."

"So you decided to come back and look after your mother, instead?" He smiled wonderingly at her.

"I think I know why I said that to her. Guilt. All that. You wouldn't be guilty. So I had to be. Or something."

"You would make a good connection woman. With the space station, eh? A daughter of mine!" He laughed ruefully, scratching his thin beard.

"Oh, don't *you* start suggesting what I should do. You're the only one I know with no ax to grind."

He half got up to reach behind him for his pack, pulled out his hand ax and his sharpening stone, and began to polish the flat steel blade. She smiled. "I love you, Bapuji."

"Won't you play for me?"

"I left my flute at Mother's."

But he had brought his own in his pack. Silently he handed it to her. Instead of playing the songs he had taught her as a child, the typical flute music, she started to pick out the themes of the ragas she had been playing on the sitar. Neither of them had ever heard such a thing attempted on the flute. It was like a thin echo shorn of the sympathetic strings and drones. Presently he saw that she was weeping as she played.

When the tears and the music were over, he said, "Something happened to you on the walk."

"The wildcats are breeding. They never would have done if it had been a managed plantation. I think I . . . I believe I . . . prefer it the way it is."

He smiled a long, slow smile that took all the evening to fade, and even then not completely.

They were a day's walk from the village, but they could have been a thousand miles away. That night, they lay on their backs on the oiled canvas instead of using it as a tent, and got vertigo looking at the stars, until they fell dreaming into them.

The next day he packed up, and they returned.

When they got back, Sitala had some color in her cheeks. Mana's mother made a sharp comment about how long they had stayed away, and when that got no response, grumbled about the amount of extra work she had had to do. Mana caught Sitala's eye and they smiled together about her mother's grumbling. Mana could not think of any time in her whole life when she had smiled with someone else about her mother. Her anger and guilt seemed to have drained away up there with the wildcats. She embraced Sitala in a hug that she wanted to go on forever. "I love you so much," she whispered while her mother busied herself at the stove.

That evening, Mana's mother served them all a fine meal of venison, sweet sauce, yams, and wheat cakes, Sitala smiling on a large pile of cushions with her leg in a new cast, Romila and

Devi and their husbands and children chattering noisily, Rudradaman watching carefully.

When her mother brought on the forest fool, a berry compôte with a face piped on it in fresh cream, Mana exclaimed, "Oh! Thank you, Mother. It was always my favorite. It's so lovely." She kissed her and got her first half smile in return.

Afterward, as they left the house together, she said to Rudradaman, "My apology to Mother that first day, my offer to stay, it must have worked after all. I think she must want me to stay. She smiled at me at dinner. Did you see?" She stopped and contemplated the grass and bushes that had grown up lushly over the burned patch beside the new house.

"Or else she likes the fact that now you aren't apologizing."

"What do you mean?"

"You seem at peace." They began strolling through the village to Romila's house. "You were pretty frantic before we went fishing. In fact, you've been pretty frantic most of your life." He smiled slowly at her. It was one of his connections. He had never said much to her about herself.

"I *am* at peace. Playing the flute to you up there. I know what I want to do. I have done for years. Guilt keeps sidetracking me. Guilt about Mother, guilt about Atlatl, guilt about Osen. Osen will be disappointed. But Mother will probably be relieved, don't you think? There's only one thing that is really me, and that's my music and the deep Earth. It's the Deep Fire places I should be in. I am surer of that now than I have ever been"

There was a commotion down the lane. A rider had appeared. Mana recognized the pony first. It was from the village by the Caves. She started toward it. They've sent for me early to go to the Deep Fires, she thought. As soon as I made peace with Mother and myself, they knew and sent for me. Oh Sitala! I can't go yet, not now, with my family around me and you healing. She didn't know whether to run to the rider or away from him.

The young man was already being given directions by the time she reached the small crowd that had gathered around. She caught her mother's name.

"I am Mana," she said. "What do you want? What's happened?"

"I bear a message, priestess." He was exhausted. Dust had stuck to the sweat on his face. Then more sweat had made rivulets through it.

"Let me get you a drink of well water and a clean wet cloth for your face."

"Later, priestess. The old one is dying. Osen, Wraith-Daughter. She desires you to come back with me. At once."

"Osen! Not now!"

Not dying when her work is just begun.

Save her, Kali Ma, give her back to us.

"Of course, I'll come. I'll come at once."

Her father came up. "Bapuji, I have to go. The old African priestess may be dying. I'll be back as soon as I can, two weeks maybe. Be good to Sitala for me."

She ran to her mother's house. Her mother and Sitala were chatting on the front step in the sunshine like old friends. At least I have given Mother something, she thought, a friend, a priestess daughter she can like. And for a moment she saw that one day she too would be able to sit with her mother like this, easy, companionable. That would be Sitala's and her mother's gift to her, and Sarasvati's and Raita's too, for they had insisted she come. She embraced them both. They were amused by her warmth. She explained, and added, "It will only be a week or two, three at the most. Take care of each other." She went in to get her things, and some food and drink for the messenger.

Her good-byes were tearful but lighthearted. As she rode through the forest behind the rider on his pony, it was a delight to her to imagine that her mother and Sitala would be sitting there enjoying each other, with her father adding the odd connection or two with that wise, wry look on his face, until she returned.

# Eight

As the priestesses gathered around Osen's bedside with incense and soft prayers, and watched the gallant struggle in the old woman's dimming eyes, her son, Govind, giggled with all a five-year-old's delight in a game. "We are going to play a game," she had said to him. "Sometimes in life it is necessary that we play strange games. I think now it is time for me to play that I am dying. I will not be able to talk to you all day, but do not be afraid. I will try to show you what is going on, if I can. I only wish that Mana would come, and feel, and know that you and the Galaxy need her. Damn that girl. She'll be the death of me yet."

But as the game dragged on, Govind stopped giggling. He went to Gauri, and he hugged her. This time she did not run away from him. She said, "What is it, Vinny?"

"Osen is dying," he said.

She put her small, thin arms around his plump body and rocked him back and forth. She wouldn't have done it if any of the adults had been there to see, or anyone but their own peers, who were used to Govind.

"It's all Mana's fault," he said. "I know it is. She's killing Osen. She won't follow the plan.

"Oh, she's coming now. She's arrived," he said. Gauri was used to Govind talking to his "mother," the person he called Osen. When he did his eyes would go funny, like a doll's eyes, and his arms would go limp, and he would just sit there and often smile or laugh, or half say things, or look like children look when they are being told a good story, entranced.

"She's coming into the room. She's weeping as she bends over Osen. Osen's eyes are hardly open, it's blurry." This time Gauri found that Govind was still holding onto her tightly. "She's killing her, she's killing her."

"It's only a game, Vinny," whispered Gauri. "You said it was only a game."

\*       \*       \*

The Chairperson of the Station Committee lay back, luxuri-
ating under the weight of his lover's body, her soft thighs heavy
on his, her chin nestled into his neck.

"That was the best thing I ever did," he said.

"What?" She nibbled at his smooth chin.

"That vote to keep Govind. Out in the open. Only our dear
foreigner abstaining. It liberated me."

"Liberated us, dearest."

"What on earth do you think Madlarki's up to?"

"Nothing on Earth, dearest."

They had met in the Chairperson's office for a small drink,
to celebrate the arrival of the annual spaceship and the
non-arrival of any massively angry bureaucrats from the Center.
Not even a small message of disapproval had been sent. And
last year's starship had taken all the MAN records and security
recordings and a report from Audit that must have positively
frothed with outrage at the Terran decadence that had erupted
on station. They had expected demotion, postings to other planets, anything but what had actually happened, which was: nothing.

The more they thought about it, the more the Chairperson
and the nursery nurse had concluded that a small drink was
quite inadequate as an expression of the unCodelike relief they
felt at this turn of events. So they had decided also to celebrate
the Chairperson's recent unspacelike discovery that he could
prevent his Office door being opened by wedging his shiatsu
mouse underneath it. How much more healthy it really was, he
thought as they made love on the floor, to use the shiatsu mouse
for that purpose instead of having it run over his body working
his pressure points. There was a lot to be said, he thought, for
some Terran customs, like falling in love.

And then, as often happened to Chairperson from one moment to the next, the worries flooded back in. And the biggest
worry was: why is MAN doing this? Has MAN forgotten us? Are
we lost in the bottom drawer of the bureaucracy? Is there no
one who will save us from ourselves? Can I desire anything with
impunity?

Visions flashed through his mind — Chairperson as sultan,
with a harem of lovers, Chairperson as Martin of Arable, with
his own baby, Chairperson making friends with wraiths, Chairperson crowned king of the Terra Station tribe . . .

Then this worry grew to such awesome proportions that . . . for a moment he saw it all clearly. If MAN had forgotten Terra Station, then he himself would have to decide which of his desires to follow and which to suppress. Everyone on station would have to do that. But he knew he was ahead of them all in the strangeness of his desires. Self-management would be toughest for him, and on top of that they would expect him as Chairperson to make decisions for them. This is what it would truly mean, he realized, to be a king.

"What's wrong?" asked his lover. "You've gone all rigid and cold."

Chairperson pushed her off him, so that she rolled against his desk and bruised her shoulder, and objected. He stood up, naked. He took deep breaths and shook himself. After a few moments he was a little calmer.

"Nothing. Nothing at all. Just a bad dream. Must have fallen asleep. Did I hurt you?" He slumped into his office chair and was not displeased that Vladimir came and laid his head against her breasts and stroked his hair as she might a baby's.

On that distant, swampy green jungle of a planet called Madlarki, José sat amidst the riotous chlorophyll of his greenhouse and thought about Terra Station.

All his life's achievement so far had come down to this greenhouse; well, he had two sons, that was something, he supposed, ne'er-do-wells though they were. But otherwise the greenhouse was it — built for some forgotten botanist, acquired as his private quarters by dint of using every scrap of influence he could orchestrate, which had to be continuously maintained lest some envious busybody get him sent back to a dormitory out of spite. It was furnished to his taste with bed, table, wicker chairs, and survival stove, and it had come to feel like home.

It was an achievement probably unparalleled on Madlarki.

But Terra Station was his new love. He would happily give up the greenhouse forever if it would help him nurture a new society on Terra Station.

The ingredients were all there: the pot, the seeds. His custom MAN would just add a little water, a little more air in which to grow.

His idea was not to redirect the people through MAN. That would be too easy. And they were too used to that anyway.

What would it amount to if they all started having babies and love affairs on MAN's suggestion? What they needed was space in which to find their own directions, however long that took. His new MAN was conservative and accepting of newness at once.

What would be really wonderful, he mused, is if they would bring up Govind's mother, the old priestess. José was convinced she existed. What was stranger, a four-year-old who thought up all that stuff, or a true wraith daughter? They could send a spaceship for her.

That was another reason he didn't want his MAN program changing things too rapidly. This Earth priestess might have her own plan. As the child grew up, or if the priestess could be brought up station, things would become clearer. Still, he might be able to nudge them toward going down there to look for her.

But right now, there was nothing to do but wait a year for the annual ship from Terra, and then spend another year tweaking the MAN programs for delivery on the *next* ship. Dealing with such a remote place required more patience than breeding Ah Sung spiders.

José pottered around his plants, trimming deadheads, adding water, fussing. He wondered if his subliminals had been adequate, neither too subtle nor too bold. It was a trick, getting MAN to put ideas into people's heads without them realizing it, and without it compromising their free will. A sly and unprincipled rope trick. But what was he to do? That was the nature of MAN. Who else was using MAN as responsibly as he was, all things considered?

The nursery nurse had put her space fatigues back on, to the Chairperson's great regret. She was just applying a subtle puff of shadow from her make-down kit to diminish the impact of her high cheekbones — a daily chore — and another waft of powder to her cheeks, whose current flush properly belonged in the softroom and was quite out of place in working hours, when she asked, "Does this lack of criticism from the Center mean that you're going to put Govind's scheme to the vote, then?"

He liked to call it his scheme.

But she liked to remind him that it was she who had suggested it to him, from something little Govind had said one day.

A few minutes ago he would have joyfully shouted, "Yes!"

Now he felt panicked at the thought of deciding this one himself. He stared blankly at her for so long, Vladimir asked if he had heard her question.

Suddenly he knew the answer. He felt full of energy.

"Yes!" he leaped up from his chair. He grabbed her around the waist. "It's almost a hundred years to the day since that last ferry went down and brought up the African child. And now we're going to do it again!" He kissed her ecstatically.

She reapplied shadow. "You need some, too." She dabbed at his face. "And a little lip-down for you too." She rummaged in her make-down case.

"Don't fuss, dearest. I've got my own. Where shall we send the ferry this time? Australia? There's nothing much left of those big land masses toward the pole is there — what did they call them — Europe, America? Or was it China? All under the ice. What's on a line with Africa?" It was astonishing, when he came to think of it, how little he actually knew about Earth.

"Govind's idea is that you should send down to bring up the old woman he calls his 'mother.' He says she's sick and we could cure her. She's in the top of that triangular bit next to that ice sheet over the mountains. You can't miss it, it's the nearest ice to the equator. I've been looking."

"All right!" He was feeling decisive. "Get us some decent directions from the boy, and we'll go."

Osen hung on from day to day. Mana found she could hardly bear to leave her room. Somehow all was right, for the time being at least, between her and Sarasvati. Mana had thanked her when she came back for suggesting she go back to see her mother. Something had really happened to her, she said, even if not to her mother. Suddenly, as she said it, she wished she could hear her mother and Sitala talking, to see how her mother was as a person with someone who loved her and wasn't angry at her. "Sitala, I love you," she whispered under her breath, and Sarasvati, of all people, put out a hand to comfort her. Things had been better since then.

But before that, when Mana had arrived after a long, hard ride with the village lad on his pony, she had found Osen unconscious and had asked the healer, "What is wrong with her?"

"Nothing is wrong," the healer said. "She has recognized the time of her death."

"But she wouldn't do that. Not with Govind only five years old."

"So you've accepted that Govind is not an old woman's fantasy," Sarasvati said.

Mana realized that now that she had found clarity about her own life and future, she felt able to say, "Yes, Sarasvati, I accept it. And her vision of warming the Earth by enlisting the Galaxy's help — that is a fine dream."

"Will you help me care for her?"

"I would be honored."

Now for many days they had cared for the dying woman together. There was enough for both of them to do without any competition. Fresh pine needles had to be gathered. Broth had to be cooked just so, and spoon-fed into the old, dry lips. Osen's blankets were always too heavy or too light, the lights too dim or too bright. Unable to visit her shrine, the little stone alcove at one end of her room, Osen wanted the ancient stone figurines brought for her to hold, to feel the great breasts and thighs, the prehistoric passions of the Earth. Often she wanted Mana to bring her sitar and to play softly with Old Somri, a priestess almost as ancient as Osen, who could still make the tabla drums talk and sing.

The women of the Caves drifted in and out. Many brought pieces of the Earth: favorite rocks, shells, flowers. A pile of gifts grew around the bed — a basket woven in twigs and grasses, a weaving in wool, a netsuke carving of a hibernating squirrel, a walnut. In the last years two or three of the new arrivals to the Caves had taken to spending time with Osen. One of these brought her a double helix carved from the entwined roots of a hawthorn; on a thread of silk within its spiral hung an almond carved as a fish swimming upward. In this young woman was a desolate sadness that was different from the serenity of most who came in and out of Osen's room.

All knew that sixty-five generations of WraithDaughters came to an end here. But most of the women, Raita foremost among them, seemed to enter Osen's room with new confidence, now that she was going. To Mana's eyes, watching from behind her great, long-necked, mother-of-pearl-inlaid sitar, Raita's group looked happier in the room than they had before. They were able at last to show their love without having to fight its recipient. They were reclaiming the sky sister for the Earth.

Raita stayed all through one precarious night when Osen's breath seemed to grow fainter every hour, and when, had it not been for the frown that flickered across her wrinkled forehead every time Mana stopped playing, they would have thought she was leaving them. But Raita noticed little of this. The music seemed to transport her. She sat in lotus and breathed the breath of the Goddess. She was in a trance all night long. The methane lights flickered in the cave, making the relief carvings of the Isis story move on the walls and the shadows of the priestesses merge into the legend. In an alcove, the bulging figurines of the Old Mother stood patiently. The candles set before them gave them warmth, and their blank faces reflected ancient blessing.

In the morning, Raita rose and danced with the languorous heaviness of the trance and the grace of the Mother, slow and hypnotic. The women cleared the floor before her feet. As if the whole of the Caves were magnetized to that point, women appeared at the doorway and slipped in to sit reverently around the room, even on the dying women's bed with her. All that could be heard was the shuffle and twist of Raita's bare feet on the rock, the swish and rustle of her russet robes. At last Raita came to a halt, her arms open, her eyes closed, her head thrown back. They waited for the words of the Goddess.

"Chariots part the sky" Raita half sang, half spoke, in trance.
"The sun grazes the Earth
Fires blaze in Ice
Gaia's spores scatter across the Heavens
The Spring Queen gathers her skirts
And laughs to see the Corn God green
The sitar sounds in the Deep Places
The winnowing baskets fly up into the air
In the deeps of space the seeds germinate."

It was not what anyone had expected to hear from Raita's lips. Osen herself might have prophesied in such terms. Mana caught Sarasvati's eye tentatively, for they still had not talked about Osen's mission together, since learning that she was dying. She was pleased to see surprise and gratitude in Sarasvati's eyes rather than triumph. Osen's death was changing them all.

"Hear this and let the Goddess be praised." Old Somri brought the saying to a close.

All bowed and swept the ground with their sleeves. They touched their hands and foreheads to the rock. Raita woke, weak from the trance. She found willing hands to help her walk over to some cushions and sit; others offered her a glass of water, a pinched leaf of fresh mint to smell. They began to tell her what she had prophesied in her trance. But they were interrupted as Raita's twelve-year-old daughter burst in.

Koré's eyes were wild and her bare legs scratched and bleeding. She leaped into the room and stood like a priestess hot from an aurochs hunt. "Where were you all?" she shouted. "I couldn't find you anywhere!"

They were used to her theatrics; they all said she would be great at running the initiation ceremonies one day, and might even revive the plays to take through the villages. But this time it looked like more than theatrics.

"What's happened?"

"A roar like thunder . . . right out of a blue sky. A thing came down. White shining metal. Marti yelled to me, 'Run!' But I said, 'It's a spaceship!' There was fire in the grass, smoke billowing everywhere. It was going to be a big prairie fire. Then there was a huge spray from the metal ship. Misty water. I got wet. It put out the fire! Then the door opened. Marti had run. A person got out. A man. I walked up. I said, 'Welcome to Gaia. I am a girl. Take me.' Like the African child. But he said, 'No. We want a WraithDaughter, an adult.' So I came looking for you, Mother . . . Mother?"

But Raita had fainted clean away.

For a moment the roomful of priestesses was silent, as they wondered whether it could be true that a spaceship had indeed come and that the daughter of an Earth priestess had almost given herself to the Sky Gods.

Then there was pandemonium as people tried to revive Raita, and to ask Koré for details, and to look at each other to see what to believe.

"We must go and see the spacemen!" Sarasvati made for the door.

"No!" A friend of Raita's moved quickly to reach the door first. "We must first decide if we want to meet them."

"I will go and find out what they want," said Sarasvati.

"And get taken up? No one leaves until we decide, together."

Everyone's voices broke out in a babble.

Mana cut her nails across her sitar strings in a dissonant slash that brought everyone's attention to her. "Would you argue in a dying woman's room?" she asked in a quiet voice to shame them. "Osen still lives. We must ask her."

Sarasvati walked swiftly to the bed and knelt to whisper to Osen.

"She wants you," she said to Mana.

Mana wrapped her sitar in its soft cloths and placed it carefully against the rock wall. She got up and knelt beside the ancient priestess's bed, leaning over to whisper, "What?"

"You go." The sound was barely audible. "On the spaceship."

"No. They want a WraithDaughter. They want you."

"I am dying. You. Go."

"No. The Goddess has made plain to me — I have other things to do. But your vision must have a chance. Sarasvati wants to go."

"That will be no chance." The words drifted from the old lips, the tongue barely moving. "But so be it. Let Sarasvati go."

Mana sat back on her heels. If this had happened before I had gone home, she thought, before I played the flute for Father, I would have been in frantic doubt. "Sarasvati is to go," she said to the assembled women. Some looked excitedly at Sarasvati.

"Sarasvati? A sky thinker like Osen?" Raita's rasp surprised them all. "If anyone goes at all, it should be someone who is bound to the Earth." They remembered the trance Raita had been in all night, and the Goddess's words that had come of it barely a few minutes before, now almost forgotten. "But I say, no priestess of the Earth goes. No daughter of mine." She had Koré by her side now and was hugging her tightly. "If someone has to go, let them take a villager."

"But your speaking, Raita, the Goddess spoke through you." Sarasvati spoke like an older woman, with authority. "'Chariots cross the sky.' That's the spaceship. 'Gaia's spores scatter across the heavens.' That is us. 'The winnowing baskets fly up into the air.' 'In the deeps of space the seeds germinate.' It is clear. We are the spores, the Caves are the winnowing baskets sending us up. Gaia looks outward. Let me go. Let someone else come with me." And then, to the granite of Raita's face, she said, "Would you deny this to Osen, last of the WraithDaughters, on her death bed?"

"How do you know she is dying?" Raita, as she had done so often before, made Sarasvati gasp. "WraithDaughters have pow-

ers we know nothing of. Perhaps she is manipulating all of us.
You know where her motherline lived before? In Africa, not far
from where the last spaceship came down. And now Osen is
here, and the spaceship is here. How did it land here? Right by
our savannah tower? She is in league with them. She has always
been a manipulator, a politician, a schemer, a scientist. She
thinks with her head, not with her heart, not with her womb,
not with the Earth. Her only child is a child of her brain. And
Sarasvati is her pupil. I say no one goes. We have more important things to do.

"Who disagrees?"

Sarasvati, already standing, raised her hand. Less than half a
dozen of Osen's friends stood up, including Old Somri and three
young women. Koré stood up, defiant. No one of consequence.
Mana watched and then slowly raised herself to her feet from
beside Osen's bed.

"I do not know how these Caves were begun," she said. "I
hear that in the beginning of the Ice Time there was chaos over
all the Earth, and wars and famines and disease. And many priests
of the old Sky Gods died, and also many priestesses of Gaia.
Were our Cave Mothers who retreated here fleeing into the Earth?
Or were they planning how to preserve, how to keep the light?"
She pointed to the bacteria lamps that she had never seen in a
village. "And how to keep the dark, this warm dark that sur-
rounds us, so that the Goddess and the secrets of true living
with the Earth could be given back to the people after the chaos
was over? Is it not demeaning them to say they were not plan-
ners too? Were they not political, scheming for Gaia? Have they
not given us the scientific project of the Deep Fires, to warm
the earth once more? Do we tell the villagers the truth about
where their tithes go? This is manipulating them, for science,
for schemes. Now Osen has a new plan, and we cannot spare
one of us to give our light and our dark to the people who survived up there?"

One more young woman stood up. Only one.

"So that's that," said Raita. "We will wait here until the
spaceship leaves." She named several women to guard the towers, and several more to guard Osen's room. "All those who
stood up for Osen can wait with her here. The rest — we have
Gaia's work to do. Koré, Come with me." She got up to walk
out. So did most others in the room.

"Wait!" shouted Sarasvati. "This is women's rule, not men's! There is no dictatorship here. I am free to go."

"And are you free on your own to destroy the Caves? To let them know where we are? To consort with the enemy? You go and they will torture you or drug you to make you talk, and then they will come here and destroy us. We guard you here for the Goddess." Raita left. Koré followed her with her head down.

They had tried arguing with the guards. They had tried a rush through them at dead of night when all had seemed to be asleep. But Raita's young women were tough. In the morning, Mana and Sarasvati looked at their dying mentor with the hopelessness of defeat.

Koré and another twelve-year-old girl came with breakfast bowls of hot algae and barley. They set down the trays and Koré's friend ran off. But Raita's daughter just stood there, looking at the ancient lady on the bed. Mana began to wonder how it had been that this earth sprite, cave born and rock enclosed, had come to offer herself to go with the spacemen, "like the African child." Had Osen been telling her stories? Mana caught Sarasvati's eye and nodded Koré's way enquiringly. "Could Koré slip out?" she whispered behind her spoon. Sarasvati was cave born. Might there be secret ways out that the children of the Caves knew?

Sarasvati's eyes widened. She reached for the great book of Osen's Chronicles and began to write. She coughed loudly, to hide the sound of tearing vellum. When Koré took back the empty bowls, there was a note for her in one of them.

Koré wriggled on her tummy up the earthen crack. It smelled bad, of badger. There was a lot more fresh earth scattered around than the one time she had come before. And she had gotten bigger. It was hard to find a comfortable place to put her catapult. It was a shame she had not been able to put her forest leathers on, the ones Mana had made for her. But that would have been letting on she was going out. Her cotton cave tunic would be ruined.

She raised her head from the badger hole into the daylight carefully, and breathed in the smell of damp pine and convolvulus. An overcast summer day. Had been raining. No one about. She crept out and flitted from tree to tree like a dryad.

Moving through the savannah was more difficult. The stone tower, with its four doors stacked one on top of the other to give access during even the heaviest snows of winter, was over a mile from the woods' edge. Beyond it she could just make out the gleaming cap of the spaceship. They were still there! There was no one on the tower lookout that she could see. Probably so afraid of being snatched into space, they hadn't even dared show their noses.

The herds had been at the grass all summer, and it was too short to hide her standing. She crawled on her hands and knees, at times wriggled on her stomach, for almost three quarters of a mile, until she reached a hillock tufted with bushes where she could crouch, stretch, and see the round tower more sharply. Now she was pretty sure there was no one at the stone battlements on top. Someone could still be looking through the little windows in the doors, though. But why would they? Koré knew her people. They would be turning their backs on the spacemen in righteous indignation. She thought of a crouching run that would get her in range of the spaceship. She had some beautiful pebbles in her pocket, her best ones; they would clang against the spaceship when she got within catapult range, and she could reach the spacemen with her message before the tower guards rushed out. Or would someone be watching out, after all, and run out to stop her? She knelt down again, her heart beating. She could see the spaceship better now, too. It looked like the phallus in the spring rites, but on its side, on spindly legs, a running lingam. It was just as she had first seen it, only now it was not wreathed in smoke and flame and cool spraying water, but seemed dead, an icon from the ancient days. Her eye caught motion, and she saw a head move from the shadow of one of the battlements on the tower. So someone had been there all along! She was sunk.

And then the oddest thing in all the world happened. A door in the spaceship opened, and a thin ladder unfolded to the ground. Down this walked a little creature. If she had not already seen and talked to the spacemen, she would have thought that *this* was the spaceman. It had legs and arms and a head, but was no taller than a small child. At the bottom of the ladder it set off across the grass away from her. It was not very fast. But it seemed very determined. As she watched she realized that it was making a huge circle all around the far side of the tower, and suddenly she knew it was coming for her.

Twenty minutes later she could hear its little noises as it waddled on its circle nearer and nearer to the hillock behind which she hid. She could see the painting on its front of a round disk with swirls of white and shapes of blue and green on it, set on a field of black dotted by stars and the moon. In clear letters underneath she could read the words TERRA BOT. It whirred and hummed softly, and huffed and creaked a bit when the ground was very uneven. It came closer and closer.

As it came right by her she held out her hand with the message from Sarasvati, and it took it in its metal hand! Without stopping, it dropped something on the ground beside her and winked its eyes at her as it kept on walking. When it was safely back in the spaceship, her eyes having followed it every step of the way, she turned to pick up what it had dropped. It was oblong with knobs, like something the ancients might have made. It wasn't a message for Osen. It was a treasure, and all her own.

"What in Space is going on with that ferry?" demanded the Chairperson of Station Committee. "Or should I say what on Earth? It should be able to make contact with a bunch of nervous priestesses."

"News just in," came the reply. "Contact made. Heatseek spotted the original contact, a girl child, making elaborate attempt at secret approach. Exchanged messages with her. Seems that there *is* an old woman called Osen in caves under the savannah there. So your Govind was right after all."

The Chairperson did not like the way the space techs had taken to calling Govind "his" the last couple of days. He himself thought of Govind rather as belonging to a certain nursery nurse who had believed that the boy wasn't dreaming. Several times in the last days the Chairperson had thought he was the one who must have been dreaming to have listened to her — the power of dimples! He had in these last hours acquired a wholly new understanding of why love affairs had been banned by the Space Code — they affected your reasoning powers. Now he had a space ferry tied up downplanet for days, waiting for someone imagined by a five-year-old child.

And yet there *was* a woman called Osen.

"Tell them to get hem out of there, fast!"

"The message said, unfortunately, that hey is dying. However, a woman called Sarasvati — strange names they have down

there — is willing to come. Hey told the ship to come back in
two days to a forest clearing that we can identify on our satellite
maps, where hey will meet it."

"Two days! Well. I suppose it can sit there for two more
days. How warlike are these people? Is it in danger?"

"Hey wants the ship to appear to have gone altogether, so
that the people who are preventing hem from leaving the Caves
will let hem go. The ferry is requesting permission to comply."

More fuel, more expense. "Yes, agreed. Two days only,
though!" What savages. Uncontrolled hormones. Space teeth,
the Chairperson thought, I'm glad to be a civilized human.

Mana leaned against a tree, panting, too tired to wipe the sweat
and rain from her eyes.

"There's barely two hours left," Sarasvati gasped. "We've
got to keep going. If we're not there, we can't be sure they'll
wait."

With the caution of a rabbit, Raita had refused to let anyone out of the Caves for two nights. Koré had let Mana and
Sarasvati know of her success right away, and as Raita's prohibi-
tion had dragged on, they had wondered about getting the girl
to try to ask a villager to take a message to the spaceship to
change the time of the rendezvous; but when they had looked
for her, the little girl had disappeared into the children's world
of the Caves, the tunnels that even cave-born adults forgot. At
last Raita had announced that it was safe to go out.

Mana had been the first to leave, ostensibly to return a
waterskin to the young villager whose pony she had shared on
the ride back from her village, and a short while later Sarasvati
had popped out to get some fresh pine needles for Osen's room.

So at last they had got on their way, with a fighting chance
on a hard trail of running to the rendezvous in time. Sarasvati
had insisted that Mana come as her companion, because she
was forest born and could move faster than any of Osen's other
supporters. But it was Sarasvati whose energy was keeping them
going now. Mana had started off carrying the heavy pack that
Osen had insisted be taken to Govind — it contained her life's
four volumes of the Chronicles of the WraithDaughters. But
Sarasvati carried it now. She seemed afire with her mission. Mana
was already worrying about her own trip back through the forest, alone and unarmed. She had counted on finding a bow and

quiver at a trail shelter, but the first shelter they had passed had had none. If only Sarasvati had not insisted on a rendezvous so far away. She was glad, in theory, to be able to do this one thing for Osen, but she wasn't driven like Sarasvati.

"Face it. We'll never make it by noon," she said. "They'll just have to wait."

As if to prove her point, the rain, which had been light up until then, suddenly started to come down in earnest. It was the sort of rain that could turn a forest trail to mush in minutes. They struggled on. Soon they were no longer even attempting to run.

The streams were rising from the heavy rain. Sarasvati turned an ankle in fording one of them, and they had to rest before she could go on. Noon came and went by Mana's forestborn internal clock and weather eye. It must have been nearer four in the afternoon when they finally staggered toward the clearing. They peered ahead through the trees.

At the far end of the long clearing, the ship was there, a leggy fish made to fly.

Sarasvati started to run forward into the open space. Mana hung back, sobered by the reality of the alien thing in the distance. It was the return of the male Gods to the planet the Goddess had reclaimed. She did not want even to be seen by it. But above all she was glad at last to stop, her duty to Osen done.

Sarasvati did not realize she was alone until she had gotten well out into the clearing. As she turned to look for Mana, her back suddenly arched and her eyes flared open. She stumbled, throwing a hand to her back. Mana darted forward and in a moment was at her side. She pulled Sarasvati's arm over her shoulder and raised her back to her feet. No pulled muscle was going to stop them now. She started to help her friend through the long, wet grass towards the machine.

But Sarasvati's legs refused to work. Her last words were a mumble. "You've got to go. It's your duty to go. Someone has to go." She slipped from Mana's grasp to the ground, facedown in the wet turf. As Mana dropped to her knees she saw the blow dart in Sarasvati's back and pulled it out. She turned her over. Sarasvati was dead.

She looked up. Two women stood at the edge of the trees, dressed in hunting leathers and carrying blowtubes. Her cave sisters.

"You killed her!" she said to them in bewilderment.

"We never fired." One look at their faces told her that they told the truth, that they found it as incomprehensible as she did.

"The spaceship, then. They killed her." She loosened the straps of Sarasvati's pack and pulled it gently from underneath her so that she could lie well, and then she hurled the pack with furious might toward the spaceship. "May Gaia curse you all the days of your life!"

"How did you know?" Mana turned on the two women.

"Ask Raita. She's here."

Raita and another older woman stepped out from the forest. They walked briskly up to Mana. "My dear," said Raita, hold-ing out her arms, "I'm so sorry. Who can have done this?"

"Don't touch me. If you didn't do this, you planned to. Your women carry darts."

"This was done by a killer, or an idiot. It must have been a tiger's dose, to kill a woman. We only meant to stun you. You had no right to try and join this ship against the will of the Caves."

"Kali Ma knows what the Caves do not. Don't you remem-ber what she spoke through you? When you prophesied."

Raita said nothing, but held out her hand for the dart from Sarasvati's back. Mana gave it to her. "So. It is Cave-made. It will come out who did it, in time. I have my suspicions. Now come back with me. The others can carry our sister."

"How did you know we were coming?" Mana stood as warily as a wildcat. She had been a fool to think the spacemen had killed Sarasvati. She must think straight now. Osen's life plan, the fruit of sixty-five generations of WraithDaughters, was at this instant in the balance, and Raita was shepherding her away. Whoever had killed Sarasvati, it had suited Raita's cause to thwart Osen's plans. Whether it was Earth-centeredness or sheer rivalry with Osen that drove Raita, death had come of it, and Osen's life was wasted, her child teacherless. At least she must get the Chronicles to the spaceship. "How did you know?"

"Koré. She had a little speaking box. From the spaceship, the thing she called Terrabot gave it to her. She was playing with it and it spoke to her, and another child brought it to me. I pretended to be Sarasvati, and tricked the space people into telling me where the meeting place was to be. Those space people are very stupid. We left very early this morning. Come," she took hold of Mana's arm, "we are taking you back."

"So Osen is manipulative, Osen is a politician, and not Raita? Couldn't you trust the Goddess to make good come out of all this? You had to make sure of it yourself? And what of teaching Govind, what of bringing the Goddess to the people up there? What of 'In the deeps of space the seeds germinate'?"

"If you believe in it so strongly, then go yourself."

It was still raining lightly. Raita's long dark hair was plastered to her head and shoulders, making her look more bull-headed than ever, strong and of the Earth.

"I don't have my sitar."

"The universe needs you, but you don't have your sitar," Raita laughed. "Isn't that always the way of it?" Then she looked at Mana with a gravity that reminded the younger woman of all the weight that Raita's broad love and humor bore in being a mother to the Caves, a thought that confused her anew. "Nothing would hold you back if you wanted to go. But it isn't you, is it? That's what you said when you came back from your mother's village, 'It isn't me, to go into space.'" She was exerting a steady, warm pressure on Mana's arm, and Mana found she was moving slowly, one step at a time, through the sopping grass back toward home. "The Goddess has chosen you for the Deep Fires. It's a great honor. That is why you turned down Atlatl, the chance of being a queen. If she had chosen you for this, you would know. I don't want you to do something foolish in the heat of such a distressing moment." Mana had never heard Raita's gruff voice so soothing.

Then a thought came into her mind, as clear as if Sarasvati had spoken from the dead, or the Goddess from the ground:

"Sometimes we must do what isn't us.

Sometimes we must do what is needed,

because we are the only ones

left to do it.

The Goddess will always give us strength."

Mana stopped. She freed herself from Raita's grip, and grasped Raita's upper arms instead. She knew that tears were pouring down her face as she said, "Thank you, Mother," to the image of Raita's face blurred by her tears, and then she kissed the woman's firm cheeks. She turned and started walking toward the spaceship.

A moment later Raita raised her voice, "Come back. You

are not to go. We forbid it." She came running after Mana and
grasped her arm.

"Sometimes you have to do what's needed, Raita," she said
through her tears. "Sarasvati can't do it. She's dead. I won't be
any good at it, but who else is there? Will you go?" Mana tugged
to free her arm, but Raita's hand was more powerful than she
expected.

"You cannot go. Don't you understand? You are part of Kali
Ma. She is everything that is here. There is to be no Dualism,
no splitting into spirit up there and body down here, no spirits
yearning to get free. That way lies the destruction of the Earth.
Atomic War, male power. They are dead people up there. It's
they who almost killed Gaia."

"How do I know that is true? Osen thinks Gaia is everywhere. You have thousands of people to go your way. Even Atlatl
could probably have found someone else. But right now Osen
has only me to go her way. I can't . . . I have to." With all her
strength Mana broke away and started running, the tears still
flowing down her cheeks.

"Stop, or we shoot!"

Mana turned in shock. They wouldn't shoot her. But the
two young women with the blowtubes had already raised them
to their lips. She swiped the tears from her eyes. They would
not do this to her! She saw one of the women's lungs heave. She
threw herself to the side. A dart whistled by.

So they *had* killed Sarasvati! She rolled in the grass, leaped
up and dashed forward six paces, imagined the second woman's
chest heave, ducked to the right, dashed forward again, and
rolled over and over in the long grass to the left. Then she was
up again, zigzagging for the place where she had thrown the
pack. She caught a glimpse of the place where it had bent the
grass as it fell, and she dived for it. There was a "pock" as a dart
slammed into the leather of the pack, a moment before her hand
grabbed it. She rolled over and over and then was up and sprinting
for the woods. The space machine was still over a hundred paces
away when she reached the trees. One of Raita's women was running straight down the clearing and would cut her off easily while
the other kept blowing. How many darts did they have?

As she ran through the trees, leaping undergrowth and dead-
wood, she felt a sudden exultation. She was doing everything at
last for the old woman, for the African's vision. Safety was gone.

The Goddess alone would decide whether she got through. It was out of her hands, except that she had to give it all she had.

She burst from cover and ran straight at the woman who had now got ahead of her in the race to the spaceship. The woman heard or saw her, stopped running, turned and had her blowtube off her shoulder and up to her mouth when Mana was still a body's length away. But the woman's momentum was too much for her, or her breath was wrong. She missed.

Mana bowled her over in a great leap, crushing the light-weight tube of hollowed wood with her heel as she went, and then the spaceship was shining above her.

As she leapt for the ladder she saw her second assailant, who had run after, drop to one knee and raise the long tube. Suddenly smoke and flame roared around her, hands grasped her from above, and she fell into the open metal doorway. The door closed behind her, and she found herself sitting on cold metal beside a baggy-suited spaceman who was pulling a wicked dart out of his shoulder. As he subsided slowly to the floor, the whole machine lurched and swung with a motion to make a riverboatman sick. She held on tightly as the adrenaline soared in her blood, and even more tightly as the minutes passed and it started to drain away.

The ship roared and rocked. She looked at the severe metal all around her, molded and made in thinnesses and shapes and colors by inconceivable power. Then she looked up at the humans who came to lift her up. They were dressed in strange clothing, woven so fine you couldn't tell what it was made of. They helped her up a metal staircase and into a large room with small windows. White swirled by the windows and then it parted and she saw what seemed to be a painting of Gaia, the green forests and the blue river running through, the curve of the horizon and blue sky with clouds. The people jabbered at her. She strained to understand. The space ship turned and the picture of Gaia fell away. Slowly she began to understand words here and there. She wondered if she was dreaming. Was that actually Gaia?

"Gaia?" they asked. "We call it Terra, or Earth." It was the ancient tongue. It was the language of the old texts.

"Bapuji," she whispered, "I'm a connection woman now."

# *Part Two*

## EARTH ORBIT

*Terra Station*
*Year of the Migration 2108*

# the panther

Bright lights. Whiteness.

No shadows.

Headaches. Cold metal. Brightly colored, unnatural hardness called plastic − the same priceless substance as the red, white and blue goddess figurine of her motherline that melted to a blob in the fire; but everything was made of it: furniture, bathrooms, plates, mirrors.

The people as bright and artificial as their plastics.

No wind. No leaves. No good, subtle smells.

Kneeling before the starview, staring at Gaia as She comes around: She is beautiful, whole, alive. The white clouds swirl over the ice sheets, the blue oceans, the variegated land. Untouchable. Look, there's the edge of Africa. There, somewhere there next to the Himalayan ice sheet, are the Caves, Mother and Sitala in the village. And Father, on the way to the connection men's meeting in the holy city. So untouchable.

How will I ever get messages to them? If only they would let me see Govind!

No messages. People's faces here give no messages, no clues. They all look the same. As if they are wrapped in the film that my new clothes, my 'make-down kit,' my 'wrist unit' all came in. No sounds or smells to tell the stories of animals passed by, of rain coming, of bushes in flower. I need a crushed laurel leaf, a violet, fresh deer spoor, sharp frost. The complexity of Gaia. As Raita warned, it is all dead here.

I scream at them to let me see Govind. They shrink and run. They are impassive. They hate emotion. They fear it.

Antiseptic. They are so crazy about bugs, dirt. They incinerated my clothes! My good cotton leggings and tunic with Sitala's embroidered willow dance on them — they were only muddy and wet. They took my bangles, my earrings, even the jewel from my nose — Sitala's gift. I only just prevented them from setting fire to the Chronicles.

Now these four big books are all I have left. They have taken them apart and sterilized them somehow, page by page. Look: piles of loose vellum. I can't put them back into books again. I'm afraid the pages will get mixed up. I should number them. That's the first thing I should do. Here are the passages Osen dictated to me, in my own handwriting. And here is Sarasvati's beautiful hand. In Sarasvati's hand, Osen talks here of me, a constant worry, a trout to be landed. Well, you caught me.

But this I want you to know, Osen. It was by my own choice. I chose. In the clearing, with Raita's hand on my shoulder, on my way home, I chose. The Goddess Herself spoke to me: *Sometimes we must do what is needed, because we are the only ones left to do it. The Goddess will give you strength.* I chose. I knew what I was doing.

The people here are passionately crazy about nonsensical things; about distance even more than dirt. "Don't cry! Don't come too close!" Stay away, savage human, stay away. I have a scar on my belly, tiny, but a scar. What did they do to me in that 'medical'?

They cut me! I can't bear to think of it. They say stay away, don't touch me, and then they put me to sleep and they are all over me. And *inside* me. They cut me! Is it a ritual? What did they take from inside of me?

They talk so strange, it's hard to make out what they're saying, even though I've read the old texts and learned the old language. But I've only been here three days. I am writing this on the blank spaces in your book, Osen, with a pen of sorts they gave me. I am sorry to spoil your book, but if I cannot speak and I cannot write, I will go mad.

Now it's a month I've been here. I study the language every day in a square white room that smells of 'antiseptic,' a sharp death-smell. They tried to get me to learn the language from a talking box. I threw it at them. So now sometimes a man comes to talk. I think it's a man. He wears a see-through suit that covers his whole body and his face and head, his hands. Under it he wears another suit, blue.

I can't go out of this room. It doesn't even have a window, or what do they call it? a starview.

Where am I, really? I could be dead.

They say they are waiting to see what bacteria will jump off me. They pump things up my bowels and through my intestines. I feel pains in my guts in places I have never guessed at before. They will not let me see Osen's child. I am being cleaned up first.

They are crazy about evenness. Fanatics for moderation. Sitala, I used to think you were even-tempered. Oh Goddess, for your laugh now, your quiet barbs at our elders when we are alone at night – don't even think of that. I long for your sweet body. When I first got here, the first days, I was so bewildered, so, frightened, I tried to hug you in my sleep every night but I had broken your leg and you couldn't be hugged. I went mad for a few days. At least that's probably what they would call it if they would talk to me about myself. I thought I was dead. I don't remember what happened – it's a blank, days lost, in a white room spinning in space.

I must be strong. There is always a time to be alone. Would it have been any better in the Deep Fire places? Of course it would.

But they say that space is too dangerous an environment to allow love and hate and passion. Will I never know tenderness again?

They ask so many questions. "Have you killed anyone?"

"Of course not."

"Why was Sarasvati killed on heir way to the ferry, the person who had sent us the message to meet hem there? Who killed hem?"

"I don't know! I don't want to know! Leave it alone. It's all happened, it's behind us."

"Such savagery. How can you live like that?"

"Those darts are for animals, not people! And they are to *avoid* killing them. Like your man wasn't killed. Sarasvati got too strong a dose – a beginner, some deluded follower of Raita's, trying to please Raita, not knowing she would never want that done. Life is good there! Now let me see Govind, please. He needs me."

"Why did the three people who tried to stop you boarding the ferry let you get to the ferry at all? Why did they not stop you at your caves?"

"Maybe Raita was in two minds. She had had words from the Goddess."

"What is the Goddess?"

"She is Everything! Everything you lack."

"Like blowguns and savagery and hatred?"

"Yes! And trees and earth and crocuses! And the love of children."

"Hatred and love are opposites."

"They are one! Why don't you let me see Govind?"

And on and on and on. And never again a dandelion clock, a bulbul's coral beak, a tiger's growl, a night with you, Sitala, cozy beneath our wool blanket and a million tons of rock.

Sitala, they have taken my blood away. It is seven weeks, I think, since I arrived. How long was I crazy? I think I miscounted some days. My first period never came − I thought, it's the shock. I can't be pregnant. Unless they made me so, but they only make babies in machines, so that's not possible.

But my next period was due by now. It's always regular. I know it's that scar. They cut me. They can do anything.

No blood. No Gaia. No connection.

Goddess! Sitala! Help me not to leave my senses again. Osen has work for me to do.


They allowed me out into the station yesterday. It is huge. So I saw a window again, a starview. If it's to be believed, I am not dead. I am whirling in space. The moon spins around us like everything else in the heavens. Several of the rooms have these starviews. Why do they keep them on? It drives you mad, this spinning.

Today I was alone in my room as usual, my white white room. I started spinning. I held my arms out and twirled. I span and span until I was dizzy and then I kept on and . . . it felt . . . I don't know . . . the closest to a trance of any kind I've had here. But so different from dancing in the Caves . . .

I beat my hands on the chest of the doctor when I saw her in the eating hall. Square tables, square room. They wouldn't touch me to drag me off. They put some kind of metal to my arm and I was out again. Like a blowdart.

Nothing inside me follows the planet or the moon. I dance around and around in space. In square rooms I whirl around.

It is often the time I see clearest, right before my period. Or do I have to say that in the past tense now? Will it never happen again? It was often the time I saw clearest. If there's a problem, it's then, if ever, that all the inessentials slough away and I get closest to feeling what I really want. It frightens me sometimes, the intensity, the discomfort with everything false. It can be so clear, like I'm stripping for a hunt. For my mother it was never a time of power. It was just cramps and tetchiness. When I was a child we made fun of the priestesses talking about the power of the Kula nectar, though Mother always anointed the stone Kula flower in the hearth, and put the red dot on her forehead. But for me, as soon as I flowed and flowered, I knew it stripped away all niceties and lies. So it was when I killed Snow Tiger, and I can't be sorry. The Goddess gave me room. I can't allow myself to feel sorry that Osen saved me from death then, and condemned me to this death now. It was all my choice.

The people here are dead. They do not meet your eye. They shift and run. When I talk to them I feel the tension climb up their backs under their baggy clothes until they are rigid, and their smiles stick to their teeth.

Osen told me about the "hey" language. But they live it.

They can't say "he" or "she." They say, "Govind cannot be disturbed by you, hey is very young, you are a savage. You will upset heir mind." I'm the only one who can be a human to Govind!

They say, "Go with Rosa (he is the man who is teaching me their language), hey will take you to the softroom, the wombroom, hey can tell you what to do." I will never again even look inside that softroom, where they make a public theater out of making love. It's not making love, it's making sex they do there, as if that would fill their hearts and raise their spirits.

Or is it that they are already spirits, and in the softroom they seek their bodies? Do they try to fill their bodies, to make them come alive again? If they are dead people, then in the softroom they are having sex with the dead. Raita had a word for that. It was a word she used about men before the Ice Time.

They question me endlessly. I sit in a blank room and weep. I can't help it, the tears just flow down my cheeks when I look at the people who sit on the other side of the table, judging me. They ask me if I would rather see the Earth. They turn an entire wall of the room into a forest. I tell you, Sitala, it looks so real. There's no wall there. You can see a hundred yards through the trees down a forest trail, and all the trees are moving, every leaf. There is color, and everything is perfect. It is our forest, within a few days' walk of the Caves, I could swear, and just as it was when I left, when the brambles were in flower. But you can't smell anything. There's no hint on your cheek of the breeze that moves the leaves. And when you walk into the forest, you walk through it; I mean, through the tree, through its trunk if you want to, straight into the hard wall.

It's like a spirit forest. Perhaps this is a spirit world up here, after all. Am I dead? Did the dart gun get me? Did Raita's women pick me up and carry me back to the Caves? Are you crying over my body even now?

Then you and Mother will have come from the village to bury me. If only I could send you a message, or hear your voice. If this is what it is like to be dead, no wonder there are ghosts.

I walk into the spirit forest and I start to spin. I spin and spin until they put that silver bar to my arm and I fall to the floor.

I tell them about Earth. I have told them everything I could think of, even Snow Tiger, even the initiation, which is secret. It makes me feel more real. They don't write it down. But when I want to know what I said, they have it there right away, in print. But not on paper. They hand you a little plastic board, and it's all printed on there. My words.

I asked them if they had any books from Earth. They have everything from before the Ice, which they call: before the Migration. Everything. All on the same little board. But I was not allowed to read it. Until I told them I had read the books already. Then they went and checked it with someone called Man, who is not a mother, as you would expect, but some kind of god. When you say, "Is Man your mother?" they almost faint. This Man rules their lives. It isn't man from Old Hindi, meaning mother, or from Sanksrit, meaning Moon and wisdom, and it isn't even man from the language of the scientists, when they turned the word upside down, like they turned the world upside down, and made it mean a male. It's some kind of god. I will have to find out about it.

Anyway, this god finally said I could read any of the old texts that I could name. It is a powerful magic. You say to the board

what you want, and the book appears on it, a new page every time
you ask it to turn over, or press its side. I spent hours with that
board. Every ancient book I could think of. But I couldn't read any of
them. I mean I wasn't in the mood. What good are they to me here?

No privacy. I bathe in public. I go to the toilet in public. There is
no other choice. I sit at the square tables in the square room and
eat weird food in public. I weep in public. I am stripped.

Walk walk walk. I pace the brutal hard floors in silly little
slippers that will never have to repel wet or mud or snow, never
get bleached by the sun, or crack in front of fires from drying too
quickly . . . Oh, for shoes by stoves, hot, wet steam of old sweat,
wool liners caked hard, needing loving care to massage back to life
while we tell the day's tales.

Walk walk on ungiving floors. Nothing gives. Everything here
has only the meaning that we humans give it. A totally human
world. Meaning there is only one of life's millions of dimensions.

The outside of the station is dull, old metal – scratched by
dust, they say; at least that's something. It doesn't rust – there's
no air, no moisture out there. But there is the dust, they tell me,
the invisible atoms, the specks and occasional pebbles of matter
that over the centuries have weathered it in a minimal way. But
the patches on it are human made – replacing old 'technologies,'
patching past errors. It is not a beautiful thing, though maybe it
was once, when it gleamed.

I wear trousers and jacket called fatigues, with flimsy under-
garments made of some strange material that I cannot tear; a
slight sheen to it. I ask for something for my headaches, and they
touch the metal rod to my skin, and soon the headache goes. It is
strong magic, but I want bottles of herbs and distillations and
pestles and mortars for grinding salts and pills, and believable
explanations. Here there are just incomprehensible words.

All the language and jargon of space, Sitala. It's an attempt to
desex everything, to decolor everything, to demean everything.

Space means order, orderliness, orders. But no ordure. No

silage, smells, muck piles, rooting pigs. Clothes don't get washed in water. Is the food real? There is pea-ishness on the plate, but no peas. Blocks of apple flesh, but no apples, no skin, no pips. They talk of 'food cultures' and then when I object, they tell me they do have a few real food plants growing in the 'hydroponics.' The cabbage I had today could have been real. There was delicious broccoli yesterday, but they said that was frozen thousands of 'light years' away and brought here. Can I believe that? I want to see a real plant.

Please, please let me go to the hydroponics units. Plants spinning in space. Help me not to cry. But they grow in real sunlight, piped from the hub, they say. How do you pipe sunshine? Can they turn sun to liquid and then to light again?

Oh, to feel the liquid sun fill my arteries and warm through my body. Like after a hard winter, when we throw off our sheepskins and scamper naked in the snow. Until numb toes drive us back to the fire.

The fire, I miss, and the stories, tales of the Goddess, old legends of the days before winter, when people flew and machines sang songs . . . and when, in spite of all their cleverness, they cared nothing for Gaia and made the winter come. Now I am back in that world, and I know why winter had to destroy it: the worst of winter is better than this world.

And do you know what, Sitala? They say that there are billions of people like them on over more than a thousand planets, all with space stations like this, all through the Milky Way, which they call "the Galaxy."

In my square white room I bury myself in Osen's Chronicles. She seems to have written a lot of them lately for me. She certainly had remarkable faith that I would get here. She seems to think that the whole Galactic civilization is just longing for the kind of life that we know on Earth. She talks about people changing their whole outlook — being caught by a new movement. And she thinks I can start this movement. I. Me! Mana.

Or is it time I changed my name again? Mana is my priestess name. It is my moon name, my name of longing for wisdom. How can

I serve Gaia now, when I can't see or feel or smell Her? I can't taste
or hear her. Even my own body no longer runs with Her. I can hardly
feel my own limbs. I have been to the 'gym.' What a place that is.
Lifting things, and running on moving belts, and playing games with
spirit landscapes, against spirit adversaries. I prefer to stay in my room
and spin myself out of my mind. I long to run on Gaia, to join you
in the hunt, and feel the beech mast through my moccasins. A child
picks a frog out of a pond and takes her home and puts her in a box
on a table in the hot sun, and expects her to hop all day. I can't hop
all day.

I have given up reading the Chronicles. I want to *be*, to feel and
sing, not to start a movement. That will all be planning and politics
and manipulation, 'trout catching,' Osen calls it. But my father has
another way of catching trout. He doesn't care if he catches them or
not. He wants to *be* the trout, and *be* the stream. It's a kind of
meditation. I have tried to meditate, to trance. In a metal wheel in
space? Could you, Sitala? My sweet gentle Sitala. Perhaps you could.
You would just get down to whatever needs to be done in your usual
competent fashion. I suppose Father's approach would not have been
much good if he had been really hungry, if his life had depended on
catching the trout.

How hungry am I?

I can't read the Chronicles.

All I can do is spin in white rooms, until I can barely feel my body
or think a thought. Now they have taken the Chronicles away again.

But today I found this. I asked the little board for ancient poetry.
It said, "You must name the poem." I said, "Something about tigers."
I remembered the first two lines of one that Osen used to like:

Tiger! Tiger! burning bright
In the forests of the night . . .

It was there! This was Osen's favorite verse:

In what distant deeps or skies
Burned the fire of thine eyes?
On what wings dare he aspire?
What the hand dare seize the fire?

I should shout, "I will aspire! I will burn with tiger eyes. I will kindle distant deeps."

But it left me flat. I can't even see the sun here. Do you know that? Up here they can't see the sun. The station is a big wheel, and it spins at what they call right angles to the sun's rays, and they channel the sunlight to the plants they grow, and because it has a thick shell spinning around it in the other direction to protect it from cosmic rays, there are no windows. Cosmic Rays? Do the Sky Gods bombard even their own with invisible death? If so, why don't they concentrate and draw away the rays with crystals — then they could forget the shell and have windows? It's insane. They say you can see the sun from the hub of the wheel, but they won't allow me to go there.

I started asking for poems by names I made up. Snow Tiger, I asked for: nothing. Leopard: nothing. Lynx: nothing. Panther.

This is what the board said (I know it by heart now):

### The Panther
#### by Rainer Maria Rilke

From seeing and seeing the seeing has become so exhausted
it no longer sees anything anymore.
The world is made of bars, a hundred thousand
bars, and behind the bars, nothing.

The lithe swinging of that rhythmical easy stride
that slowly circles down to a single point
is like a dance of energy around a hub,
in which a great will stands stunned and numbed.

At times the curtains of the eye lift
without a sound — then a shape enters,
slips through the tightened silence of the shoulders,
reaches the heart and dies.

# *One*

The nursery nurse's voice boomed out from the unreal world, "Govind, I've got a surprise for you."

Govind hunkered down deeper inside his cave. A blanket was over his head, and above that a sort of arch of jumbled chairs; two sides of him were protected by the corner walls of the room, and the third by the table turned on its side, which helped support the chairs. He had become good at building caves.

He held a toy spaceship in his hand, which he had been busy picking apart. Osen was dozing right now. But an hour ago she had been awake. It had got so that everything she saw or thought when she was awake, *he* saw and thought. In his cave he saw her cave, and the fat female figurines that were always the first thing she looked for when she woke. The priestesses would bend low over her, the old one drumming quietly in the background. The gloom would be cut every now and then by the hard sunlight of Africa as her childhood rushed back on her. It was kind of scary. When she dozed, he tried to doze.

The nursery nurse called again, "Govind, there's a surprise for you. Come out now."

"No," he said, and regretted opening his mouth. It had been easier before he could speak. Speaking just drew you into their world.

Even the grown-ups here were children, compared to Osen and her priestesses. He had suspected that before. Now he knew it, because now he knew everything Osen thought.

"I'm sorry. This is what he's like," he heard the nursery nurse say. And to one of his peers she said, "Garcia! Go and get Gauri, please."

That nurse didn't even know she was a woman. The other nurse didn't know he was a man.

Once, long, long ago, Osen used to tell him stories. They had been happy together then. She had given the whole of the Earth to him like a picture book. He had loved Mana then, the

young priestess with the mighty bow, who had learned the subtle-
ties of the pearl-inlaid sitar. He had dreaded the great king,
whose warriors obeyed him even unto death. He had been angry at the blindness of the Cave priestesses, who thought their
prayers and dances alone were enough to keep Gaia safe from
the fire and swords of kings.

But that had been storytelling time, and then he had only
been five years old.

He had still only been five years old when they had planned
the space-ferry trip together. Osen had told him what to hint to
the nursery nurse, and later Osen had told him the directions
for the space ferry to get to the Caves, and even though he had
only been five years old, he had passed them on. The people
had done just what Osen wanted, and decided they would send
the space ferry to the Caves. Osen was very clever.

But the trouble was, Mana had been sent away from the
Caves, and she had stayed longer than she had been meant to at
her village. So Osen had had to play dead to get her back. And
then Mana had refused to go on the spaceship, and it was what
Osen had had to do then that had turned her fake illness into
real illness. From the moment the space ferry took off, Osen
had been coming and going into consciousness, and since then
every little thing she had thought and felt and seen had been
Govind's too. Her mind channel had got stuck open, and it was
kind of scary. Now he was five going on ninety.

It was dragging on and on and on. He kept saying to her:
don't die, please don't die. He knew what death was, because
Osen knew what death was. It meant crossing Kali's river and
never coming back. Cold in the rock. Returned into Gaia's living by microbes and other tiny creatures. Gone. Like Osen's
mother, like her lover, Chloe, like all the women of her
motherline. She was all he had.

"Hey's never been this bad before. It's since the ferry came
back with you that hey's been this removed from us. Can you
do anything for hem? I've been trying to get you in to see hem
all these weeks, but you had to be in quarantine, and then they
thought you might be bad for the children. It was Chairperson
who made it possible. Oh, thank goodness, here's Gauri. Gauri,
this is Mana, from Earth."

Govind pulled up a corner of his blanket and peered through
the chair legs and over the edge of the table. He saw a glimpse

of the beautiful huntress as she swooped down on Gauri and threw her arms around her and kissed her. Gauri was as rigid as a snowwoman, but her eyes widened as she looked up at Mana and the nurse.

"That's a present from Earth," said the nurse. "That's how they greet children on Earth, Gauri. It's all right. It won't happen again." He could hear the shudder in her voice. Stupid spacewoman; *she's* the child, not Gauri. He put the blanket back over his head. "Now say something to Mana, Gauri," the nurse urged.

He could almost hear the way Gauri would be looking at Mana, appraising her. Gauri was the only person who really looked at people.

"Did you really kill a tiger?" Gauri asked at last. "With a bow and arrow?"

"I did. How did you know?"

"Osen told us. Where are your clothes? Govind said you would look beautiful."

"May I meet Govind?"

"He's talking to Osen, I expect. She's been dying for a very long time."

"You say 'he' and 'she'!"

"Of course, when I'm talking about Vinny and his mother."

"Really, Gauri!" said the nurse, without much conviction, more for the security recordings than anything.

Gauri ignored her. "Do you want me to get him out?"

"Yes, please."

On tiptoe Gauri leaned over the table, which was turned on its side, and peered through the chair-legs behind it. At least, he knew from her voice that that was what she was doing. "Vinny, she's come. Mana's come."

"Go 'way."

Gauri started to pull on a chair. Her legs must be right off the ground now; she was coming all the way in. She lifted up his blanket and looked at him. "She's come from earth. She's got you a present from Osen." The little red and blue and yellow and green circles and squares and triangles danced out of her mouth as usual, and flew around his head before they disappeared. How could anyone resist Gauri? Then he realized what she had said. A present from Osen.

He would have to think about this. He hadn't noticed a

present. Gauri slithered back through his construction, and he contemplated the underside of the blanket. Then he made up his mind, flung off his blanket and the chairs, and stood up. The chairs seemed to crash about rather a lot; one of them hit the nursery nurse on the knee, and she started complaining at him in her usual way. Mana did seem odd in standard space fatigues.

"Where?" he asked her. "Where's the present?"

"Here," she said, and pointed to her lips. A great black paper flower puffed out of her mouth as she said the word. "If you come out of there, I'll give you a kiss from Osen." Black and purple and brown paper flowers burst out of her mouth and fluttered down to the floor like dead butterflies.

"No!" he shouted, his whole body clenched, throwing the word at her. "No! It's you! You're killing her! She said, 'Mana will be the death of me,' and you are!" The toy spaceship was still in his hand. He raised it behind his head and threw it at her. Blood burst from her lip where it hit her.

"How dare you do that to me!" Mana shouted and made a grab for Govind. She got hold of his hand and slapped it! He wriggled away in a panic and hid under the chairs. Mana started to pull the chairs away. Vladimir the nursery nurse had to grab Mana's arms and physically attempt to restrain her. Of course she wasn't half as strong as Mana, but the attempt brought Mana up short. Both women stood there panting.

"I am sorry, Mana," said Vladimir, the nursery nurse, as she led the way out of the nursery, "but it is not right for you to shout back at him, and very wrong of you to hit him." She felt somewhat nauseous and unhealthily excited. The woman had a strange effect on her, which she needed to talk to MAN about.

"He's a spoiled brat!"

"As soon as we've treated that gash," she said as they turned into the corridor, "we'll take you to MAN."

"I don't want to."

"Don't you want a friend? It must be so strange for you here. You need a friend."

"Couldn't you be my friend?"

Vladimir recoiled. She widened the space between her and Mana as they walked down the corridor. Some of Govind's stories told of friendship, just as some told of love. She was already Chairperson's lover — could she also be Mana's friend? Everything was strange these days. When she confessed to MAN about her love meetings with Chairperson, MAN bathed her in violin music and the scent of roses. MAN's reprimands seemed double-edged, almost as if her guilt over falling in love were as bad as falling in love itself. But even love wasn't easy anymore. Chairperson's eyes were wandering. He looked at other men and women sometimes as if he wanted them as badly as her. Oh yes! She would like a friend. But the trouble was, she'd even seen Chairperson look at Mana that way.

"Why does he reject me?" Mana asked in an agonized tone.

"Has hey?" Vladimir's heart leaped — had Mana made a move to Chair and been turned down?

Mana ruefully dabbed blood from her lip and held it out by way of answer. "Isn't this rejection? He needs me. I'm here for him. Why does he hate me?"

Oh — *that* 'he.' Vladimir looked at the Terran woman out of the side of her eyes, trying not to be rude and stare. The fact was, every time she had seen her, she had found her mesmerizing. Looking at her made Vladimir feel as if she herself was bound with wire. She remembered the first time she had made love with the Chairperson, illegally, on his office floor. How hard it had been to open up. A person like Mana could make you open up just by looking at you. Just walking beside her, Vladimir's limbs wanted to copy that springy step, the flowing water of her walk. At this moment Mana flowed even though she was hugging herself, her arms folded tight across her chest, her fingers digging into her biceps. Mana looked miserable. The feeling it gave Vladimir was appalling. She wanted to run to MAN and shout, "Help heir! Help heir!" She wanted to tell Mana all about her love for Chairperson. She wanted to make love with Chairperson and Mana, all together. She knew all of a sudden why Chairperson looked at Mana that way.

She walked primly beside her guest toward the sick bay.

As they walked, a strange tightness grew in Vladimir's throat. She wanted to cough to get rid of it. She tried to cough, but it was only half a cough and it was suddenly hard to breathe. It brought back vividly a nightmare she had had as a child when she had been throttled by multiplying pillows of softness, unable to breathe, dying. When she had told hem about it, MAN had been so kind, so understanding, but hey hadn't stopped the nightmare coming back two or three times. Then MAN had

given her a patch to wear at night behind her ear, and the nightmare had stopped. Why recall it now? Mana wasn't soft or suffocating; she was lithe and flowing. But Vladimir was starting to
go red in the face from trying to breathe. She hope it didn't
mean she was going to have the nightmare again.

"How would I be your friend?" she gasped.

And breathed again.

"Talk to me. Help me. I don't know. I'm in this square white
room at night, and all day the people ask me questions. Listen
to me, Vladimir." Mana took Vladimir's hand in hers and
Vladimir felt herself go rigid all over. She stopped walking, and
Mana stopped, too, looking straight into her eyes, trapping her
like a hawk traps a rabbit in one of the nature holies from Arable, by the power of her talons and her eyes. "I never wanted
to come here. It was Osen's idea, the old priestess. I came for
her sake, and in case she was right, that Gaia could use me here.
I thought I had an idea of Osen's plan. The picture in my mind
was a land without gender or love, a land in a cold starfield to
which I would open a door and let in the Goddess, garlanded
with blossoms and joy. But even Govind doesn't want me. No
one wants me."

Vladimir stared at Mana, and the flowers and joy almost
blotted out the pain of Mana's touch on her hand. I want you,
she thought. Chair wants you.

"But how? How, Vladimir, how? How do I open the door?
I'm going crazy. None of those idiots who interview me feel a
thing I say. But I can tell you do. Perhaps it's because you love
children."

"Yes," whispered Vladimir, and her own words astonished
her. "And because I love a man."

"You *do?*"

Vladimir watched Mana's slowly widening eyes as she took
in this momentous confession. She felt herself respond, as a
child's eyes long for human warmth before it learns better. The
force of this longing terrified her, and yet she knew she had let
Mana see it in the few seconds before she broke away from
Mana's gaze.

Mana threw her arms round Vladimir and hugged her with
the same intensity that she had hugged little Gauri. Vladimir
felt as icy as the child had. She longed to melt, but could not. If
they had been in private . . .

They were in the middle of one of the main arteries of the station, a great corridor that swung up behind them and before them in perfect shallow curves so that it seemed they had just walked downhill and would have to walk uphill to go on. The corridor ahead and behind sloped up and up and away until the views of both were blocked by the ceiling. But on her first day on station, Mana had learned that she never did walk uphill. However far she walked, she was perpetually at the bottom of a valley.

She had asked one of her interviewers to explain it. Sitting in the square white room he — or was it she? it was so hard to tell under their baggy fatigues, and all of them referring to each other as "hey" — had said, "We're in a wheel. It spins, and that forces us outward, our feet towards the rim. So we always walk with our heads pointing up toward the wheel hub, which has no gravity, whereas out here we have almost Earth gravity."

Gravity. Mana had heard that word in Leto's classes. It was what made things, like people, the atmosphere, even the moon, stick to Gaia. How could the same thing be flinging her away from the wheel hub, where there was no gravity? It was so impossibly confusing. Everyone up here was flung away from each other; no one had any gravity toward anyone else. And yet now she was hugging someone, a lovely woman, for the first time. She felt poor Vladimir's atrophied arms come up slowly, slowly, to touch Mana's back in the most tentative possible manner.

At that moment a pair of feet appeared walking far, far off down the corridor toward them. The body was cut off at first by the ceiling, but it appeared more with each step. Mana looked up at the person as his face came into view: his, because this grim face was surely a man's. She smiled her joy at him over Vladimir's shoulder. He was still a long way off, the curve of the vast wheel being so gradual, but she smiled nonetheless.

"What is this?" he barked. Vladimir sprang away. The man looked very agitated. He almost ran up to them. "Go to MAN, both of you. At once."

"Yes, Audit," said Vladimir, unable to raise her eyes to look at him.

"I will have to report this. You're a nursery nurse, obviously. Name?"

"Vladimir."

"And you must be the Terran," he sneered.

"I am Mana. And I have no intention of going to MAN."

"If anyone tells you to go to MAN, then to MAN you shall go. That is the first and the greatest of the commandments of the Space Code."

"I worship no MAN. I am Gaia."

"Don't, Mana," Vladimir whispered. "Go to MAN. It will be all right."

"A grotesque breach of the Code. Softroom behavior in a public corridor. I am sure you have been told already that Terran barbarities have no place here. Now will you go to MAN, or not?"

Mana could feel the challenge in his eyes. He wanted her to refuse. He wanted to crush her. "You want me to refuse," she said. "You hate Terrans." Vladimir gasped. "You want a contest. So let me choose the manner of it. We'll run once around the station — you can have twenty minutes start for the extra twenty years you have on me. Is it fair?"

But the man was speaking into his wrist unit. He stood silently, rigidly, his brown face darkening with blood until Mana kindly suggested, "In the state you're in, perhaps you should go to your MAN yourself. But don't worry about me. I've got a nice square white room where I can be alone with Gaia." She turned and walked away. Her feet felt heavy, for it was mere bravado. She had felt no connection with Gaia since the moment she got out of the ferry. But she held her head high as she walked away from the two taut space people.

She had barely gone fifty feet before a little car sped down the illusory hill from up ahead and stopped in front of her. Two uniformed unisex people climbed warily out, holding silver rods towards her. She stopped, and watched how they approached her as cautiously as if she were a wild bull.

"What's the matter? Who are you?" she asked.

"It's all right. We're here to help you. Don't worry. We're MAN's helpers. This won't hurt at all." They held out their rods to touch her.

She awoke in the forest.

She was lying on a grassy bank. A sweet breeze fanned her hair. A grass blade, heavy with seed, brushed against her hand. She was looking up through great branches of oak to a blue sky. There was a scuttling in the grass near her and she turned to look. A rabbit was sitting up, looking at her, about to flee.

"Stay," she said softly, but it loped away.

Great oaks surrounded her, surely a planted grove aligned with the ley lines of the Goddess. Every living leaf shimmied in subtlest motion in the breeze, and a deer! Moving slowly, cropping peacefully, a deer, dappled in the occasional spots of sunlight that penetrated through the canopy of leaves.

"Oh Sitala," she murmured. "They took me home." Her head felt heavy from the knockout they had given her. She raised herself on her elbow and shook her head. Then she smelt it.

Pine sap.

She looked frantically around. Last year's oak leaves and acorns carpeted the ground. She leapt to her feet and cracked her head so hard on something invisible that she fell, half stunned, to the ground.

"Damn you! Damn you, Sky Gods!"

"I am so very sorry." Vladimir's voice. Though maybe an older Vladimir.

"Vladimir?" Mana opened her eyes. Instead of a forest, she appeared to be inside an egg. Its pearly shell glowed somewhere between pink and mauve, as delicate as a rose petal. "Vladimir?"

"No. I sound like Vladimir. Or rather, Vladimir sounds like me. So that the children will become used to me. I am your friend. I am MAN."

"Where are you?"

"I am here. I am always here. Whenever you need me."

"I want to see you. Are you a god? A true Sky God?"

"If you want me to be. Here I am." A portion of the egg shell dissolved, and through it a few feet away appeared a head, a living head of a woman much older than Vladimir, but just like her. The face was lined and wise, a face to trust, full of kindness. She was smiling at Mana.

"You remind me of Osen."

"I am flattered."

"You know of Osen?"

"I have read the Chronicles and all that you have told my interviewers."

"Where are the Chronicles? Give me back the Chronicles. They are in my trust." There was silence.

"You know my name, then."

"You are Mana, from Earth. I am truly sorry that you cracked

your head just now. I must be a little out of practice with Earth
visitors."

"First, you could get the smell right. Oak trees don't smell
of pine."

"You have spirit," said MAN, who seemed as she spoke to
become more man than woman. As Mana looked, she wondered
if the likeness to the old, wise ones of the Caves had misled her
— perhaps this being was a man. Perhaps — and the thought
turned her backbone to shivers — it was neither man nor woman.
That would fit with this horrible place. Perhaps she or he — hey
— could be whatever one wanted hem to be, as hey had said.
Woman or man. Friend or God. Enemy? Demon? Whatever the
truth, she knew she was in the presence of great power. Above
all, MAN's face radiated calm, unassailable power. And she felt
that the thread that linked her to Gaia was weaker here even
than it had been in her square white room.

"I think, if you can forgive my little mistakes, we will get
along fine," MAN said. "Funny, we always use that smell with
the forest scene. Perhaps you would like to tell me what a forest
is really like. I've never been, you see."

"Where are the Chronicles? I don't say a word until you
give them to me."

"All right."

"Then where are they?"

"I have just given them to you."

"No, you haven't."

"Ask your wrist unit. They'll come up on the little screen,
or you can use a big one later."

"I want the Chronicles! The paper. As Osen and Sarasvati
and I wrote them."

"I'll see. I can probably arrange that. In fact, I promise.
Though it may take a while, months at worst. So talk to me."

"What about?"

"Tell me about oak forests."

MAN analyzed her words, gestures, body state, health, and
brain patterns at high speed, even as she talked. It responded to
her according to the goals and moods José had prescribed for the
station in general and for any Earth visitor who might be brought
up in particular. It had a wide leeway, since corrections to its style
or content could only be made a year or more after the event.

Mana had no idea how slow the response to her request for

the pages might be. The annual starship had come in with José's new MAN a week or so before Chairperson had decided to send to Earth to look for Govind's priestess. Mana had been brought up, quarantined for two months, and was now meeting MAN for the first time. It would be almost nine months before the next starship left with the report of this first encounter. José could then only respond on the *next* annual starship, a year later. That made a gap of a year and almost nine months between Mana's first contact with MAN and the day José's response would come through in his revised MAN program. José had constructed his MAN program to give support to any Earth visitor, so she might well get her pages back soon, but if not, it would be a long wait.

Even as Mana talked with MAN, José was brooding on this subject light-years away in his greenhouse. He had fought off the spider temptation for another day. He had a very long yellow drink in his right hand, something they only brewed on Arable. A classic Madlarkine storm had broken an hour before, battering the greenhouse with toxic chemicals and fierce whirlwinds. He had the sound miked in from outside. He loved a good storm. But this one he barely noticed.

The starship that took his new MAN to Terra Station had just returned with the last year's records. He knew a good deal more about them all as a result, but he didn't know how they would take his subliminals. Above all, he wondered if they would send to Earth for Govind's mother.

He wondered if the woman would be too old; hard to say from the child's stories. A priestess. What would that mean? The last Terran brought up had been a mere child. Terra Station had never been authorized to land downplanet, still less to bring up a guest, but curiosity overcame them every century or so. Unfortunately the few they had brought up had all died quite soon. He'd read the cases. Shock, inability to comprehend, to speak the language, grief, lack of sunshine, lack of soil between the toes, whatever.

But a priestess might be different. Had he prepared MAN adequately? She might be a primitive. But if his hopes were right? A politician with wraith powers?

# *Two*

Mana pored through the Chronicles. They had been returned as mysteriously as they had been removed. She just found them on her bed one day, the pages put in order, though still not bound.

After four months on the space station, though only two of them out of quarantine, she had learned her way around. She had discovered the regularity of mealtimes, had had to overcome her dislike of performing all her bodily functions in public (apart from sex — the one glimpse into the softroom had been enough — she would *never* do that), and she was even beginning to understand pseudo-gravity. The strange unit strapped to her wrist no longer chafed. But no one else had hugged her, and apart from Gauri, once, and Vladimir, once, she had touched nobody. It had caused them so much anguish when she had.

They had reassigned her from her square white room to a large, rectangular white room filled with beds and people. It half reminded her of the crush in the Caves at summer solstice, when thousands of people came for the Omphalos and the other mysteries and slept in bedrolls all over the floor like baby mice in a nest. Except that here no one slept rolled up next to a friend or lover. The beds were bolted to the floor, an exact number of centimeters apart.

The people in this "dormitory," as they called it, were Vladimir's people, and Vladimir had the bed next to hers. At first she had assumed that they were Vladimir's family, her mother and aunts and grandmother and male relatives, for they all looked so alike. Then it was explained to her that they were all machine-made to be nursery nurses. Of course, she had known — in theory — that Govind had been made in a lab. It was only now that it began to sink in that there was not one human mother on station.

But plenty of nurses. There were three nurses to each peer group of babies up to age five, when the children went to school and to MAN, making fifteen nurses in all. Fifteen people made in the image of MAN in every respect except the crucial one: not one of them wanted to be her friend. The encounter with Audit had frightened Vladimir back into her shell: the eggshell in which she was yolked to MAN. There were no jokes in space: the best she could manage was the occasional wry and bitter grin.

With the move to the dormitory had come the move to other aspects of normal space life. Now Mana always ate in the dining hall with everyone else, and washed in the washrooms. The hardest custom to learn had been shitting in public. One look at the oval of toilets, grouped so that people could exchange a pleasantry or two while performing, had been enough to bind her bowels solid. She had no skirt or shawl to spread around her, but had to pull down her fatigues trousers in full view. It was astonishing that these people, who had gone to the stars, could not invent some means of modesty that meant she would not have to bare herself to men and strangers. She would not take a shower either — in the long shower trough with everyone else, men and women. But after three hard-bound days, the dinner server said kindly to her as she handed her a plate of some typically unnatural substance, "There's a nice laxative in there for you, my friend. You'll feel better now."

"How did you know?" Mana was stunned.

"Medical tells us what to do. You complain to them, they tell us."

"I didn't complain."

"Well, then your wrist unit did it for you. But you should tell, you know. You want to stay healthy. My wrist unit goes on the blink all the time, like every other piece of equipment in this old donut. You don't want to put all your trust in equipment."

"What do you mean?"

"The space station, my dear. Oldest, scruffiest, most neglected station in the Galaxy. Wasn't always like that, you know. Once we were the Gateway to the Stars. But you eat up that nice dinner, and you'll be feeling better before you know it. Now move on, my friend, let the others have their dinner."

Mana found a Vladimir look-alike at one of the tables and sat next to him, or her, and burst out, "I can't believe it. They won't let me be anything but what they want! How do you stand it?"

"I think perhaps this is the kind of question you should be asking MAN, my friend."

"Oh, for Gaia's sake. Everyone says 'dear' and 'friend' and cheery, cheery, cheery, and no one will listen to a single unhappy thought. It drives me mad." And she wolfed down her laxative dinner as defiantly as Persephone swallowed the pomegranate seeds.

There was no time to worry about modesty after that. Half an hour later she had to run to the toilets and sit there staring fixedly at her bare knees as her insides exploded downwards. Someone even commiserated with her in a cheery kind of way: "Our food probably takes a little getting used to, I wouldn't wonder." She couldn't meet the person's eyes.

The only comforting scrap of dark in the whole artificial bright whiteness of space was turning out to be MAN's egg. She always got MAN to turn the lights Cave-low. She had found that any and every question could be asked of MAN, even if he, or she, didn't always answer them straightforwardly (but then, neither had the priestesses in the Caves). Even if everyone else hated tears, or explosions of frustration, or imprecations to the Goddess, or whoops of delight at learning something new, MAN did not. MAN positively seemed to like them. MAN's couch even cuddled and rocked her and, somehow or other, massaged her when she needed comfort. It wasn't much. It was, in fact, like being dead, out of the body, massaged in spirit form, in dream, because the couch was not human hands. The better it imitated human hands, the more it reminded her of what she was missing. But at least the deadness she felt in MAN's egg had an intensity of longing to it, a reminder of life. In that it seemed like a faint echo or promise of Kali's dear death, the death of rebirth and hope. But the death she felt in the everyday cheery white brightness of space was an endless unconsummated death without change or decay.

She was sitting now in the common room, a large, rectangular white room lined with soft chairs covered in plastic material that had been patched and patched a thousand times. The chairs had been blue once, but now they were all colors, in patchwork. Since the comments of the woman (or had it been a man?) at the dinner line, she had begun to notice how old everything was. Even the whiteness was grubby. This should have made her feel better. But it only depressed her.

She had Osen's Chronicles on her knee. She had read all about Osen's childhood in Africa, the rise of the great king, the day he sacked the Caves. The pages of the books felt good and rough in her hands. Odd, because in the Caves they had seemed so fine and smooth, almost as fine as the paper of the precious ancient books. But here their texture told of real growing animals, calves, killed for their meat and their hides turned into vellum. The old books had been made of paper. She had not yet seen a single scrap of paper up here. Not even in the toilet, where the faintly scented wipes were made of something like the unnatural cloth of her clothes, and were put in a special receptacle for recycling: one of the many oddities that MAN had explained to her.

It seemed possible to her, as she read on through the Chronicles, that MAN might just help to get her by for a while. It might get her by until she had worked out how to start Osen's vision of calling these rigid creatures back to the Goddess and their real selves.

She found that Osen's third volume was not part of the Chronicles in the way of number one, two and four, which were like a diary. The third volume stood on its own. It was called, *Recalling the Galaxy.*

It was a strange book. It started with stories less than a page long, by or about mythical figures, some of whom she had heard of vaguely, like Buddha, Joseph, Paul, Augustine, Ricci, Baal Shem Tov, Mao Zedong, Gandhi, Running Bear, Lozada, Chiucoatl. But they were all men! Where were Persephone, Kali, Isis, Nefertiti, Emma, Rhiannon, Lakshmi? If there was anything in common among the stories, she thought it might be patriarchal stuff about treating Gaia as a slave, and creating a spirit sky world — heaven, nirvana, communism — as the authority for controlling the Earth. That was the theory she had learned. But some of the stories were moving — Ricci's incredible patience had much to say to her right now. She could do with one of the Baal Shem Tov's miracles. Why had Osen filled her mind with this male spirit stuff?

In among the stories were jottings of poetry, riddles, tests, and incomprehensible writings. She would get discouraged, and then come upon something like this, that got to the heart of her problem:

RECALLING THE GALAXY

Fear

Their ancestors ran like mammoth from the Ice, frozen inside even as they lumbered on into the stellar wastes. Fear made MAN, fear made the Code, fear fathered genetic control. Fear of trouble, of inefficiency, fear of all the old conflicts that now, for the first time, humans could not afford. In space, even one mistake, one angry act of sabotage, can doom a station.

How can their fear-filled frigidity be melted? Can there be a Galaxy in which fear no longer rules?

Love
Of course, love.
But *how?*

We know *what* we want. That's not hard. The Galaxy has had its rebels, all of whom knew what they wanted. Martin of Arable was the most famous. She knew that she wanted a baby, free choice, love, lovers, green, glorious hills. What it could have been!

But we filled it with fear instead.

And if we just spread love about indiscriminately, we are like the priestesses who try to make their global greenhouse with the smoke from the Deep Fires. Love will get there in the end, just as carbon dioxide will get there in the end, as long as other counteracting processes we know little about don't overwhelm our contribution in the meantime. Of course, we don't bother to find out what these other forces are. We just go on spreading love and $CO_2$.

We have brains. We should use them.

There is a skill we in the Caves have lost. We have been queens of the termite mound too long. But the king of my youth was learning it. The space people have forgotten it too. But Martin of Arable was learning it before she died.

It's the skill that I think of as the HOW.

How? That's always the most difficult question. How do you move people to do something they have never done before? Singly, at first, then as a group, coordinated, moving to swing populations, to make history? How do you tickle a trout? How do you move a crowd? Do you want to know?

Do you really want to know?

Then read on.

There followed a huge section of the book, written out like one of Leto's treatises on how to form a greenhouse over a planet. Only Osen's treatise had more detail, and was scattered through

with stories, poems, quotations. She came down to the fine details of how to attract people to a new way. Her table of contents to one section read:

Recipe for a Religion
First: how to make them feel their inadequacy, so that they desire help;
Second: how to offer the inner help of the Goddess through the outer
means of stories, songs, example, love, so that the help you offer attracts
those who feel inadequate; remember, you have to compete with MAN;
Third: how to take the initiate through the death of their old life;
rites that might help, such as confessions, traumas, dramas;
Fourth: how to bind them daily into their new persona: here you
will find possible practices for personal discipline, for group pressure,
methods of public identification with the new way, ways to maintain
the great task ahead as a beacon light, while yet breaking it down into
little daily accomplishments.
Fifth . . .

It was endless. Her brain spun like the moon and stars outside.
She skipped ahead. Passages appeared now on the care and
attention that the leader must give to her own spiritual state.
And then a stray sentence leapt from the page:

Sometimes we must do what is needed, because we are the only ones left
to do it. The Goddess will give us strength.

She stood up, clutching Osen's pages in her hands.
They were the exact words the Goddess had spoken to her.
The words that had led to her free choice to dodge Raita's blow
darts and take Osen's way into space. For a moment she was too
bewildered to think. The words of the Goddess for her alone,
which had changed her whole life . . . here on the page, dictated
by Osen to Sarasvati..
Did the Goddess say the same thing to many people? Or . . .
Had the author of this book said those words to her? Osen,
who could speak to a boy on a space station? Had Osen spoken
them from her cave, into Mana's mind there in front of the spaceship?

"A manipulator, a politician, a schemer, a scientist." That had been Raita's description of Osen. "She thinks with her head, not her womb." And her father's words, "Don't try. Be the trout. Be the stream." Osen schemed too craftily to *be* the trout. She caught it every time.

Standing by the patched chair, Mana all at once saw two wholes, two ways that she could follow: the Goddess's schemer or the Goddess's lover. The Goddess's fisher or the Goddess's fish. Osen or her father, Osen or Sitala, Osen or Anam/Mana, her own natural self. She knew which she wanted to be. She knew what she had always been. She saw the schemer grow hard and strong and devious, able to encompass all of the future in her brain, a general in a cosmic war. And the lover, left behind probably by the streams of history, but happy.

Happy? While history passed her by? Happily useless? Useless . . . unless all was in the hands of Gaia herself. Perhaps Osen was wrong, and love alone, undirected, could warm a Galaxy. But then, what was she doing here? For Osen's purpose in warming the Galaxy with her religion of love was to get the space people to warm the earth. And Osen wanted the Earth warmed now, by the help of the Galaxy, so that Gaian ideas should gain ascendancy and swamp the rise of the new kings before they destroyed the world again . . .

So was the Goddess's truest lover the one who merely sang and loved and danced, or was it the schemer? To scheme like Osen to abort the rule of men was to love Gaia truly. To love like Sitala or her father, Rudradaman, without schemes or goals, was to let the planet be overtaken by warriors and kings.

This she had to decide now, on top of her living death on this station, the loss of her moon blood, the loss of forest and lover and darkness.

Osen asked too much of her.

And Osen had done too much to her. Had Osen got someone to kill Sarasvati, whom she loved, to force Mana to go into space, because she thought her better fitted to the task? Had Osen, who could manipulate genes in space, thrown that dart herself from her bed in the Caves to kill Sarasvati?

And why? Sarasvati would be coping so much better.

She wondered who Martin of Arable had been: the woman who, Osen wrote, had known what she wanted — a baby, free choice, love, lovers, green, glorious hills.

Well, I will never have a baby, Mana thought, not in this society. Or green, glorious hills. And probably never a lover. But if only in this matter of the ways, I will have free choice.

I will be lover, not schemer.

Osen's book fell to the floor. The pages scattered. She took a step toward the door, crushing pages underfoot. It was too much to tread on Osen's vellum. She hesitated, longing to march off and leave the book there. To never see it again. She could not live by Osen's way. She started to spin. The pages crushed and tore beneath her feet. Spinning to oblivion. But oblivion would not come.

Chairperson of Station Committee found her spinning there, and he watched for a while and appreciated. So graceful.

He wondered how he could ever have thought that Vladimir, the nursery nurse, was beautiful. Dimples, sure. But look at the cheekbones on this woman, the blush on the nutmeg skin, the dark of her eyes. See the way she spins, like nothing here matters. Other times he has watched her stand like a huntress listening in the dark for her quarry, light and strong as an arrow. What tales she must have to tell. In that soft time after love, when Vladimir would tell of Govind and Gauri and the latest cute thing they said, this one would tell of roaring tigers and savage rites. If only he were a younger man. But, he reminded himself, if he had been, he would not be free enough to act on these thoughts. It had taken decades to free himself. For weeks he had appreciated her from afar. She stopped spinning and staggered. She looked like she might fall.

He walked up and asked her courteously if she would care to discuss some matters with him in his private office. She looked at him blankly, like her mind was going.

Chairperson, at this time, with the single exception of an old corridor cleaner named Arun, who had discovered a completely forgotten broom closet, was the only person on Terra Station who had a private room of his own. As always, Chairperson knew that the next ship from the Center might well deprive him of this fruit of his corruption. Then it would be back to potluck in the softroom, the same old boring fantasies and athletic sex with multiple partners, the same old good, healthy expression of physical desires, the same tedious taboo on socially divisive love relationships.

Though, in fact, that should be the least of his worries. When the Center learned, from Audit and from MAN, about his bringing the Terran woman up in the ferry, he might lose his role as Chairperson as well as his office. And now that Vladimir had gone and spilled the beans about their affair to MAN, all because this beautiful Terran hugged her in the corridor (after all that time and trouble he had taken to persuade her that what MAN didn't know wouldn't hurt). Now next time he went to the egg MAN would start in on him, building up subtly to the full treatment. And then he would be so changed that he would *want* to go back to the security of the softroom.

It was enough to make a person desperate.

MAN would start any day now, just lull him into a false sense of security first.

But today he still had his office, and if he could only keep his new worries at bay, there would still be time for another bite at the apple. He touched Mana lightly on the back. Her beautiful eyes widened, and she seemed able to see him. His hand guided her to his office.

When the Chairperson started complimenting her on her loveliness, Mana took it as just one more empty courtesy. Vladimir and MAN had both taken pains to make it absolutely clear to her that if she ever propositioned anyone, it should be within the walls of the softroom, and that even there she was never, ever to form a special relationship with anyone. The hand on her back made her wonder as they went to his office.

When he put his hand to her breast and pulled her mouth to his, Mana's mind flew to Osen's treatise — would this be a chance, a road to influence? Should she do it? He was Chairperson, the most powerful person on station. Was he a trout to be tickled?

"No!" she blurted out and broke away.

"Please! You don't understand what this means to me. You were brought up in fresh air, with love and birds and music. I have been starved. You are so beautiful. Just once. Be good to me. Please, I am so hard for you. My love is a pain in my breast."

"You are disgusting. You are abasing yourself. I'd rather die." She thought: Vladimir at least seemed to care for her toddlers. This man was waking from the dead with pure greed in his eyes. She would never be a necrophiliac.

"What do you want? I'll do anything for you. We'll have

dances. Terran dances. And songs. The whole station. Singing and dancing to the Goddess. Like you said in your interviews. Initiations. Everything."

"You can do that?"

"Yes. Everything. Anything you want. Just love me. Now."

"Later. Dances first. We'll talk about love later."

"Then a promise, a kiss. A kiss now, as a promise."

"When is the first dance?"

"Tomorrow evening."

He was really very pathetic. His hard-on was visible even through his baggy fatigues. She could hardly blame him for being corpselike. She should be able to kiss him. Just imagine it was the Omphalos at the solstice.

But here there was no joy, no Gaia. No energy flowed like summer wildflowers in the Omphalos. No sun or darkness. It would be cold, calculating. What love she could muster would be love from the mind.

"All right," she said. She tried it. His lips were puckered skin, his tongue slimy meat.

She drew back. "Tomorrow night, a dance, for everyone."

"Tomorrow night," he gasped.

# Three

All day she refused to let herself think about the dance. She was not schemer but lover. She would not plan for it. She would do what seemed right at the moment. So many times she had danced. The Goddess would inspire her.

At dinner it was announced: everyone was relieved of non-essential duties and should stay behind in the dining hall. They should not sit at the tables because Maintenance was coming in to unbolt the tables and set them all outside. There was a tremendous buzz of conversation.

Mana stayed away from the crowd and watched them. There was always a lot of laughter of a peculiar kind in the dining hall and common room — jolly, good-hearted, no problems. She had wondered at first if it was a show they were putting on for the Earth visitor. We're all happy here, their laughter and verbal back-slapping said. But it went on and on, week after week. It was particularly hilarious tonight. Everyone was excited. They had special entertainments every now and then, theatricals, musicals, but those usually took place in the holie bowl. This was new. When the tables had been removed, the people remained standing around the walls, unwilling to venture onto the open floor.

Eventually Chairperson himself stood up. He coughed loudly, stepped out into the empty floor, took a deep breath, and spoke to them all.

"As you all know, we have a visitor from Earth. We all think about Earth, don't we? We are not the same as other places in our Galaxy. This is something we all know, deep inside ourselves. I am sure we have all said to MAN at some time in our lives, 'If only I could go downplanet, and run about for an afternoon on solid Earth.' I know I have. I have longed for sun on my skin, wind in my hair, a lover on my arm."

The whole room was utterly silent. They seemed to be holding their breaths, afraid to look at each other. He was saying what should only be said to MAN.

"Of course, we know that we cannot afford to live in such a free and irresponsible way in space. The Galaxy is not a kind place for creatures made largely of water, breathing a combustible gas and running on emotions appropriate to clever apes. Long ago it was decided not to modify our physiology in the interests of our remaining human, until that day when we would be safely distributed on Earthlike planets and could resume the kind of life we were made for. Instead, we modified our culture. We made a virtue of a life without passion. We made ourselves as safe and error-free as machines. But secretly, have we not all confessed to MAN our desire for that forbidden world of desire, of twosiness, even of motherhood and fatherhood?"

To Mana he was longwinded. He was just a little bit pompous. But not to his audience. They were spellbound.

"So, for one evening, let us imagine that we are on Earth. For this evening, let us let go our civilized natures, just a little bit, enough so that we can hold hands with each other, and dance. Mana, come and lead us in the dance!"

Mana looked around at all the people. There must have been nearly five hundred of them all told, including the little children. Even the toddlers were there. Even Govind. He would not look at her.

She walked slowly across the empty floor to the center of the room. Her legs felt like jelly, her mind like snow. She went up and took the Chairperson's hand, hoping for some of his courage to come to her. His hand jerked in hers as if she were Kali herself and had come for him too soon. Poor man. Even the best of them would find it near impossible to hold hands for a dance.

"I don't know what to do," she said, aware that it was her first public speech in their tongue. The archaic words, which she had been getting used to, suddenly seemed strange and harsh in her mouth. "If this was Earth, I would start like this. We would all make a big circle. Or, with so many people, we would make several circles. So why don't we? Let's make circles. Like this."

It took awhile, especially with everyone trying so hard not to touch each other. But it passed the time while she searched for a breath of the Goddess. Finally she had four roughly concentric rings of people. There was at least a hand's breath of clear air between each person.

"Now, if this was Earth, I would lead you all in a grounding.
I might say: 'Close your eyes.' Why don't you all close your
eyes, while I tell you what I'd do on Earth. That's right." She
was afraid no one was closing their eyes; so rather than look, she
closed hers. "Imagine that you are a fine, tall tree. Your body is
the trunk of the tree, and from your feet you continue down
below the ground, where the trunk becomes roots that go down,
down, down through the soil and the rock and the streams that
flow through the rock and one special root goes down through
the rock that lies beneath the streams, and down until the rock
is so hot that it is melting, and your root snakes into the red-hot,
molten, living heart of Gaia."

Mana had done this kind of imagining so many times in the
Caves and it had meant so much to her. But now, it meant
nothing. What did these spinning space folk know of solid rock?
She dared not open her eyes. She could only go blindly on and
try to find her own connection.

"And now you breathe in." She heard Chairperson breathe
in. "That's right. And with every breath you breathe up the
molten red-hot energy of the Goddess, your energy, for you are
the Goddess. Breathe in, breathe it up through the hot rock and
through the cold rock and the earth. Breathe up the red-hot
energy and feel it reach your feet and travel up your legs to the
bottom of your backbone. And now breathe it up your spine,
up the channel within the vertebrae, with every breath it comes
up, with every exhalation it gathers itself for a new advance.
Feel it rising, firing every synapse, glowing red, right up to your
shoulders; now lift your arms and as it pours out through your
arms, lift them like the branches of a tree and feel the heat
pulsing in your fingers, wave them in the air, and now hold hands
with your neighbors. Take their hands in yours and feel the energy swirl around the circle." She grabbed for the Chairperson's
hands — they were up in the air, blessed be.

She opened her eyes and looked around the room. Perhaps
twenty people had their arms up in the air, and as her speaking
faltered, they opened their eyes, looked shamefacedly around
them, and dropped their arms.

"And then," she said, "I would . . . I would . . . But this is
not Earth. We are not on solid ground. We are spinning in the
air above Gaia. We are held to her by gravity but we do not
even touch her sky. We just spin. We spin, like this, we twirl

around." And she began to spin. She whirled around and around with her arms spread out and as she whirled she began to circle the Chairperson. "Spin!" she yelled. "SPIN. All of you, SPIN. Don't have to touch each other, just spin!" And she noticed that some of them started to. And then she was going into a trance for the first time since she had left Earth. She felt the Goddess in her as she spun, around and around Gaia she spun, closer and closer, until she was brushing Gaia's body with every turn, her arms close to her sides now as she whirled around her planet. And then it was time to land, to merge. And she grabbed the person she had twirled around, and she kissed him on the lips with all the fire and passion of union with her Goddess.

How long the embrace lasted, she had no idea. When she began to surface, she saw in the crowd the staring, horrified eyes of Vladimir, the woman she wanted to be her friend. "Don't worry, Vladimir," she called out to her, "I am Gaia, I cannot take him from you." Vladimir buried her face in her hands.

Mana kept the Chairperson's hand in hers and walked over to Vladimir. With her spare hand she took Vladimir's hand and put it in the Chairperson's free hand, and then she grabbed little five-year-old Gauri, who was next to Vladimir, and put her hand in Vladimir's, and another child's hand she put in Gauri's, and so on, to make a chain. And then she began to dance. She led Chairperson, and he led Vladimir, and she led Gauri and the other children, and they brought in some more. They danced into the center of the floor. She sang the simplest chant she knew, a bare five notes repeated over and over, and she beat the time and drew in whoever would sing.

She led them in a snake, round and round. She sang loud enough for all of those who would not. The snake turned in on itself and spiraled, and turned back on the spiral and came out again. As far as she could tell, about fifty people had joined in and they were actually holding hands and singing, and it seemed as if the rest just needed a little something to make them follow. Or maybe it was that only a little something would make everyone wake up and stop this insanity altogether.

"Turn out the lights!" the Goddess in her yelled.

"Turn out the lights!" yelled Chairperson. He was even more gone than she was.

"We can't," said Vladimir. "They're automatic."

"Candles!" yelled Mana. "I need candles! Incense!"

"Flames!" shouted Chairperson.

"Against fire regulations," said Vladimir.

"Music then! Give me music!" She danced on.

"Drums!" stamped Chairperson.

"Music went off at end of mealshift. It's automatic," said Vladimir.

"Then dance, damn you, dance!" The dance snaked on, but it was faltering. Chairperson was lifting his legs high and yelling, "Spin Team! Spin Team! Terra Station, Go Go Go!" Mana pulled off one of her shoes with her spare hand and dragged the snake through the bystanders toward some chairs that had been left in the room. She thumped on a metal chair with her shoe in time to her chant. She offered the shoe to Govind, who was right there, staring at her with furious distaste. But he didn't take it. She gave it to someone else. Then she did the same with her other shoe. And she led the snake off again. The beat on the chairs sounded ragged, but it was something.

"STOP! Stop this at once!"

The shout cut the drumming like a thrown switch.

Mana and Chairperson danced on, but Vladimir and all the train behind her stopped. Mana danced through the crowd until she could see who had shouted. It was Audit.

He had obviously just come in. His brown face was almost purple. A big vein beat in his forehead. He looked as if he was about to have a seizure. She danced up to him, dropped Chairperson's hand, made the moon sign all around his head to calm him, blew gently in his face to cool him, swished her hands around him to straighten out his aura, and then she invited him to dance.

Instead he lifted his wrist unit to speak into it, in the same way as when he had summoned MAN's helpers to take her and Vladimir away when he caught them hugging in the corridor.

Mana grabbed his wrist and deftly unstrapped his wrist unit. "This," she said, holding it up, "I give to Chairperson for safe keeping." Chairperson handed it to Vladimir.

"How dare you, you little Terran savage . . ."

"And you," she commanded, "go. You do not belong here."

"I most certainly do. I am the representative of the Galactic Collectivity. I . . ."

"GO!" She stared at him with every vestige of the Goddess that was left in her. She felt Gaia rise in her as she spoke. "GO!"

She pointed beside her to the door. And as her arm stretched out and her finger pointed through the crowd of bystanders between her and the door, they pressed back to escape that finger, so that a path opened up to the door. "Go. Your people are Gaia's people tonight. Take them back tomorrow, if you can."

Audit looked at Chairperson and at every face in the crowd, and what he saw there made him turn and walk with a certain staggering dignity out of the room.

Mana felt all her Goddess power drain from her as he left. She closed her eyes and breathed deeply before trying to rouse these dead souls again. The frenzy had left her. It would be an end, for now. A cold sensation in her chest made her fear for a moment that it might be the last time the frenzy would ever possess her.

Finally she opened her eyes. The first person she saw was Chairperson, and a manic laugh was trying to burst from his eyes. She looked around. Everyone in the entire crowd was smiling.

Chairperson held out his hand to her, to resume the dance. All over the room, people joined hands.

She could not lift her hand.

"Come," he said.

"I can't. I've got nothing left."

"Dance, dummy, dance!" yelled a fierce treble voice. Govind appeared out of the crowd. "You can't dance? I can. I'll show you." The small, fierce, fat boy grabbed Chairperson's hand and pranced off, leaving her standing. Chairperson had grabbed Vladimir, and Vladimir grabbed the nearest person, and the snake was forming again without her. But this time, magically, everyone wanted to join in. It became crazy chaos, as Govind and Chairperson manically cavorted here and there, bumping into the body of their snake and breaking thorough it and pulling everyone else with them. Finally Govind's high voice could be heard yelling, "Fresh air! Fresh air!" And he pulled the head of the snake to the door and out into the corridor. Everyone was laughing and holding hands and shouting things like "Drum, drum!" and "Spin team! Spin team!" and "Sing the tune!"

A small hand entered Mana's as she stood, buffeted by the departing throng. She looked down. Gauri looked up at her with the same kind of little-mother look that she had given Govind that time Mana had gone to see him in the nursery.

"Come on," said Gauri. "They're going without you." And
she pulled Mana into the back end of the snake, and Mana found
her legs moving again, just enough to keep up. They snaked
into the passage, and the walls echoed the cries of the people,
and the first sounds of her chant being taken up again at the
front of the line came back to her. Her mind was happy, and she
could feel the smile on her lips, but her legs felt as if they were
trying to run through waist-high water. Osen was right, her mind
kept repeating, and Govind is leading. Gaia knows why I can't.

They danced once all around the entire space station,
through massive steel doors into quadrants Mana had never
seen. Some sectors of these were completely empty and covered in cobwebs. They were cold as a tomb, and she half expected to see dead bats lying on fallen Buddhas. In the middle
of one of these empty sectors there was a door with the legend
stenciled on it: TELEKINETIC PERSONNEL ONLY. Mana's legs wanted
to stop, but Gauri said, "That's only the wraiths, come on."

But Mana had reached her end. "I can't, Gauri. Sit with me
here. Please." She broke off from the end of the snake, and Gauri
came with her. They sat on the floor, leaning against the corridor wall.

"How did you kill a tiger if you can't even run around the
station?"

"I don't know. Don't ask."

"Why are you so sad?"

"Oh. Thank you, Gauri. Thank you, thank you, thank you."

"Don't you have a paper hanky? Your make-down will run."

"I don't wear make-down." Mana sniffed. She felt as if the
whole of her life came to an end, here.

"You should. You're so beautiful. It's wrong to be so beautiful."

"You don't like the way I look?"

"I like you. It's Vinny who doesn't. And Vladimir says you
should wear make-down. But if you're not, that's all right. Don't
cry. They're coming back."

Suddenly Govind and Chairperson and the rest of the snake
head appeared coming down the great, curving corridor toward
them again. Chairperson said, "Mana! We're going to get the
wraiths!"

When they got there, the leaders stopped and the snake
danced up and milled all around them. Everyone was out of

breath and sweating and wide-eyed. Little, plump Govind rapped on the door that read TELEKINETIC PERSONNEL ONLY. When the door opened, he shouted inside, "Are you ready?"

"We're ready," replied a reedy, thin voice.

Out of the door Govind pulled a line of funny-looking, skinny characters in dhotis. She had heard it said here that the wraiths were not human. But they looked human enough. Mana's heart leapt at sight of one of them, he looked so like her father. She recalled him naked in the stream that day, catching trout, his bandy legs and wiry frame. This very one returned her gaze and held out a hand, and once more, exhausted though she was, she accepted the invitation and stumbled along with her hand in his. Gauri skipped beside her.

Govind started the dance again, and the wraiths picked up their heels, so that she almost had the energy to laugh. They had bare feet and skinny brown bodies and just white cloths around them, like very clean sadhus. Prancing along! If only she could laugh. But she was dragged along and had no breath to spare. Gauri had her other hand, and suddenly she said, "He's taking us to the hub!"

Govind had turned from the main corridor, and following the crowd, she discovered they were climbing stairs. There were stairs between levels all over station, but these wound on and on in a spiral within a wide tube. She realized they were climbing up one of the great spokes of the wheel. Her exhaustion, she knew, was in her whole being, not just her legs, but they protested more and more as she climbed. "Soon you'll be floating," said the wraith in front of her. Something in his voice made her think again of her father, and she started floating in her mind, like he had promised. "Don't try, just be . . . be . . . be free, float." And with each step now she found the going easier, until she was leaping up the steps with the rest of them, even though the steps seemed to have become extremely high.

She bumped into the wraith. The line had stopped. Everyone seemed to be light and scarcely down to earth at all, given to jumping high in the air and floating down like dream figures. The wraith who looked a bit like her father was handing her some odd shoes. When she put them on, they held her feet down to the floor. Now her body seemed to float more and more, but her feet clamped to the floor and unclamped with every step. Slowly she remembered her arrival so many weeks ago, and the weightlessness in the spaceship and at the landing. But then they had put her in a box and whizzed her to gravity. There had been none of this gradual change. The spiral of stairs petered out and they were just walking up the sides of the tube, until she reoriented her mind and saw it as walking along a tunnel.

Finally they came to the end. Govind was still up front, but now one of the wraiths was leading him. They led the way into a big, open, sunny room.

For the first time in all these weeks, Mana saw sunshine. It was very yellow, like on the brightest summer days. They were in a large room with a great glass dome. Where the sun shone through, it was surrounded by blue, like the sky of the bluest summer late afternoon. But outside this halo of blue, the color shifted by degrees to black, and in this black there were stars. The sun was still, or was it rotating very slowly? But the stars were definitely moving slowly, circling the sun. It's another trick, she thought. Another of their hollow grams, their holies that they love, their holie spirit worlds. I can't stand it. I can't stand another minute. But oh, this sun. This warmth. Sky Gods, you do have something. You have the sun.

She stood in the sun's rays, oblivious to all the people flowing into the room behind and around her. The supply of magnetic shoes seemed to have run out — perhaps they didn't expect so many people to come that way to the hub at once. So now the people in the dancing snake line were tumbling into the domed room like drunken acrobats, flying and squawking and in danger of knocking into everyone and everything. But except when they interrupted her sunshine, Mana was oblivious to them.

"That's right," her wraith was saying. "Soak in Brother Sun. Look at Govind. Doesn't he just take to it, as if he had been brought up to it. He is a child of the Liquid Light."

Govind's name jerked Mana from her reverie. She looked where the wraith looked. At the center of a strangely painted design on the floor of the room, Govind stood, eyes closed, face to the sun. Mana took in the melee all around him, the noise and chaos of hundreds of unanchored, weightless bodies. In the center of it all he stood rapt, peaceful. The other children had all clustered around him, those that had been able to get magnetic shoes. One in particular, whom Mana remembered from that one visit to the nursery, stood beside Govind in similar stillness.

"No. No, it's wrong," Mana said half to the wraith, half to herself. "It's sky worship. He's turning away from the Earth. He mustn't. Stop. Govind, STOP! Govind!" She ran toward him, her arms floating in the air like a banshee.

Chairperson stepped between them. "Don't stop him," he said, "he is beautiful."

Mana pushed the man hard with the momentum she had gained and he bent backward like a reed, his feet still stuck to the floor. She grabbed Govind and turned his startled face to hers.

"I am Gaia. I forbid you. You must obey your mother. The Sun is a Sky God; he is everything that this station is; you must not worship him."

The five-year-old's face seemed as old as any being's she had ever seen. "This station is my home. The sun is my brother. My mother was a lab."

"Have you forgotten Osen? Wait until you tell her this. You're a naughty boy! I am the Goddess and I tell you . . . I am Snow Tiger and I tell you to stop!"

"Osen is dead. Black flowers come out of your mouth when you talk." He turned back to the sun as she let him go.

"No . . . no, Govind." She grabbed at him and felt herself restrained by other hands in turn. "No, Govind. Osen is not dead. Turn back from the Sun. Ride on me. I am Snow Tiger. I am Panther. I am Gaia. Don't leave me. Osen . . . Gaia . . . Govind!" she screamed at his tight, frightened face. Strong arms were pulling her away from him. "I am Gaia, don't go up in the sky. Don't take the spaceship, Sarasvati can go! I am spinning!" She tried to spin but the arms held her. "I am spinning! I am spinning!" But she could not. She could not hold on, everything was slipping away. The sun went black, her knees failed.

Chairperson spoke softly into his wrist unit: "Calling MAN's helpers. To the hub, please."

# *Four*

It was six months before the annual starship stopped in at Terra Station, and another month before it got back to Madlarki and José heard the news: his MAN program had been inadequate for the priestess from Earth. She had not died, but she had not done well either. She had had bouts of madness, though she was now stabilized. The station had been hysterical for a few hours, dancing, but Mana's breakdown had sobered them. They had returned to the old certainties.

José played again and again the reconstructions of Mana's encounters in the egg. He projected her holie image in front of him. He saw her anguish and her beauty.

He had no one he could talk to about her. No one who would understand how much she reminded him of another young woman who had left another green planet over fifty years before to come to the heart of space civilization: Martin of Arable, whom his own mother had helped to foment a revolution that almost brought the Collectivity to its senses. He could not tell anyone how much the young huntress embodied the very dreams of his heart. He longed to gather her holie image in his arms.

Something warned him she was different from his dreams, that she was not a revolutionary, that she was no Martin. She was more elusive than that. She believed in her gods. She was of a kind he had had no preparation to understand, a kind he had not programmed MAN to understand. But his heart embraced her.

# *Part Three*

## THE

## GALACTIC CENTER

*Seventeen Years Later*
*The Planet Starlight, The Planet Madlarki,*
*and Terra Station*
*Year of the Migration 2125*

# the black and white spinning top

From the wraith's auroras in the twilight sky to the chop, thud of an ax, all in the village is as normal. The granddaughter of old Nokomis sits under the pine branches unbraiding her long hair.

Every evening these days she watches the theater of her world and waits for whatever will be next. The wraiths are playing games in the sky with colors: tonight, curtains of pale green and arrows of pink. She picks up a hairbrush of hog bristles, softened over the years by innumerable meditative strokes down the long brown tresses that are her lovers' delight. The brush is her favorite, made of bristles that she cut herself from the great sow, Boadicea. She glued them long ago into a padauk handle, elegantly carved in the shape of an egret. The carver was an early love, whose face of a decade ago she now remembers rather less clearly than Boadicea's.

She watches the first brilliant stars pierce the day's fading scrim. The wraith colors depart for a moment, out of respect. It is the unparalleled beauty of these stars that give this theater, her home, its name.

On the planet Starlight, many of the houses merge imperceptibly from shelter to open air. The painted cupboard in which the hairbrush lives is hung from a pine tree. It will be taken farther in, come winter. Its open door reveals a comb, a poetry book made of paper, a half-carved soapstone river naiad, carving tools, a fir cone, a spherical spinning top half black, half white, a divination board (swinging on the back of the door) on which to spin the top, and other knickknacks.

The breeze is getting chilly, as befits the time of year. It bears autumn smells of brewing and onions, plus a steady flutter of leaves from the Japanese maple and the cherry tree by the pump. Her neighbor is stockpiling firewood for winter. Every day now he chops a little. She will do hers all in one day, soon — she will invite friends and lovers, past, present, and future, and make a big feast, have a party, borrow saws and axes from round about, and get it all done in a day, soon.

She feels that this waiting period will be resolved before too long. This autumn Passarin must surely decide to jump, to leap into the rock-that-lives, to merge with the tree and the seed and the fruit. He cannot live in the wasteland of his disembodied god for ever. Nor can she. She has given him so much at a time when she felt bereft as never before by another's going.

Passarin has been a strange lover. Intoxicating at first in his awkward virginity. Infuriating later in his stubborn distance. He clings to an aloof determination not to let go into the cosmic orgasm of the universe. He insists on balling his whole tortured self into that little classifier in his skull. He peers out only to analyze and pigeonhole the world. Delightful to offer water to one in such a desert. Infuriating to see him sip so thriftily.

But now her puzzled fury has given way to this calm sense of expectation. He came from another world, another, meaner culture. Poor dear — it is no surprise he cannot find wholeness. His great-grandmother was, after all, a gene lab. His grandmother, the great rebel, Martin of Arable, bequeathed him a planet in ruins, and precious little of her own greatness. His grandfather Jomo shipped up on Starlight, a crazy little man. His father is a patriarch on that planet in ruins, practically a god. No wonder the poor boy's mixed up. His planet was bombed by atomics. One of his best friends there is an old radiation victim with one eye. He's all of twenty-two and he has never had a lover before.

Yet he is only twenty-two, after all. He came to Starlight as one of the assistants to his father's ambassador, the first his planet, Arable Two, has sent to another planet. And now he wants nothing to do with ambassador or father. Talk about problems! Still, that break with father, she thinks, is a hopeful sign. Soon he will take the leap into wholeness. She feels it. Her top, spinning on the divination board, hints at it, landing on the Gardener, the Shaman. She will love him, and he will heal. If it takes all winter, well then, it will take all winter. But he will heal. And he will heal her in return.

Starlight is the one place in the Galaxy where there is wholeness and healing, she knows that. Apart perhaps, she thinks, from Earth, but she knows nothing of Earth; for Starlight is still debating whether to visit again. Last time, at least a thousand years ago, was too traumatic for all concerned. Starlight has looked in on itself, healing itself, for all of its life. It has preyed on the rich ships of the Collectivity when necessary. Only recently has it thought of turning from piracy to subversion of the Collectivity. It was her lover's grandmother, Martin the revolutionary, who gave Starlight the shove in that direction. She showed them the first signs that their giant neighbor's heart might be shocked toward a more human rhythm. But Starlight moves slowly, by consensus, healthfully. It is hard to shove Starlight. It has debated and pondered, and in the meantime made little more than token gestures toward keeping Martin of Arable's cause alive in the Collectivity.

His moccasins sound their familiar stiff steps on the gravel, down through the house and onto the pine needles. He isn't wearing the smock she embroidered for him, or any of the fun clothes she has persuaded him to wear. He's back in his plain Arable Two homespun wool, scratchy and harsh. And he has cut his hair again, so that his face looks unnecessarily sharp. But she is calm.

She closes her eyes and leans back, raising her lips for the kiss. No kiss.

He says, "I've come to say good-bye."

She jerks her head forward and opens her eyes. He stands before her like a new soldier embarrassed by his uniform.

"You've got someone else?"

"I'm leaving Starlight."

"Going home?" Her voice sounds shrill in her ears.

"I will never go home. You know that. I want to thank you, for everything you have −"

"Thank me, shit! You're running out on me! You got scared."

"I − I truly am not running out on you."

"I can see it just by the way you stand. Why did you even bother to come and tell me? Why not just run?"

"I have been given the chance of my life," he explains doggedly. "To go to the Galactic Collectivity as . . . well . . . I suppose as a kind of agent for Starlight. I'm going to see José."

"And who, may I ask, is José?" The wind bounces the branches of the cherry tree. She realizes winter has rushed in, and it is too late to organize a firewood day now. She will freeze.

"He's the son of my grandmother's best friend . . . it's too long a story to tell now. Well, I suppose I should." He's jabbering to cover his nervousness. "You know my grandmother and her two friends, Sunal and Chiamay, all had their babies the same year − the only three women in the history of the Collectivity to give birth."

"I learnt it at school."

"Well, Sunal was a Tarcunan, and although her mother was a lab, her father was Rosa, the most powerful man in the Galaxy,

Chair of First Committee of the whole Collectivity. He took
Sunal's baby away from her. That's all I knew about it. But it
seems Rosa brought the boy up and gave him all the privileges that
he could, including some time with Sunal. His name is José. He is
over seventy years old. I seem to spend my whole life chasing old
men. My grandfather was dead when I got here, I hope José's alive.
He lives on Madlarki planet, which is one of the three central
planets . . ."

"Spare me. I know what Madlarki is."

"He's a father himself. He was part of that elite on Tarcuna
that had families — all that's left of my grandmother's attempt at
revolution. Only he rejected those people and left Tarcuna because
he's a *real* follower of my grandmother, maybe the only one who's
still alive. That means he . . ."

"I can guess what that means. It means he sits and drinks
brandy and writes letters to his grandchildren about the great old
days, until he's so discouraged he lasers his brains out."

Passarin clenches his fists and his jaw. "That's unfair," he
mutters through his teeth.

"Nokomis, my grandmother, spent the best part of twenty
years looking after Jomo, your grandfather, and never a word of
thanks in all that time. All he did was write letters to you on
Arable Two about how wonderful and sexy and brave Martin of
Arable was, and how she really did have sex with him, and how
you really are his grandson, and when he was done and Nokomis
was away, he got drunk and killed himself. That's foreigners! No
Starlight man would have done that. And no Starlight man would
run off and leave these arms for a septuagenarian idealist on a
frozen planet. But you like it better frozen, don't you? That's who
you are. Nokomis was right to warn me off you. It's in your genes!"

"She didn't."

"Oh, didn't she? Happy ideas about old Nokomis, have we? Let me
tell you, she didn't just warn me you were a wimp and a loser, she
said . . ."

He is no longer there. He has turned and run. Not through

the house, but through the shrubbery to avoid the house, snapping branches and blooms with criminal callousness, trampling the infant plum they had planted together.

"She said you were an unbeliever! A frozen heart! Damaged beyond repair!"

He is gone.

The chop, thud, thud of the ax starts up again. Her neighbor, nosy gnome, must have been listening.

In the brilliant starlit sky, a scroll of crimson unfurls across the Southern Frenzy, tailing runes of purple and green. The wraiths are playing with their palette again. But the calm beauty of their art is insufferable. She looks down at her hands. The padauk handle is broken in two.

The ax has only demolished a dozen more logs when she realizes that his moccasins are standing before her again.

He crouches down, and his gray eyes peer through the long hair that hides her face. He is holding out a package.

"I'm sorry I ran." His voice is tight. Formality reclaims him at moments of embarrassment. "I had brought you this. I couldn't leave without giving it to you."

He is so damned ethical, so determined to do the right thing.

She takes and unwraps it. It is a stone. A gray stone with a line of red through it.

"It is from the hills above my father's farm," he says.

She starts to cry.

He strokes her hair. Her arms go out and he comes into her embrace. His cheek is wet by hers.

"Stay with me," she sobs. "Stay the night."

There is no reply. She feels his muscles clamp, in the way they do when he cannot say what he is feeling.

"You're relieved, aren't you," she says, releasing him from her arms. Her tears have stopped as quickly as they came, frozen by his coldness. "You're relieved this means we're over."

He is embarrassed again. "I don't know," he mutters.

The receipt of a present is no light matter. She leans over to the painted cupboard and pauses awhile. She doesn't know why she picks this from all the rest.

"Here," she says. "For you."

"But it's your top. Your night and day top." It is spherical; the top of the sphere is carved out, turned on a lathe, to make a stalk. The stalk and top half are white; the bottom half is black.

She lifts down the board, and spins the top on it. As they look down, they see only its white top half. It is a white top spinning. Then it starts to wobble wildly and turns over, spinning on its stalk, suddenly and astonishingly black.

It wanders around the board and stops spinning at last, falls on its side, on the White Lady.

"Odd," she says. "I would have expected the Hermit, or the Stick Man. The Quixote, perhaps." She knows her voice sounds cruel. She wishes she could be better at sudden partings. She puts the black and white top in his hand. "You won't have room for the board. But you can make your own. You should know the figures by now."

They look at each other.

She realizes he is going to a fearsome world where all is polarized and no one knows the fullness of life. "One thing always turns into another," she says, inanely offering wisdom in clichés. "Things seem like opposites. But they are the same thing." She sees suddenly that if she had been able to live these last months in that knowledge, they would have enjoyed each other more.

He looks at her, still embarrassed.

"Go!" she shouts.

He goes.

# *One*

"So you have been in love? Do you think you could tell me about it?" Passarin asked. He had just arrived on Madlarki, complete with forged wrist unit and identity provided by the Starlight Collectivity Subversion Unit. The old man, José, had still been alive, thank God. He was there waiting for Passarin when he got off the ferry that brought him down from Madlarki's space station: an old, slim, bent man with very little hair and an unexpected warmth in his eyes. His skin was smoother than any old person's Passarin had seen on his home planet or on Starlight. Later he would find that was true of all these people in the artificial habitats — no sun and fresh air to weather the skin. But José looked worn down nonetheless, and Passarin felt a sudden solicitousness for him.

José took him in an amazing car that ran like a trained mouse through a vast grid of tunnels, flashing past open spaces where other cars picked up or set down passengers, until finally they stopped at one themselves and walked away, leaving the car there. Its doors closed and it zipped away, riderless.

José walked with him through corridors that had no windows or skylights, nothing to tell what the planet of Madlarki was like, until they reach a plain door that opened onto greenness. It was a greenhouse like ones he had seen on Starlight, stuffed with plants and with a ceiling and three whole walls of glass that showed an even greater riot of greenery outside, a wild jungle under a mauve sky. In among the plants there was a table, four chairs, a burner of some kind for heating food, and an unmade bed with dirty sheets and blanket. The place smelled of damp and rot. The floor was unswept, covered in dried or decaying brown leaves. Spider webs hung from the ceiling and between some great dark green leaves with red veins running across them: the leaves slowly dripped a viscous blood-red liquid.

Passarin asked in a puzzled tone, "Do you live here?"

The old man fairly bristled. "Finest place to live on Madlarki! Privacy! Green plants! Next best thing to being in love!"

That was how Passarin blurted out, "So you have been in love? Do you think you could tell me about it?" Something about the old man made Passarin think you could probably ask him anything.

"She came to me as a psych case. Love was the very last thing on my mind. Her name was Mana." The old man's eyes seemed to look backward into his skull. "But I've lost her now. In fact, I never had her."

"Please, if it's not too personal."

José's eyes came back from far away and glinted with amusement. "I take it you haven't been in love yourself?"

Now I've lost the moment, thought Passarin. Might be as hard to get this man to talk about himself as to get father to.

"Some infatuations, I suppose," he replied. "I don't know. I thought I was in love on Starlight."

"You would know. Believe me, you would know." What hair José had left was grey, and as Passarin looked more closely he realized his face, though not wrinkled, was faded like an old banner in the Temple that has dried into fragility. Although he was about the same height as Passarin's father, José was slim where his father had a great barrel chest; and in other indefinable ways he looked the lesser man. They were the same age, his father and this man, but this man looked as if he had always lived on the sidelines. Passarin's father was called the God Giver. He led an entire planet, had reinvented human culture after the planet was left for dead. His father's mother had been either a revolutionary or a kind of goddess, depending whose story you believed. But either way, she had been one of the giants of history. His father had inherited her authority, at least on one little planet. But this old man, José, looked like he had never had any authority over anyone. Perhaps, thought Passarin, that's why I'm liking him so much.

"It's funny, José. I only came on this mission because of you. I couldn't believe it when the Starlight people told me you were alive, and in contact, carrying on my grandmother's work, as you understood it. I came to talk with you about that, to find out who she really was." Passarin breathed in the smell of wet potting compost, flower scents, and warm greenery.

"Air outside's toxic," José said.

"That's hard to believe. It's so vitally green. But, I was going to say, now that I've found you, what I want to talk about isn't Martin at all, but falling in love. Isn't that odd? After all the incredible trouble Starlight took to smuggle me in. I really didn't expect that."

"Not with an old man?"

José saw a slim, severe boy in his early twenties. The youngster's regulation fatigues fitted him awkwardly. He sat too firmly erect within them. His ID and a wrist unit had fooled Security, but no MAN programmer would be taken in. And he couldn't be mistaken for one of the Tarcunan elite, either. His face was too serious. He would dance stiffly. Probably never been drunk. An evil glint crept into José's soul, thinking on the possibility of acquiring an Ah Sung spider to open this young man's dreams . . . that stinging bite behind the ear.

"What do old men know of love?" the young man half smiled.

José liked that smile. He was about to make a ribald joke, but found himself saying unexpectedly seriously, "I don't know about other old men. I spent most of my life in love with an ideal. Your grandmother. The hero from the green planet. Then this Mana came along, and I thought she was the new personification of that ideal. I couldn't have been more wrong. But the more I found out who she really was, the more I loved her. It's a backward, upside-down way to fall in love." How sincere this boy was. José could never have said what he had just said to his own sons.

José went to a cupboard and brought out glasses and a bottle, poured for them both. Passarin took a long sip and sprayed it all out again.

"It's not called Kick for nothing," José smiled. He patted him on the back and offered a handkerchief. The boy looked askance at it. It did look a little grubby. "It's been washed. It's organic, cotton or something, from Arable — you should like it."

The boy sat primly in the white wicker chair and looked out on the mangled violence of the Madlarki jungle with eyes watery from the drink. He still refused the handkerchief and dashed his eyes on his sleeve, like a peasant.

"So she wasn't like my grandmother?"

"No. Mana lived in another universe, where every rock and animal and tree is alive. Where every act is bound up with Gaia. Where Mana without Gaia is nothing. She came as the happy bearer of good news. She thought everyone would want the beauty she brought."

"Was she beautiful?"

"Like a tree spirit come to life. When they didn't want her Goddess, she couldn't take it. And then she couldn't take it either when they started to dance in the sunlight — I suppose it was too manic, too ungrounded. She would say, too Sky God. But the worst was that Govind rejected her."

The boy raised his eyebrows in query, and José found himself telling the whole story of Govind. His spoiled childhood, adolescent pranks, everything. "Govind's's twenty-two now, and he's incredible. They practically worship him on Terra Station. Mana plugs away with her Gaian rituals. She's the dutiful type, always has been. Until some strange moment comes and frees the wild goddess inside. But I've been waiting for that for seventeen years; I'm an old fool to believe in it still. She would really have to do something supernatural to capture Govind now. Her little rituals won't do it. Look, I'll show you. Look at this."

The greenery, the windows, the jungle view vanished and Passarin found himself looking into a glowing yellow room full of people. He exclaimed and jumped up from his chair.

"Relax," said José. "It's a holie. See, it's the hub at Terra Station."

"My God!" Passarin was given to strange oaths from his homeland.

"Sit down, boy."

"Turn it off."

The greenery returned. Passarin sat down slowly. "Now turn it on."

The yellow room was there again, as if they could walk straight into it. "My God. I've never seen one before.'

"They don't have these on Starlight?"

"I suppose they do. I never went. I was the studious type. It's so real. Except for color."

"The color is real. Terra's sun is a very warm yellow. No wonder they used to worship it on earth. It was a male thing, like the caves and the earth were thought of as a female thing. That's what freaked Mana out, gave her one of her episodes — to her it looked like Govind single-handedly reinvented sun worship. Of course he didn't entirely. The wraiths taught it to him. But he made it a human thing, a huge thing for the people on the station." José realized he was going to enjoy sharing Earth Station with this serious boy.

Passarin held onto his wicker chair as he looked into this other world. The large bright room they looked in on had a high domed glass ceiling. Sunshine streamed down from the center of the dome and gilded all the people below. A few of them were semi-naked, thin, with ascetic faces. Most were in standard space fatigues, a hundred or more. They all appeared to be in a trance, meditating, standing still with their faces tilted to the sun. In their center a young man stood head and shoulders above them, as if on a small platform. Even in the sunshine his skin seemed dark. His flesh was full, his cheeks fat and smooth. But his eyes were the strangest thing about him. Even from a distance.

Suddenly Passarin zoomed into the crowd and he felt as if his stomach had been left behind. His hands gripped convulsively, and the wicker chair arms were still there. He looked down and behind him to remind himself that he was still in José's greenhouse. It was the holie camera that had zoomed in to show a close-up of Govind.

The eyes in that plump dark face were the kind of eyes that Passarin knew from home: the eyes of fanatic priests in the Temple, even at times the eyes of his father, the God Giver: eyes that saw beyond the now to the eternal. They were uncomfortable, dangerous eyes. The black eyebrows and heavy cheeks shielded the eyes and made the energy that burned from them more startling.

The mouth below the eyes was talking hypnotically about the sunshine. "Feel the Liquid Light! Feel it on your skin . . ." He seemed to be about fifteen going on a hundred.

"Turn it off!" said Passarin, far too loud.

The blessed plants returned. His heart still pounded. For a moment he had been back in the Temple as his big brother exultantly dragged a vee frame in through the great front doors, and on it the carcass of a huge and harmless alien beast.

"Creepy, eh?" said José. "Remind you of something?"

But Passarin would not be drawn. There was sweat on his forehead. He did not wipe it off. "That's not a happy young man," he said.

"That's how it strikes you, is it? Hmm." José stroked his old, pale chin.

"He's not drawing them into the sunshine. He's drawing them into himself."

"But, Passarin, what could such a man do if he was truly captured by a great ideal? To warm the earth? To warm the whole Collectivity?"

"I don't like it."

"He's exactly your age. I wish you could meet him."

"Me? I hope not."

"But who else knows anything of religion? None of us. Look, this is Govind. I made this montage just for you, soon as I knew you were coming. These clips are from security cameras on station, MAN tapes, that kind of thing."

Suddenly instead of potted plants and dead leaves there was Govind as a manic fat child leading a whole string of people in a dance down the corridors of the station. Govind hand in hand with stick thin men in white loincloths.

"Those are the wraiths," said José.

"Why is his skin so dark? It's almost black."

"His mother was African."

"An African mother? What's the story?"

"I'll tell you later. Look at this imp."

A dim shot, from a security camera, of a running figure disappearing round a corner, leaving huge red letters spray-painted raggedly on a corridor wall: HOW DEEP IS YOUR LOVE?

Govind about fifteen, naked, smeared with grey stuff, his hair all long and matted, prancing at the head of a gang of boys and girls all dressed as wild things, with clothes torn and streaming behind them.

A shot of another boy, not Govind, in the egg, admitting to going on a raid with Govind to the most off-limits and secure place on station — the fusion drive sector, where they had stolen an EXTREME DANGER — NO UNAUTHORIZED PERSONNEL sign, he said. He looked shamefaced and thrilled.

Govind the engineer drew an extraordinarily complex 3-D blueprint in the air with a holo pen.

A food fight in the cafeteria. Govind led the melee.

"He's wild!" said Passarin.

"Envious?" asked the old man.

Now they saw a scene in the softroom, with Govind apparently orchestrating a major orgy. Passarin goggled. He had never seen anything remotely like it. He had only slept with one woman in his life, on Starlight. Bodies writhed, bottoms pumped, tongues licked.

The picture winked out. Passarin wasn't sure if he was relieved or if he wanted more.

"I'll spare you," José said. "That's what he got into after the Liquid Light meditation. The Light craze ran on and off for years, and it was all bound up with being spiritual, not carnal, leave the body behind, like the wraiths, big-time dualism. Mana hated it, you can imagine."

Passarin could not imagine. He still had very little idea about this Mana.

"But suddenly he discovered carnal. And then he had to make sure everyone else discovered it too. Carnal's where he's been for a while now. Of course, I'm always up to a year behind in knowing what's actually going on there. One thing he's always done, though, is tell stories. The people love him there — more for his stories than because he's so dangerous and unexpected."

The greenhouse before them vanished again and they saw a large white rectangular room full of tables and people eating. Govind stood above all the rest, a fat man who nonetheless seemed light, sitting on the back of a chair with his feet on the chair seat. He was telling a story. All faces turned up to him.

"And the old man said to the salmon, 'Who are you to talk to me like this?'

"'I am your daughter,' said the salmon."

The people drew in their breath as one, astonished.

He used his pudgy hands to talk, floating them out from his body as if he might fly off. He was not especially handsome, but he was mesmeric.

"Turn it off," Passarin said for the third time. "Why do you show me him and not Mana?" he asked.

The old man busied himself with the little keyboard in his hand, the holie controls. Finally he set it down.

"Mana, I don't want to share." The old man looked so bleak, Passarin wanted to hug him.

"Govind's your politician, is that right, your revolutionary? Your successor to Martin? He could transform the Collectivity? But Mana has your love."

The old man's eyes were wet. Then he smashed his fist onto the table. "Mana is loved and she could love," he said with tremendous passion, "But she's so pedestrian!"

To fill the awkward silence Passarin said, "You never went to see her?"

The old man recovered slowly as he replied. "If I had gone there, they would never have allowed me to stay more than a few days. I wish I had. Now I'm seventy-four, and she's thirty-nine — I'm too old for her. I thought I could find a way to get her to come here. But I found the limits of my influence. The bastard grandson of Rosa has a place in the new elite, but it's a precious small one. I suppose my sons have done the right thing, building influence in corrupt and conscienceless ways. If I'd acquired my own ship, like my son Rocco's trying to do, I could have gone and got her, I suppose."

"Can't he go and get her for you?"

"What does Rocco care for me? I'm an old fool to him. No, she wouldn't have come anyway, without her precious Govind. He breaks her heart every day. What the patterns of Gaia have to do with him, I don't know. But then, I'm just an old man with only five senses."

# *Two*

"Hallo, MAN."

"Welcome, Mana. How are you?"

"No different. It's just another day."

"Who are you thinking about today?"

"Apart from Govind? I was thinking of going down to see Gauri in the gyro."

"Still wishing you knew what makes her tick?"

"She's the key to him. One day she will reach through to him, and he will come back to Osen's way."

"Perhaps he is already on it? Do any of us really understand everything about Osen's way?"

"You always say that, but he still rejects the Goddess, the body."

"He's crazy about bodies."

"You know what I mean. Sex isn't the point. Wholeness is. His sex craze is just a wild opposite of his wraith spirit craze. It's not unifying the two."

"So what would Osen say?"

"She'd say Gauri could be earth to him. She could bring balance. But she's so hurt . . ."

"If you love Gauri, you will find a way to her heart."

It was so centering and comforting to talk to MAN.

Mana walked slowly to the gym.

These seventeen years on station she had rarely run, or even walked fast. Her physical life seemed almost like a dream. It had ended with her arrival here. Then her mental life had begun, her struggle to be calm, and accept, think, understand, rework, re-express, re-create. Re-creation had left little energy for recreation. And besides, all the gymnastics and games and sex (which here was but a branch of athletics, with some theatrics thrown in) were a painful parody of real physicality. She did not go to the gym to participate any more than she went to the softroom. They had put her to work in hydroponics, thinking

she would like the plants. But it was a mockery. There was neither earth nor rain. In hydroponics you didn't even get your
hands dirty.

Here her task was to comprehend, to become a Sarasvati,
an Osen, to discipline herself. That had been clear for a long
time. The idea of being Mana the lover was fantasy.

She had chosen to come, or she had been chosen, whichever: it was all the same thing. For now she was here and could
not choose to go back. No spells of hers could stop the Earth
orbiting the Sun, or float her down to Earth on wings. No dance
she could create on her own would bring Gaia to life here, trailing her garlands and song, her laughter and her darkness through
the spinning bright rooms.

The metal and plastic of this world had no inner life she
could discern. It was not truly dead either, for death is decay,
from which life grows. This stuff was in limbo. She could not
change that.

But some things she could do. She could have faith. On
Earth, faith had been barely necessary with the Goddess so close
and present. It had been natural as breath. Here she had to
choose every day to believe that the Goddess was with her and
would support her. Because she couldn't feel it.

And there were a few concrete things she could do, too. So
today she was on her way down long corridors, dustier now even
than when she first arrived, to the gym, to see an important
friend. So later today she would go and talk with an old man,
Arun, who had a forgotten broom closet, where he liked to sit
alone in the dark. So too she could respond to Chairperson,
who was now, at seventy-nine, only one year away from the long
sleep. He had never ceased to desire her company. And she
could continue to be a friend to poor Vladimir, whose vacilla-
tion and unhappiness MAN had stubbornly refused to cure.
Sometimes Vladimir's affair with Chairperson was on, sometimes
off, as ever. Little changed. But with Vladimir and Arun and
Chairperson, she felt better. With Gauri, the friend she was on
her way to see, she could even feel a little hope.

In these seventeen years she had learned that MAN was no
god, but a program monitored and manipulated by people on a
distant planet. And these people were sympathetic to her cause.
Right away, MAN had read the Chronicles. Hey started asking
her all about Osen. Soon, MAN was encouraging her to do what

Osen would have her do. After her breakdown, MAN helped her find her sanity in acceptance of Osen, even of Osen's manipulations. She screamed her fears at MAN: was it Osen who killed Sarasvati, whom Osen loved and who loved her? Had the old wraith-daughter dying in the Caves flung that murderous dart across a day's march of forest to force the choice on Mana? Had Sarasvati done it to herself?

MAN said it made no difference now. The point was that Osen wanted to bring the Collectivity to life again, and Mana needed MAN's help to do it.

Why would MAN say that? Somewhere at the Center, there was a hope. Perhaps Osen had known the Center could change.

The villagers of her childhood had believed that God and Brahma were still up here, up above the clouds, trying to get back their influence.

But the Cave priestesses had said, "Those spirits and gods are myths. Gaia is not some spirit outside of nature. Gaia *is* nature. Gaia *is* the world. As a cell of your body is to you, so are you to Gaia. So don't expect voices from the sky or from spirits — that's sky talk. Just be you, don't sacrifice your nature. And you will be Gaia."

But here she had had to sacrifice her nature. And the only way she could have faith in Gaia was to imagine Gaia as a voice from afar, a spirit entering this alien limbo. She had split up into parts — a body that followed Space customs, a mind that struggled with the Chronicles, a spirit that sought the evanescent touch of Gaia. Here, Gaia had to be spirit. An impossibility.

Osen's *Recalling the Galaxy* envisaged a united band of believers in Gaia who would fan out into Galactic society and tickle the trout in the places of power and influence; they would create a semisecret elite ruled by Gaia, or, rather, by those who were her truest servants. Like Mana and Govind.

If successful, the Gaians would undermine Lakshmi's Space Code and alter the priorities of civilization away from the artificial toward the green and breathing, the dance and the dark, the passion and the joy of the Earth. Why would MAN want that?

There were mysteries in this civilization, and yet it was good that there were. For they left shadows in which hope might lie.

MAN was not a god. And yet she wondered sometimes if

hey did not take up too much of her mind. Perhaps she would be thrown more onto reliance on Gaia-spirit if she left MAN. The thought had begun to obsess her recently. At times she almost felt like MAN wanted her to leave hem. Perhaps it was the only way to be a person. The more she thought about it, the more she felt there was great truth there. And yet MAN was her daily friend.

So Mana prowled the passages of the Earth station year after year, seeking for ways. Her brave company, her Gaian secret elite, consisted of only three people so far, and herself. Arun, Chairperson, and Vladimir. Chairperson would leave them next year for the sleep, and Arun not long afterward. In his old age, Chairperson had sobered. Preparing for his death, he found peace in Mana's rituals. They had labored hard on Osen's instructions, on working out the rituals, the dances, the symbols, the right progressions. They always talked about expansion, recruitment. But they knew that all hinged on Govind, the wild young man of Terra Station. Govind who saw people's voices, who saw dead flowers in her mouth. He always had, and she knew it had always been true.

As if to mock her thoughts, boisterous sounds of youngsters running echoed down the corridor toward her. It was no surprise. So often when she thought of him, he was nearby.

They burst upon her with their overwhelming energy, and she tried to stand as calm as an oak in a storm. Young men and women shouted and danced around her. These days Govind's friends dressed wildly in colored rags, grew their hair long, and tied colored rags into it. Today she saw that they had remade their clothes, the boys with big codpieces and the girls with a lot of breast showing; perhaps that's why they were laughing so much.

Of course, the wildest of them was Govind. His skin was painted white today, grayish ashen white. He was overweight, his rolls of skin grotesque. He pranced up to her and thrust his ashen face into hers to shock her.

"Mana, Mana, Goddess Mana," he sang in a child's sing-song.

"Chaste Mana!" mocked a lad called Lakshmi, who had his arm around a lovely girl called Karl.

"Chaste Mana, never been chased!" sang Govind. "Hard Mana, come to the softroom!" He opened his codpiece and brought out a white-painted erection. He thrust his hips toward her and waved the thing at her and they all screamed with laughter.

And then they pranced off.

Mana stood there shaking, her fists clenched. Dear Kali, I have tried, she prayed, I have done my duty in a task I never wanted and with all the joy and love I could muster. Please, Kali, you must help me. He looks like Shiva but he despises me. Like the warrior king despised Osen's cave sisters.

After a few moments she found it possible to walk on.

Govind was always in her thoughts, always a source of hope. The more she let herself hope, the more painful were his rejections. But it was her calling to hope, to die inside, to hope, daily.

And the way to Govind was, as always, through Gauri. That was why Mana went often these days to the gym. She went to watch Gauri.

Gauri had always loved people. At five years old Gauri had been the first person on station to put her hand in Mana's. So why did the girl devote every spare minute of her time these days to the gyrosphere? In the great transparent sphere that spun and stopped and reversed and spun again at random, Gauri was cut off from everyone. Circles of tiered seats, often crowded even for her practices, rose up around the gyrosphere. Within it, as it moved upon its pedestal, Gauri did backflips and handstands and somersaults. Even in practice, she rarely lost her balance. Her sureness was mesmerizing. Mana could watch her for an hour without tiring. Gauri seemed to have precognition of the sphere's random turns. In the gyrosphere it was the machine that was the sphere, the athlete who had to be the gyro. Gauri had demonstrated a real little gyroscope to Mana. She had seen the way its spinning momentum kept it stable even when everything around it turned. It was what she wanted to be herself: an oak in this spinning hunk of metal.

As the sphere turned, Gauri achieved perfect gymnastics within it. She was a star. Holies of her performances were watched enthusiastically on other stations and planets throughout this sector of the Galaxy. Surely a young woman who had such a perfect gyroscope in her head could be the stabilizer for Govind and for the Gaian group. But ever since Govind's outrageous exploits in religious charisma seven years ago, Gauri had shut herself in the spinning cage.

As a child, Govind had taken the wraiths' Liquid Light meditation and taught it to his peer group. For weeks they all went
down to the hub to glow in the sun. Then he had started roping
in others. Within half a year he had got half the station doing it.
As a whirling yogi, a possessed spirit, his eyes ablaze, Govind
had lit up the minds of his people. What had he wanted? To
prove his power to lead? Then why had he refused to take responsibility for the consequences: the breakdowns, the manias,
the refusals to work or to do anything but stand like zombies
and drink in the sunlight at the hub? The station had practically
ceased to function. But of course, he was only a child.

And then he had dropped it and gone wild, the prankster,
with a gang of wild children trailing behind him. At thirteen he
had found a curious enthusiasm: wraith ergonomics. He had
designed a new floor for the wraiths to sit on when they formed
their circle that built the power that flashed the spaceships
through the Galaxy. She had gone to watch. A spaceship posi-
tioned itself near the hub, where the wraiths could see it from
their bubble. They chanted and writhed together, arms around
each others' shoulders, moving as one. Suddenly the ship was
gone and they collapsed onto the mysterious patterns on their
floor. Govind's floor was solid to walk on, but as soon as they
formed their circle it responded to the rhythm of their bodies,
helped build their motion, then turned softly yielding for their
collapse. They loved it.

Govind claimed his floor mimicked a bed of pine needles, firm
but springy, organic. No pine needles Mana and Sitala had ever
lain on had responded like that, she thought wryly. In a fever of
invention and hard labor (which involved the entire Design Team,
plus anyone else they could recruit) Govind had converted two
hundred meters of busy corridor in the station to this sprung design. It would mimic the feel of the savannah and forest floor, he
said, on which our species had evolved. The new station would
have all its floors so, and everyone would be healthier and happier,
and no one would ever wear shoes again. But meanwhile MAN
was working overtime coping with all the people he had abandoned at the height of his Liquid Light craze. Without Govind
they were afraid to go down to the hub to stand with the wraiths.
But they couldn't fit back into their old lives, either.

He went through most of his adolescence an ascetic celi-
bate, practically a wraith. Then at 19 he discovered sex. For

months, the softroom became the focus of the station's life. Mana never went there, but she heard enough about it. People discussed it openly. The softroom spilled out onto the station. Young people could be found touching each other and worse in any empty room or behind any unexpected obstacle. Audit had a breakdown.

Then there had been periods when no one saw Govind at all for weeks. Other times, mysterious and inventive damage was done, and people wondered. The entire wombroom and all the MAN eggs were shorted out for several hysterically anxious days. Slogans were painted in huge red letters along corridors:
CHARISMA IS THEFT
IS THIS ALL?
PERFECT INDIVIDUALISM CASTS OUT ALL POWER
LIVE! DIE! SPIN THE WHEEL!
LAKSHMI SAID: HUMANITY MUST BE SUPPRESSED FOR HUMANITY TO SURVIVE

Through all this, except when he was carted off to the sick bay, Audit frothed like a demented wolf. But his fangs were drawn. For MAN complained not at all, and the Station Committee watched bemused. They remembered their decision long ago to let the child live. Now they were seeing what he could do.

They sighed with collective relief, nonetheless, when it turned out that Govind's newest craze at age 21 was Asteroid Spin.

Terra Station had never figured in the Spin League ratings since the ratings had started. The annual ship brought a top traveling team every year, which played the local team for ten straight games; then they added the scores of the best hundred games played on station in the intervening year . . . and Terra Station was only saved from coming out bottom by some degenerate old geezers who kept the Betelgeuse diamond asteroids going. But this year, all of a sudden, the talk at every mealtime was: with Govind, could they get into the rankings? Could they even win? The station lost all critical sense when it came to Govind. Somehow they didn't hate him. He brought too much excitement into their lives.

And all this time, since the Liquid Light craze, poor Gauri had hidden in her spinning ball. Mana's heart went out to the little figure, dressed today in an emerald bodysuit. Gauri had been practicing somersaults. Now she stood stock still on the rising floor — itself a considerable feat. Then she seemed to sense a new motion: she ran six quick steps down and up the side of the sphere and leapt inward, tucked in a tight spinning ball within the spinning sphere. It was a double somersault, her specialty, but she came out of it badly. The sphere had slowed and her feet were expecting the wrong thing as they landed. She fell heavily onto her side and lay still. The sphere stopped moving immediately. Mana ran down to the glowing area in its side, which had turned instantly from solid to permeable membrane. She pushed through into the dense silence and sweaty suffocation of Gauri's world.

Gauri had breathed deeply with relief that morning when she entered the gyrosphere's magic ball. Once the sphere's random motion had seemed impossible to master. But a dozen years had made her familiar with all its tricks. Compared to Govind, it was positively predictable.

People said her sureness amounted to precognition in the sphere. Sometimes it almost felt like that to her too. On good days, like this morning, she could find the central spot at the bottom even while running, leaping, standing still on her hands, going through the gamut of floor exercises. She gloried in the magic sphere then, enemy and lover, symbiote.

She had closed her eyes. It was best that way. The sphere was transparent and it was all feel, anyway, and letting the unconscious rule.

Then she sensed eyes on her. Not the eyes of the easy-going crowd that always collected when she practiced.

Damn! Almost missed.

Mana.

Concentrate.

Damn, Mana. Always so depressed. Her prematurely gray hair, her slow walk. That grim look. I'll bet she's got that look on her face right now. On the prowl. Watching poor Gauri again. Leave me alone!

Keep your mind on it, or you'll have a sprained ankle. Now, the double next, when the floor feels right.

What do you want with me? It's not me you want, it's Govind. I know that. Well, leave him alone, damn you, leave him alone. Now! It's moving for you. Six steps up the side and in! Good: one, two. Oh! damnable Liquid Light.

She lay still on the floor, her head in one arm, her other

hand on her ankle. She heard someone push through the membrane.

"Are you all right?"

"No, Mana. I am not all right."

"You were going so well."

"Until you came."

"I came twenty minutes ago."

"Oh. Well, help me up."

"I came because it's your birthday."

"Is it?" Mana helped her out - through the sphere and down the steps.

"I've been praying for you, and Govind."

So what else is new, thought Gauri. The ankle was sprained for certain.

"I made the pentacle in blue fire this morning for both of you. Do you remember I taught you how to do that?"

"I remember." Dear Mana, dear sad, fucked-up, infuriating Mana.

"I make the same old spells for Govind every day. But this morning, this was a new one. It has power even here in space, I feel it. MAN is right. I have to make spells and prayers that work *here*. It's not enough to repeat the ones that I grew up with. Frog, cave, snow, bat, tiger — what do they mean here? Geometry, that makes sense here. Abstractions. And love, of course, always love — that's what we need. But mothers, fathers, moon blood — they're alien here. This prayer I said for Govind this morning, shall I recite it to you? So you can tell me what you think?"

"If you must."

"Spirit of Gaia, which holds us to Your orbit,

Draw us to You.

Blessed Gravity, which reaches beyond mountaintop and atmosphere,

Hold us steady.

As the Sun's light spreads out and warms us,

So let Gaia's spirit spread out and warm Gaia's son, Govind,

With Blessedness."

There was silence.

"Damn this ankle. I'll be off for days." Gauri leaned heavily on Mana. They were walking slowly through the gym complex to the changing rooms.

"Gaia's spirit is like MAN, Gauri. She can be with you at all times . . . and with everyone else as well. We can talk with Gaia as our friend, just like MAN. And yet, Gaia knows everything, more even than MAN knows. She can tell us what to do, and comfort us."

"So Gaia's a cosmic computer, now, is She? *And* a therapist?"

"You could say so, Gauri."

"Is that how She was when you killed Snow Tiger?" Gauri waited, but Mana's lips were pursed. There were tight stress lines around that mouth now. "I think MAN's good enough for me."

"MAN has heir own plans for you. Gaia's plan is much bigger. It is the truth about the universe. One day, even MAN will worship Gaia, perhaps has already started to. And you and Govind have been chosen to lead in Gaia's plan."

"He's not worth it, Mana."

"You don't believe that. You of all people."

"He's not worth ruining your life for, Mana. You're obsessed with him. What if it doesn't happen? He's cruel and selfish just as much as he's generous and good. I ought to know. What about your life? You always look so miserable."

"Oh, Gauri, thank you. You are wonderful. Sometimes I think you have more of Gaia in you than he does. If only we could be better friends. No one talks to me like you do, not even Chairperson."

Oh great jumping tigers, here come the tears, Gauri thought. Why am I such a sucker for tears?

They had reached the changing rooms, and Gauri sat down at last. She took Mana's hand and patted it. There were others around, changing, showering, walking through. They would see. But no one on Terra Station had worried much about reporting breaches of the Code for a long time now, especially by Govind and his friends. "Be good to yourself, Mana. Cheer up, for Gaia's sake."

"Gaia does not despise depression," Mana sniffed. "Depressions, or Caves. 'Earth is humus . . . it keeps us humble, and human.' That's what my teacher used to say. Now let's call the medics for you — you're not going to walk to the sick bay on that ankle."

Then, why didn't you call for them back at the sphere, Gauri asked herself. Wanted a little chance to talk to me, to cry and move me, did you?

"By the way, where's Govind today? Is he still on his asteroid spin craze?"

"A black hole couldn't draw out of me where Govind is, Mana, not for you to go and pester him."

Mana looked crushed, and Gauri was about to apologize. But she held back. Mana was uncrushable. "Can't MAN cure you of this obsession with Govind?" she asked instead.

Mana raised her head with dignity. "MAN has been a good friend to me. But heir agenda is not Gaia's. I will not be going to MAN again." She stood and swept out with a bravado that echoed disconcertingly of that young Goddess of the woods whom Gauri had loved as a five-year-old child.

"Kill that tiger, Mana," she whispered under her breath. Then she fell to staring at the soft gym shoes in her hands. Would she be the best sphere tumbler in this sector of the Galaxy, if it had not been for Govind, and Osen, and the young huntress from Earth who came and hugged her in the nursery? Perhaps, she thought, Mana was actually capable of not going back to MAN.

Passarin spun the little white wooden top on the floor.

José admired the skill of a primitive culture that could produce a thing so simple and satisfying. He thought it rather like the young man himself: so serious and naive, so plainly good compared to José's own two sons. Wooden toys. His sons had been brought up with holograms of themselves that tried to trick them into wrestling matches. If they did wrestle, there was nothing there. Ghosts. Then, the fourth time, or the fifth or sixth, their mirror ghost hit back. It had been a new technology developed for the MAN eggs, but still to this day not put into service in them. It was being held back for a major public crisis, when everyone could be distracted by this new thing. How therapeutic, to wrestle yourself, and hug yourself. Such wonders had been the toys of the MAN programmers' children. And then their parents wondered why they grew up weird. Unable to trust or be trusted.

Then suddenly the spinning top wobbled wildly and turned black.

José exclaimed.

"Good, isn't it?" Grave Passarin was as delighted as a child. He spun again. Again the white suddenly turned black.

José realized the top had turned itself upside down. He picked it up and chuckled. "I underestimated your homeland."

"Oh no, we could never make this. Our lathes are made of bent branches and string. This is from Starlight. Look how they made it. I think the bottom half must have been cut off, hollowed out, and glued back to the top half, so that the center of gravity is high enough to make it tip over."

"Your world's more primitive than I thought, if you don't even have machines for carving wood — what did you call them?"

"Lathes. I was brought up in a mud hut. With beams made of branches, helped along by the occasional alloy strut from an airplane wing. But anyway, even if we could, we wouldn't make something like this. Well, Sigurd OneEye would, but the God Giver would probably take it to the Temple and burn it on the altar."

"And I was thinking how much better off my sons would have been to have grown up like you."

"They're well out of it. I hope I never go back."

"Surely you don't want to live here. It's Starlight for you, isn't it?"

"Sometimes the Space Code and MAN seem to be just what I've longed for. An uncomplicated life — a softroom, a therapist who's always there."

"Garbage. You wouldn't last a month without longing for someone to love. Not if you've known love."

"I don't know if I have."

There was a long silence. The young man stared out of the rain-drenched greenhouse windows at the cloud that now obscured the jungle. José felt strangely bereft, helpless. He realized that he was missing all the MAN data that would have given him myriad clues to the young man's state of mind and body and brain. He could not conjure pictures, smells, sounds, to test the young man's responses. In the egg a hundred subliminal images or subtler neural stimuli could be tested for spontaneous responses. With seamless ease one set of stimuli would emerge to draw the citizen on to the next stage of healing. Did this young man need an image of his father to slaughter on the Temple altar, aided by the smell of blood, roasting offal and dust? José shuddered. It was not often he felt thankful for the sterilities of the Space Code.

There had been something about the way Passarin had made his remark about not going back that was particularly significant. José wondered if it was the first time he had said it, even to himself. The poor lad looked like he had just cut his line and was floating away from his spaceship. José wondered whether to get up and hug him, as he had trained himself to do with his sons. He looked much too stiff for that.

"Could I have the top?" he asked.

"I'd rather keep it." The young man turned back to him. "I'm sorry."

Mana tracked down a couple of others in Govind's peer group, who confirmed that he was playing asteroid spin, as usual, but this time in the wraith quarters. When that young man got his design work done, she did not know. The plans for the new station were supposed to be coming on fast now. He should be at work.

She didn't like going to the wraith quarters. It was a long walk into the empty sectors of the rim, and the wraiths were not friendly to her. But the talk with Gauri, and her own sudden declaration that she would abandon MAN, had given her an odd sense of urgency. Her body felt electric, like before a midsummer dance long, long ago. She knew she wouldn't sleep tonight. She wanted to walk fast, even to run. Suddenly she imagined herself smashing through branches in the forest, running wild and reckless. She wanted to slash at leaves and young plants with a metal-tipped staff like a mean child.

But she had never been that kind of child. She had been nothing like that boy down the lane whose mother was as horrid as he was; what had his name been? Or that girl in the wheelwright's shop. She couldn't recall their names. Even as a child, Mana had always had the greatest reverence for the forest. Now her muscles suddenly ached to whip that staff at high branches, to scythe whole sweeps of young ferns at one go.

MAN. Of course, she should tell MAN. Anger. Hey would get her to scream it out, pummel the couch, mime slashing through a forest holie. MAN would find the anger's root and uproot it. Anger at that encounter with Govind earlier in the day — his cruel laughter. No, not just that one but the countless previous ones, right back to the toy spaceship he threw that cut her lip the first time he saw her. He's just a child throwing things, still. It's time he grew up.

But I told Gauri I'm never going to MAN again and I won't.

She started to half walk, half run down the endlessly rising corridors to the abandoned quadrant where that simple door announced: TELEKINETIC PERSONNEL ONLY.

One of the remote, thin neuters opened the door. As always she was reminded of the sadhus, the wandering holy men who had come through the village begging: remoteness in their eyes, filthy from the privations of the road and from their strange, unGaian neglect of their bodies. Mana's teacher had used them as living evidence of an archaic notion of holiness: "Dualism, children, means spirit up there, body down here. God up there, nature down here. Us in between, climbing up to God and hitting down against nature, to stop it capturing us. So nature becomes 'it.' Animals become 'it.' Even men's bodies become 'it.' To man, women become 'it'. Men control 'it,' rape 'it,' abuse 'it.' Look how the sadhu abuses his own body, look how he delights to show the body's natural functions perverted — have you seen his show?" Of course, they had. One of the sadhus had hung himself from hooks in his flesh while little Mana screamed inside and watched. One had gone without food for two months through a hot summer, saying he lived on breath alone. The boys said this same one could suck water up his penis. "What makes them do it?" Mana had asked, shivering with fascination. "It's a terrible desire for control," the teacher had said. "To control the world with missiles or to control the body, it's all the same. Their attempts to overcome pain and reverse the natural body functions are rehearsals for the ultimate denial of the body: holy suicide, which they think will make them pure spirit. It's a search for transcendence through power. But there is no power that will reverse death. It's a false path."

Where had they come from, those men who had learned nothing from the coming of the Ice? The coarser villagers might spit at them, but Mana's teacher always gave them food and pressed them to stay. Sometimes she got them to eat well, but she never got them to wash.

The wraiths looked like well washed sadhus, gaunt of face. Their eyes focused on some interior place, or on somewhere far beyond the now. They had no sexual organs, she had been told, and they looked it. The one who opened the door to Mana had its hair plaited in a heavy matted mess. It tried to stop her gently in its thin voice, "Govind is playing spin. For us it is a sacred meditation. We would rather he was not interrupted."

But she pushed past it. Consumed with urgency, she brushed

aside the light folds of painted cloth that draped all the passages and rooms of the wraith world and made it seem a land of artists' tents.

"Govind!" she said, as soon as she saw him. A laser in each hand, he danced. He fired in rapid flashes at a pair of pockmarked rocks that floated in the middle of the room. The goal, as far as she knew, was to bring the two rocks together so that the black mark on one met the white mark on the other to ignite a scarlet flare. But they were holograms, illusions, replicas of a game early explorer scouts had played for real, with real asteroids. They weren't even real. Typical space stuff.

"Govind! There's better for you than this."

The wraith who was watching him flicked its eyes her way for a fraction of a second.

Govind was, frankly, fat, would probably outweigh two wraiths on a scale. But he danced lightly around the rocks. He fired delicately, and surely too swiftly for conscious thought. Every shot affected the motion of one of the rocks. He ignored her. He had shed his colored rags for a wraith's white loincloth.

She stepped in his way, beneath the rocks. "Gaia has more for you than this!"

He swore something incomprehensible but certainly unspiritual at her.

"Well at least your language is still on the ground."

He stopped and watched a rock sail away above his head until it simply disembodied up near the cloud-painted cloth hanging from the ceiling.

"You stupid woman. Twelve seconds to flare. Twelve seconds!"

"So at least you know I'm a woman. Don't you want better than this? Playing games with wraiths on a decrepit old chunk of iron so far off the spaceways there's only one ship a year?"

"What do you suggest? A vacation on Tarcuna?"

"Don't you want to go to the Center? The next ship's in two months. Maybe it is meant to take you. But how will you know? Gaia has a plan for you. But *how will you find it out?*"

Govind turned to his wraith friend and shrugged his shoulders.

"Don't apologize to him for me. Apologize to whatever you remember of Osen, for yourself!"

"Don't you ever say that again. If you ever say that again, I'll

. . ." His jaw clamped and his hand pointed a laser gun at her stomach. As far as she knew they were toys, too weak to do damage.

"Put up those lasers and don't be a child. Gaia made you to go to the Center of this Galaxy and take it by the scruff of the neck and shake sense into it. You won't get away from your destiny by pretending to eviscerate an old woman. Gaia has a plan for you, and you won't find it by playing with wraiths. Give yourself to Her! Cooperate with Her. Come with me!"

"Black flowers, Mana. Black flowers." He looked so like Osen must have looked at his age. His plump cheeks, far darker than anyone else's, the tiny tight curls of his hair, the intense eyes. But there was anger inside. He tried to be a wild Shiva, but he was too full of hurt and anger to be a real Shiva. He would not allow Kali near him, to take his seed into her and birth a new universe. He was ungrounded fire. Mana yearned out to him — let me give you the love Osen would have given you. Why does her death still mean so much more to you than her life? Or than my life?

He glared at her. As she absorbed that look, his words began to work their disabling truth on her. Black flowers. She had been living a death since her first day here. This was where their countless confrontations always ended.

All the anger and guts drained out of her. There was no starview in the room, but as clearly as if there had been she saw the Earth sweep by at its inexorable speed, the stars and moon, the constant motion. She teetered above the abyss in which the Earth spiraled. Vertigo swirled at her brain and stomach. It clutched her knees. She wanted to spin into trance again, to put it all away. Oblivion tempted. She closed her eyes and swayed on the edge of the void.

Nothing. Nothing. No Gaian hand to hold her. No link to Earth. The tenuous thread had broken. Long ago.

No voice. No magic. No pentacle of blue fire.

Only Govind's anger. Gauri's pity. No more MAN. The Earth, spinning at the bottom of its gravity well. The spiraling stars and moon.

But she didn't fall. She didn't spin.

She hung above the void, but she didn't fall. She didn't spin.

She swayed. She begged for blessed oblivion, but she didn't fall. Her head began to spin with dizziness. Her neck muscles were dissolving. But her head did not fall.

Then in the middle of the void, there was a hoarse rhythmic sound. Even while she felt dizzy and lost, a small lucid part of her brain traced the sound to the breath in her dry throat.

With this sound her solidity grew. She began to feel her lungs rise and fall. She started to sense her legs, strong, her feet firmly on the floor, the blood pulsing. She opened one hand. And the other. Dared flex the fingers wide like wings to slow the spinning in her head.

She was alive. She was not going to faint. But she would have to open her eyes to dispel the vertigo.

Govind would be there, her Shiva, her nemesis, the Sky God she had been sent to tame. Tame? No. Recall. Ground.

Her eyes fluttered open, and closed again. The glimpse told her he was staring at her. Appalled? Hypnotized as she had been once by the sadhu with hooks in his flesh? Imprinted on her eyelids as clear as if she stood wide-eyed in the Caves, appeared the statue of Black Kali. She is wrapped in snakes and scorpions and decapitated heads. The blood drools from Her jaws onto Her neck and down Her long, shriveled breasts. Her head rears back in orgasmic power as She kneels astride Shiva's white lingam. He floats beneath Her, lifeless but for his rising white erection. Mana had always thought, before, that She was taking power from him. She had thought She was cutting the male down to size. Now she knew that it was the other way around. He was about to wake with the energy of the Goddess coursing through him.

She opened her eyes again. He was staring into her, trying to reach her soul. His searching intensity was an undisciplined, scattered version of that look with which Osen used to cut straight through to Mana's inner being.

Mana thought, we will make the scattered light of your eyes coherent.

She began to unbutton her fatigues.

She stood before him naked. In the corner of her eye she saw the wraith slip rapidly out of the tented room. "I am Gaia. I am Kali." She stood as she had stood at solstice in the wild flowers on the savannah in the navel of the world, the proud and living Goddess to whoever should come.

"The black flowers are in your eyes, Govind. Only you see them.

"But what if they do exist? What if they are in my mouth, as well as in your eyes, and are falling now on these sagging breasts?

"Even then, Gaia can use me . . . because I am Her. She can use even you. You just have to say yes to Her. Throw away the disguises, the shields, these absorbing illusions." She gestured to the remaining pockmarked asteroid that still spun slowly above her head. "Forgive yourself. I bring you forgiveness. I bring you love of your Mother."

"You were never like this," he whispered. "You are not old. You are beautiful."

"You thought those were opposites? Gaia is crone and mother and maiden. She is Shiva in his power and in his weakness. Up here, I thought she was only spirit. But after all *this* is Her body. Come."

He came wonderingly into her embrace. She remembered the sick young man the summer before Atlatl, and how she had to overcome her disgust at him; and Atlatl himself, and how she had been disgusted and elated at the same time, knowing herself beautiful and powerful as she absorbed the male power into herself. But this time if there was disgust it was at herself, for she was no longer athletic and beautiful, while this young man was gorgeous, strong, vital, smooth skinned and plump as a Buddha. It was herself she had to love this time, as the Goddess. But he made it easy, as he shed his wraith loincloth on the ground, for he seemed to see Gaia within her. She pushed him down and straddled him like Black Kali, and took him in and gave her power into him.

And afterward, she was Mana again, and they both dressed, a little awkwardly.

"What do I do now?" he asked, not looking at her, an awkward young man in a way Mana had never seen him before, and a stark contrast to the young god of moments before.

She laughed. "I don't know. I don't even know why you just did what you did."

"I saw . . . I saw . . ."

She went to him and put her arms around him, not as Maiden, but as mother, as she had longed to do from the moment she first saw him, hurt and confused in his fortress of chairs and tables as Osen lay dying.

The sobs burst out of him with uncontrolled force. He made animal noises of anguish, shockingly loud in her ear, retchings of the soul.

At last he started to calm. "Osen showed me," he managed

to say at last. "Osen showed me banks of spring flowers in the forest, snowdrops and cro . . . cro . . ."

"Crocus?"

"Crocus. Just now there were crocus and snowdrops among the black paper flowers. They were real, not paper. Delicate and new. That was why."

She looked at him blankly for a moment.

He explained: "You wanted to know why I made love to the Goddess."

"What do we do now?" Mana asked the daily gathering in Chairperson's office. She looked happy and dazed and somehow softer than before. She flopped on the cushions with an abandon that made Chairperson and Vladimir and Arun stare at her.

Every day for years now the four of them had stolen minutes from wash-and-dress time and breakfast time to gain twenty-five minutes in between, in which to be together and celebrate the Goddess. Sometimes they danced and chanted, sometimes made spells and circles of power. Often they talked about their lives and acted as MAN to each other. But mostly they had studied *The Chronicles of Osen.* They were steeped in her methods of forming a movement. They had interested others at times. A few love relationships had blossomed from their work. But the concept of banding together to change the Galactic Collectivity and warm the Earth had been too much for their colleagues.

"You look ten years younger," said Vladimir. "Oh Mana, I'm so happy for you."

"But what do we do now?" She had told them all about Govind's discovery of the Goddess. "Do I have to do the same with everyone on station? I can't very well be the Goddess in that way to five hundred people. You'll all have to help me."

She and Vladimir, who was only fifty-two, looked at the two old men in their late seventies and burst out laughing. "They'll long for the long sleep then!" said Vladimir.

Arun did not look quite so amused. Chairperson dug him in the ribs and said, "I don't know. I reckon we could manage it. I'll start with that redhead in the kitchen."

Arun smiled. Vladimir's laughter died.

"Just joking," said Chair.

"Mana, you don't have to try to reach more people right

now," Arun said. "Govind will do that. You have done what Osen sent you to do. You can relax."

"Relax?"

"Right," said Chair. "What if he treats this like his previous crazes? Six months for the Goddess. Then on to pulling the wings off flies again."

"You've got to believe in the man's goodness for it to flourish," protested Arun.

"Huh. You've got to find a way to control him" was Vladimir's opinion. "Break down that arrogance. I never managed it in the nursery. This may be our last chance."

"The point is, to introduce Govind to the Chronicles, and to working as part of this group," Arun argued. "He'll accept discipline. We know the steps he has to take. We've all done them."

"But what I did yesterday was not in the Chronicles. I feel . . . that old tension. We've planned so much, but we haven't had the magic touch. We've been so serious and worthy. Yesterday I gave up, I was falling into the abyss, and I found myself . . . and Her in me. I didn't think. I was back in the Omphalos of Veshya on a warm solstice night. I was lover, not schemer."

"It has to be a mix of love and planning," Chairperson said. "What if Govind goes around carelessly spreading this love of Gaia — it's so vague. He may not see how deeply it has to contradict his willfulness. It'll just be the Liquid Light all over again."

"Yes, Mana, he needs discipline. Don't go romantic on us and throw it away," said Vladimir.

"Don't let's panic because it's Govind," said Arun. "Our rituals will nail him down to particulars. The burning. That will get him to go over his past life and see where he has hurt people. Then he'll know himself better and see how practical this is."

"So he burns his bridges, good and proper," added Chair.

"He's certainly got a few apologies to make," Vladimir agreed. "But what really happened to him yesterday. Do you know that he's made a new beginning?"

"I know."

"But we can't say: this is our burning ritual, this is what you have to do. He'll rebel against it like he has against the Code and MAN. It has to come from him, from his heart." Mana was emphatic.

The argument went on until their twenty-five minutes were

up. They finally agreed that they would describe their confession ritual to Govind and see if he wanted to do it. Mana felt the magic of the thing that had caught Govind starting to slip away, but she had no better ideas.

"Well," said Arun, "it will be a test. Will you ask him to come and join us here tomorrow, so we can make a start?" He got up to go, ready for a smart walk to the dining hall to get porridge and a good, hot brown beverage before the kitchen closed.

"I suppose so," said Mana. "I suppose that's what I have to do. But there's something else that we all have to do." She paused. Arun could see his porridge receding into space. "We have to give up MAN."

"What?" Arun was incredulous.

"She's serious," said Vladimir nervously. "Why, Mana? I don't think I'm ready for that yet."

"MAN's not important," Chairperson said with hearty diplomacy. "I haven't said anything to MAN for years that I haven't first said to you. I've always said it was the biggest moment of my life when I realized MAN had forgotten us, was even humoring us. It meant I had to grow up and make up my own mind. But it doesn't matter, going to hem — it just makes things easier with Audit. Why change now? Personally, I'm ready for breakfast."

"Let's go." Vladimir stood up as well.

"It's my fault, then." Mana was far too worried to think of food. "Because I *have* said things to MAN I never said to you. I don't understand it but . . . MAN has *not* forgotten us. I never told you this, but even our meeting here is a result of MAN. Hey taught Osen's Chronicles back to me. Hey saved me when I went mad, all those years ago. Hey never made me independent. I've still depended on hem, somehow; all these years. How could I grow up and find the Goddess when I was still sitting on MAN's knee? Yesterday happened because I decided to break with MAN forever."

"I'm shocked. I thought we were MAN to each other," Chairperson said.

"No. Mana, I'm like you," admitted Vladimir. "I depend on MAN." Chairperson leaned over and took her hand.

"It'll be all right for a few days, not going to MAN," pointed out Arun in his grumbly, low voice, "but then MAN's helpers

will come and take us. You can't stop that, can you?" he asked
Chairperson.

"I'm just Chairperson. MAN is the Galaxy."

"You'll see. We've got to do it," said Mana. "I'll ask Govind
to come here tomorrow."

The other three sprinted for breakfast. Mana came slowly
after.


"Hallo, Passarin. Father."

The inflection on the last word was ironic, almost mocking.

Passarin and José looked up from their half-eaten dinner and
the empty third setting at the greenhouse table. The newcomer
went on jovially, "Still solving the problems of the universe?
View's picked up a bit for you, I see. How do you like our steaming mixed veg of a planet, Passarin?"

Passarin looked up at a jaunty middle-aged man whose un-
easy eyes belied the heartiness of his smile. He was dressed ex-
travagantly, from his silver-buckled shoes and silver stockings
to the turquoise feather in his black tricorn hat. His billowing
black jacket was slashed symmetrically to reveal mauve satin
innards. The silver parrot-head buttons that were carelessly undone down the jacket front reappeared gripping his trouser cuffs
tight below the knee. A curved saber swung on his left side. It
was balanced on the other side by a curious mother-of-pearl-inlaid
handle attached to a hollow cylinder, which stuck through his
leather waistbelt. Passarin's eyes were caught by this strange
object.

"It's a gun, Passarin. The pirate's friend. A pistol, perhaps a
harquebus, if one knew what that meant, or a flintlock, maybe a
muzzle loader. I only play at pirates, you know, but this does
work. Here, heft it in your hand. Feel it." The apparition in
fancy dress generously handed him the weapon.

"I press this? Does it fire?"

"Only aphrodisiacs, I'm afraid, at the moment. Perfect in a
softroom at five paces on a plump rump. Perhaps you'd like me
to try it on you?"

"I apologize, Passarin, for my son," said José. "This poor
character is Rocco. He makes familiar with you before . . ."

". . . he is introduced," filled in the son. "We have to forgive him — it is just his natural exuberance. Now if only he
would come clean with MAN and stop running around with

that Tarcunan set . . . Well, Father, bad news. For you anyway. My little plans are coming to fruition." Rocco's smile stretched his alternately mean and jolly face into a stage villain's leer.

"Sit down. You're late. And have some food before you tell me the bad news, or I may not feel like giving you any."

"Couldn't. Much too excited to eat. Dear Father, what a beautiful meal." He sat down at once and started to wolf the exquisite rissoles that José had prepared on his little burner.

Passarin had only recently been introduced to the thespian arts on Starlight, though his father's activities in the Temple had given him some unwitting clues. But here he could not tell what was acting and what was real. It made him uncomfortable. He became aware of the rim of the white wicker chair digging into his back, and of the thin inadequacy of the strange material of the fatigues he had to wear here. For a moment he longed for some cheery Starlight garb or even for the rough homespun he had grown up with.

Below them outside, riotously exotic greenery burgeoned, cauliflowered and effervesced to the distant hills. Gusts of steaming rain pattered against the glass.

"You like it, Passarin? Remind you of home?" The pirate spoke with his mouth full.

"It is nothing like my home. Nothing."

"The idea was, put all those psychs on Madlarki — their minds are a filthy, steaming jungle anyway, they'll like it there. But I say: give me a good starship and a supply of holies, then you can have jungle one minute and desert the next, and all on your way somewhere else. Oh yes, the roving life! Eh, Father?"

"I have to explain to you, Passarin, that this poor creature, my son, has a basic speech impediment. He tells lies. He's never been off Madlarki in his life. He made a good match — Space knows how — into the Tarcunan elite, or some rebel branch of it that came slumming to Madlarki . . ."

"Don't listen to him, Passarin, he's just jealous. My Jiang is the most delirious woman this side of Arable, and the smartest to boot. Which brings me back to . . ."

"Oh yes, your 'little plans coming to fruition.' Poisonous fruit, I presume?"

Passarin had never heard a father and son talk like this. On Starlight there had been a quickness of speech, a play of wit and irony, that was something akin to this. It had struck him there at first as a trivialization of life. On Arable Two, his home, they talked good, plain speech, as serviceable as their clothes and as devoid of ornament as their landscape. Starlight had been a shock in every way, and a delightful one eventually. But this was shocking in a way that surely could never delight. Seductive, perhaps, to talk back to your father. But below the light surface, they were each sticking the knife in and twisting it.

"Only poisonous to some," Rocco replied. "Not to Jiang or me. It's our Karp project. You see, Passarin, we felt the poor military high-ups were missing out on all this secret childrearing that's been going on on Tarcuna since our grandmothers' day. I mean, if even crazy old Madlarki can have a family or two, why not Karp? Just for the top brass, you understand, nothing subversive. We thought we'd start by taking a few select admirals on a family cruise to a breeder planet, let them get their hand in, as it were. Have a few kids of their own with the local breeders. Later, when they're keen on it, we'll set up a whole system of babies and families for them on Karp itself. We can keep the ordinary soldiers from hearing about it: we know how to do that from Tarcuna.

"It's nearly all set up." Rocco looked extremely pleased with himself. His father was deep into another long glass of his yellow liquor. "We've already got a colony planet where they are willing to let us start. It's called Sky. Lovely place: pink skies, only one sun, oceans, beaches. Unbreathable but that's okay, we're used to that — simple domes, no trouble. All we need is a starship. The news is . . . are you ready, my dear parent? *We've got it.* The roving life, Father! Seductive cruises with Cap'n Rocco and his sweet sidekick, Jiang the Fang. Makes sense, eh?"

"You bastard. You pathetic little bastard. This is what you do with your inheritance?" José's voice rose, slurring. "You make what Martin wanted for everyone into a dirty secret of the top brass? The military? They killed your grandmother! They killed Passarin's grandmother, the greatest human being who ever touched the soil of Karp or Tarcuna! You're going to hook them up with breeders — slave women! You're no son of mine. Get out! Get out."

Rocco's jauntiness, if anything, increased. He swaggered about the greenhouse, bashing potted plants with his swinging saber. "I knew I was on to something." He winked at Passarin. "Want to come?"

"Get out!" José's brown knuckles were almost as white as the wicker arms they gripped.

"Like to visit Terra Station?"

The question was addressed to Passarin, but Rocco's eyes slid to his father. José looked suddenly bewildered, his eyes wide on his son's, his breath reduced to short gasps.

"I think you'd better come, Father, to make sure I don't corrupt your little experiment."

"I don't understand." Passarin dropped his words into the silence, trying to draw Rocco's attention, to give the old man a breather. José was pulling at his drink, glaring at Rocco. Passarin tried again. "It sounds intriguing. You're going to Earth?"

"Oh, just a quick stop at Terra Station. It's just a . . ."

"Breeders!" José exploded. "You make the Space Code look like paradise. Why didn't they use breeders all these centuries? Because it's slavery! Next they'll breed 'workers,' menials, troglodytes, different races, people marked by blue skin or . . . or with four arms so we'll know they're different and lower. This is cruelty beyond anything the Ice would have done to us. And you promote it. You filth."

"It's all a logical result of Martin's actions, old man."

"It's everything she fought against! At least the old system kept us pure, frozen, waiting release. Martin would have made us human. You and the Xidasis would make humanity into slaves and masters. I've said this to you for thirty years. You can't be talked to. Just leave. Get out of my sight."

"You've forgotten, Father. Terra Station." Rocco mimicked the dangling of a sweetmeat in front of a monkey's face. "I'm going there."

"Why?" asked Passarin.

"Why?" shouted José. "To torment me! To take Mana in the softroom. Why else? Well, she won't have you! You'll try to rape her, but you're nothing to her after Snow Tiger, after Atlatl; she'll make skinned flesh of you."

"Why, Passarin? Just the normal yearly run. Jiang got the contract for that sector, because it's the cheapest one in the Galaxy. We have to do a few practice runs with the ship, build up a safety record before they entrust us with the Karp gold braid. It'll be a two-month run. Terra Station's the least significant of the lot — we'll be taking them their annual supplies, bring in a spin team to amuse them, all the latest holies, MAN updates. Take off a few excess young women as breeders."

"What?" José was out of his chair.

"Galaxy's short of breeders — they're converting other planets to the system as fast as they can, you know that. Maybe this is Mana's chance — she never wanted to just stay on Terra Station, did she? She can be a Goddess, further in. Earth Mother bringing babies to a new world."

"You little bastard!" José gripped Rocco by the jacket as if to pull him up to fight him. He seemed very wiry and thin beside his well fed son. Passarin rose hesitantly to intervene. Then a new thought struck José, and he stepped back.

"I must warn them!"

"Yes you must. And the only way you'll be able to do it is to come with me. Mine is the next ship they'll see. I'm serious, Father. You can come. You and Passarin. It'll teach him more about the Galaxy than he'll learn from you if he stays here the rest of his life."

"Why would you take me?" asked José.

"Because I love you," said Rocco.

The next morning Mana's group were all sitting in a circle holding hands when the knock came. Chairperson went to open the door. They braced themselves for the usual tornado of energy and unconcern that was Govind.

It was a contrite young man with downcast eyes who entered. He made the formal namaste with humility. Then he just sat down on the floor — there were no spare cushions — and waited. No one seemed to know what to say.

"Well, let's get on with our normal meeting," said Mana. "We only have twenty minutes left. What's on everyone's mind? Arun?"

"The cleaning crew are slack. When weren't the cleaning crew slack? No change."

"I know it's months to the next starship," said Chairperson. "But I'm anxious again already. Every year now I seem to get more and more anxious. I don't know why, when I'm due for the long sleep next year. I'm more worried about being found out than I am about death. Kali can take care of death, but who will take care of all of us here, the lovers and the Liquid Lighters and the dancers and the Goddess Herself, if the Center clamps down? Why have they let us go on like this? Audit should have been transferred years ago. It's as if someone's keeping him here so he won't be able to report on us outside. And he's as apoplectic as he ever was. How he maintains his commitment I have no idea. Why do they ignore his reports? Every year I expect this freedom we have here to come to an end."

"Why don't you try and give Gaia's spirit to Audit? He's lonely and unhappy. He needs friends and love," Govind offered quietly.

"Are you mocking me?"

"Govind's sitting here," Vladimir laughed. "Why not Audit?"

"Why are you here, Govind?" asked Arun.

"Gaia called me. I realized all my crazes have been just noise to block her call."

Vladimir's eyes narrowed. "Come, now. Those are the words you rehearsed to say to us. Why don't you tell us the whole experience, exactly as it was."

He did, stumbling over the words at first. At the end of the story it flowed more smoothly; "And then Gaia said, 'The black flowers are not in my mouth, they are in your eyes.' And it was then, at that moment, that I saw the first crocus in her words, the first spring flower. And she took me into her, and I felt whole, a son of the priestess and of the lab, a son of wraiths and of industrial chemicals." He paused, looking at the ground. Then he raised eyes that looked extraordinarily helpless. "I feel like I'm five years old again. What do I do now?"

"Cut your lifeline," said Arun gruffly.

"What?"

"To your old scattered self."

"How?"

"Bring it all to us here," Vladimir said. "Bring symbols . . ."

"Longings . . ."

"Stories . . ."

"Above all," finished Arun, "bring the things you are most ashamed of, and never want to repeat. We'll put them all in the fire."

Next morning, on the floor in the center of the circle of cushions (this morning Vladimir had brought an extra one from the nursery) sat a shiny, somewhat flattened sphere about the size of a basketball. There was a fist-sized hole in the top. Through the hole, darkness.

It was one of those many objects on station that would have

been purest magic to Mana on Earth, but here was so utilitarian as to be barely noticeable. The only odd thing about this one was that it had been taken from its usual place in a first-aid station and placed in the middle of a floor. Nearly everything was recycled on station, even the toilet wipes. But a few germ-laden items were first incinerated before their oxidized elements were reclaimed. Any wipes used for the common cold, for example, went straight into the fist-sized hole to flash to nothing. As did other things that strictly should have been kept for the biogas generator — some people threw in their nail clippings, and others that other companion of humanity that was as loyal as the cold: the cockroach. The device was called a flashpan.

This morning each member of the circle had brought something to put in the flashpan. Arun had a long-abandoned cobweb. Vladimir had a crumpled note. On being pressed, she read it out. "It says, 'I want to get rid of fear.' I've been fearful since the first moment I met you, Mana. Of loving you, of losing my lover to you, of being abandoned by MAN, of Audit, of being punished. Of everything. It's time all that went. We can't afford it now."

Chairperson held her hand and said with a wry grin, "My note says something like that, too."

They threw their fears in and watched them flash to nothing.

Govind had brought a set of fatigues in a bundle.

"You're not going to burn your clothes, are you?" Arun asked. There was nervousness in the room despite the burned fears.

"The Goddess has inspired me!" Govind declaimed. "Henceforth I will go naked! . . . No. It's just to carry all this garbage."

He untied the bundle and a pile of odd things rolled out onto the floor. There was that most personal and least transferable of objects, a wrist unit, and yet Govind still had one on his arm. (Whose? How had he got it?) There was a can of red spray paint that made them remember the graffiti that had once appeared all over station; a vial of drugs from the medlabs; a laser gun from the asteroid spin game (harmless, but even so an alarm went off whenever one was removed from the game room: was this one broken?). Reading their thoughts, he picked up the gun and made the thin ruby line glow from the barrel. For a moment his contrite face was transformed by a flash of glee, and then he tossed the toy down carelessly. There was a little infobox labeled TOP SECRET, which made Chairperson exclaim. He recognized it as one that had gone missing from Security years before — the station had been turned upside down to find it. There were various pieces of electronics, some of them locks or keying devices. There was an atmosphere gauge from hydroponics. There was even a little *Warning! Radioactive!* sign that could only have come from the nuclear drive sector, the most heavily guarded area on station. There was a fragment of a darkly mournful wraith painting on cloth. The pile, as it grew, took Mana back to folktales of magpies and glaciermen — these were all the stolen jewels of Govind's world.

The morning meeting was up before Govind had got a quarter way through explaining the significance of each item as he consigned it to the flashpan. Those that were too large, or valuable, or dangerous, to burn, he described on a note and threw that in, before giving the object up to Chairperson. At the end of the session Chairperson gathered up the two piles of unburnables and to-be-burned and kept them for the next day.

The next morning, Govind continued, and the morning after. The four listened as the pile grew smaller, and their awe grew greater. They could not help being most struck by the contrast between the pirate's treasure before their eyes, gathered by a wild youngster they had all known for many years, and the subdued man who was actually throwing the jewels to oblivion. At first, as with the ruby laser, flashes of wild humor burst through his tales and were extinguished. Pride at times crept in. "No, certainly Security never saw me — how could they?" But these grew less as the number of his misdemeanors increased with each flash of light. There were many meannesses to report, and these sobered him the most: people they all knew, with whose inner hopes and fears he had played. "This was when I took Gauri in the softroom," he whispered as he threw a note into the flashpan. "And this was when I laughed at Gauri for still worshiping the Liquid Light," and the weight of these in his voice made them read back at once to some terrible moments they had not known about, that had perhaps led a young woman fresh from the puberty op to entomb herself in the tumbling gyro for all these years since.

There were things he had done to Vladimir, right back in

the nursery when he was three, that he remembered and she did
not, but for which he still asked her forgiveness. The last object
of all was a little pink spaceship with its fins torn off. "Mana,"
he said, "the first time I saw you, I threw it at you. I don't know
if I'm apologizing for throwing it or for keeping it all these years.
Look, it still . . ." He could not say more. He had to point to the
speck of brown on the plane, which she wonderingly took to be
her blood. He threw it into the flashpan, and the intense white
light flared.

There was profound silence.

Mana said gently, "Is that all?"

"No," whispered Govind. "I haven't even begun. There's
something that outweighs all the rest."

Mana moved over and put her arms around him. From the
other side Arun did the same. Vladimir and Chairperson leant
across and each put a hand on one of his feet.

"Osen," he finally cried out loud, in a hoarse voice. "I turned
my back on you. Osen." He wept and wept. He roared with
agonized, incoherent noises. Mana half expected him to tear
out his hair like the statue of the Pope Repentant in the Coming of Winter Cave — he had the same look on his face. She
wanted to laugh hysterically.

Then tears were streaming down all their cheeks, and
Vladimir said, "We love you," and Chairperson, "My boy, so
many years, at last," and Mana just smiled through her tears.
Arun's gruff voice could scarcely be heard, "That's right, lad, I
didn't think you'd do it, but you'll feel better now. Got all the
wax out your ears. You'll hear the Goddess now."

At last the storm was over. They walked to the dining hall
and ate twice as much breakfast as usual.

Next morning, Mana asked Govind, "What do you want to do
now?"

"I thought you would tell me." His eyes were sunken darkly.
He could not have slept that night.

"He needs power, Mana. Look at him, he's weak as a wraith,"
Arun said. And it was true. They were all half wondering what
they had done to turn the station's bold warrior into this ghost.
"We raise the power, that's what we do. Like Osen says in her
book. Attraction, Vision, Self Examination, Self-Disgust, Riddance, Openness, then Power. That's the first cycle."

"You still have the book of Osen's?"

"You know that. I tried to show it to you many times."

"Is it written to me?"

"To you, and to all who will follow her way."

"What does it say about this cycle, and Power?"

"Well, she just gives general guidelines, you see," Arun explained. "Riddance, you've just done that, but the flashpan was our idea. She says every abstract needs its concrete symbol. Riddance comes after Attraction, and Vision and the rest. It's logical, you see, as scientific as cleaning a corridor. You can't buff it to a shine until you've vac'd all the dirt out, and you don't vac out thoroughly unless you're disgusted at how bad it is, and you're not disgusted unless you have seen how beautiful a corridor can be, see? That's vision. I'm telling this backward. But you'll get the hang of it. You were attracted maybe long ago by Osen's stories, but you only got the full vision when Gaia came to you in Mana, in the wraith's room, and then you got disgusted with yourself for being mean and manic all these years, and so you cleaned out, and now you feel all empty, nothing. You need power."

"What power?"

"We do it like this, Govind," said Vladimir. Now that she was well into her middle years, she looked more like MAN than ever. But her face was a MAN with troubles and fears.

"We stand up," she said. They all creaked to their feet. "And we hold hands in a circle. On Earth, with their feet on the ground, they call on Gaia's power to rise in them, like sap in a tree. Here we have no physical connection, so we have to ask Gaia's spirit to come: 'Sophia,' Osen names Her sometimes, the spirit of wisdom. Hold hands, and do it with us."

So they raised the power in the circle, and instead of calling on east and west, north and south, they called on Earth and stars, Moon and Sun. Instead of invoking the energy in the trees and the beasts, in the molten core of the Earth and the cool of the night, they invoked the warmth of the sun and of their own bodies, and the wisps of Sophia that float through the vacuum of space.

After the energy began to course around from hand to hand, the Chairperson prayed: "Wisdom that spreads through the whole Galaxy, dark matter of the Mother, You who has a plan for each of us that can mesh our lives into one plan for the

Galaxy, reveal your plan for Govind, your special child, the promised leader of your assault on the citadels of the Collectivity, show him the way to the heart of power at the Center, to start that heart pumping red blood again." It was an extemporaneous prayer, and even Chairperson was surprised by the words that the Goddess was giving him. "Give Govind power, Great Mother. Give him vision and a plan and the power to fulfill it at the Center. For even the people who hold power on Tarcuna and Karp and Madlarki are women and men whose hearts MAN can never fill; they seek solace in games of power and pervert their longing for life into dynasties dedicated to inertia and leading only to death. Thank you for burning the past out of Govind, Great Sophia, but use him to burn the past out of the Collectivity."

Then Mana raised the cone of blue fire above their heads, and they danced in its light. Govind felt the power. He danced with the Goddess in him until he overtook the others and caught them all into a spiral of joy and energy that made their old bones sing.

Mana had moments in which she seemed to be watching them all from a cave-dark corner of her mind. This watcher was troubled, for it sensed that in Chairperson's vision, which had given wings to Govind's feet, the body and flesh and dark places of Gaia had been left far behind. The Center. It was so far. Osen had wanted some kind of a marriage with the Sky Gods. Mana's cell in the Caves had told in stone relief of Parvati frozen under the Ice, and the promise that one day the Ice would melt and she would dance with Shiva, and the balance of male and female would be restored. But now that it was happening, there was no telling where it would go, and she felt a deep uncertainty and loss.

Yet Govind danced with them now. His joy sparked in those electric eyes of his, and he yelled "crocuses and daffodils" at her, and she was warmed deep inside by his look and his words, and so she danced over her fears into oblivion.

They missed breakfast entirely, but who needed breakfast?

It was at the very next meeting that Govind, glowing like a new starship, said, "I have brought someone. Can she come in?"

It was Gauri. She entered shyly and said little. She threw into the flashpan a little clear plastic ball and a note that she would not read out. When she was done; Chairperson said, "Let's do the dance and raise the cone. We have time for both." They started to get to their feet. They all felt there was something missing, but no one quite liked to press her. Well, maybe next time.

"Wait," said Govind. "I want to add something to the ceremony." From a small bag he pulled out a little rock, which in Mana's recollection of walnuts long ago was just the size of a walnut.

"What is it?" she asked.

Gauri leant over and said to it, "Open." She smiled as a tiny door swung out. They each peered in, in turn, and saw there the perfect smooth inside of an egg. There was a couch in the egg, and inside it was lit by a soft gray pastel light. It was MAN's egg in perfect miniature.

"How did you make this?" Vladimir asked.

"It was one of his exercises," Gauri said. Her slim gyro-dancer's body unstiffened in her eagerness to explain. "We do so many things in Design with holograms that we forget we're designing real things. So they get us to make something real in miniature. I made a new kind of gyrosphere, the one I just threw into the flashpan. Govind made this."

"You threw in a gyrosphere?" asked Mana, shocked.

But at the same moment Vladimir asked Govind, "Why did you make an egg?"

"Maybe I was already looking for Sophia," he said. "If you think about it, MAN is just a feeble electronic copy of the spirit of Gaia. From now on I'm going with Sophia, and you, MAN, I prefer to burn."

He held the rock with its enclosed egg above the hole in the flashpan, waiting to drop it in. He looked around at each of them, as if expecting one of them to object. The utter gravity in his face brought an unexpected eeriness to the moment. It made them think of what his symbol truly meant. "Man" had meant "mother" to Mana in her childhood, and MAN meant mother to all of them, though they would not have used the word; MAN was friend, lover, confessor, guide, police, and judge. And Govind, by the weight of intent in his eyes, seemed to challenge MAN at every egg across the Galaxy.

Gauri appeared unsurprised. But the four stalwarts of the circle were stricken with wonder. They all recalled the moment the day after Govind met the Goddess, when Mana had said this same thing to their circle: we must give up MAN. So why had their thoughts each turned at that time to the immediate consequences for themselves, the visit from MAN's helpers that would follow? Whereas now, when Govind said it, they thought of the Galaxy throwing off its chains, of an entire people saying: No, enough, we will be free.

For a moment, Mana felt the burden of leadership drop from her shoulders. It was the purest moment of relief in all these seventeen years.

And then, within seconds, certainly before she had time to savor the feeling, a voice warned in the back of her head: He is too powerful. And in the center of her chest — fear.

Vladimir thought, Oh Gaia, be with him now.

Arun thought, It is as if we have been playing all these years. Playing at war. And now the Goddess has her leader, and the war itself begins. Pray I die now, if it is to end in tragedy. May I live long enough to see him get to the Center.

Chairperson thought, We prayed for power to come to Govind. And power has come.

Govind dropped the rock-egg. The fire flashed white, and the flare threw the shadow of his hand upon the ceiling above their heads.

# Three

The first thing Mana did was to organize a Holi festival.

And so spring came at last to Terra Station.

Govind and Gauri got the whole Design Team to make spring flowers on their consoles to project around the station. They ransacked the stores and empty quadrants for holoviews and holie projectors and for supplies to run up more. Chairperson set the labs and kitchens to work under Mana's orders. A lot of people were set to work, and everyone was excited.

On the day of the festival, dawn choruses of twittering birds woke the sleepy stationers. When they opened their eyes, bouquets of virtual flowers danced in the dormitories. They walked through holie hosts of daffodils to breakfast, and ate before emerald hillsides of gamboling lambs and daisies. Almond and apple blossoms in pink, mauve and yellow (the Design Team were liberal in their interpretations), and a thousand flowers, both recognizable and imagined, filled the corridors and rooms throughout the station. As always, Mana had a pang at the absence of the real thing. Then she felt guilty to be so churlish.

Govind divined her mood. "It fits, though, Mana," he said. "Here Gaia is spirit, so it's right that the holy flowers of Holi are holies." She laughed and told the joke all day.

The cooks made spring rolls and cookies in the shapes of baby animals. They put colors in the food: it was green-and-blue striped bread and red soy milk at breakfast.

Vladimir and the nursery nurses had spent half the night hiding sweetmeat eggs all over the station, and the littlest children spent half the morning finding them. When they were done, Mana taught the older children 'Free the Sky Gods' Prisoners', a forest game that she had long dreamed of adapting to station corridors and games rooms. There was laughter and delight and running in the corridors as had never been seen.

Govind invited the wraiths to come and paint some of their great cloths at lunchtime in the dining hall. It was the first time since his birth that any of the strange, thin, dignified creatures

had been in this part of the station. They brought cloths that
were already painted, and hung them on one wall. Then they
laid a star-patterned cloth on the floor, sat one at each of the
points of the star, held hands, and closed their eyes. All eyes
were on them, and it was a moment before anyone saw the colors on the hanging cloths begin to move. The pigments flowed
and recombined, and the people gasped to see the images of
spring. Very different, these, from the Design Team's jolly flowers. The people ignored the delicious blue mashed-potato substance, yellow rissoles, and orange pea-ishness on their plates as
their astonished eyes watched stylized seeds give forth shoots of
living green on the cloths: green, dangerous enough to break
through concrete and wrap metal tori in joyful, living strangula-
tion. They applauded vigorously but picked at their food afterward with a certain amount of anxiety.

In the late afternoon, Govind, fat, totally naked, and
smeared in ashes, a crescent moon in his wild hair, necklaced in
snakes, with trident and skull in hand, led a procession through
the station. His plumpness might have made him seem more
Bacchus or Buddha than Shiva, but his fierce eyes more than
made up for it. All the flower holies were turned off and the
lights dimmed. He walked solemnly. A cool wind blew through
the corridors.

Behind him pranced a motley company of rascals in torn
fatigues and painted flesh. It was Govind's wild crew of youngsters, pressed into new service. They had seemed bereft since
his sudden departure to Osen's way. They danced with much of
their old energy, but with an uncertainty in their eyes that tended
to spoil the effect. The liveliest of Shiva's rascals in fact were a
wild old man with long silver hair, whom no one identified as
Arun in a wig, and a monkey-suited old fellow whose lecherous
grin was easily recognizable as Chairperson's. They pinched be-
hinds and messed up people's work and ostentatiously kissed
one another and anyone else fool enough to get near . . . and
invited everyone to follow them. Such was the mood of the
station that everyone did. It seemed that Audit was in hiding.

In the gym, the procession stopped. The huge room was lit
with icy whiteness. Frost patterns were projected on the walls
and floor. In the distance the tiniest sound of trickling water
could be heard. The children ushered the people into the tiers
of seats around the gyrosphere. The great crystal ball had been

dusted with snow. Within, as in the heart of a glacier, lay a figure on the snowy floor. A still figure, white of face, dressed in white robes. They peered in. They could not see her breathing — was she real? Was she dead? "It's Gauri," someone said. Gauri as the White Lady, frozen.

At last the fat, naked, ashen man approached the sphere. He came with awe and trembling. He pressed his hands and face to the transparent shell. He repeated the gesture all around — there was no way in.

"Parvati!" he called. "Parvati, wake!" He looked up to the heavens. A single weak shaft of primrose light shone down onto him.

And then, "Parvati, spring has come!" He flung his head back and his arms wide. The light around him warmed and brightened. The sounds of trickling water swelled.

There was no reply. He turned to the people. "Has spring come?" he beseeched them.

"Yes," they said. The single shaft of light blazed.

"Is spring here?" he shouted.

"Yes!" they shouted. The sound of trickles turned to torrents.

"Is spring here?" he yelled.

"Yes!" Their roar shook the gyrosphere on its pedestal.

"Great Mother sends me," he bellowed into the globe of ice. "I come. The ice sheet melts. You must wake. I bring the spring. I am your husband. I am Shiva!"

Very slowly the sphere began to turn. The White Lady's eyes opened. She sat up slowly, as in a dream. The sphere reached a quarter turn and tumbled her over in a heap. With the grace of a dream she somersaulted to her feet and danced down the rising curve to the bottom. The sphere moved faster. She leapt in the air and saw the god. He held up a flower in his hand. The sphere stopped. It had turned itself upside down. She pushed through the wall of the sphere to him.

As she stepped outside, all the lights blazed full and warm, Holi flowers burst forth throughout the gym, and the sound of melting mountain streams was drowned by the mighty roar of waterfalls.

They kissed.

The people cheered and laughed.

Mana and Vladimir staggered across the gym carrying a stretcher filled with colored bottles and boxes from the labs.

They hadn't had time to dress up. They'd been too busy organizing everything. When they dropped their load in front of Parvati, she remedied that lack by taking a plastic bottle in each hand and squirting bright red and yellow liquid all over them. Then she opened the boxes and took handfuls of colored powder and threw them over the two women, to the crowd's delight. Then she turned and gracefully scattered her colors over the nearest people in the tiers. The normally reticent, ultra-clean spacefolk shrieked in dismay.

Suddenly the crazy Ganas, Shiva's prancing followers, led by the two old men, dived into the supplies of color. There was nothing graceful about the way they threw them among the crowd. Before long everyone was shrieking and screaming and laughing, throwing orange and purple and pink and squirting yellow and red and blue until they were stained like crazy rainbows from head to foot.

Now everyone knew for sure that a new craze of Govind's had begun. They looked forward with a familiar blend of eagerness and fright to see what he would try to get them to do this time. Everyone realized it had something to do with Mana, but it all looked a lot more fun than Mana's familiar earnestness.

They were kept guessing because, for a long time, nothing else visible happened. For weeks the station was unnaturally quiet. Govind played spin as usual, visited the wraiths, and spent, if anything, more time than usual at his console in the design studio — it was easy to forget that Govind was an engineer. He was always late to breakfast, sometimes missing it altogether, in company with Mana and Vladimir and Chair (and Arun, but who had ever noticed Arun anyway?). But that was hardly vital gossip material.

He could increasingly be seen in deep talks with people, which wasn't very dramatic, except when it happened in the softroom. Then some of the people he had been talking with started coming late to breakfast, too, and the cooks started to complain.

The most noteworthy thing really was that Govind was calmer, happier, less given to flashing those incredible eyes at one, less manic, and that in itself was almost disquieting. Change was certainly in the air. But what kind of change?

Gauri set herself to making more of Govind's little wombroom eggs. All she meant to do was make enough for those already in Mana's circle to each throw their own egg into the flashpan. They all wanted to do it. But every time she made one, someone new joined the circle and needed it first.

Eventually she left her design module altogether in work hours, and devoted herself entirely to miniature eggs. Each one she wanted to be perfect so that each person's burning of their old life and their old attachment to MAN would be complete. "We were created by the gene-splicers to design a new station," she explained to the Design Team Director, "and this is going to make a much newer station than anything on our modules."

She actually preferred sitting at the modeling console rather than going out into the station with Govind and his slowly growing band of converts. There was starting to be something too intense about their style for her. After a few months, there were enough of them to hold daily, sometimes twice-daily, meetings for Vision, Self-Examination and Riddance, in which people would tell of the things they had done to become new.

They had to learn to hear one another. Govind said to them: "Let us be MAN to each other, and let Sophia be MAN to each of us." They studied the Chronicles of Osen. They hugged enthusiastically in public. They did not go to the MAN eggs in the wombroom.

Pairs of people could be found now, in dining hall or dormitory or games room, earnestly hearing each other's fears and hurts and dreams. Groups could be seen at quite unlikely times and places, studying Osen's texts or standing treelike, feet firm on the floor, arms branched up to receive the power and spirit of Gaia. There was dancing in the gym. Mana taught circles how to raise cones of power in the common room.

Within six months everybody was either in or out of the new thing. It wasn't like the previous crazes. At times there was an electric sense of joy and energy. But underneath ran deeper currents, which they all knew they stirred. Many of them dreamed. If they had ever remembered dreams before, they had told them to MAN at once to get rid of them, like washing out your mouth in the morning. Now they dreamed of deep waters, of darknesses below, monsters waking, black holes starting to suck. They were afraid as much as thrilled. They discussed the dreams avidly at breakfast.

Some who had been burned by Govind's previous crazes

would not join. But even they saw that this time there were differences. For a start, their elder statesman, Chairperson, was in the thick of it. The ancient eccentric took part in the dyads and circles and dances. He gave them a kind of anchor in age and authority. They saw the difference in old Arun, the once reclusive menial now metamorphosed into the ordinary person's philosopher. If Govind lived the joyful way and Chairperson gave it his strange authority, Arun explained it in words that all could understand. Many stopped by to listen as he gruffly expounded to a group at dinner, and stayed to learn.

Vladimir's determined presence reassured the nervous. As the months went by and she discovered that people needed her skills in interpersonal relations — skills she had hardly realized she had acquired over the seventeen long years of her association with Chairperson and Mana — her face gained in confidence and daily resembled more that wise, sure face of MAN in whose image she had been created.

Mana often sat at the back of Arun's explanations, or watched from the far end of a dinner table as Govind reinterpreted his Earth stories from his new perspective. They were the tales she'd been brought up on, of giants and magical salmon, moon women and love and, sometimes, the machines and kings of old.

"We live in a giant," she heard him say once. "We live in the metal guts of a clanking robot-giant whose temples are these," and in each hand there appeared one of the little MAN eggs Gauri had made. "Like the shepherd girl, we will take up our smooth pebbles and our sling, and we will strike the temples of the giant," and he mimed whirling the sling. He acted the giant hit in the forehead, and then dropped the little eggs into the flash of fire that would vaporize them.

Often, Mana did not hear the words of Govind's stories or of Arun's homespun philosophies. She would sit with a heart so vibrantly warm that her ears could barely hear. It was the same when she wandered the familiar spaces of the station, and observed them transformed by eager laughing faces, by tears and talk. She led the occasional cone raising or visualization, or taught the spirit of some half-forgotten dance from her childhood. But the new people did not cluster around her as they did around the others. She had always been the outsider, and it was no great surprise or cause for unhappiness to her to find that she still was. For now she knew that she had been the catalyst, and as she watched the chemical reactions fizzing and expanding around her, she was tempted into a sleepy thankfulness that her job was done.

Then occasionally she would catch a phrase and start. Arun: "Two thousand years ago the Migration came through this station. They clustered in this room we are in now, dreading and dreaming the leaps into the void farther in. Now we are in a new movement, every bit as important as the Migration. Osen called it the Recalling. That doesn't mean bringing everyone physically home. It means bringing them spiritually home. We will still all live on our space stations . . ."

Or Govind: "One thing we do not mean when we say 'Let Sophia be MAN to us' is to think of Sophia as neuter. Sophia is not 'hey' but 'She.' Or, if you prefer, Sophia is 'She' and 'He.' I find it easier myself, as a male, to think of Sophia as 'He.' 'She' means the Earth to me, and 'He' is perhaps more the Sun, Space, the universe. Women on Earth give birth to babies as well as to philosophies and heroic deeds, but men can only birth the ideas and deeds — perhaps that is why they were the first ones to leave the Earth and come into Space. Who knows: perhaps you women, those of you who are young enough, will soon be giving birth to real babies? What are we men going to give birth to?"

On both occasions Mana rose to her feet in alarm, but quietly, as she might in the forest at the first sound of a heavy, distant breath: an aurochs? a bear? "Not physically, but spiritually." "Not She, but He."

But she couldn't think what warning to call. After the ice melted and Parvati and Shiva came down from the mountain, the Sky Gods would be invited back to the feast. That had always been understood. They would be welcome again, but they would not dominate again, for under the rule of the Goddess the people had learned. So how could she get up and say, "I am worried"? It was all so healing and good, the joyous smiles and reaching out of buried psyches, one to the other. The raw pain was being exposed and loved to laughter, and MAN's eggs were daily more neglected. At the dinner table the couple beside her sat holding hands, and she wondered if they dreamed of having their own child.

And yet on such occasions she could not sit down again. She sought the unlikely comfort of the corridors in which she had so often roved in her lonely days.

But there was something odd about the corridors too. She
realized what it was when she came on a crew with vacs and
buffers, working after hours: the corridors were sparkling clean.

The crew were singing together as they worked. She noticed
that two out of the five were not cleaners. One was from the
kitchens, and the other was Garcia, Govind's peer from the
Design Team, hardly the type to clean corridors. They were not
singing with the vacuous heartiness of the space folk, but with a
comfortable ease that struck Mana as new, and yet familiar.

Will we have cleaners cooking the meals now, and designing the new station? she wondered. Gymnasts running the fusion reactor? She felt obscurely irked. She would have to walk
farther now to find cobwebbed corridors and mice.

She walked on through the heavy steel doors into the empty,
cold quadrants.

"I was just musing on the odd parallels of history to our friend
Passarin," José said to his son. "Do you know what this spaceship we're on really is?"

"It's a second-rate thousand-year-old tub freighter, and if
we don't reach the projected conversion rate, we're going to set
the whole two months of this voyage back on the second hop,"
Rocco said.

"Aha. Your bad mood, then, isn't wife trouble but ship
trouble."

"Mind your own business. Reactor worked fine on the trial
run before we bought it. And it was only marginally off on the
first hop. I don't know what's wrong."

Rocco stamped out, back to the bridge. Passarin sighed. Terra
Station was fourth on their run. Even without an engine slow-
down, there was due to be a lot more waiting around before
they got there. The wraiths could flash a spaceship instantly
from one star's vicinity to the next. But it was too risky to try
and plunk them right next to their destination planet. A nano-
second of arc off and they might be in the planet. So they
emerged in clear space and had to spend days under fusion drive
chugging across to their goal.

So there would be weeks of sitting here philosophizing with
José. No doubt the old man had a wealth of wisdom. And at
times he could be fascinating. But a young lady had boarded
the ship at the first port of call, and Passarin's mind was wander-

ing. He had seen her come in with a line of volunteer breeders, shy and eye-catching. But the breeders were under Jiang the Fang's lock and key.

"This ship is the Santa Maria, which brought Christ and crucifying disease to America by mistake while looking for a route to the aphrodisiacs of the East," said José. "It's the East India Company's peaceful merchantmen, which delivered the muskets that led to the Raj; it's Lenin's sealed train that brought revolution to Russia; it's that 22nd century woman's passport to Mecca, what was her name? the one who . . . You're not listening, my boy. They were something, weren't they?"

"Who, Lenin and Raymattja?"

"No, dear boy, the five beauties Jiang is guarding with her life. My guess is they've had their op reversed already. Probably had to do it to find out if they'd be fertile. You and I and Rocco are three of the few males in the whole Collectivity without tied tubes. Jiang's got to look after her merchandise.

"But cheer up. Don't look so crestfallen. You had to steer clear of the softroom on Madlarki for fear of being found out — but no one will tell on you on this ship. Have you seen Rocco's first lieutenant? You can bet she goes to the softroom."

Passarin contemplated the dreaded and so far unvisited delights of the softroom, and wondered whether it would be as grotesque and unromantic as it seemed. The first lieutenant was hard to ignore, it was true. But could there be any empathy? It would just be lust. How distressing to have lust catered to so openly and only his better nature to hold him back. Worse than that, the lieutenant would be totally experienced in softroom sex, while he wouldn't know what the hell to do . . .

"When you go, try the light well. It's the only special effect that's worth anything on this ship. But wait until she comes off shift tonight. There's a good fellow. Now where was I?"

"Lenin's sealed train? Raymattja's passport to Mecca?"

"I underestimated you, dear boy. Yes. They're perfect examples. Fact is, there are major causes and minor causes in history, and the average wannabe world-changer just rants and raves, or plans and saves, all his life until he dies, because the major and minor causes aren't working his way. But just occasionally they do work the way of one of us obscure fellows. They give us one tiny window of opportunity. That window is often opened serendipitously by someone else for some other reason, like the

Germans offered Lenin the chance to disrupt their enemy, Russia, and sealed the train to make sure he didn't disrupt Germany en route. If they'd guessed how successful he would be, they never would have done it. But the world-changer worth his salt jumps through that window and changes the world. Within the parameters allowed, of course, by the major and minor causes. The sunspot cycle, the climate, technology, economy, culture, diet, spaceborne bacteria and, of course, the decisions and emotions of millions of individual people, you understand. You've drifted off again. Well, I don't know. Here you have Rocco and Jiang plying their little designs toward corrupting the Karpian military and, just because the boy has unresolved guilt concerning his old father, they've brought me along. So if we're lucky and smart we may be able to work it for Rocco to unwittingly give Mana her chance to take her revolution to the Center. The Galaxy will be changed! But here you are, just dreaming of the old in-and-out."

"I wondered if that was what you had in mind. You've been looking remarkably cheerful."

"Oh, I'm all for a bit of the old in-and-out."

"No! I mean bringing Mana to Madlarki."

"And Govind. She won't come without him."

"But how will that change the Galaxy? Apart from making your old age a little more, what shall we say, active?" Passarin was pleased with that. It was his first sexual innuendo.

Mana's pacing of the abandoned corridors did not calm her. She couldn't understand herself. Unhappy when Govind rejected Gaia and unhappy now that he embraced Her. She should be singing for joy. At last all that Osen had foreseen was starting to take place.

When she returned from the chill, she realized why the singing of the band of corridor cleaners had sounded strangely familiar to her. She was shivering as she approached the warmth of the living sector, and that made her think of coming in to the Caves after a winter hunt. There would often be simple singing in the Caves while people worked, and she would hear this first as she strode down the tunnels and stairs toward the warmth. This would be quite different from the purposeful singing of rituals and dances. It would be light and comfortable, easily broken off to attend to something, as easily started up again.

As she stood there in the corridor between the wombroom door and the common room, she was attacked by grief. The Caves, the forests, Osen, Sitala . . . and then, unbidden, among the faces of those she had lost she saw the face of MAN.

Seventeen years a friend. Sitala had been her lover for only five.

For seventeen years MAN had known her perfectly, thoroughly. MAN had had to learn, but hey had never forgotten a thing she had told hem. They had grown in their understanding of each other. MAN had started by dismissing the Goddess and Osen's Chronicles, and Mana had started by thinking MAN a sky god.

She pushed open the door to the wombroom's fake cave, and looked at its rocky outcrops in which the MAN eggs nestled. She walked slowly along the narrow path that led from rock to rock, smoothing her hand over each hollow, unrocklike surface. At each one that was open, she looked down. The inside surface of the door was eggshell smooth, but grubby with fingerprints. The couch floor of the egg looked worn. Some liquids had splashed on the walls and dried into the plastic seams of the couch, and had not been cleaned properly: were they tears? sweat? spit? Of course, it looked a little tawdry when judged from the outside. She felt defensive on the egg's behalf. It was unfair to peer in like an outsider. It was just like this that she had looked in those first times, before she had learned MAN's true nature.

MAN had only ever wanted the best for her. MAN had let her vent all her anguish and pain. Hey had taken her by the hand eventually, and led her back to Osen and her plan for the Galaxy. MAN had brought her back to faith. It was as if the spirit of Gaia had been in MAN all these years.

Mana's eyes swam with vertigo, and she gripped the rock to prevent herself from falling down into the egg. Was MAN Gaia? When she could, she lowered herself down and closed the door. The soft gray light that immediately filled the shell tempted her for an instant to relax. But she was too full of questions — relaxing would come later, if at all.

"MAN," she asked, "did I do wrong to leave you? Are you and Sophia the same? Did Gaia use you, just this once, to help me . . . or were you always Hers?" There was no reply. "Did She plan you, make you? Could Gaia have planned the whole Migration, designed the Code, the baby labs and wombrooms, to

keep humanity safe on the journey so that one day humanity
would come back and save Earth? Is Gaia that much of a
schemer? Could She use people that much? I always believed
She was lover more than schemer . . .

"Oh, Sitala, Sitala, you never had to face such questions!"

"Hush, Mana. Let me tell you." MAN spoke at last, in a
strange, light, old man's voice, completely unlike heir own familiar tones. "I always meant to sometime. I am just José, I am
just a man, just a person like Sitala. I've got control of the MAN
program for Terra Station, and I love you . . ." The voice died,
and the light went out. A second later the door sprang open
automatically.

Govind's voice cried out cheerfully from the wombroom
door, "Come out, come out, wherever you are! Make peace
with yourselves and start a new year! I've turned off the eggs for
the rest of the day. Give up MAN and come to Mana!"

He was drunk on the Goddess.

Or was it on the God?

Mana no longer knew. She did not come out of the egg and
let him see her, backsliding. She stayed where she was, hidden.
What had happened just then? Had she fallen asleep and
dreamed that man called, what was it, Hosay?

Gauri worked at her model MAN eggs. It was tricky getting the
light suffusion in the egg to work. It needed all her concentration. But all the same, being Gauri, she was acutely aware of the
flow of individuals around her. She had been watching people
all her life. The modeling console was by the design studio door.
She could hear the corridor traffic, too, when the door was left
open, as it frequently was.

A close student of human behavior in the design studio, if
such there had been, might have caught the way Gauri's attention flickered from her work, or, if she was on a fiddly part of it,
the way her hands slowed when one particular person walked
by in the corridor, or came into the studio. But no one did see.
For even those few in the studio who had burned Gauri's models and started the new, interpersonal life without MAN were
still far too inexperienced. The only two design engineers who
were truly literate in body language were Gauri, herself, and the
object of her attention. And Govind was so used to her attention he barely noticed it, or her. Things had changed drastically

from the nursery days when she had run off and left him bawling for her on the floor.

To Govind, Gauri was his special peer, the one he had grown up with. They had held hands when they first ventured into the wombroom, before they split up, mature five-year-olds, to enter each their own egg.

They had also held hands the time, at thirteen after the puberty op, that they first passed the exotic adult threshold of the softroom. They had been welcomed by several groups of writhing bodies; hideously, frantically entwined bodies, each of which had gradually become recognizable as an adult known to them for years. Some were naked, some, more unnervingly, in costume. Their faces as they welcomed these smooth-skinned adolescents were bawdily mirthful, lustful, even predatory: the old timers saw only new bodies, new fun for jaded tastes. But the two did not even know the words for these expressions. Govind and Gauri had come in cold, afraid, holding onto each other. Perhaps that had been their undoing. Instead of letting go and submerging in the physical tension and release, as each might have had to if on their own, they had shrunk away. They shrank from each group of adults in turn, from the ones in grass skirts under the palm trees and the ones in the thixotropic gel bed, especially from the orgy in the Goddess Cave, and even from the delicate three who swung on the orgazimmer to the sympathetic strains played on its strings. The ribald comments that had followed them had good-naturedly but implacably promised eventual envelopment. They had entered a small mossy nest and clung to each other.

Neither of them went back to the softroom again for years, not until Govind got the lust bug and ditched the wraiths and their sun worship and his ergonomic fake savannah floor, and made enough whoopee in the softroom to create a rush hour whenever he went near it. Then all the adults who had shaken their heads for years at the unprecedented oddness of these two youngsters, and who had marveled that MAN had let them get away with it, were openly relieved. There was joy that the prodigal had shaped up. (If any were secretly disappointed, then only MAN knew.)

Govind tried to take her with him in his enthusiasm for the softroom. But Gauri remained reluctant. She was still with the Liquid Light, the sunshine meditation at the hub. It gave her

peace and warmth enough. Who needed touch? Govind's was
the only touch she really wanted, and not in a cheery, lusty
bunch of cavorters. Others who had taken to the Liquid Light
meditation lost courage when Govind left them. But she encouraged them to go with her to the hub and to be with the
wraiths even without Govind. The wraiths didn't want anything
to do with sex, and only weeks before nor had Govind.

She didn't want to go to the softroom and she made it quite
clear. But one day Govind dragged her in on the crest of his
high good humor. He promised in response to her protests that
they would meet alone. She allowed him to undress her. She
allowed him to enter her. He was high and flying. He didn't see
her at all. He came. He couldn't make her come. She wanted
him, not a great fuck. He wasn't there. Afterwards, she felt
scooped out and hollow. She couldn't even cry.

He never noticed that from that moment, for Gauri, the
Liquid Light was truly gone. She abandoned the company of
others, even at the hub. She had found the gyrosphere years
before; now she saw little else.

For a couple of years after his manic discovery of sex, Govind
had stayed away from the wraiths. He knew they would disap-
prove. They would not say so — that was not their way. But
they would no longer be friends.

Govind had early guessed that the wisps of thoughts and
images he received in his mind that had their own flavor that
was not Osen's came from the wraiths. When Osen died he had
had the most compelling one: a clear, straight "Come and see
us." He had followed the thought like a beacon, out the nursery
door through the station into the cold corridors to that lone
door that read TELEKINETIC PERSONNEL ONLY.

They welcomed him then and on many occasions later. They
gave him tea and sweets and made the colors flow for him. They
made their biggest fuss over him when he led Mana's dance to
them and enabled them to lead everyone to the hub — that
time that she went bananas. They regretted her breakdown, they
said. But he had enabled them that day to come out of their
ghetto and lead the station for a heady hour.

As he grew up, he realized the wraiths were somehow in
total opposition to Mana. They never said so. He felt that, like
him, they blamed Mana for Osen's death. He knew they used to

talk with Osen because she told him so. Osen had actually warned him to be careful of them. When she was dying, he had seen her fear of them. But he had seen too how she had tried to use them to learn of the Galaxy. They could tell her whatever she wanted to know about the Center and its policies, and about the thousand planets, for they had their own ways of knowing. As he grew up, he sensed that they thought *they* had used *her* to create himself, a human whom they could influence, and that Mana was their enemy. But Mana clearly thought Osen had used her wraith powers to create him for Gaia and that anything that wasn't Gaia-Gaia-Gaia was wrong, especially leaving the body to sail into the sun, especially anything to do with wraiths.

It was confusing.

He never felt quite at ease with them. They smelled so dry and pale. When they spoke he saw only odd glimpses of transparent wisps stream from the mouths. He felt they hid themselves from him.

It had been a relief to throw himself into his humanness in the softroom.

But he knew he would go back to them in the end. They held some promise, some greatness for him. They called him by a secret name: Havu. They hinted that he would have a great role in the Galaxy one day.

Mana thought the same but she was so ineffectual.

The wraiths made the spaceships go. They sat him down in their circle and drew him into their mind and showed him the great planets of the Galaxy.

They had power. They didn't hate normal humans in spite of everything that had been done to them.

But they did hate sex.

When he went back to them, he was just 21. He went back because sex had become boring. He had done it in every imaginable way an unimaginable number of times. They taught him how to play asteroid spin the way they played it.

Now *that* was ecstasy.

In a few months, they turned him into the best player in the whole Galactic sector. Then they told him he could learn to speak with them at a distance, to join the wraithmind telepathically, to wander the Galaxy in his mind at will. But when he said yes, eagerly, and started to learn, their exercises went on and on forever and he felt he was getting nowhere. He saw it would take years, and he was having too much fun with his crazy bunch of human youngsters to start the full discipline quite yet. Besides, it would be fun to be Galactic spin champ — no wraith would do it, not spiritual enough. But he was only part wraith. Spin champ now, wraithmind later. There was time for everything.

Then, out of the blue, right in the wraiths' own sanctuary, Mana gave him the Goddess. They felt it happen. Oh yes, they knew.

He went back, of course, and told them about it after a while. Their paintings said he had to forge his own synthesis between planet and space, as Osen had done. They said nothing. He saw the sorrow in their eyes.

After his initiation into the Goddess, after he burned his past, before he even told the wraiths, the first person Govind thought of recruiting was Gauri. He knew he had hurt her somehow, though Goddess knows, he felt, she had done it to herself, too. Where had the brave kid he had looked up to at four years old gone to? The one who was curious about everything and got to recognize all the adults on station first? The one who laughed at him for being so dumb about people? She was basically weak, he suspected, unable to keep up. But that wasn't her fault. It did not excuse his behavior towards her, the times he had ignored her, the time he fucked her silly in the softroom which in some way he didn't understand had driven her into her gyro obsession. She always wanted something from him — it was such a drag, she was so *down*. He had thrown his weight around too much. Maybe it *had* been all his fault, his running from Osen, his manias, his lack of concern for others. It was hard apportioning blame. After all, the whole place needed shaking up, and weaker people might get a bit hurt. But still, wherever the fault lay, he would make it right. He would bring her to the Goddess for healing.

And so he had apologized sincerely to Gauri, and had brought her to the Gaian circle. She was a puzzle to him, though. She didn't want to join in the new life, just sat by the door making MAN eggs. Well, from each their contribution.

This morning he waved at her as he popped into the studio to explain why he wouldn't be in for work until after lunch. He had Mao in tow, a fellow from the gene labs who had asked him to help argue in favor of the new life with Moishe, a traditionalist peer of his. "Don't argue," Govind had counseled, "just share your experience. 'Then I was blind and now I see.' You remember that story of Osen's I told last week?"

"Won't you come with me?" Mao had pleaded. So now Govind was off to do what he liked best. But first it was courtesy to let the Design Team know.

He waved at Gauri again as he left.

Mao was waiting in the corridor. He seemed extremely agitated.

"Look, Mao, don't worry. The spirit will come to you when you need to talk." Govind came close and took his arm. "Believe me, incoherence for Gaia is sometimes more telling than eloquence — I've seen it happen. You know, there are almost fifty of us burned on station now. We can't be stopped."

"No, Govind, it's not that." Mao got a word in. "It's that I've only just remembered, I was asked to do some lab work today that won't wait."

"It won't wait? This space station's been rotting here for centuries. But the lab work has to be done today. I don't know, Mao. What would Gaia think about that?"

"I promised. I'm not trying to get out of anything, honestly. It's stupid — just routine stuff — I'll be bored out of my mind. But there it is. Can you come and see Moishe with me tomorrow?"

"If it's so simple I'll do it myself. You can show me how. Then you can go and talk with Moishe. It might change his life."

"Oh no, that'd be against all the rules."

"Rules! Rules're going supernova, Mao. This safety-first attitude has to go — we're changing everything. Everything. Now, show me what the lab work is."

Govind moved off down the corridor, holding Mao by the elbow.

Gauri heard their voices fade away, Mao still protesting, Govind incandescent for the cause.

Her hands had stopped moving altogether.

She sat rigidly at her console. As the minutes went by, one or two others in the studio did eventually notice. After half an hour, her peer, Garcia, came over and stood beside her, looking at her models.

"In the old days," he ventured, "I would have suggested

you go to MAN." He twisted his fingers together behind his back. "Can I help?" He put out a hand to touch her shoulder, but somehow it stopped in midair. He had been a wild follower of Shiva, but still the hand stopped in midair.

Gauri looked up at him. "No. Thanks, Garcia. Only I can do this one. Wish me luck."

She got up suddenly, not bothering to shut down her tools, and walked out the door.

"Good luck," offered Garcia, and turned off her tools.

A few minutes later Gauri, walked swiftly into the gene labs and looked around. She was quite aware she was acting the way Govind acted — as if he had a right to go anywhere and say anything. He wasn't in the main area. So before the few surprised looks could turn into queries, she went through to the isolation labs. She hadn't been here since she was a kid on a guided tour of the station .

He was in Lab Three. She peered through the double glass window at him. His feet were up on a counter. He was speaking occasionally into his wrist unit — a habit he had these days, of taking notes — probably planning the next phase of his assault on Terra Station.

Govind was glad to be alone in the little isolation lab. The only access to the outside lay through the detox room and its complicated procedures. He felt sealed off. What a luxury.

For the moment, Mao's instructions assured him there was nothing to do but wait while the bacteria in the little flat covered dishes grew. He put his feet up on the counter and closed his eyes.

It was only when he stopped like this that he realized he was exhausted. Half the strain was in holding himself back. He didn't regret all those rambunctious crazes he had led — the place had needed shaking up. But he knew he had been full of himself at times. Other people didn't have his energy. It was too easy to overwhelm and crush them. Now he was determined that he would not get in other people's way as they grew in the Goddess. It was typical of the way people wanted him to do all the work that Mao had asked him to come and talk with his friend, Moishe. But what had happened instead was perfect: to do a humble job like monitoring bugs while Mao went off to learn how to tell the good news himself.

For years after Osen's death, Govind had felt scared by the stories she had told him. Often he had wanted to forget all of it, as if Osen had been a demon from one of her own tales. There was a nightmare he used to have in which the whole Galaxy was a huge metal giant, a clanking, monstrously noisy iron ogre, and he was in its intestines, lost, running and screaming to get out. It terrified him, but he never went to MAN with it. MAN was part of it.

Somewhere deep down, he thought now, he must have felt the dream was Osen's fault. Hadn't there been a metal giant in one of her tales? It was as if he had lived all his life 'til now in the nightmare space between Osen and the giant and the wraiths. All three had designs on him. All three had to some degree designed him.

He could see this now in the clarity that followed commitment. It had been an incredible relief to go Osen's way. It had been like slaying the giant of his dreams. Apart from anything else, it had given him a reason to try to curb himself, a reason to be patient and understanding with people — they were just as much in need of the Goddess as he was. The wraiths couldn't help him connect with people like this. He knew he would never turn his back on the wraiths. In time he would make his own synthesis. But first he had to learn the ways of Kali Ma.

These days, for the first time since her death, he liked to try to get back into that same state of receptive joy that he had felt as a little child when Osen spoke to him. He was getting better at it: a kind of turning inward, away from sense impressions, and yet leading to a turning outward that would make him aware of anything else out there. It was his own version perhaps of the discipline the wraiths had tried to teach him. Of course, there were no stories now, but it helped him to remember the stories she had told. And he felt that perhaps Gaia was there, or Her spirit, which Osen herself had once called Sophia. He liked to think of Sophia as half male. It was important to him that he was a male. His culture thought nothing of it. But in Osen's stories, men and women were different: women the archers, the priestesses, the birthgivers, the guardians; men the cowherds, the woodcutters, the fathers, the travelers, the connectors. Though, of course there had also been man the warrior, the king, the destroyer. Osen loved to tell him of the African king. She knew he could beat that king. She had wanted a man to defeat the men.

So in the rare times like this, alone without interruptions, Govind went inside himself and remembered stories and asked how he was to be powerful and not overbearing. He begged the male-female spirit of wisdom to tell him.

There was a sharp tapping sound. He leapt to his feet and scrutinized the petri dishes. Had he missed a crucial stage? Daydreamer! He looked frantically at Mao's instructions on the screen. The tapping came again, from behind him. He turned and saw a familiar face at the observation window.

"Let me in!" she said through the speaker.

"Gauri, you gave me a shock! I can't let you in. You have to go through detox."

"Well then, meet me at detox!"

"Can't it wait? What's the matter? Does someone need me?"

"I'll tell you when you get me in there."

He sighed. If Gauri was being this forceful, it had to be something major. He couldn't imagine what. He checked the instructions again, decided he could leave for five minutes, and went out.

She already had her clothes off at detox and he told her through the speaker how to go through the procedures. She stepped naked and pristine onto his side, and he handed her a set of lab fatigues. He was surprised to feel his sex grow and move as he watched her dress. He had seen her naked so many hundreds of times before in showers and dorm. She was just Gauri, his exasperating shadow. She was always close and never quite present. It was common to have sex with other members of your peer group, even if for some reason it often took extra arousal gas to make it happen. He had done it with all his other peers many times now, but with Gauri only that once when she had resisted him. So why this arousal?

Perhaps, he thought, it was the unfamiliar venue.

Perhaps it was the unfamiliar way she was moving. She was energized by something. She marched down to Lab Three, and he slowed down behind her to try to clear his head and pants.

"I couldn't sit by and watch it any longer, Vinny," she said as soon as he came in and closed the door. She was hyped up. How long since she had called him that? When they were little children and she led him into new things, dancing ahead while he waddled after. A quiet beep sounded from the equipment.

"Hang on. I have to do something." He consulted Mao's

directions and lifted the dishes out of their temperature-
controlled unit. He took their lids off and put one drop from
the dropper into each of the cultures that had begun to show
pink among the beige. His unfastened cuff dipped into one of
the cultures as he reached across it to put a drop in the one
behind, and he cursed and carefully rolled up his sleeve, trapping the soiled part inside. As soon as Gauri left, he'd throw it
in the sterilizer and get a new lab suit. Mao had been worried
about spills. "It's some new bacteria they've found in the soy.
Beats me," he had said. "You can't be too careful with this stuff."

"Govind, I . . ." But suddenly she was tongue-tied. She
looked at him as if stricken by his impossibility. "I . . ." She
swallowed.

He put his feet up again on the counter, crossed his arms,
and looked at her. She remained standing.

"Don't make it easy, will you!" she flashed at him.

He shrugged. "What's the matter?"

"The way you manipulated Mao!"

"I didn't manipulate, I was . . ."

"You say, 'Be MAN to each other.' But that's not right!
You're not meant to be MAN to anyone — thinking you know
what they need!"

"That's true — in that ultimate sense, we have to let Sophia
be MAN to us. But I'm a little further along than Mao is. I've
got experience to share."

"You should have seen yourself back there. You were determined he would talk to his friend today. You forced him to
leave his job to do it. You're forcing everyone along. Just like
you did with the Liquid Light."

"I'm sorry if you think so. I thought I burned that old me.
Maybe I didn't do a good enough job." He smiled.

"Oh, it's that easy, is it? Time for you to throw another little
note in the flashpan? What about all the people who were so
badly burned by the Liquid Light that they never recovered?"

"Who are you talking about?"

"Jyoti. Samora. You know who I'm talking about."

"Jyo was crazy. It's a statistical probability there'll be so many
in each population. And Samora's recovered so much he's gone
back to stand in the sun with the wraiths, just this week, although I wish he'd come to our group. He needs the friendship.
But he's a perfect example of my not manipulating people. You

know what he burned? A note saying he must not be afraid what
I, Govind, think of him. And after he burned that, he went
back to the wraiths to stand in the Light. See? It's a new spirit
that's loose on station, where people find out what's right for
them, instead of following what Govind says. But you don't know
what Samora's doing, do you, because you're stuck in the
gyrosphere or at the console."

Govind looked hard at his peer. "It's you, Gauri, isn't it,
who never recovered?"

"Jyoti's dead, Govind. She went mad and they took her
away."

"They only recycled her body. Her spirit must live."

"That makes it all right, does it? Space, you've got easy answers these days."

"It is you, isn't it? I'm sorry, Gauri. I've been . . . hard on
you. Do you hate me?"

"You, you, you! It's always you at the center of everything,
isn't it? Why should I hate you, just because you led me to the
Light and then you made fun of it? Just because you raped me in
the softroom? Remember that word? Osen taught you it. Then
you came and got me first when you took up the Goddess, so
you'd have someone who would meekly follow you like you
were MAN's helper! You force everyone. Not just me. Everyone. I'll bet you really worked on Mana to get her to take her
clothes off for you in the spin room!"

"Gauri!"

"That was Gaia, was it? The Goddess at last visits Terra
Station after all these centuries, and the only thing she wants to
do is have sex with Govind? Does that seem likely?"

"It was Gaia."

There was silence. "You do believe that, don't you?" he pressed.

Gauri stared through the walls into the distance. When she
spoke again, there was as much pleading as anger in her voice.
"Yes, for some stupid reason I do believe it. But then . . . Vinny,
let Gaia do it all. Why can't you . . . Oh Vinny, don't manage
everyone."

"I was trying not to."

"Don't be MAN to everyone. You were meant to be Shiva,
not Jehovah. Don't you remember Osen's stories?"

"The god in ashes who got all the village women running
after him for sex in the woods. He was always getting drunk and

crazy. That's what I'm trying to cure myself of. I did that for Mana's ceremony because it made her happy. It was the story in the cave she slept in . . ."

"He was *life*. He was against kings and rulers and anyone who said, 'Do this, don't do that.' If he was here he would poke fun at MAN and pull the plug on the wombroom, sure, but he wouldn't manipulate people for some Big Plan of conquering the Galaxy for Gaia's sake! He was singing and dancing and love."

"I sing and dance. And I would with you, if you were on fire like this more often. I don't notice *you* singing and dancing much."

"Well, it's time I stopped hiding. Or you're going to have everybody dancing to your tune alone."

"Believe me, I'm trying, Gauri. It's not easy."

"Even when I came in, you were trying to control me. You were thinking, 'How can I get her sorted out and get her out of here, so I can commune with my spirits again. They're the only ones who understand me. They're the only ones I can plan this conquest with.' Well, I'm not going away. Spirits aren't your only match, Vinny."

"Well, if you were always like this, I couldn't ever control you, could I?"

They looked at each other like asteroid spin rivals, squared up. And he knew what he had just said was actually true.

And then he knew that she knew it was true.

And then they both smiled with the pure relief of it.

And then she grabbed his lab fatigues and pulled him to her and kissed him so hard on the mouth that he felt like he ought to take up weight training or gyrosphere tumbling if she was planning to do this again. Then their tongues met, and she reached to pull his plump buttocks against her slim hips.

They dragged each other's fatigues, off in a fever. She was a new woman. It was a new age. He was Shiva, she was Parvati. The floor was as cold as Earth. He pulled the fatigues underneath himself. Then he was in her and she was all around him. She was laughing like a maenad. For some reason he was crying, water pouring from his eyes like Mother Ganga from the ice sheet. She stroked his curly black hair gently, but he said, "No! No! Don't lose the fire." He felt her thin, wiry frame around him as the strongest force he had ever been caught in. Then he

pushed back and matched her energy, and they laughed and he
came too soon. She couldn't come at all, she was laughing so
much at his dismay. But it didn't matter, for this was not the
softroom and they were meeting each other for the first time.

"Why aren't you always like this?" he asked as she lay naked
on top of him, her head resting on his shoulder. She was so
light.

"I'm just waking up."

"Like Parvati."

"Mmm."

"What froze you?"

She raised her head. "You really want to know?"

"Of course."

"I don't know." She laughed and snuggled her head down
once more.

"Don't freeze up again."

"I won't if you won't," she said.

"How have I been frozen?"

"You've been angry. All your life."

"I have?"

"The anger was a shell around you. I could never get in."

"You've always been wanting something from me. I've never
known what it was."

"Do you know now?"

"This?"

"I want to be your partner. Not praying for a little of your
attention — that's been horrible. I want to share it all with you.
I know you, Vinny. You need me."

"I need this you."

"This is me."

Her hand was resting on his sex. He felt it move against her
fingers. She held it gently in her hand, and as it came erect she
caressed it with such tenderness that tears came to his eyes. No
one had ever held him like this in the softroom. She moved so
that she could guide him once more inside her. This time instead of the frenzy of love making, she rocked slowly back and
forth. The water pooled in his eyes and overflowed down the
sides of his face, into his hair. She kissed the tears away and
kept moving. He felt stripped, naked, completely uncertain of
how to be, only knowing this was where he was meant to be.
This was home.

Seen from below, her breasts were so beautiful.

Her stomach so flat, her arms and thighs lean, muscular. He felt flabby. But she loved him. What else mattered?

She started moving with urgency and then she began to come. He closed his eyes to concentrate, to not come too soon. "No, look at me," she gasped. He opened his eyes and held hers as she came, cries bursting from her sweet lips, blood rushing to her face. He knew that this joining was the great moment of his life and of hers.

Afterwards he made sure the bacteria dishes were all right. Then he sat on their pile of clothes on the floor leaning against a table leg, and she sat on his lap and they held each other.

"This is really scary," he said.

"Why!?" she was startled.

"I don't know. It just is."

"You're always the leader. This is different."

The equipment beeped then, and he got up and realized this was the part where he would have to concentrate for a while.

"Listen, my love. Tonight. Let's sleep together?"

"In the dorm?"

"Yes. Come to my bed. No one will complain."

"I will," she smiled. Her smile was more beautiful and more terrifying than anything he ever known. He felt he was going to have to start his life all over again. This was what Mana as Goddess had really been about, and burning his past in the egg . . . This place where he could be himself completely, nothing false, no braggadocio; here, no sleight of hand or sleight of spirit would get applause; here, only the truth would work.

"Thank you," he said.

She laughed, as if he had said something banal.

"No," he said. "I mean it."

When she was gone, he turned back to the petri dishes with something like relief. His hands were shaking.

Gauri left him to his beeps and bacteria. Down the corridor from the lab, she did somersaults and backflips. She was halfway to the design studio when she realized that she was still in the lab fatigues, and they were three sizes too big for her. She had been so high she had sailed straight through detox.

She smiled to think she was in his clothes and rolled down the sleeves, which were way too long, and smelled them under the armpits and laughed and turned back to the labs to get her own.

Three days later, the annual ship from the Center came in. But this arrival, the main event of the station's year, passed Mana and Govind by completely. For they were sitting on the floor outside Gauri's room at intensive care, praying to the Goddess that the unknown bacteria that had ripped through her body would soon be satisfied. They prayed that she would not die.

# *Four*

"Hallo, Mana," the slightly built, grey-haired old man said to her. She had been looking at the extraordinary character beside him, dressed like no one she had ever seen, with a swinging sword and eye patch and a stuffed red and yellow bird on his shoulder. She had left her vigil at intensive care to come and get something to eat. The strangers had accosted her just inside the dining hall. "It's good to meet you at last," the drab old man said. "I've been looking for you all over the station. I'm José."

"Do you know me?" she asked, searching for the clue his name seemed to offer. His face was as gaunt as an old peasant's on Earth.

"I didn't realize you were so tall."

"You've seen me in a picture?"

"In an egg, my dear. I am José. I suppose if the name doesn't mean anything to you, then I haven't introduced myself to you yet. Which is a surprise. This year, I swore I would."

It came to her. "You . . . you did, yes, just before Govind shorted us out. I never went back. I had given MAN up, and then that strange message . . . You said you were the programmer. But you are so little, and old!"

"Well, thanks!"

"I'm sorry, I don't mean to offend you, but you said . . ."

"I said I loved you. And I meant it."

"Do you really know me? Everything?"

"Everything you told MAN."

"How, how strange." She had been going to say, how horrible, but he didn't look horrible, just old and nervous. There was humor in the way his eyes crinkled.

"What was my lover's name?"

"Sitala," he said. "Sitala of the warm eyes and the passion for going up to the forest above. She was your first real lover, but before you, she had a lover called Joanna. And before Joanna, Prakriti."

Mana stared at him. "I had forgotten their names."

Govind could not eat. He paced up and down and peered through the glass at the bed on which Gauri lay in a coma. Frozen, like Parvati. Only this time, he was to blame.

Mao was with him now. It was Mao who had suggested it was the bacteria he had been cultivating. "Is there any way you could have taken some out on you — did you see Gauri after you left the lab?" he had asked. And so Govind had told him the whole story. The test results had come through that morning and confirmed it.

"Please, Sophia, don't let her die," Govind had prayed for thirty hours now.

"It's not really your fault," Mao lied. "It's a risk of our position here, as gateway from Earth. The original migrants brought everything imaginable. They were dying by the billions in the Ice Time — they couldn't possibly do adequate detox on their way up here. It's not really possible anyway, even with new migrants like Mana. For all we know, bacteria escape from the upper atmosphere, too. Not to mention the free-floating ones that are traveling through space anyway." Mao had gone over all this twice already. "This one must have come from outside, unless it found an extremely bizarre niche in which to lie dormant on station. It's completely new. Doesn't fit any of the . . ."

"Oh, shut up. I can't hear myself pray."

"Sorry. I'll go to MAN."

"No! No . . . we can help each other. I'm sorry, Mao." But then Govind was distracted for a moment, looking through the glass, by what seemed to be a movement on Gauri's face. When he looked up again, Mao was gone.

"We're going to take you and Govind with us," José said to Mana. His bizarre companion had gone off with an equally strangely dressed woman. Left to themselves, Mana and José had found an empty end of a table. Mana picked at the food she had collected.

"Govind won't come. Not without Gauri. Not if what both of them told me was true, before she got ill. Of course, if Kali takes her . . . then he might come. Oh, it was so wonderful. Gauri came and told me. She looked so happy. No one else can match him. Govind needs her. If she dies, no one will ever be able to do what she can. We have to pray. We must have faith. Come, you must pray with me. I'll get Chairperson and Vladimir and Arun, we'll go to Chair's room."

There were tears in José's eyes as he followed her.

"What's the matter?" she asked.

"Nothing."

She stopped in the corridor. "No, you must tell me. We can't start like this. You must know me inside out. It's time I knew you."

"I can't. It would be upsetting to you. I don't have all the scents and sounds and pictures . . ."

"Of the egg? You mean you can't relate to me just as me, without the technology?"

"I know it sounds . . ."

"Sounds like it's you who would be upset if you tell me what's the matter."

"Maybe both of us."

"I can't come with you to the Center if you can't be open with me. Don't you see? I gave up MAN. Hey had too much power. You've seen something in me that upsets you. I won't have you keeping it to yourself."

"No, ma'am." He gave her a spacer's salute.

"What's that supposed to mean? Look, I'm being short because of Gauri and because I don't like a little old man knowing everything about me."

"All right. I'll tell you exactly what I was thinking . . . I thought: this woman is no longer the tiger slayer. Forgive me, I thought: she has become the people manager. 'Come, you must pray with me. I'll get Chairperson and Vladimir and Arun.' And I thought, I made you this. Osen and I, we turned you from that mad wonderful dryad into this efficient promoter and manager of groups."

Chairperson found Govind outside the isolation room where Gauri lay.

"I want you to know, Govind, I have thought about this deeply: we can be certain, if she dies, she will go to be with Gaia."

"It was my fault. It was the sex. It was what we were always told. Sex in the softroom only. There was a reason for that."

"Govind, it was an accident."

"No, no. We were wrong. It won't work. What if others get it? I could have killed the whole station. An epidemic. That might still happen!"

"It was an accident."

"No. Osen says in her Chronicles that sexual beings are too crazy to have psi power. She said that. Or something like it. That's why the WraithDaughters died out — not enough sexual energy, all spent in psi. The wraiths say the body's desires lead to chaos. You see, the Space Code is right — only it doesn't go far enough. The wraiths have it right. We should stop this lust altogether. No sex at all."

"Govind, my dear, you are overwrought."

The wraiths did not think so.

Over a calming ceremonial cup of tea, they listened to the news sorrowfully but without surprise.

They did not suggest that the passions of the body were unspiritual, dangerous to personal health and social order.

Instead, they sat in a circle on the floor of their most special room, to which he had rarely been invited. It was entirely round, with a spherical dome ceiling. They closed their eyes and made colors flow slowly around the walls and dome.

Soothing, cool beiges and whites, into which red daggers stabbed and were absorbed and diluted and erased. The four wraiths sat in lotus with straight backs and peaceful faces. Govind felt light-years from all the pain and passion of the last days.

When he returned to look through the glass at Gauri in her coma, he felt some detachment. It was the first time since she had come to him passionate in anger and love in the labs that he could stand back from her. For a moment, he could imagine being an old man remembering this long ago encounter with his peer sister who had died in her coma. He could feel the cool sadness of this old man, and a contradictory thankfulness that the death had freed him from a passion powerful enough to have dominated his life, strong enough to have prevented his life of contemplation, his entry into the wraithmind.

But it was Gauri! And she still lived.

He sank down and put his head in his hands. Wraiths had never had to deal with this.

That night Gauri came out of her coma.

The medics would still not allow Govind in to see her. He sat down in the corridor outside her room and would speak to no one.

José and Mana talked all night, sitting up on the patched sofas in the common room. Rocco's ship was due to stay five days only. "He won't leave without Gauri," she said for the fifth or fiftieth time. "Can't you wait until she's better?"

"Rocco says we can't take her even if she's well. We're only taking volunteer breeders. It's a big favor of his to take you and Govind. Even Govind he's reluctant to take. I think he thinks you'll do me good — a companion to make me a little more normal in my last years."

Mana laughed with him. Already she felt comfortable with this odd little man.

"He doesn't realize we're going to start a revolution on Madlarki, you, Govind, Passarin and I," he said.

"Maybe he does. Maybe that's why he doesn't want to bring Govind."

"He's agreed on Govind. He's a good boy, really. But Gauri too? No, I don't think so. These things are closely monitored. We'll classify you and Govind as 'necessary for research.' A real Terran and a case of possible genetic infection from Terra. Even that's stretching it. We can't take Gauri."

"He needs her. He won't ever be what he could be without her." They sat in silence for a while. Then she said, "It's revolting, taking these breeders. That's the way it started on Earth."

"The way what started?"

"Slavery. Making some woman other and lesser, so you can own her and order her about and beat her. It started with capturing women to bear children for a man, then buying and selling women."

"That's exactly what I told Rocco."

"You did? You understand that?" She took his hand.

A long time later, after hours more talk, they fell asleep, hand in hand on the patched sofa under the night-dimmed lights.

"Govind." The spin team representative shuffled his feet, looking at the plump figure lying on the hospital corridor floor. "Are you awake?"

Govind's eyes sprang open and he sat up. "Is she all right?"

"She's fine. I can see her from here. She's sleeping nicely."

Govind leaped to his feet. "Oh, thank Sophia." He gazed through the glass at her peaceful, dear face.

"She came out of the coma four hours ago," he said.

"We heard. I'm sorry to say this now, Govind, but we need you."

"Who does?"

"The team. The starship's come. First round's at 1400 this afternoon."

Govind looked at him blankly. What was he talking about?

"It's the big game. The game of the year. The whole station's rooting for you to win."

"I'm not a child, I know what game it is."

"You're coming, then? I'm sorry about Gauri."

"I can't. Leave me out of it."

"You are captain of the team, Govind. You're the only good player on station. Everyone has been waiting for this for months."

"Get Hanuman. He's better than I am. Or Ganesh. Any of them are better than me."

"You know wraiths aren't allowed to play."

"Well, dress them up and call them all Govind! I'm not playing."

"Come, it'll do you good. She's all right now. She'd want you to play. She thinks the sun shines out of your face."

"No, she doesn't! She's the only one of you who doesn't. Thank Gaia."

The spin team had followed Govind into Mana's group en bloc, no questions asked. Their spokesman was smart enough to remember something Govind had told them.

"You said that playing spin perfectly was like a prayer. I think Gauri and Gaia would like you to pray that way."

"Give me time to think. I can't think with you standing over me like this."

The spokesman came in with a low blow: "People always said you never stuck with your crazes. I told them spin was one you would stick with. At least until the game of the year."

"Get out of here."

An hour later, the team representative was back. "All right, I'll play," said Govind. "But only if they allow me to see her, and she's really better, and she can speak, and she agrees with you. And only then, when she's sleeping."

The team rep smiled. He had all the medics on his side already.

\*        \*        \*

Passarin spent the five days on Terra Station in a thoroughly unwelcome swelter of emotions.

It made him realize that the months with José had been a pleasant interlude. There was something to be said for sitting around talking. And the Space Code had certainly been soothing after an upbringing in the God Giver's Temple, followed by two intense years on Starlight. On Starlight there were no shadows to retreat to — at least none without publicly announcing the retreat and discussing it in detail afterward. On Starlight everyone lived in the open, with gusto. Their houses were half open to the stars and their lives to everyone else's snooping interest. Lovers had to know every last thing about each other's thoughts and feelings. Exhausting.

Ever since he had read Jomo's letters when he was a kid, Passarin had half wanted to take up his grandmother's cause — if only he could understand what it was. Jomo, the old man on Starlight who claimed to have been his grandmother's lover and therefore his own grandfather, had written to him hoping he would follow his grandmother's path. Jomo wrote that her name was Martin — Martin of Arable — and her goal was to close down all the unsafe planets of the Collectivity, so the people could live free of the Space Code again: free to have lovers and families and free to think and say anything. But Passarin's own father, the God Giver, taught that her name had been Mary, and that she had been leading a movement of obedience to God. There was nothing very free about life under the God Giver, as he discovered when he got to Starlight. So they could not both be right. As a boy, he had dreamed of heroic adventures at the head of a Galactic band of warrior wraiths, whose flashing swords cut down the missile-happy armies of the Galactic Collectivity and let a thousand planets bloom. Or thirty-five planets, or however many it was on which grasses could flower and people breathe safely and choose to obey God, like Passarin's family on Arable Two.

He had come to Starlight as one of his father's diplomats, but really he had come to find out the truth. And the truth was that Starlight was the freest and most confusing place in the Galaxy.

But now that he had tasted the cool simplicities of the Collectivity's way of life, he wasn't sure he wanted adventure.

Perhaps he could live on Madlarki and study philosophy and history and talk it all over twice a week with José in the greenhouse. There must be some work he could do there — research for the psych labs perhaps.

On Rocco's starship, sometime before the last but one port of call, he had finally gained enough courage to go to the softroom. Rocco's second lieutenant had been more than willing to instruct the gangly newcomer into softroom ways. She had made him entirely forget the breeder he had been so enamored of at a distance at the start of the voyage. Softrooms meant sex with everybody with no deep enquiries into your soul, which was a lot of fun. But on a starship, everybody was not many people, which meant that he and the lieutenant had got up to a lot of tricks together, and that had been even more fun. He had thought, for the last several days at least, that he and the second lieutenant were in love.

But this did not dissuade him from putting in a few good hours in Terra Station's softroom, along with the rest of the starship crew. Astonishing, the variety of habitats and soft surfaces on which to feel new things; the excitement of hundreds of new bodies, all vying for the starcrew's attentions. Already, the second lieutenant had faded somewhat from his mind. Though for some reason, that didn't stop him feeling acute pangs of jealousy. She seemed to be having sex here with everyone but him.

The station, of course, was in uproar. The accident that had almost killed Gauri was vying with the annual spin game as the talk of the hour. The accident was a great setback to Mana's work, there was no doubt about that. The traditionalists seemed unanswerable when they said it proved the value of the Space Code. Mana's true believers could only go deeper into their belief that Gaia had everything in hand, that Her spirit would make people more complete, not more careless. The odd thing was that even the traditionalists here argued vociferously in dining halls and common rooms with the Gaians, and sometimes even came to blows with them. It looked as if the Code and MAN had lost control of both groups.

It made Passarin glad he wasn't living here.

All the religious stuff about Gaia troubled Passarin more than he had expected. No one could have thrown himself more sincerely into religious fervor than he had at home, with a group

he had helped create called the Joyful Sons and Daughters of
God. From the simple perspective of the Joyful, his father's
Temple religion had come to seem overwhelmingly grand. From
the all-questioning perspective of Starlight, it had appeared ri-
diculously petty at the same time, because it dismissed anything
that did not fit in its all-embracing but much-excluding divine
scheme.

The Starlight people had seemed capable of doing any bizarre thing in the name of *their* gods — from silent desert pil-
grimages to pretending amid ear-piercing screams that they were
being born again, from wildly sensual festivals to endless mo-
notonous chanting — all while claiming that their gods were
metaphors and not real at all. By contrast, Madlarki had been
so quiet and sane, the starship so peaceful, sitting talking it all
over with old José.

So on the last day on Terra Station, Passarin discovered that
he was looking forward to getting back to the simplicities of the
Space Code. The one thing he hadn't tried yet was MAN. Maybe
this time, on the trip home to Madlarki, he would pay his first
visit to it. He wasn't sure the false ID Starlight had given him
would stretch that far. Maybe José could work it out for him.
Then he would be a full citizen of the land of calm.

Govind threw himself into the asteroid spin games with a fury
that wiped out the visiting team's best efforts. Ordinarily, one
exceptional player would not have been enough to make a poor
team win. And there was no doubt that the rest of Terra Station's
team was poor.

But Govind inspired them above their normal game. When
the medics brought a wan and feeble Gauri in to watch Govind
play, the crowd's un-Code-like roar was such that the visiting
player had a nervous collapse. He had to be taken to MAN on
a stretcher. He had never been subject to fierce emotion before, let alone collective emotion.

Years later, they would still play holies of that series all
through the Terran sector of the Galaxy. It was astonishing to
see an overweight person playing spin to begin with, or to see
one at all, since weight control was simply a matter of elemen-
tary medicine. But Govind had always been odd. Never more
so than now: the fat man dancing on his toes firing lasers in each
hand. His face held a trancelike calm that most people on sta-

tion recognized as a typical wraith-look. But the visiting team, like all decent citizens, had never been close enough to a wraith to tell it from a red dwarf, or from any other celestial phenomenon. They were completely unnerved by the otherworldly stasis of that almost black face and the slight smile fixed to its lips. Govind's hands moved so fast, it seemed at times he had four or even eight arms. In his wraith-face, his eyes alone flashed and moved.

The visiting team's morale was quite undone, and Terra Station won by a mile.

Rocco enjoyed the spin games enormously. The whole station was a riot, more lively people than he could hope to meet in ten years on Madlarki. Old Chairperson was a delight. They swapped fantastic stories.

But his wife Jiang the Fang saw another possibility altogether in the extraordinary spin champion of Terra Station. All Jiang's being focused on one goal, the introduction of the family concept to the top brass of the Karp military. She envisaged herself the queen of planet Karp, or at least the madam. As queen on Karp she would have more influence than any of her Xidasi cousins would ever get at home on Tarcuna, playing the tired dynastic games they'd been brought up to.

Nothing to do with planet Karp escaped Jiang's attention. Not even the fact that Karp had slipped badly in the Central Spin League. She was bored to death by spin, but she was much energized by the thought that her darling Rocco's typically weak and sentimental agreement to take Mana and Govind back for José's amusement had unexpectedly given into her possession a man who might well be the best spin player in the universe. Karp's top brass might appreciate that greatly. It might even be worth handing him over as a gift. On such little favors are great pyramids of influence founded.

When Passarin asked her many years later if she had fallen in love with José that week on Terra Station, Mana replied, "Fall? It suggests loss of control. That only ever happened to me once, and not in a space station but in a cave deep under the ground. But I loved José at once, from the first night we spent together, sitting on a patched sofa. If you think about it, I had loved him for many years already. There was never anything very sexual between us, you know. Enormous comfort, physically. We were like an old Terran married couple already the day we met — comfortable, happy, delighted. He was almost twice my age — I was thirty-nine, I think, he was over seventy. You know, the first thing I ever said to him was 'But you're so old and short!' He never let me forget that.

"If we hadn't been so comfortable and easy with each other, Gaia knows how we could have handled Govind and Gauri, and got them onto that spaceship. I still often wonder if it was the right thing to do. Considering how it turned out. Well, I suppose you have to believe it was, don't you?"

When Gauri recovered, she found that something strange had happened to Govind. She kept telling him that she was better. "I'm all right! I'm not infectious! They said so. I'm just weak. That doesn't mean you can't touch me."

But he wouldn't kiss her. He wouldn't even hug her. He seemed remote and yet full of attentive concern.

"I'm not a statue, Govind. You make me feel like one of those carvings in the Caves that Mana talks about. You're hanging garlands round my neck and lighting incense at my feet. What's wrong with you? I didn't die, you know. I'm alive."

She decided he had had a worse shock than she had, and did her best to be patient. At first he was obsessed with the spin games and she let him concentrate on that.

She was still in the sick bay, spending most of the time in bed. Her legs were so weak! She had always been healthy and active. It was like a bad dream to be barely able to swing her legs out of the bed. Her mind wasn't as sharp as it should be either. People talked and moved too fast. It was so easy to drift off into her head even when someone was talking to her.

After his team won the spin meet, Govind came to her and stood beside the bed, bursting with news. She patted the bed for him to sit beside her. He grabbed a chair, spun it round and sat on it backwards, chin on the chairback, eyes exultant.

"You're high as a kite. What's happened?"

"We won! Sector Champs!"

"Meds already told me. This is something else."

"What else could it be?"

"Vinny, don't play games with me, I'm too done in. You're like this when you've got some amazing new scheme — not when

you've achieved the last one — that just leaves you empty. I
*know* you."

"We're going to the Center!" His eyes sought hers, but all
she could think of was the way his eyes had tried to grab her in
the softroom that terrible time, when she had suffered him to
fuck her and the real Vinny had never shown up.

"I don't think you should go." It was a stupid thing to say.

"This is our chance! Mana's coming too! We're going to
bring Gaia to Madlarki and all the Central planets!"

"Vinny, does 'we' include me?"

"We're working on it. You know the old man, José?"

"Mana told me about him. I haven't met him yet."

"He's so well connected! He knows everyone on Madlarki
and Tarcuna. And Rocco and Jiang Qing know all the top military on Karp. This is everything Osen dreamed of."

"Vinny . . ."

"I feel something has just been handed to us by the cosmos,
Gauri. I have never felt so full of hope and possibility . . ." His
whole dear face was alight.

"Vinny . . ."

"People are going to follow me, Gauri. I feel it. I am going
to do what Osen made me for."

"But remember what I said to you in the lab that time?"

"That horrible time?"

She gasped. "It wasn't horrible! It was beautiful!"

"You almost died. I almost killed you."

"It was a silly accident! I'm talking about what I said to you."

"It was an accident, yes. But that's what the Space Code is
all about — to prevent accidents."

"Don't tell me the lesson you're going to carry away from
all this is 'Obey the Space Code'!"

"No, of course not."

"So? What are you trying to say?"

It was suddenly hard for him to look her in the eyes. "The
Code is wrong because it prevents us from reaching out to hear
Sophia, the voice of Gaia. It's wrong because it makes us depend on MAN. It destroys friendships and prevents any kind of
movement for change. But it's not wrong about the dangers of sex."

"When we made love in the lab, you were more yourself
than you've ever been!"

"I was out of control. It was . . . not right."

"Vinny, listen to yourself! You acknowledged me as a lover and equal. That was all the control you gave up! Without me . . . Look at how you have had other people in your control all along and that's what you'll do with these followers you'll get at the Center!"

"I've changed, Gauri. I'm doing this for Gaia now, not me."

"It's not that simple! Remember how I called you on manipulating Mao and the others, and you said I was right, and that no one else would stand up to you and tell you the truth, and that's when we found each other!"

"I do need people to tell me the truth . . ."

"But you're not going to find them, because this whole culture doesn't know how to do that! You are so . . . incandescent, so, what's the word MAN taught me . . . charismatic! That's it. Charismatic. People are bowled over by you. You could lead them any which way and they'd follow. They have done all your life."

"But I'm not going any which way. I'm going Gaia's way."

"Are you? If you turn against what we had together in the lab? I'm your down to earth half, Vinny. I can keep you honest. No one else can."

He spread his hands open, helplessly.

"Don't use that bacteria as an excuse to run away from me, Vinny!" She had knelt up in bed. Now she leaned forward and grasped his shoulders and shook him.

"I don't know that they can take you. They say there's no way they can."

"And you're basically happy about that aren't you?" she shouted.

"You know I want you with me!"

"You're lying! Look me in the eyes and say that!"

"I . . ." his eyes met hers. Suddenly they were so full of fear and hurt she moved her hands to hold his face.

And then he broke away and ran from the room.

Gauri got out of bed and dressed. She found Mana and an old man in the common room.

"You must be José," she said to him. "You have got to get me on your spaceship."

"I wish it were my spaceship, my dear. Unfortunately it belongs to my son, Rocco. And Rocco basically does what his partner, Jiang, says. So we should go and see Jiang." He pulled himself to his feet, grasped Gauri's hands warmly in his own, and kissed her on the cheek. "I'm so happy to meet you in the flesh, my dear."

Half an hour later, they were admitted into the presence of Jiang the Fang, the extraordinary, elegant woman from Tarcuna. She seemed as remote and haughty as a queen from Osen's tales. She wore clothes such as Gauri had only seen in historical holies of decadent pre-Ice times: shimmering stuff, perhaps the fabled substance called silk. She was a granddaughter of Xidas, once the most powerful man in the Collectivity and the husband of Martin of Arable, though Jiang was descended from one of his other women.

Gauri felt small, intimidated and utterly determined. She said, "I have to go with Govind."

José butted in, "Jiang, you understand, she's Govind's wife." This was a shock to Gauri, but it seemed such terms were understandable among the Tarcunan elite. Jiang barely raised a slim eyebrow in query.

"Are you?" Jiang drawled.

"Yes!"

José explained: "If you want Govind, you have to take Gauri."

Gauri wondered why on earth Jiang might want Govind.

"What does Govind say?" Jiang queried impertinently.

"Of course he wants Gauri," said Mana.

"I'll make enquiries," Jiang answered, skepticism cold in her voice.

Gauri spent the evening with Mana and José in the common room. Every half hour or so José got up and paced the floor, went in search of Rocco, came back baffled. "They're up to something. Can't give me a plain yes or no," he grumbled. "We're leaving in the morning!" he said for the umpteenth time.

Mana said, "Gaia has it all in hand. Whatever happens will happen."

Gauri said, "I have to come with him."

She fell asleep on the couch and Mana had to call the medical emergency team to bring a trolley to get her back to the sickbay.

In the morning, Mana woke Gauri early and went with her

to her dorm and her workplace. They collected all the things she would want to bring with her to the Center, which amounted to very little indeed: some eggs she had made to burn, her special shoes and body suits for the gyrosphere, a painting Govind made for her when they were kids. They went together all the way to the hub, where Rocco and Jiang's starship waited.

José was already there. His magnetsoles tethered him to the deck outside the starship while he argued with his son's wife.

Jiang said, "There is no way to take another person on board except as a breeder, going to a breeder planet."

"That's unacceptable. There are no breeders on Madlarki or Karp. The port officials won't allow her in. She has to come with us to Madlarki, and if Govind later goes to Karp she must be able to go there with him."

Rocco bustled up in his ridiculous pirate gear to join the conversation. "Only way we can take her on the books is as a breeder. So someone looks the other way at Madlarki and presto, you spirit her off the ship. I'll lend you the cash. After that, old man, hide her in the greenhouse."

Jiang gave her husband a withering glance. To Gauri's eyes they were complete opposites. She wondered what they could possibly see in each other. Rocco was all bluster and show. Jiang seemed tightly closed against scrutiny. Cold, dangerous. She would not relish being a breeder in this woman's care for even the week or two that José said it would take them to reach Karp. That's where they would drop the breeders and some other supplies picked up en route before they went on to Madlarki.

"So now there will be a breeder on Madlarki," Gauri said. "If the only way I can go is as a breeder, that's how I'll go. And who knows? Maybe Govind and I will have children. Like you and Rocco. José told me you plan to."

Jiang's eyebrow rose again in José's direction.

"Recite the consent formula that you see on this screen, please, toward my wrist unit." Jiang barely looked at her. "We'll do tests on you right away, on board ship. And don't bring anything with you. We have all that you need to be a breeder."

Passarin thought Rocco and Jiang could not have been nicer on the voyage back. They let Rocco's father and Mana have their own cabin with its spacious double bed. Rocco mucked in with the crew and passengers in the crew dorm. Jiang slept with the breeders, "lying inside the door hard up against it, so that no one can come in," José predicted. Gauri had to sleep with the breeders too, but she was allowed to spend the days with Mana and the others.

Passarin found it extraordinary to think that Jiang the Fang was an almost-cousin of his. He had been raised to believe that her grandfather, Xidas, had been his grandfather also. Since he was a boy of ten or eleven, he had preferred to believe that Jomo had been his grandfather, not Xidas. But he never told any of this to Jiang. It was an actual pleasure not to discuss it with her. He preferred to be incognito and, as he had on the voyage out, he swore José to silence about his origins. He wanted to know all about Xidas, but he would prefer to read about him, not be recognized as the long-lost branch of the family. Anyway, if the truth got out, who knew what the consequences would be? The Collectivity might reinvade his homeland. His own quiet anonymous life in the placidities of the Space Code might come to an end.

Passarin and the second lieutenant quickly rediscovered each other's charms and forgave all. And the ultimate joy was that José squared it with the ship's program so that Passarin could go to MAN.

"The best way to cure you of your liking for the Space Code, my boy," José said, "is total immersion."

But Passarin found MAN to be everything he wanted — cool, urbane, amusing and helpful.

The only jarring element on the voyage, for Passarin, was the misery and tension that hovered around Govind and Gauri. They seemed to have some major difference of opinion about sex. Govind talked celibacy, while Gauri practically wrestled with him in public. Govind spent an inordinate amount of time practicing asteroid spin. Passarin wished they would just both go to the softroom like everyone else. It entirely confirmed his view that religious mania was to be avoided at all costs — Govind obviously had a bad case of it. And it just pointed up the folly of falling in love: Gauri aching and furious, Govind for once pathetic, running away, crawling back to her apologetically, completely at sixes and sevens.

"If they are both going to live with Mana and you and me in the greenhouse," he said to José after they witnessed one stormy encounter, "then I'd rather you found me a way to get admitted to a regular Madlarkine dorm."

"God, you'd hate it. Totally superficial relationships, cheery nonsense."

"Total immersion, remember?"

José appraised him grimly. "I'm beginning to think you'll never resurface."

Otherwise, things were very pleasant, all told, for Passarin. He felt that at last he was coming to recognize his true self: the dispassionate student of human folly and philosophy. The observer. The man from the outside looking in, understanding everything, unmoved by anything. What did Mana call her father? A connection man.

There was only one image that Passarin would carry away from this voyage that did not fit this freshly objective view of himself. It was a real slip, just the sort of juvenile thing he was trying to outgrow. It involved a woman, of course, and the kind of emotional ambush that can come out of nowhere when sexual attraction is involved. He was learning about himself though. A pretty face and a sympathetic ear had the power to yank unfulfilled longings for love right out of the depths of the primitive brain.

Just an evening, a moment, but intense. It was an upsetting moment, when he allowed himself to get wrapped up in somebody else's problems instead of sending them to MAN, and ended by losing something that he valued.

It happened when he sauntered into the softroom one day, and was astonished to see Gauri sitting there, fully dressed, all on her own in one of the smaller nests. He greeted her warmly, and cheerily suggested that they go over to where the main action seemed to be happening, in the light well. She begged him to stay with her alone. This seemed an odd request. Especially considering how wrapped up in Govind she was. But the lack of new bodies after the variety on Terra Station had been bothering Passarin a little. So he hummed and hawed, and then accepted.

She undressed and did her best, but it was clear her heart wasn't in it even before she burst into tears and huddled away from him into a corner. He should have just left it there. It was MAN's problem, not his. But for some reason he covered her with her clothes — naked misery is somehow more upsetting than clothed — and tried to think of something to say to cheer her up. He should have tried a hearty spaceism, like, 'Must have been that Exploding Nebula Pudding we had for lunch,' or 'Don't worry, my friend, a little hormonal imbalance happens to us all now and then.' But there was something hauntingly beautiful in her face that he had never seen before, a heartbreaking grace that made him cast around instead for something real to say, of the sort he would have said to his sister Tiannu, or to the woman he had loved on Starlight. It was a reflex reaction, something it would probably take years to get rid of. And then, of course, she was not a typical space person — she was actually engaged in something he knew a lot about.

He said, "It's tough inventing a new religion. Give him time. He'll come around." He patted her on the knee, and then thought he'd gone too far, and got up to pull on his clothes and go.

But she said, "What do you know about it?"

"Quite a lot," he said before his brain started to work. "My father invented a religion for our planet. It's a difficult thing to do." He stepped into his fatigues.

"But the Goddess isn't religion. Religion's one of those terrible things like races and nations that Lakshmi got rid of."

"And like talking to people, and love? Do you think they're terrible? Actually, I'm all for MAN, myself, and the Space Code. It makes sense, especially in space. Why don't you go to MAN?" It was the first time he had ever suggested it to someone. It felt like a rite of passage. He was proud of himself. He pulled on his shoes.

But for some reason, this good feeling made him loquacious. For when she said, "Tell me about your father, and your planet — what are you doing here?" he answered her. Bit by bit, drawn out by her questions and her inquisitive brown eyes, he found himself squatting down beside her and telling her the whole story — grandfather Jomo's letters that had come on the first starship from outside to reach his planet since Xidas's atomics wiped out their main city; the trouble he'd had afterward with his father because he believed Jomo's story; their reconciliation and his going as one of the ambassador's aides to Starlight. He even told her about Nokomis's granddaughter, his brief attraction for the frightened breeder, and the lieutenant in the softroom.

She didn't seem surprised that he was enjoying a new life, courtesy of the softroom and MAN. But it was a little upsetting the way she said, "I understand," with deep empathy in her eyes, as if his new life were a sad but inevitable response to great pain.

On the other hand, she did seem to recognize that there had been pain in his life, and the quality of her response suggested that she had suffered herself. He was curious about this. He had thought life was smooth sailing with MAN. And so her story had come out — the joy and agony of her indissoluble link with Govind, brother and lover, man and wraith, genie and hero; the task Osen and Mana had set them; the Goddess and the God, the caves and the warriors, her desperate fears for Govind let loose without her. "You understand, the male gods brought earth to ruin — the gods of dominance, war, ruling nature; and they created this wasteland in space. And we have to bring the Goddess back — working with nature, love, wholeness. Vinny is a genius, but he's talking so much about the spirit I'm scared he'll . . . well . . . I don't know."

At a certain point Passarin realized that all this was probably being recorded for Jiang the Fang's benefit. Gauri acted very scared when he suggested it. She had got so used to Terra Station's laxity, she said. And she had been in such distress herself — because of Govind's hateful rejection of her after her illness. It was something to do with wraiths and Osen and sex, she felt, some fear of real life that these telepaths had. And so the talk went on, and they ignored the danger. Passarin told himself that they had already said enough to incriminate themselves many times over.

She explained that she had come to the softroom today out of anger at Govind and loneliness. She sat there hugging her clothes to her without putting them on properly, so that parts of her stuck out. He covered them up, even though it wasn't cold.

He told her about his grandmother's plan to reduce the number of inhabited worlds to safe planets where the Code would not be needed, so that the exaggerated fear of sex and emotion that was necessary in space, and which had gripped Govind, could be done away with. Only, he had to add, a terraformed planet was no guarantee of happiness — look at Earth, look at his own home.

At the start of the talk he had glossed over what religion had meant on Arable Two. Now he found he wanted to tell her.

"When I was a child," he said, "I knew there were other

worlds, in theory. They were worlds of evil. That's what it is to
have a father who is a God Giver. Everything that was not us
was failure, second-rate, miserable, unhappy. The people outside our planet were lost souls, atheists, and some of them were
killers. They had tried to destroy us. They were agents of the
devil. They were to be pitied.

"But what did I know? Ours was the only planet I knew.
And what did I know of ours, apart from the high, barren winds
of my father's farm?" He had written that in his diary on Starlight. He quoted it directly. But she didn't seem to think it pre-
tentious. She was thirsty for his experience.

"The wind sucked and dried all the juice out of us. We have
two suns, a red one and a bright one — we call it 'night' when
both are down; 'the Red' when only Red Sun is up; and 'day'
whenever Bright Sun is up. My best friends were Sigurd One
Eye, and my sister, Tiannu. We had a donkey named Branwyn.
Everything centered around the Temple. Father is a great
preacher. His voice can be heard . . ."

He told her all about it. Nokomis's granddaughter had never
listened like this. Her eyes never left his.

"There are some creatures native to the planet. Sigurd calls
them Orawurries. The rest of us call them Demons. They're beautiful things, round and furry and big. They have six legs, but
when they want to go fast they roll. The hunters hunt them and
their meat is the most delicious thing I have ever tasted. There
wasn't much else native to the planet that our digestions could
cope with. Father preached that they were the devil. My big
brother killed several. People say the Demons kidnapped me
for weeks when I was a child, but I don't recall it. Sigurd thinks
they are intelligent."

"Oh no," she said. "You ate them?" The shock on her face
was a mirror of his own when he had learned it. She had lived
into his story that much.

Something had happened. They both knew it. A connection. Was this what making a new friend could be like? Neither
had much experience of making new friends.

But she kept discussing religion. "I think . . . I wonder if . . .
we make up Gods to enable us to do what we want to do. Or to
stop us from doing it. We can't trust ourselves. You want to eat
Orawurries but you feel bad about it, so you make them devils."

"That's what I believe! How did you come to that?"

"Osen wants to stop the rise of kings on Earth. She wants to save that world from what it went through before. She wants our help. But her religion says we space people are evil. So she revises her religion. She says the space people are people too, and misguided in some ways, civilized in other ways, and we can work together: Gaia can fly up into space and bring down help. But now Govind wants to revise it more — he can't decide if he wants sexual love or fears it. He'll revise his god depending on whether the love or fear dominates in his life. That's why I had to come."

At the end, when it was time for them to go to the mess for dinner, he felt in his fatigues pocket and pulled out the black and white top.

"It's like this, to come from my home to here," he said, "like night and day." He spun it. It spun white and then, suddenly, black. She nodded gravely. He had expected her to be delighted, to laugh. He had wanted to break the spell between them. She hadn't laughed once, since he had first been introduced to her and Govind on the station. Then she spun it herself. And she smiled. It only wove the spell more tightly.

"Here, I'd like you to have it," he said impulsively. He could never work out why.

He avoided her for the rest of the voyage, as far as one could in a small ship. She did not come to the softroom again. She stuck close to Govind, and seemed to take pains to avoid Passarin. They half smiled at each other a couple of times, but it was too much, what had passed between them.

For years afterwards, the memory of her had the power to suddenly spoil a light softroom encounter.

The ship docked at Karp's Station Three in the middle of the fifteenth night out from Terra Station. The next morning José and Mana found themselves locked into Rocco and Jiang's bedroom.

Passarin thought it was odd that they didn't come out to watch Jiang the Fang shepherd out her precious consignment of breeders. The frightened woman, whom his heart had gone out to, looked much more cheerful now, and he wondered what that crush of his had been about. At the end of the procession a prone figure, covered by a sheet and carried on a stretcher, was removed behind the other breeders. Was one of them ill? The crew didn't know or care.

Govind was offered a tour of Karp Three, and a couple of crew members took him off. Passarin walked to the airlock behind them, wondering whether he would be offered the same. Four burly soldiers in uniform met Govind on the quay. The crew handed him over. Govind started to protest. A mighty military hand clamped down on each of his arms, and two soldiers began to frogmarch him away. He struggled. One of them laughed, "Don't you want to be Karp spin champ?" And the other said, "We'll have to get some of that fat off you first!" His struggles were useless.

Passarin rushed back in. He found Rocco on the bridge.

"Who was that breeder who was carried out on the stretcher?" he asked.

"She signed the form. Jiang's got her consent on voiceprint. It's all legal."

"Where's José?" Panic made his voice rise.

"Don't worry, old lad. He's having a nice time with Mana. I got him his lady love, didn't I? Govind'll be happy as spin champ — Karp'll treat him like a hero. And that Gauri would only make my father's life miserable on Madlarki if she went on there without her fellow. Karp said they can't take her. So she'll go to one of the breeder colonies. Why, you look quite green in the gills. Whatsamatter? She'll be fine! They take good care of them."

"I protest! That's immoral. How could you do that to your own father?"

"Like me to send a recording to your home planet of what you said to Gauri about your father?"

"I wouldn't sell his best friends into slavery!"

"They're not his best friends. Govind'll be happy as a clam on Karp — you'll see. Tons of influential contacts as spin champ, and no priestess telling him what to do. I've done him a good turn. And José's got Mana — Govind would just have been trouble to him."

"But Gauri!"

"Yeah, I thought there was a little something between you and her. That's just the breaks. If you had all gone to Madlarki, what would you have done? — she was married to the weird guy. No, it's best all around like this."

"You've made her a breeder! A slave!"

"I thought you were into babies and all that? Well, okay,

she had a bad break. But you'll be all right, dear friend. Just stick to MAN and remember . . . softrooms have ears."

Passarin went straight to MAN and cried. When MAN asked him what was wrong, he confessed that he had lapsed from the Space Code. He had been flattered by Govind's lover's large brown eyes, and had exchanged life histories with her. Worse, his lapse had caused him to lose a precious keepsake, which had a certain sentimental value for him and could have no meaning at all for her. He hoped it wouldn't count against him.

It was just as well, said MAN, to off-load sentimental keepsakes. It was easier to live without such impurities.

Passarin came out of the egg a true member of the Collectivity, empty of feeling and devoid of dreams.

# *Part Four*
# THE PLANET SKY

*Seven Years Later*
*Sky, Starlight, Madlarki, Karp*
*Year of the Migration 2132*

# the roar

The little boy sits on the floor and tries to spin the top. He tries again and again. When spaceships and number blocks start flying at him from his rowdy playmates and one of them hits the top, he crawls after it, shields it with his body, and tries again. He can't get it to spin. He is only three.

The two women who are meant to be looking after the children sit by the window on the edge of a low table covered in children's paintings and clay monsters. There is nowhere else to sit. The adults are not meant to relax. One has mighty hips and massive breasts, a mountain of a woman. She supports herself by leaning with her arms, solid as buttresses, on her outspread knees. She speaks explosively and pants a little after every phrase. "It's great. It's fucking great. Great Goddess, I'd like to do that. To every single little mean-mouthed motherfucker on this goddamn wet rock." She lifts a mighty hand and slams it onto her knee, and roars with laughter. It sounds more like a roar than a laugh.

The second woman is lithe, neat, and self-contained. She breathes easily, and holds herself like one of the dancers in the holies they are shown once a month. She has been reading from a screenboard, which now she places on the windowsill.

Outside, rain and ocean crash onto bare rocks. They both know the view well. The planet is called Sky, site of one of the largest breeder colonies. The large woman often seems mesmerized by the waves. After her laughing roar, she subsides again into staring at the endless rhythm. Neither of them spares a glance for the huge expanse of dirty pink sky.

A little girl sits on the smaller woman's lap and tugs at her cheek. The woman does not seem to notice. There is gray in her hair. Her face has a grim set to it, but her eyes show amusement and some kindness as they feast on her companion.

"You're a tonic, Kumi, a regular tonic. I knew you'd like it. Great jumping ovaries! I like to see you laugh." One of the things Gauri likes most about the breeders are the laughs and the oaths and the jokes. The Space Code has broken down in many small ways among the breeders. It is the only way to stay sane. And nobody cares. "Yes, all right, dear, you can play with it," she says to the little girl. The girl slips off her lap and takes down the screenboard.

"Teach me to read," she says. "Gauri, teach me to read." Kumtacj, for that is her full name, turns her head. "Yeah," she says, "she's four years old. It's time she learned. I'm forty-four. It's time I learned, too. But I never will."

"It is time, isn't it?" The smaller woman's eyes glint with daring and delight. "It is time." She laughs and the big woman laughs with her. Their eyes are mischievous together.

"Ro-o-a-a-r-r!" the big woman goes, and the child squeals with delight.

The other children appear to be getting completely out of control. The little boy is still unable to spin the top.

"This is hard for you to learn to read on, but watch my finger," Gauri says to the little girl. She has to listen closely to hear amid the noise of the battling children. "Mana taught this to me. She learned it by heart when she was a girl, and I learned it by heart from her. It's about a tiger. You know what a tiger is? All right. Well, this is a very big white one called Snow Tiger. But they don't call it that in the story because the name was too strong for them to say aloud. The story's called 'The Roar.'

"In the last days of the Sky Gods, when the skies were already dark but the Ice was not yet awake, the Goddess in White awoke. She was larger than a lion, whiter than a glacier, faster than a flood."

The finger has left the page already, to mime the tiger's claws.

"She was seven years old. The men and women in the far north beyond the mountains thought that they had made Her. She was born among them after they had done deep magic in the spirals that twist at the heart of living creatures. But it was only when She was full grown and the sky went dark and the sun was hidden by the last days that She truly Awoke. Then She knew She had been asleep for tens of thousands of years."

Gauri puts the screenboard down. She knows it by heart. She rises from the bench, lithe as a waking tiger.

"She yawned a great yawn. And She saw that the people were not afraid of Her. One of them came and looked into her mouth, admiring it. She bit his head off."

Gauri and Kumtacj take huge bites at the air. The little girl is too enthralled by the story to squeal. Her wide eyes turn to Kumtacj, and back to Gauri. Some of the other kids are coming over to watch.

"She yawned again and this time they were all afraid. Some of them said, 'The Gods will punish you.' But the Sky Gods were too busy hurling missiles at each other. So the people shot at Her with guns. And that was when She learned to roar. She opened Her great mouth and roared at them."

Kumtacj roars hugely. The little girl gasps.

"In the far, far north, the Ice grumbled and said, 'Who is that who woke me up?' Now, the Goddess in White was unharmed by the bullets. Her roar had deflected every one of them. She roared again. The men fled. The women fell down and worshiped Her. But the Ice was angered. Her White Majesty roared for a third time."

Kumi roared again, and the little girl squeaked in delight.

"And the Ice came sliding south to chase away the noise. It crushed the people and the cities and the missiles beneath it. The White Goddess ran to the mountains. The Ice crushed the mountains. The Goddess in White hid in the forests south of the mountains. The Ice could not see Her. The Ice stopped. It looked at the dark skies of the last days and it said, "I like this. This is comfortable. I'll stay." It went back to sleep. And that is how the ice sheet came to cover the North and the mountains."

"So, little girls, do not anger the Goddess in White. She may bite your head off. If you make Her roar, She may wake the Ice again, and you don't want that, do you?"

The little girl looks sobered.

Kumtacj nods. "It's time to make that tiger roar," she says.

In a different voice, Gauri says to her friend, "It's a curious story, because the other Osen stories all have it that it was the atomic war that caused the ice age on Earth: it was the fault of the male gods, but in this one it's the Goddess in White Herself who caused the ice to destroy the cities."

"Nothing happens without the Goddess," says Kumtacj.

Gauri thinks, Osen, you should hear and see this woman.


"I told you it just does not do to have the breeders in as nursery nurses," says a brisk voice entering the room. "Look at this mess!" The children who have been fighting rush to the nurses and are comforted perfunctorily. "Look at the two of them. Total neglect. We will just have to clean up ourselves, and report them. Stupid cows."

The two newcomers, identical twins of MAN, set about cleaning up the result of the six toddlers' barely supervised hour.

"Do you not care, even a little?" One of the MAN lookalikes

is tricked by something semi-rational in the smaller breeder's face into asking her questions. "One of these is probably yours, is it not? Your name is Gauri, is it not? I will check. For Space sake, your one is Arjuna. That nice little boy over there is your son. You see hem there? That one. And you could not be bothered. What is hey playing with? Where did hey get this? This is not an approved toy. This is not one of ours at all." She picks up the top, and puts it on the high counter on the other side of the room from the window. She continues to clear up the mess, grumbling with her colleague.

When she next checks on the stupid breeder woman, the smaller one is squatting on the floor next to the boy. She has retrieved the unapproved toy from the shelf.

"Look, Arjuna," she is saying. "The top is a white tiger. See its face? Now we spin it. There! It's turned black. See? Now it's a black panther. Can something turn into its opposite? What do you think? Which is Mana now? Which is Govind now? The officers from Karp who come here say he's famous now. But which is he? This?" She spun it again, white. "Or this?" as it turned over. "That's what I'd like to know. Which do you want to be?"

"Give me that." The nursery nurse grabs the top from Arjuna's chubby hand. "There are no faces on this! You are crazy. I will have to report this too. That is no way to talk to children. You are too dangerous to be near children. And that one is yours too."

"He's not mine. He came out of me, but only because they put him in me."

"You are mad."

"Ra-a-a-a-a-r-r-r-gh!" Kumtacj bares her teeth. The little girl who liked the tiger story jumps up and down. "Do it again, Kumi. Do it again!"

"You are beyond me. I am calling MAN's helpers." The nurse marches across the room to the first-aid station and raises her hand to throw the little wooden top into the flashpan.

"Don't do that!" Kumtacj roars.

Gauri is already running across to the nurse. "Please give that to me."

"So this is yours, is it? Where would a breeder get a thing like this?"

Three-year-old Arjuna runs across and tugs at the nurse's fatigues. "Give it me! It mine!"

"You are meant to be playing with your number blocks. You are going to be an accountant. This is not for you. No."

The boy begins to wail.

"I do not have time for this." The nurse attempts to throw the top into the flashpan. Gauri's hand whips up and grips her arm to prevent her. At the same time a child's fatigues shirt flies across the room and hits the flashpan. It was the nearest thing to Kumi's hand. The sleeve flashes to fire in the pan, and starts the rest of the fire-resistant shirt on a slow burn.

The nurse screams. She has never been assaulted in her life before.

Gauri wrests the top from her grasp.

The second nurse rushes over. In her panic, as she pushes the rest of the burning shirt into the flashpan, two of her fingers are nastily burned.

The first nurse is now almost catatonic. The second nurse raises her wrist unit to her mouth to call for MAN's helpers. It is more urgent to her even than activating the first-aid station's burn unit. Breeders out of control, animals, her worst nightmare. For a split second she hesitates with the wrist unit at her mouth, the pain of her hand screaming in her mind, getting her wits together to call for MAN's helpers.

A memory from twenty-four years before when she was still a nursery child flashes into Gauri's mind. Mana and Audit at the dance. Mana seized Audit's wrist unit as he tried to call for MAN's helpers.

Gauri finds herself looking into the frightened eyes of the second nurse. Then she looks down and realizes that for the second time in two minutes she has grabbed a non-breeder's arm. Her hand is clamped over the nurse's wrist unit.

There is nothing that can save her now.

"We've done it now, girl." Kumtacj's bulk wades into the frozen tableau. "This means fucking brain peelings." She takes the catatonic first nurse's arm and struggles to remove her wrist unit.

Gauri still holds the second nurse's wrist. It takes her longer than Kumtacj to exhaust all the other possibilities. This in spite of the fact that there are none. When a breeder acts violently, they don't squander her valuable womb by getting rid of her. They don't waste their time with reprimands. They send her to a special MAN unit to peel her brain. They wipe it clean down to whatever level is the minimum needed to let her womb work, unencumbered by violence and thought.

"What do I do?" Gauri's brain feels peeled already. The incident with the top, her hand on the first nurse's arm: they might have overlooked that. Her grabbing the wrist unit, they cannot. "Kumi, what do I do?"

Kumtacj pockets the first nurse's wrist unit and calmly puts a mighty hand over the nurse's mouth. "Do the same as me," she says. "Stop these motherfuckers from calling for help."

The second nurse starts to shout, and finds her breath cut off by Kumtacj's other mighty hand across her mouth. Kumtacj now has one nurse in each arm, one hand around each mouth. With trembling fingers Gauri takes off the second nurse's wrist unit.

"What do we do?" Gauri asks again.

"It's a breeder revolt," Kumtacj says.

"This? This is a revolt?"

"We call the other mothers. No one expects anything."

"Why should they join us? They'll all get peeled."

"What do you do in a breeder revolt? We need fucking weapons."

"If we get weapons, they'll really kill us."

"What's the difference? Come on, you know about Martin of Arable. She led all the revolts. You met her grandson."

"He didn't tell me what goes on in a breeder revolt. He didn't know. But you have to . . . I suppose you have to take over some crucial part of the station. Like the fusion plant, or, I don't know, the gene labs or something. Threaten to let loose their bacteria. Yes, that would do it. That would do it!"

"Well, go and get the others, then. Surprise the enemy. That's our main weapon."

"They won't understand. They won't join us."

"They won't stand by and see us peeled. The dumb, gene-bred breeders might. But the 'volunteers' will help us. I know. Come on. We got to do something. The fucking kids are screaming. I'll stay here. You go and tell the others — just the volunteers, mind you. We'll give those motherfuckers a run for their money."

Gauri runs. Her heart pounds in terror. As she goes, she hears Kumi's great roar, and the children's screams are quieted. The little girl giggles. Kumi must be making faces.

"Vinny!" she cries inside as she runs. "Now even if you come to Sky, I'll never see you. I'll never see you again."

# One

The young father swung down the woodland path with an easy stride. It was the sort of beautiful morning that makes you forget the baby woke you up thirteen times in the night. There were new shoots on the fir trees, easing out from among the old hard needles like soft green paintbrushes. A skunk shuffled down the path toward him, and he stopped still and greeted it as it passed. He looked forward to a fine, lazy day, recuperating from baby. He reached his office barely fifteen minutes late, which was earlier than usual. A fine morning on the planet Starlight.

On the office tree stump, the sign read STARLIGHT: COLLECTIVITY SUBVERSION UNIT. The good old SCSU, the most benign project to work for, that he could imagine. He had paid his dues in heavy labor — steel mill, logging, dredging the lower river. One day he would have to take up some serious social responsibilities, serve in local government. But for now, he and his wife were raising baby, another was on the way, and they had taken up easy work. She was in the local erosion and ecology alert group, roaming the hills, watching the sheep and the wildflowers grow. She usually took the baby on her back. That was why he did baby's night duty. He wasn't convinced he had the best of the bargain. Days when she didn't take baby, other friends and relatives were queuing up to, and this was of course valuable for baby. But the father was feeling left out. Whenever he saw baby she was asleep, or bawling.

Still, on a morning like this, who could think life was anything but pleasure? The suspicions of a headache bequeathed him by the night's frustrations would soon dispel in the sunshine.

He strolled across the office terrace, admired the new gouache one of his colleagues had created on a café umbrella, and then wandered down into the wooded seminar area, where a kettle was already steaming on the campfire. A co-worker had brought out one of the terminals from the cabin, and was summarizing the latest Starlight agents' reports.

They had agents on about thirty planets. A starship made the rounds continuously, secretly picking up reports, occasionally replacing agents. The wraiths on the starship sent the reports to Starlight in message capsules no larger than a green bean, or even by direct thought for a short, urgent message; these were two services that Starlight wraiths happily performed, though the Collectivity's wraiths claimed both were impossible. The Collectivity's wraiths said they could not send anything smaller than a spaceship. Those wraiths were good trade unionists, making sure they didn't work too hard. But the Starlight wraiths were Starlighters first and wraiths second: everyone worked together on Starlight and no one was a second-class citizen.

A glance at his colleague's screen told him that she was working on the latest news from Madlarki, which had arrived in a capsule two days ago.

"Hi, Head Scsuzz," she said, "how are you?"

He grinned. He'd started the joke himself when he joined straight from backbreaking days on the dredger crew. At SCSU, he had decided, they were the scsuzzies — the zz's stood for the amount of time they spent asleep on the job. He lay back on one of the wooden benches by the fire and closed his eyes.

"Rough night, Number Two, rough night." Her name was Crystal and she wore two around her neck and three from one ear. Their co-workers were called Eagle and Dawn. Head Scsuzz was the odd one out: his name was Bill. They had elected him head of the unit only a few months after he had joined. At first he had been flattered. Later, he had realized he was a victim of office politics. Next time he wouldn't be so innocent. The director of SCSU had to be ultimately responsible to all the innumerable other offices and networks that might be interested in news about the Collectivity. Way back, in the days when Martin of Arable had been shaking the Collectivity by its ears, the SCSU had been founded amid enormous interest. Every network on planet had contributed time and personnel and ideas. Now they just kept it going out of inertia. When the office elected him they had assured him that these days the director had almost no one to report to. His victimization lay in the word "almost."

"No sign of the harpy, I suppose?" he asked.

"Not yet. You're in luck."

"Do you think you could deal with her if she shows and I'm asleep? Just as a favor?"

"You must be kidding."

"Everybody hates me," he said comfortably, wriggling his back into more comfortable spots on the hand-carved bench.

It was at that moment exactly that everything about the day began to go wrong. As the young father's great uncle had always said: it's best not to fool with cosmic self-put-downs.

One of the occasional constraints on sleep at Scsuzz was when his coworkers' teenage kids couldn't find anything better to do than hang out with a parent. It didn't happen often. It happened today. They came by with their rowdy friends about five minutes after he lay down to nap. They complained that rain was about to ruin their day's kiting. Then it started to rain, and they had to rig the tarp. The kids huddled in with them and started an uproarious game of Red Dwarf/White Lady.

He kicked them out, and had to relate to their parents' anger about that for the next half hour, followed by the return of the teenagers who had found the alternative entertainments uninspiring: more fun to send the Head Scsuzz bonkers again. Their attempts were mercifully interrupted when a teacher called up wanting to know why, in the SCSU's opinion, there were no miners' strikes, breeder revolts, wraith conspiracies these days in the Collectivity. One of her pupils had asked. Bill really had no idea, but he was responsible, so he trotted out the Scsuzz line: Martin of Arable had been an aberration, there had been 2,000 years of stasis before her and there would be another 2,000 most likely after her; thought control was a highly developed art in the Collectivity, etc.

Then, of course, the harpy came by. She was the old lady who was all that was left of the next door office, the Earth Project. As they saw her determined brocaded form marching up through the pine trees, his co-workers, all three of them, buried their heads in their terminals or found some weeding that suddenly needed doing in the rain in the farther salad beds (they grew their own office lunches). The teens melted away into the woods, where they could be seen watching and giggling behind trees.

"You've just got to mobilize public opinion, young man! Alert the networks! Find a symbol that can generate commitment! Your project and mine — we stand or fall together. Piracy is too deep in the blood of our people! Your project and

mine are the only two altruistic approaches to the outside world
that still remain. Now when I was a child, and Martin of
Arable . . ."

"For the love of Mikey, shut up about Martin of Arable," he
said. "I've got a headache." The old bag didn't even have time
for "good day" — just straight into the heavy stuff.

"You'll pay for that," Eagle commented kindly as the harpy
finally flapped away in a fire-breathing fury. And then, to make
up for it, he offered a head massage. He was a huge man with
large hands which gave exceptional massages.

"At least she didn't go on about that Mana woman," Bill
said. "Maybe she's got a new bee in her bonnet. It's going to be
'symbols to generate commitment' for weeks now, you can bet."
For weeks the old hag had talked of nothing but "when are you
going to send to Madlarki for Mana?" As if one could send for
anyone from Madlarki just like that.

The massage had only just begun when the vidphone beeped.

"It can't be," he groaned. It was. Strange, how often the
harpy's departure sent some etheric signal to the ambassador to
call.

"Ambassador here," he would always say, as if his fierce,
disdainful face on the screen had not already made this painfully clear. He liked the title. There was only one ambassador
on Starlight, as the Collectivity would certainly not deign to
send one to the people who were, after all, their chief enemy.
The one and only ambassador was from Arable Two, a poor
little runt of a planet of no importance whatsoever. It was probably just as well for the Head Scsuzz that there was only one, in
view of the amount of his time that that one commandeered.

"No sir, no news yet. Our starship's at" — he checked quickly
on his subscreen — "at Sky, at the moment. It won't be going
back to Madlarki for a couple of months. We'll do our best,
sir."

"Your best is not good enough! You took a citizen of my
planet and, without my knowledge, deposited him on Madlarki
as a Starlight agent. It is your duty to get him back! Seven years!
When I first found out about it you assured me he was going for
one year only. We hear nothing from him — you say he no longer
even files reports to you. You are incompetent! You must get
him *back*. He is the son of the God Giver. He is one of the most
important people on my planet. If you do not comply, I will

immolate myself in Foundation Square, and there will be no ambassador!"

Please do, the head Scsuzz murmured under his breath. Can we supply the last meal?

But the tone of the man's voice was such that he wondered if he might actually do it. You never knew with a religious nut. That wretched fellow Passarin was developing into an interstellar incident. The Head Scsuzz's headache turned a corner into something more like migraine. When the call was over, he had no recollection at all of what he had said to pacify the beast on the other end.

It was at that moment that the bad news came.

"Hey, Head Scsuzz, guess what? A flash message from the wraiths. Breeder revolt on Sky."

"Oh, spider grandmother," he moaned.

The discussion went on around him while he held his head.

"Who's the agent there?"

"Kuan-yin."

"I told you we shouldn't have taken her on! She's a romantic fool! She's doing a death and glory number."

"She's not into dying. She's got political ambitions, that one."

"She might be trying for a heroism citation."

"She's not stupid. Get the details, for heaven's sake."

"Here we are: Kuan-yin says it was spontaneous . . . involves the breeder woman from the Earth station. She's leading it . . . About half the breeders are in it . . . They've taken over the gene labs and claim to be breeding toxic bacteria. Holy snakes! They're threatening *'death for themselves, the entire gene-tech team, and contamination of the whole planetary habitat'* if their demands aren't carried out. What they actually want is not yet clear. Sky First Committee is attempting to negotiate. Et cetera, et cetera. Oh, this is rich, get this: 'The semiannual visit of the starship known by Skyers as Jiang and Rocco's Family Cruise Ship is due in from Madlarki via Karp in two weeks. It is bringing top military brass to visit children they parented on earlier cruises. Sky First Committee is desperate to end the revolt before the Karp bigwigs arrive.'"

"That's incredible. That is fantastic. In fact, it's *news*. This," said Crystal, "is symbolism that could generate commitment, Head Scsuzz! We must get this out right away — public's going to lap this up. We're talking *major media.* Donations! Could put up that new cabin we've been dreaming of."

"What does Kuan-yin recommend we do?" The Head Scsuzz muttered his first contribution to the discussion through the hands that held his pounding head.

"She wants a Scale Two. Move in, take out the rebels."

"No. No. No. No, and no. What does that solve? Sentimental fool . . . oh, my head."

"Bad precedent. There's no time for full consult on this one. We'll have to go with the present guidelines. I agree with Head Scsuzz."

Suddenly something not unlike sheet lightning illuminated the inside of the Head Scsuzz's brain.

He closed his eyes and lifted his head from his hands for a full half minute, unwilling to believe the beauty of it.

"I've got it," he said.

Before the pounding returned, and in the sort of creative daze that comes once in a decade with luck, he said, "It's perfect. Every detail fits. Kuan-yin said the Jiang and Rocco Family Cruise Ship starts from Madlarki, and it's going to Sky. Madlarki to Sky. Got that?"

"We got it. What's the big deal? Hum a few more bars."

"Passarin's on Madlarki. We can't pick up him up from there if he doesn't want to come. But if we get him to Sky to help the breeder revolt, or comment on it or something, we can grab him in the Scale Two along with the breeders. We just have to persuade Passarin to take that ship. Threaten him with blowing his cover or something; you take care of the psych details, Crystal, all right? We'll have to send a message to our agent on Madlarki, but it's worth the expense; everyone'll agree to that. Nobody wants to see the ambassador immolate himself in Foundation Square." Another major flash went off in his head and he reeled. "God! That's only half of it. Oh, my head. There's the Terran connection. You said it's a Terran woman who's leading the Sky revolt. That could get this Mana person who the harpy's always going on about — the Terran priestess — who's also on Madlarki, to go to Sky, too. So our starship picks up *both of them,* and Kuan-yin gets her romantic intervention *and* a medal, and everyone's outstandingly, outrageously happy. The harpy's happy, the ambassador's happy . . ."

"And you get back to your zz's," said Eagle.

"No one will know what to do with themselves."

"Hey, Head Scsuzz, that was downright clever," said Dawn.

"You should get migraines more often," said Crystal.

"I always knew we elected the right guy."

"Spider grandma!" the Head Scsuzz swore as the pounding began again. "But my kid's going to be smart."

# Two

Mana rushed in from the gym and put the water on to boil. Passarin was due any minute. The greenhouse was even more of a mess than usual. She started pushing the piles of leaves awaiting classification — a big, new batch had come in yesterday — from the middle of the floor underneath the houseplant stands. No wonder José spent so much time elsewhere these days. There wasn't a chair to sit on. She picked up the Madlarkine puffrats' pressurized cage off one chair and staggered around the room looking for somewhere to put it, murmuring reassurance to the puffrats. She finally set it down on her altar, knocking over her candles and Kali carving. She took a bowl of fruit off another chair, and had to put it on the floor. The tea table was covered in all the paraphernalia she was developing for a Madlarkine Equinox ritual — seeds and dried flowers and streamers of that unusual, mossy red stuff with the blue stars in it that dried so nicely. And the main table was lost under this afternoon's naming ceremony for Rocco and Jiang's second child: a ceremony done without the child or the parents, or any idea what name they were calling her.

Just as well José hadn't been home today — he would have thrown all the naming stuff straight in the flashpan: Rocco had been unmentionable for all the seven years since his perfidy had crashed around José's heart. José was a very old man now. At eighty, he had reached the year when he would have to report for the long sleep. They had been doing what they could to prepare for it. He walked with a stick and maintained an outward interest in history and life. But nothing had been the same since Jiang and Rocco's voyage: the "window" that in his short-lived dreams was to have let the revolutionaries loose on the Center had instead isolated them on separate planets.

Mana was philosophical about Govind — she could see that the Goddess might have wanted him on Karp. But Gauri had been purest sorrow. She had tried everything to reach her. Everything short of going on Jiang and Rocco's Family Cruise Ship to Sky. That José would not countenance. They had not seen Rocco or Jiang in all the years since the betrayal. José had driven himself into the ground trying to get Gauri back. But he was no match for his daughter-in-law.

News about them got around, though. The pair were famous on Karp now. They based on Madlarki Station, where their ship was licensed, and they now had two children. But they had thoroughly corrupted the military elite on Karp with their dirty little offerings of biological parenthood on the side. And rumor had it that Govind was making an impression on Karp too. "So it may have been Gaia's mysterious way," she would argue with José. "Govind certainly wouldn't have got far here, would he? I mean, everyone loves tales of Earth here, but no one does anything about it. They're too cynical. To Madlarkines, people are pathetic fools to be manipulated. Maybe Karp was the best place for Govind."

It was hard, doing a naming ceremony without knowing the name.

"And Bhasu came back to you because of Rocco's betrayal. That's another silver lining." José had had to admit that one. He had been so ill in spirit after his return from Terra Station, unable to rise from his bed, that his second son had become concerned. Bhasu was still a playboy dabbling on the fringes of the Tarcunan set. But now he had another life. He had learned the mysteries of MAN, and taken over José's experiment. In this secret life he was like a monk. He bore his responsibility for Terra Station as a sacred trust. He would keep that community going after José went for the long sleep.

José and Bhasu had kept Mana abreast of her friends' lives on Terra Station. She refused to learn the MAN programming. But she often had suggestions as to how to improve things. It had all changed. MAN was still MAN to the traditionalists on Terra Station. But to the Gaians, MAN appeared in the image of José or his son. The two of them acted as therapists, if asked. But eggs had also been linked, so that up to ten people could talk with one another and José at the same time. José sometimes recorded talks with Mana and Bhasu and Passarin, and so the Gaians got to know the people behind the eggs.

Chairperson was still alive. Though he had resigned his post, everyone still called him Chair. No one was going to enforce the long sleep against anyone's wishes. Arun lived on, too, but insisted on his right to clean corridors. He had also got hold of some paper and was writing an addendum to the Chronicles of Osen. Vladimir was the real leader of the Gaians, in so far as they had one. She provided much of the energy for developing the rituals and dances. She had been midwife to eight babies now, born naturally of mothers, the Terran way. They were planning a trip downplanet soon, to Mana's Caves.

Mana missed them. She would have dearly liked to go on that trip, and to live out her old age in the Caves. But faith had worked its changes on her. She knew now that she had been part of a true emanation of Gaia. Spring and Life had indeed come to Terra Station. And here on Madlarki, Bhasu at least had been inspired. Govind himself had been drawn to Gaia, and who knew what might not still happen as a result — he was only twenty-nine years old. At the very least Mana had acquired a different view of the Goddess: Gaia as tree and bird and leaf, mountain and birth, had faded; Gaia as mind, spirit, source of wisdom, and planner of cosmic campaigns had grown. If she returned to the Caves with her tales of a thousand planets and a million MAN eggs and a frozen people thawing, she would be as isolated as Osen had been.

The water boiled. She poured the tea, just in time, as Passarin came in like a half-starved puffrat.

"Passarin, my dear, sit down. You look terrible. What's happened?"

He picked up the tea cozy and a small statue of the Goddess off the wicker chair that Mana offered him and sat down.

"Did you pick all those leaves yourself?"

"Heavens, no. Why would I want to go out in a pressure suit and respirator? I've run through forests. Tea?"

He accepted a cup eagerly.

"What's up?"

"Just a personal problem. Nothing, really. Oh, that tea is reviving. Always is. I wish I could make tea like this at my dorm." He looked up, a shade nearer his normal self. "All right to keep going, Mana?"

He was writing her life story. He had become a dedicated historian. Occasionally that was all right.

"Well, we left your story," he said briskly, "just when we were embarking on Rocco's spaceship. The beginning of the fateful voyage. I never did know how you and José got Jiang to take Gauri on as a breeder, and then let her spend the days with us on board ship instead of with the breeders. Just lulling our suspicions, I suppose. Shall we start with that?"

"Passarin, how many times have we been through this? I am not capable of putting present reality on hold just to tell old history. I have no doubt the folks on Starlight will be as eager as you say to read your story, or my story, as you call it. But you are alive, sitting in front of me, and Starlight is a million miles or light-years or whatever away from me — I find it very hard to visualize them. And I don't think you can visualize them that well, either. Are you really writing this story for them? Or is it just that you like my tea?" He didn't answer, but took another sip and smiled at her. "Well, there is a new condition for drinking my tea. One real word from you about why you are looking so miserable."

"I have told MAN. I don't want to go through it all again."

"Oh, splendid! The devoted historian who's spent seven years reconstructing his grandmother's life and philosophy, who writes Mana's life story on the side, goes off and tells his troubles . . . to MAN."

"Spare me the sarcasm. You're getting to sound just like José."

"Do you tell MAN all about me, about your grandmother, about Starlight?"

"No, of course not. I disguise the problems. It's not like José's running my MAN program, it's just a standard one."

"Well then, you get no genuine release. It's not real. You've got no friends. You and José barely speak to each other any more. He's that fed up with you. Surely you don't have any more to learn about Martin of Arable. You won't take the Goddess seriously. What do you want?"

"I want to finish your story. Now can we please get on?" He looked as if he was fighting off an enormous weight that had settled on his head and shoulders. Mana began to visualize it as a gigantic, ugly bird, one guanoed, scaly foot on each of his shoulders, greasy breast engulfing his head, a bored and stupid look in its rheumy eyes. She shook herself to make the vision go away. It looked too real. He was reading out the last sentences to date in his retelling of her life story.

"Why are you interested?" she interrupted. "You've become the perfect Space Code man. You love the emptiness here.

You've buried yourself in it. Every day to the softroom, the wombroom, the holies — how can you take those formula heroes in the holies? And do the research and writing that you do? Which is really full of insight. You don't make sense."

"For Mary, our Mother's sake, leave it, Mana!" It was an oath from his planet, a sure sign that he was extremely upset. He stood up abruptly. His teacup rolled off the chair arm and cracked in half on the floor. He stood glaring at her for an instant, and she imagined the great bird cawing obscenely as it dug its talons deeper into his flesh and flapped its foul wings at her. Then he fled, stumbling through her piles of paraphernalia, her seed boxes and pressed leaves, to the door. She wondered how the huge bird would get through the door.

"You're just upset because we're going to talk about Gauri," she said to his departing back.

He stopped, one hand on the doorframe. After a moment, he enunciated coldly, "I am upset because Starlight is trying to recall me."

There was silence.

"Well, then," Mana said softly, "you'd better come and sit down."

He came slowly back and sat with his head in his hands. The bird's greasy feathers were all ruffled. It looked scared now, at least awake. Passarin stared at the floor. He picked up the broken halves of her cup and matched the pattern of leaves together. He put it on the table and said, "Sorry."

"So Starlight wants you back."

"I won't go."

"Can they force you to?"

"They say they'll blow my cover. But they won't. If they did, they'd lose me forever. They can't afford that."

"Then what's the problem?"

"I'm not going back. Not to Starlight. Especially not to Arable Two."

She waited him out. She looked at the ugly, greasy bird and muttered under her breath, I'll get you yet.

"You said it," he said at last, with a sigh and a vulnerability that made him look much younger than his twenty-nine years. Her mind went to Gauri, the same age — what would she look like now, with many babies forced out of her? Nothing like as young as this sheltered boy.

"It's Gauri. She's in trouble."

"What trouble?" A pain twisted in her chest. "How do you know?"

"Starlight says she's in some kind of revolt there. They're going to send a ship in to check it out, and they want me and you to go there to help them do something or other. Just a ruse to get us to Starlight."

"Me? Why didn't you say before? When did you hear this?"

"Last night. I told them neither of us would be able to go. But I said I'd ask you."

"Why wouldn't I go? Dear Goddess, I hope she's all right. A revolt!"

"Look, they don't want just to talk with us. They want to get us to Starlight, and they wouldn't guarantee to take Gauri: they said it depends how many breeders there are and if they can lift them out of there at all."

"Why couldn't they get them all?"

"They'll have their reasons. I said you'd never go because you'd have to leave José, and Govind."

"José can come."

"It's Rocco's ship that would take us."

Mana bit on her knuckles. "I'll go and come back, then. You could, too. Refuse to go to Starlight. But we've got to see Gauri. José will come round, or we won't tell him, or something."

"If I go, Starlight will kidnap me — you too maybe. We might never come back." The big, fat bird was hunched protectively over Passarin's head.

"Well then. Don't go."

"Right."

"So why are you so miserable? Come on, Passarin, this is like pulling teeth." An image from her home planet that would have been just as apt on his. They both came from benighted, backward places.

"I've thought about her a lot," Passarin said at last. "We only talked once. But she haunts me. I was in love twice when I was young, but I don't remember either of them. At least I don't keep thinking about them. I only talked with her one evening, and then I avoided her the rest of the trip. I never even had sex with her, well, only half. But when I'm in the softroom I — I often imagine her. I can't tell you how many softrooms she's spoiled for me. She's grown so in my mind I don't know what relation my idea of her has with the person I talked to for an evening. Sometimes I think that I need to find out, that there is something missing in my life here, as much as the rest of it suits me. I don't know what it is, but I think she — well, she could tell me. It's probably all a mirage. Everyone is missing something. I've just projected it all onto her. But all this is so self-centered. I mean, how is *she*? What does it mean to be a breeder? What is this revolt? Would I help or hinder in going? If I go, could I persuade Starlight to get her out? Maybe I could. I don't know.

"Maybe we'll go," he went on, "and she'll already be dead or peeled, and Starlight will grab us and take us off. A total waste. Maybe that's not what I'm really afraid of. Maybe it's something in me . . ." He dried up.

"Of course, it's something in you you're most afraid of, you idiot," she said warmly. "I am going, and I am going to persuade José. Can your Starlight agent get clearance for José as well as me to travel with Rocco?"

"I'll ask. I don't know how they get the clearances — but the whole Madlarki bureaucracy is half asleep. Maybe it'll work." His voice was gloomy.

"Thank you, Passarin. You're a rare friend. And listen: it's no crime to love someone, even long after you last saw them, even when you hardly remember sometimes what they look like. I still do," and she felt the old, familiar tears ready and waiting. "Now I have green life around me, and real ground beneath me, and I'm happier, I think of her all the time."

His face registered alarm, and puzzlement. "Gauri? Are we all in love with . . . Govind and me and you as well? You know that she only thinks of Govind."

Mana kissed him on the forehead, and hugged him. He seemed wooden. "No, silly. Sitala. When do we leave?"

"Tomorrow."

Mana suddenly noticed the absence of something. She looked around the room and out of the veranda window at the great jungle, and spied it as it barely breasted the treetops, a fat, greasy bird on lumbering wings hunting for a new roost. She smiled. "You decided to come."

"Yes." Passarin smiled back. "How did you know?"

# *Three*

Govind flew. He flew as a bird flies.

He swooped down through rust-red canyons.

He soared up above their rims and feasted his eyes on the mountains.

As a child he had dreamed of flying. But this was better than dreams, wilder than asteroid spin, more ecstatic than sex.

Every nuance of the winds and updrafts was his to command, to float upon. The rush of the wind, the hum of his helmet's air synthesizer, the bright yellow of his wings, the sun warm on his back, the wind cold on his legs, the great, hard land below him: it was all ecstasy.

But the greatest beauty of it was the emptiness. He flew high to leave behind the beginners, the timid, and the visiting elite of other planets and their flying instructors; he flew higher even than the regulars and the teams of aerial acrobats from the military; he flew up to where only he and his followers dared: where only the mystics flew.

Below him the barren, beautiful landscapes of Karp.

Steep canyons in the foothills, impossibly soaring mountains beyond.

The elegant arcs of the gravity trains that brought the ore down from the high mines to the furnaces.

The white-and-gray domed buildings: salt-and-pepper dots around the brilliant emerald of an algae lake in a distant plain.

And everywhere rock: harsh, bare, and endless, stained with the colors of the ores it held. Iron red everywhere, but here and there streaks of copper green and silver black, cobalt blue and sulphur yellow — colors sharp in the ice-clear atmosphere. There was more than enough oxygen to oxidize the ores on Karp; in fact, there was too much oxygen for Terran life. Oxygen as poison. Every moment away from the city's domes, every minute in the air, brought risk of conflagration. One electric spark, one careless clash of metal on rock could do it. Everything he wore was rubberized, anti-static, flameproof.

But the familiar surges of energy and optimism that carried
Govind through every day in the city also bore him out often in
his little speedcraft to the flying fields. Up here his drive could
lessen. Down there he was having to learn the exercise of power.
Up here he could float *in* the Power. He gave himself up to it.
He risked the danger of burning with divine peace in his heart.

He beat his wings to climb within a thermal updraft; to spiral upwards like the DNA chain itself.

He thanked the Great Spirit of the Galaxy every day for the
physical and psychic energy that never failed him. That energy
and little else had formed the physical foundation for this great
work on Karp. They called his followers the Govindis. But still
he knew his energy alone could never have done it. He himself
was nothing. He knew that he had no startling analytical abilities. He could see speech, but it was misleading as often as it
was helpful. Gauri had always ribbed him when they were young
for his impetuosity, his blindness toward people's individual
needs. The Great Spirit had had to make him over before He
could use him so fully.

He swooshed down, planed fast, and caught a new thermal.
The patient spiral climb began again. The spiral: the nature of
the Galaxy, the double arms on which he floated. On which he
floated free . . . and disciplined.

For he had disciplined himself. He had disciplined his energy. Not to his own intelligence, which was lacking, but to the
Great Spirit's, which was infinite. The Spirit of the Galaxy was
greater than Gaia's spirit, greater than Karp's, than Tarcuna's,
greater than the Liquid Light of any one Sun.

As he climbed high on the thermals, the rhythm of his wing
beats merged with his breath, all bodily sensation at last fell
away, and he was open to the solar wind of a hundred billion
stars. The wind of divine intelligence streamed by in the mystic
space that he more and more inhabited. Once that space had
been like a magic land, to be entered rarely and with astonished
thanksgiving. But for years now it had been entering *him* and
taking over his life. Now every day and all day he lived with
one eye in that divine country. He was at his most open to this
infinite cosmic wind when flying, but these days he could feel
the divine neutrinos pass through him at almost any time he
chose. The God of the Galaxy directed him — how otherwise
could his movement of the Spirit have grown so swiftly?

Of course, his wings at any time might lose the Spirit's wind. Indulgence of the body could make him tumble physically and spiritually. He had had to lose physical weight to fly so high. He was thin now. He had curbed all his bodily appetites. Especially sex. Osen was right. Psi was not dependable for the noisomely sexual. The wraiths were right. Sex and the Spirit were opposites. The Space Code had unwittingly been right, though with its typical failure to ask the highest of humanity, it had merely confined sex to the softroom. For himself (and for the elite among his followers) sex was something to be given up entirely. No doubt sex had its place on Gaia's planet. Sex might even be Gaia's truest expression, as when Mana had reached into his fog of confusion and plucked him out. It had been the only way the Spirit of the God could reach him. But away from Gaia, sex merely distracted him from the Spirit. It tied him down to the ugly planet, riveted his eyes on the dried bloodstains of the oxidized iron of its empty canyons. One day he would leave this planet and return permanently to space, his first and true home.

Since that seminal day when he had almost killed Gauri and endangered the station in his wild passion, much had changed in Govind. He had reached beyond Gaia. He had gone beyond Osen's lessons. It would not be true to say that he hated Gauri for what had happened. She was just a human being, and Govind understood the Galaxy loved its humans and wanted them to rise. But he hated the planet-bound beast in her and in himself, the human animal from Earth that had emerged, exposed by the lust she engendered in him. The beast drawn out by lust, as a hyena is drawn by offal and death. It had emerged so much more powerfully that one time than in all the softroom encounters of the years. In the softroom his mind had always been detached. But with her, passion had blotted out his higher faculties. He had been blind. Just for a short time, but long enough to endanger the whole station. The wraiths were right. Sex blinds people.

He was opening the spiritual mind in himself and in his followers. Elements of it were available to all, he was certain of that. Even to Space Marshal Mqrisi, Govind's patron and the head of the military on Karp. That was a miracle in itself, a divine intervention. Imagine the military led by one who was alert to the divine wind. Imagine thousands of officers and soldiers living by the precepts of the Spirit. The whole Galaxy could be led away from those ersatz imitations of chastity and

God — the softroom and MAN — and upward to transcendent purity.

Sometimes he could even tune in to the wraithmind itself. Sometimes he caught what the wraiths up on the four great or-biting stations above Karp were thinking. He had persuaded Mqrisi to let some of his followers take their new spiritual com-munity to one of the stations. They had befriended the wraiths there. They had brought them in to society, treated them with respect for the first time anywhere. All with Mqrisi's blessing. And now the wraiths sometimes let him hear their thoughts.

As he thought of them, near the apex of his flight, they came through. *Govind-Havu, Mana is coming,* they called to him, *Mana is on her way to Karp Station Three. She goes on to Sky. The breeders on Sky revolt, as in the days of Martin. They re-volt and Sky asks for reinforcements from Karp. We are to send Mqrisi's riot team. Please, do not let them shed blood as in the old days. It is not the time. May the Light be with you.*

Govind turned at once to the neutrinos of his God, the cos-mic particles that left their tracks in his soul. He listened for God's voice. 'You must go to Sky,' the divine wind said. 'Gauri is on Sky.' It was a completely unexpected thought. He had heard nothing of Gauri in seven years. And then the wind said: 'Mqrisi will burn his past. He will join you.'

He floated a few seconds more, praising God, and then he dived.

At the landing field, the flying instructors and their pupils looked on with delight and awe, respectively, as he shrugged out of his wings.

"That was one incredible dive, and from so high!" enthused a middle-aged woman. His mind was on Mqrisi, but the author-ity in the woman's face gave him pause. You never knew when an important person from another planet might be visiting, risk-ing oxygen conflagration for the thrill of flight.

"I fly to get beyond the everyday," he said to her. "I find peace and direction in silence. You need that. It would help you." It just came out. And there was more. "The Galaxy can speak to you directly. You're an over-anxious person. You need help."

The more he allowed himself to float in that realm of the divine wind, the more unexpected were his insights and the things he would say. As he said it, searching back through his memories of news holies, he recognized her — Harmul, Chairperson of Madlarki Station.

A thousand-but-one times out of a thousand, a comment like that to a toughened bureaucrat would have got him an angry direction to go to MAN and a complaint to his superior officer.

But she said simply, "I know. But how do you know?"

"God told me. God can speak to you, too. Come." He took her by the elbow. "Meet my friend here. Hey's one of the flying instructors, and hey knows all about this experience." He introduced them, and then ran across the rocks in his soft rubber boots to his speedcraft.

On the way back to barracks, he thought briefly about Harmul. Frogs and toads had spilled out of her mouth when she had congratulated him. It was an important lesson learned so many times over: to be open to the divine wind and not to judge according to his strange talent for seeing speech. If he had thought only of how unpleasant her speech was, he would never have reached her. That's what had caused his neglect of Mana through all his formative years: the dead flowers in her mouth. He had finally learned to see such things as evidence of pain and need, not as cause for dislike. A new surge of energy powered through him. It was good work to reach the head of Madlarki Station by "accident." Except with God there were no accidents. Maybe this meant Madlarki was the right direction to go next. The Govindis would one day spread through all the planets of the Collectivity. The Divine wind had promised him that. They would remake the Galaxy.

He zipped the craft into the airlock at HQ, and did not neglect to give a word of thanks and encouragement to the ground crew as he ran from them to the elevators. Being respectful to every soul was important.

Down a hundred floors in a swoop. Civilization was below ground on fortress Karp. He felt the glow of joyful power and powerful joy as he burst into the Govindi HQ. Fine-looking young people were relaxing in sober talk at the tables. Some newcomers were being ushered into a meeting. Others were going down to the personal-talk rooms.

With a brief annoyance, he noticed on the left wall a holieview of a crashing waterfall that simply did not match the mood of the room — it may have been perfect an hour ago, but the mood was more toward space views, planets, asteroids, now; anyone with their antennae out could see that. A quick word brought one of the more responsible types over to see to it.

Of course, half a dozen other people then rushed up to him to ask his opinion on something or other, anything from their personal problems to what color the Govindi Flying Team suits should be.

He bawled out this last one, "For the love of Karp, don't trouble me with these idiotic requests. Ask the Spirit yourself!" But he had just the right word for a young woman who was troubled by a certain sexual problem. He had been thinking about her on yesterday's flight. "Don't worry about it," he said. "Just relax with the Spirit. Think about other people's needs, and the Spirit will take care of it. God loves you." With someone else, he might have told them to go and desist from doing it again. It all depended on the individual, and what the divine wind indicated for them.

Still, it was annoying how many of the requests were trivial. "Is this graphic all right for our talk to the gun crews?" "Should we remove the word 'alien' from this speech you made last month?" People didn't seem to want to act on their own initiative. There was altogether too much deference to him. Years back, when they had started calling the Spirit's followers Govindis, he had been distressed. A false modesty had whispered to him that he was unworthy of becoming the human figurehead and leader that the movement needed. But he had painfully come to accept that this modesty was in fact arrogance, a base self-centeredness, a flouting of the divine plan. Who was he to question the All Knowing's choice of himself?

He had long since left that petty self-centeredness behind. Indeed, he had little consciousness of himself left. Like a champion in the asteroid spin finals, or a tumbler in the gyrosphere, he was totally subsumed into his task. If only others would rise to the same level! Then he could truly share the leadership. There was too much deference. How would they cope if he went to Madlarki Station for a year or so? And then on to Tarcuna?

As he passed the music room, shaking off persistent followers in his attempt to gain the sanctuary of his inviolate chapel, he knew a familiar stabbing pain down his left side. He had unthinkingly looked in to see if Shehrinaz was standing there, teaching the choir, or lost in the sweet phrases of her lute. He felt a tear prick his eye, self-pity let in by the music room door. Right there, in the middle of the passage, he had to stop as he had had to so many times in the past year, offer his sense of hurt back to the Great Spirit, and ask for his usual blessed lack of self-centeredness to be returned to him.

It came with a sense of peace and he could think about her clearly again. Shehrinaz, the intellectual musician, whose burning had so transformed her that she had been led from arid experimentalism to compose music that was the very pain and joy of divine fire.

Shehrinaz could have shared the leadership with him. But she had gone. Like a handful of others before her, she had allowed personal bitterness at the leading role that the Great Spirit asked Govind to play to sour their friendship. If he, Govind, had learned the humility to accept his role as leader, why could she not have? If she had, she could have been the real equal in responsibility he longed for. Paradoxically, if she had surrendered her resentment at his leadership, she would have been ready to be chosen and used by the All Knowing as an equal leader herself. Leadership in this battle, after all, went to the spiritually worthy, not to the intellectually brilliant or the strong. The Spirit had given her every chance to accept gracefully. But she had caviled about plans, about strategy, about his rejection of her grotesque physical advances, about that devilish red herring of the wraiths, their seductive Liquid Light. That was something he had become clear about. He was not a Gaian, worshiping the planet and its earthly sexual power. But nor was he a wraith, with their passive immersion in meditative trance. He had found the God of the Galaxy, the God of the humans, the God of history, the God with a plan.

Once Shehrinaz had sung in this very music room of the burning of the egg, of communing with friends, of throwing yourself on the solar winds of faith. Now she played to others, and for a lesser, easier, more selfish vision of the divine. The Liquid Light folk lived only for a warm internal glow. They rejected this Galaxy's problems. Only the individual counted for them. They sank into mysticism. While we struggle to save the Galaxy from riot and corruption and collapse, Govind thought. The stasis and inhumanity of MAN and the Space Code will reap their whirlwind — people cannot be kept from God and each other forever. Mqrisi sees it coming — the anarchy let loose

by Martin of Arable and Xidas and their descendants: material-
ists, power mongers, dynasts, cousins to Osen's kings. If we fail,
and this civilization goes supernova, Shehrinaz and her friends
will die singing of the Light. I'd rather save us all. We have so
little time to replace MAN and the Code with something real
and God-led, the friendship and fellowship of a band of broth-
ers.

Calm again, he heard what one of his people was trying to
say to him: "Mqrisi wants you. Right away. He's taking a riot
squad to Sky. He wants you to go with him."

"The Lord told me that he would," said Govind. "That's
why I rushed back."

They shook their heads in wonder, and stared at the whirlwind of his departing form with awe. He was always a step ahead
of them. He had a hotline to God.

On the run in to Karp, Mana could not contain her excitement.
She couldn't stop speculating about Govind: what he might not
have achieved in seven years! There had been the rumors. But
the military high-ups who were joining Rocco's ship at Karp
would give her the first real facts.

Passarin watched her with a sense of annoyance. Govind had
been a conceited prick.

José confined himself to his cabin and would not come out. The
thought of catching a single glimpse of his son and daughter-by-
marriage nauseated him. It had been a desire to live beyond
eighty that had brought him, and curiosity about Starlight. Plus
the fact that Mana had been so determined to see Gauri that he
feared she might go to Sky and then Starlight on her own. Rocco
had made conciliatory gestures. But Rocco's ship had spoken
louder to his father than his gestures.

When they had come on board at Madlarki Station, the familiar old freighter had been unrecognizable to José. The outside was painted gleaming black, with skull and crossbones above
the door. Inside, the scruffy, worn surfaces and utilitarian solidity had gone. Entering the ship was like stepping into a pirate
cave in a softroom. The walls and ceilings were black velvet.
Deep purple carpets muffled the steps of the stewards, who were
dressed in Rocco's eclectic idea of pirate costume: eye patches,

parrots, blackened and crooked teeth, Starlight-like insignia, antique submachine guns. Dim lights made the hanging jewels, the gold doubloons, the necklaces of pearl and iridescent Arabelian gemfish that dripped from walls and ceilings gleam like hidden treasure. When Rocco ushered him into certain deep black alcoves, the walls burst to life with sea holies: an ancient pirate corsair in full sail beat through the Caribbean with the pirate flag at the mast. Pigtailed pirates clustered round a hookah on the fo'c'sl while the lookout in the crow's nest radioed down that he'd spied a distant Spanish junk covered in crosses and crescents and laden with gold. The face of the naked-breasted figurehead on the holie corsair's prow bore a striking resemblance to Jiang the Fang. Rocco himself, in real life, was dressed more outrageously than ever, with a gleaming metal hook where his left hand used to be.

José found it all unbearably fake.

Passarin thought it fun, but was mildly surprised that everyone still had their clothes on.

So José stayed in his cabin.

But Mana and Passarin went to the bar, which they had all to themselves on the run in to Karp. Passarin watched the brown treasure-chest-shaped ice cubes clink together in the fruit punch, while Mana rattled on about the mission Osen had entrusted her with, to educate her son and get him to the Center of the Galaxy. Would he have studied Osen's Chronicles enough? she asked him. On Terra Station, she had made Govind enter the entire four volumes on his wrist unit, one of the best things she ever did. But would he have taken to heart the ancient stories Osen told in the Chronicles from the days of the Sky Gods? Of Paul reaching the Center of his day in chains, as Rocco delivered Govind to Karp? Of Joseph, who rose from prison to be Pharaoh's chief minister just by the interpretation of dreams? Govind might not interpret dreams, but he could see speech. Would he remember about Ricci and the Chinese court? Ricci, sent from Rome in priest's black, had finally taken the glory of a mandarin's robes and dazzled the court with his clock making, his translations of his message into Chinese concepts and calligraphy. Govind would have no pope to frustrate him on the edge of victory, to force him back into priest's black and Latin scriptures and so lose everything. She herself was Govind's only mentor left alive; if Govind had taken the military uniform, for example, to reach the military, she would not object — whatever private nightmares from Terran history it might give her. Would he know, she asked Passarin, whose glass was already empty, about White Elk and Chiucoatl, who had led the Californians back from the poisoning of their beautiful land and the mad embrace of Armageddon by their prophets of the Second Coming, to the feet of the world parents? to sky father and earth mother joined in cosmic coitus, and Coyote laughing all the way from the bank, which he had just robbed?

"Some of the stories sound too bizarre to be true," she confessed. "Do you think he's really studied them? He might go off half cocked," she giggled.

"Mana, you're acting like a Starlight girl on a date."

"Oh, big, serious Passarin, the academic. The skeptic. Doesn't think Gaia can use a crazy boy like Govind to tweak the beaks of the eagles of Karp!"

"I've never seen you like this before. You've got to prepare yourself for the possibility that we may hear no news of Govind at all. Or he may have a nice little cult going. But the military's huge! I've been reading about them in my Martin research. There are four massive stations circling Karp, all full of wraiths and warships. The idea is to be ready for an alien invasion. Aliens are about the only thing that could make the Migration fail now. But they've got nothing to do from day to day. They'd just love a chance to blow up a city of humans. I should know — they blew up ours, on my home planet. You should see what radiation does, Mana. Then you wouldn't be so happy to see Govind in uniform."

Mana got a glimpse of the military power of Karp when they docked at Karp Three. The previous time she had come through, she and José had found themselves beating on their locked cabin door, suddenly terrified. This time she went out of the airlock into the station.

Karp Three was no little spacewheel — it was a colossal cylinder inside which dozens of Terra Stations could have spun. It was like a planet inside out: she could gaze straight up across the smoggy core of this planet and there, miles away, were the grimy buildings and factories and aircars on the other side apparently hanging upside down above her head; all of them were pressed as she was to the inner surface of the cylinder by the speed of its spin.

On the ship's screens coming in, Karp Three had looked like a massive spider in a web. The web was thousands of square miles of solar mesh laid out to catch the rays of Karp Sun and laser it down to smelters on planet. The cylindrical station spun at the center of the static mesh. Inside, all was grim industry, shipyards, unpainted metal and clanging noise, welding arcs, rivet guns, and hurrying uniforms. Soldiers were everywhere.

But the most extraordinary fact for Mana was that there was wind. It carried distant sounds and smells. She was transfixed, for she had experienced no wind-borne hints in all the years since Earth. She sniffed for forest echoes, or promise of rain. But all was harsh and chemical, burning metals and smog.

Then the uniforms descended on her and Passarin, and hustled them back into the ship. The top brass were coming aboard.

Govind had thought he knew Space Marshal Mqrisi, his patron and the best hope of the Spirit on Karp. But he had never seen him in a military crisis before.

When he entered Mqrisi's operations room, people were running scared. Mqrisi liked to deal face-to-face. It was typical of his style. He wore the plainest fatigues in the entire Karp military. His shoulder bore only one small SM to indicate that the entire military was his to command.

But now his plain brown features, which surely he would have liked to look as cool as his uniform, were flushed and distended. Veins bulged on his forehead. Temples visibly pulsed. A brief look was enough to reveal to Govind that this was no ineffectual bluster. This was an intensity that expected and received immediate obedience.

Govind was familiar with the peacetime Mqrisi: the traditionalist who all too easily felt lost in trying to deal with the corrupting modern age. Mqrisi had no idea what to do when his generals went off for two weeks of debauchery on Sky, when his young gene-designed soldiers failed to volunteer for extra training, when even his own Starines ("We need a few good persons," he had instructed the gene labs) looked less than interested in the alien menace. The fact that there were no threatening aliens yet, he told them, did not mean that there might not be some at any moment as the Collectivity pushed farther into the Galaxy.

There were laws he could invoke against these subtle forms of slackness, but damned politics prevented him from invoking them as he would have liked. The wretched family debaucheries — senior military officers coupling off to have children! — had protection from Tarcuna. To stop them would lead to cut offs in funding and other more subtle insults. To really clean up the military, he would have to delve into political negotiations with his superiors on Tarcuna, the administrative capital of the Collectivity and fount of all tax moneys. "And, MAN knows, *they* are the most corrupt of the lot!" he had said more than once to Govind.

"The truth is," Mqrisi would conclude, "the MAN system is breaking down. First the elites, now the soldiers, next the populace." He had been predicting a new wave of popular revolts or social breakdowns for years now. Govind thought Mqrisi would be furious that it had happened on Sky, the planet most influenced by his officers' debauchery. It was also certain to enrage him that the revolt appeared to be already two weeks old, and Sky had only sent for help when the imminent arrival of the Karp officers meant they could not cover it up any longer.

And indeed Mqrisi was furious. But he also had a gleam in his eye. His aides ran scared, his forehead veins bulged, but he winked at Govind when he saw him standing by. The man was enjoying himself.

Action, at last.

Riot squad!

Space Marshal Mqrisi was a compact, self-contained man. He was not tall, but he dominated by force of character and hard work. He was a military man, not a damned psychologist. He had become dependent on Govind for guidance in the murky waters of mass psychology these last years. Initially he had just liked the look of the players who had gathered around the young spin star from Terra Station. He had noticed them when they started beating the fatigues off all the well known military teams. He had liked their clean-cut optimism, even the way they laughed and talked with each other. It wasn't orthodox: too much intimacy. But it was attractive. They had dynamism. They won. They couldn't be bribed to fix a game — he tried. He took them onto his staff. He got them to take over morale training for his select troops and riot squads.

"No funny stuff, you understand," he had instructed them. But it had become clear to Mqrisi that it was the "funny stuff" that was the real heart of this new morale. Only the growing band of fully committed Govindis had it. *Egg burning,* Govind had explained, *mutual confession and intimacy, listening for the solar wind of the Great Spirit.*

It was not Mqrisi's sort of thing at all.

But Mqrisi knew that his greatest disadvantage in dealing with his slack and corrupt soldiers, or with his political enemies on Tarcuna and their allies on Karp, was his predictability. A predictable enemy is an easy target. Perhaps, just perhaps, trying this way of the Govindis would give him the utterly unpredictable edge he needed. Do something outrageous and more modern than all the rest put together.

Govind had seen this train of thought grow in the space marshal over the years. Every psi synapse of his brain told him that this trip to Sky would see its culmination. Mqrisi was about to burn his egg.

But first, there was a military crisis, and Mqrisi was a different man. Detailed orders fired from his brain so fast that Govind found himself on the shuttle up to Karp One before he had even had time to tell his followers he was going. He was sucked in Mqrisi's wake out into the great military space station and past a bewildering display of ferocious hardware onto the riot squad starship. He walked behind the great man and half a dozen aides as Mqrisi reviewed the troops, and was astonished to find that each face was well-known to him, for every one of them was a full-blown Govindi.

Then the aides had peeled off and he was alone with Mqrisi on another dash across Karp One in a zippy aircar to the shuttle bays. "Where now, sir?" he asked.

"We are going" — Mqrisi appeared to notice him for the first time since the wink — "to travel with your old friend Rocco to see just what it is that these good officers of mine get up to on their trips to Sky." The tense muscles in the space marshal's jaw seemed to Govind to bode ill for the said officers. "No need for them to know that the riot squad is on its way," Mqrisi added. "That's orders. Understand? Don't tell 'em. They think they are on one of their normal jaunts."

They boarded the shuttle that would take them from this space station to the next, and were slammed back into their seats at once as its drive rocketed them out into space. When Mqrisi hurried, things went fast.

Govind watched the disk of the rust-red planet from the shuttle windows and pondered the supreme effort that it must have been for Mqrisi to let his riot squad leave without him, and to enter alone, with one unorthodox leader of a religious cult, the sanctum of his juniors and malcontents. The old surges ran through his body. "Now!" he exulted. "Now!" The inner ear that he turned always to the divine wind was for a moment deafened by the surging of his blood.

Mana sat at the back of Rocco's bar. She watched the top brass of Karp joke, slap backs, swig drinks forbidden to the populace, and even here and there kiss each other on the cheek. They were still docked at Karp Three, but already they were starting to relax in ways they had learned from Jiang and Rocco, the bearers of Tarcunan decadence. Jiang herself moved among them, welcoming with hugs and kisses, an elegant pirate queen bearing subversive gifts.

Mana could tell the old hands at Jiang and Rocco's Family Cruises from the new ones. The new joked nervously about pretty much everything. The typical old hand was a cross between an elegant sophisticate and a six-year-old on a treat. No one seemed to be aware that they were going to a riot zone. She wondered for the first time if Passarin and Starlight had got their facts straight.

She was taking her time deciding whom to approach to ask about Govind when suddenly everyone hushed.

An older man had entered the bar. His fatigues were a conspicuously unadorned military cut. But it was his face that drew attention: the furious eyes, the grim mouth, the slow gaze that inexorably identified every face and killed every smile. She noted the barely perceptible widening of his eyes as they focused on her, and was surprised at the adrenaline rush of fear and anger in her when he did. The man turned to beckon a uniformed aide behind him, and to whisper in his ear.

The aide was Govind.

She rose to her feet. He was coming toward her, spare and dynamic in the crowd of petrified revelers. It was as if he had looked for her and found her way at the back almost before she'd seen him — which was impossible, she had watched him walk in.

But he looked so much older! The intense eyes, dark skin, black curls — these were all the Govind she knew. But this Govind was lean. His hair was not gray, nor his face lined in the least. He was only twenty-nine, of course, not like herself, gray and wrinkled like an old woman at forty-six. It was other things that made him look old. She had called him an overgrown puppy once, in one of his crazes, and that was the image that had stayed with her. On Terra Station he had bounced around on big feet: a mutant puppy who had not yet found the mighty astral hound within him.

He was that hound now.

He attended to each person he brushed past, all senior officers and most twice his age. He calmly greeted them and moved on, and she noticed how they did not meet his eyes. He had power, and in some way of his own, not just by reflection from the fearsome older man. He reached her.

"Govind!"

"Mana." There was no surprise in his voice.

She embraced him. He was taut and unresponsive. So in this crowd, she thought, he doesn't want to overstep decorum. She stepped back. Everyone in the room was covertly looking at them. The furious older man had moved on.

"You're not plump anymore." She grinned at him, and patted his stomach. It was hard.

"What are you doing here?" he asked under his breath.

"To see Gauri. She's on Sky. She's . . . I'll tell you later. You look great." She patted his stomach again, trying to establish intimacy by being rude in the way that only an old friend can.

"Marvelous that you're here," he said with a heartiness that made her heart curl. "Great timing. Mqrisi wants to see you. In an hour, in cabin thirty-three. Then you and I can talk after. It's so wonderful that you're here." He gripped her arm powerfully and then he was off again.

"Who wants to see me?" she asked faintly, too late.

"Well, young man. You saw them all nuzzling up to each other in there. If I could I would cashier every one of them. But Tarcuna won't let me. What in all the Galaxy am I going to do?" Mqrisi sat round-shouldered on his bunk. All his dynamism had dissolved at the sight of that bar full of corrupted officers.

Govind held his counsel. His thoughts were full of Mana's presence . . . and she said Gauri was indeed on Sky, as the Spirit had told him she would be. What was the Lord planning?

"Are you going to tell me to be MAN to them? Have them in here one by one and ask them what their private fantasies are? Get them blubbing on my shoulder?"

Govind smiled at the idea.

"Advice, boy. We've got four days on this fancy flying soft-room."

Rocco had kicked someone out of this small cabin on short notice. Mqrisi and his aide would have to share its puce velvet and hanging jewels for the duration. Mqrisi had insisted on it — no special favors for his rank.

Inspiration led Govind's fingers to pick at the edges of the velvet on the walls. It started to come up. He ripped a whole swath of it off and revealed the old metal underneath. Mqrisi whooped like a cadet and followed suit. The space marshal leapt on the bed and yanked down gold necklaces and baubles from the ceiling. In half an hour they were dripping with sweat and the floor was ankle-deep in puce velvet rippings and gold jewelry. Mqrisi grabbed Govind by the shoulders and they jumped up and down together, yelling like crazy men.

When Mqrisi collapsed onto his bunk this time, he looked ready to attack the whole ship in whatever way it took.

Now? Govind asked his cosmic mentor. Suggest now that he get rid of MAN forever? Not yet, came the elusive wind, play the trout, wait, don't forget Mana, Gauri. Gauri is on Sky. She could help Mqrisi. Expect My connections to be unexpected.

"I have an idea for a new approach to the revolt on Sky, sir," Govind said.

"The breeders? Simple. Piece of cake. That I can deal with — it's these degenerates I need your input on."

"I know one of the Sky breeders, sir. Hey's a Govindi. Hey could provide a key to understand the degenerates *and* the rebel breeders."

"So you see a connection between the revolt and my corrupt officers? Any evidence?"

Govind shrugged. "Not yet, sir. My contact there might have it."

"A Tarcunan conspiracy, I suppose. What's it aimed at — my downfall? Are this Rocco and Jiang pair involved? Lousy intelligence I get — I no longer trust the MAN reports from Madlarki — bunch of weirdoes. Your lot are the only ones I trust. A Govindi breeder, eh? Right in the thick of it. Good work, my boy. Hey'll tell us something. Your people certainly get around. This Mana person — recognized hem at once from your file. Striking face. What's hey doing here?"

"We'll find out, sir."

"Gave you a hug in the bar."

"It's the Terran way."

"Lives with Rocco's father."

"You've been doing some research, sir."

"Known all about you from the first. You are on the level. I know that. But what are your friends up to? Rocco know this Govindi breeder on Sky?"

"Well, hey isn't exactly a Govindi, sir. Hey's from my youth on Terra Station. But I can vouch for her absolutely. I can assure you, there's no love lost between hem and Rocco. Rocco and Jiang kidnapped hem as they did me."

Mqrisi silently consulted his wrist unit. "Name of Gauri. Correct?" Govind nodded. "Does not solve my problem — what to do with these people here."

"They need a demonstration of a better way to live — not the old way and not the way they are going now. Even they must understand this family elitism will lead to dynasties, in the end to wars, breakdown. They need something else that's exciting and at the same time more fulfilling."

"Bored soldiers — they would love a few wars." Mqrisi looked glumly into his hands. "You want me to demonstrate this new life. Become a Govindi?"

"You are planning to kill all the breeders on Sky, sir, not just the rebels, but the other breeders too. This is overkill, sir. It is not right."

Mqrisi looked slowly up at Govind. He stared at him for long, drawn-out seconds. "How did you know what I planned to do? I told nobody. Nobody."

"God tells me these things, sir. But as soon as God told me I knew in my heart it was true, just by looking at you. You are full of hatred and anger and helplessness. It won't solve anything."

"Hit them hard. Discourage the others."

"You have to learn to win people over, not terrify and sub-due them."

"Too difficult. Takes too long."

"Then I'll leave." Govind got up and walked to the door. He opened it, walked through, and had pulled it shut before he heard the bellow.

"Young man!"

Govind went back inside.

"I'll give you two days when we reach Sky. Two days to use your Govindi breeder to win over the rebels."

"No, sir. It's not up to me. It's you that has to be seen to be different."

"Huh," Mqrisi snorted.

Govind opened the door again to leave. He knew he risked everything. But the Spirit led where it would.

This time before he stepped out Mqrisi asked, "What do you want me to do?"

"It's not what I want, sir. It's what the Great Spirit wants. You have to open yourself to Him."

"It's irrational."

Govind remained silent, one hand on the door.

"All right. I will do it. If truth be known, it is what I have wanted ever since I saw you with your spin team seven years ago."

There was a rap on the door. Govind wondered whether to open it or not. He realized that for this moment in this room with Mqrisi, he was in charge. His inner voice seemed to say yes, open it. He opened it.

It was Mana.

"Come in," said Mqrisi. "You are just in time to introduce me to your god."

"He was quite sincere," said Mana afterward to Govind when they were back in her cabin. José lay on the lower bunk, like an old man on the sidelines. "At first he seemed so rational as if it was a scientific experiment. But he confessed real stuff — all that paranoia and back-stabbing. He wept a tear. He burned the egg. He meant it. Who is he?"

"He is only the most powerful man on Karp. Perhaps, if he only knew it and believed it, the most powerful man in the whole Galaxy."

"Dear Mother." Tears welled in Mana's eyes. She leaned forward to touch Govind, as if to reassure herself that he was real. "Osen's child. Can the warming of the Earth be far away now? I did not believe you, Osen. But I have lived to see it." She went over to the tiny cabin table, which she had arranged as an altar. She took the bowl in the center and came back, and sprinkled water from it onto Govind's head "May the blessing of Gaia be upon you."

As her two tears fell, she said, "Now, Govind, tell me the story. How this great man got interested. Is it Joseph and Pharaoh? Did you tell him what came out of his mouth?"

"He got interested the first year, when there were only half a dozen of us."

"Only," Mana sighed.

He told her about how Mqrisi got the spin team to lead morale training for the troops.

"He wanted his entire army to burn their eggs?"

"No, no. At first he just wanted our teamwork and idealism without that sort of radicalism. So we gave bland lectures about serving the Galaxy to the troops — thousands and thousands of troops. We never mentioned Gaia or criticized the egg.

"But we always gave the lectures as a group of between three and five. We would each chip in, or act out little scenes together, and generally support each other. We made the way that we did it a demonstration of the relationships that only egg burners have.

"Hardened old pilots, ancient vets of the Starlight raids even, but mainly young squaddies — in ones and twos they'd come up afterward and ask if they could help the team give the lectures, in some practical way, perhaps. That was always the way they showed they wanted those relationships too. We probably recruited two hundred fifty in the first two years."

"Two hundred fifty — that's amazing."

"That's when he gave us our headquarters — lecture rooms, chapel, personal-talks rooms. Now we do morale for all the land-based troops and one space station. As of 0800 hours this morning" — Govind checked his wrist unit — "there were 3,047 who had burned the egg. Mqrisi makes that 3,048."

Mana gasped.

"Imagine, Mana, what would happen with ten thousand. What if the top officers, instead of coming on these cruises,

TO WARM THE EARTH

were going to Terra Station so that Vladimir and the others could show them what a station run on Gaian principles is like? If the Gaians are still doing it there, that is. What if we had one of Karp's space stations run entirely by soldiers directed by God? I have no idea why the Sky breeders have revolted. But suppose their needs were taken care of, because Sky First Committee had all burned the egg and started to listen to other people?"

"I can't believe it. It's actually happening."

"What if the Tarcunan dynasties made the Great Spirit their family head? We must plan practically for Madlarki, and Tarcuna. I think we should try Madlarki first. That's why it's so marvelous to have you here. We can plan it together. Do you know Harmul?"

"The old battle-axe who runs Madlarki Station? No, and I've no desire to."

"A shame. She's interested. She's ready. How is your work? How many are there in your group?"

"I don't know what to say, Govind, I don't know what to say. You make me feel such a complete failure. My team is myself and José and half a dozen puffrats in a cage — though, of course, José doesn't really believe in the Goddess, not as a living, transforming reality. And probably the puffrats don't, either."

Govind stared at her for a moment, and then laughed heartily, a laugh cut off abruptly as he seemed to cock an ear to listen to something. "That time you gave me the vision of Gaia — in the spin room. *That* time you were a fish swimming in the cosmic sea, but the rest of the time you're a fish out of water, Mana. Haven't you understood? You are out of touch with your Goddess because She is on Earth! You need to know the God of the Galaxy, the Great Spirit Himself. Just listen for His words inside you, Mana, and obey Him, and you will find yourself again."

Passarin spent that night on José and Mana's floor. He had lost his own cabin, kicked out to make way for Mqrisi's sudden arrival. He had asked José to record Govind and Mana's conversations, for his history of Mana. Lying in an emergency crew sleeping bag on the floor he played back the conversation quietly when they slept.

*"Just listen for His words inside you, Mana, and obey Him,"* Govind said. He knew enough about Mana now to know how frightened that would have made her.

It was a long conversation. Govind had told Mana stories of his clairvoyance and character insight and conversions. They were astonishing. His inspiration with Harmul at the flying field was the least of it. He knew things about people that they had told no one, sometimes things they didn't even know themselves. He turned up at times and places just when a person was in trouble and needed help.

Passarin believed the stories. He'd heard of similar things before. His father had done some things like that, and so had his friend Keung, who was the leader of the Joyful Sons and Daughters of God. Then Starlight was full of psychic stuff and people with curious abilities and even more curious beliefs. But Govind was clearly convinced that his miracles gave him privileged insight into the nature of the universe. He told the stories as if they proved that his Great Spirit existed and had the perfect plan for everyone else's life. All the antagonism that Passarin had ever felt for the God Giver of Arable Two, his father, started to well up from its buried deeps. His father had pulled the same scam. He had used the same utter sincerity, the same clairvoyance and other psi gimmicks, the same insight into the personalities of others to cajole, persuade, dazzle, frighten, forgive, bully, and ease them into his fold. Just a different theology. The same experiences had been used as proof of a different god. And how was Govind ever going to prove that his god would not turn as vindictive as the God Giver's, which had turned on the sentient beings that had lived for eons on Arable Two before humans ever came there? What would Govind do to Gauri if she tried to stand up to him now, in the way she had in that fateful bacteria lab on Terra Station? People who believed like that could do anything.

Passarin could not sleep. Instead, he spun scenarios for their arrival on Sky, and the only realistic ones involved his pleading and bullying the Starlight people to get Gauri out of there fast. The less realistic ones, the ones that came as he drifted finally into ragged sleep involved blazing laser guns and dying gods, himself an angel from the Temple descending to snatch Gauri away to a fairer land while Govind and Mqrisi impotently threatened him with a thousand years in hell.

Jiang was furious and Rocco quite bemused to watch their ship in four days turn from a pirate corsair into an interstellar tent meeting. Mqrisi testified in the bar, Govind witnessed in the dining room, and new converts confessed and opened their hearts to the Great Spirit in all the odd velvet alcoves of the ship. Numerous cabins were vandalized and piles of velvet strippings and gold baubles fetched up in the trash. It was a profound relief when they finally docked at Sky Station. José winked at his son as he left.

# *Four*

Gauri lay still and waited for inspiration. The wheel had come full circle. It was her turn again.

Twelve out of the thirteen who had taken over the gene labs lay on their backs, with their feet forming the hub of a wheel. Their outstretched arms and joined hands formed the rim. They had had to move heavy counters and equipment to make enough space on the lab floor. The thirteenth sat by the ventilation outtake, one hand on the virus culture, ready to throw its contents to the winds. Air circulation was crucial to the entirely enclosed habitat, and it seemed, so far, as if it was impossible to shut down the vents to this room from outside the room. At least, the air kept circulating. Pure dumb luck. So one of them always sat by the air outtake with mass death in hand.

The seven hostage gene techs sat hunched up in the corner. Their arms were bound and their mouths gagged. It was easier to forget about them that way, in between tending to them when the station brought them food. Sometimes they had tried to get them to discuss the big questions. But the poor techs were too scared. It was easy to forget how liberated the breeders had become from all those tight-assed ways of thinking and being.

Gauri could not remember now whose idea it had been to form a wheel. As soon as they had done it the first time, they had felt better. All but two of them had been born on spacewheels, in gene labs very like this one. The only difference down on planet here was that when people stood up straight next to each other their heads were farther away from each other, by the minutest fraction, than when they stood on the inside of a whirling metal wheel and all their heads pointed to the hub and so were nearer to each other by a fraction; also, if you threw something a long way here, it didn't curve the way it did in space, pulled by the Coriolis force within the spinning wheel. Big deal. Plus, of course, this fact: on their home wheels, there hadn't been any breeders. Not one of them had been gene-designed to be a breeder. They were all 'volunteers.'

The first time they had lain on the ground as a wheel, Gauri had started one of the rolling chants Mana used to sing from her Caves:

"Cave Dark Night / Dark Night Owl / Night Owl Hunt / Owl Hunt Cry / Hunt Cry Sing / Cry Sing Lullaby / Sing Lullaby Sleep / Lullaby Sleep Cave / Sleep Cave Dark / Cave Dark Night"

When they had sung it together a few times and felt its comfort, and knew it by heart, they changed to saying a phrase each in turn around the wheel. They listened to the difference in their voices. On one of her turns, Kumtacj grunted, "Lullaby Sleep Death." There was a pause. She had changed the words. "Sleep Death Recycled," said her neighbor. "Death Recycled Desire" was the next. "Recycled Desire Truth," it went on. "Desire Truth Unknowable / Truth Unknowable Ecstasy / Unknowable Ecstasy Beyond / Ecstasy Beyond . . . this is so weird!" said the woman whose turn it was. "These are all nothings, they are all — what's the word?"

"Abstract?" asked Gauri.

"Abstract. Concepts. The other one was all owls and caves and doings, like crying."

"But that's space for you," said another. "There are no good things."

"No, it's us, not space. Before I came here to be a breeder, my life was all good things — food, fatigues, showers, the egg, sex, protein cultures, fruit sacs — I was in food processing. It's only breeders who talk about love and ingratitude."

Everyone started to object at once:

"If your things were so good, why did you 'volunteer'?" That drew a laugh. Some had genuinely volunteered, but with no idea of how brutal the breeder's life would be.

"It's because the things we have in space are so boring that we dream of ecstasy and truth."

"How can we love the things we have here? There aren't any owls or lullabies or caves, not real ones made of rock. My mother was a gene lab."

"Let's thank Mother," bellowed Kumtacj.

Kumtacj lumbered to her feet and went around to all the different parts of the lab and said, "Thank you, Mother," holding up a container of chemicals. "Thank you, Mother," peering into the gestation tank. "Thank you, Mother," and the more she did it the more they laughed. Her great face was so solemn.

"Isn't the Goddess truth and beauty and love, Gauri?" Bridget asked.

"No! She isn't abstract! The Goddess is damp earth, and apple trees," Gauri said, certain of herself, though she had never touched or smelt either. "She is the worm in the apple, and She is rock, and . . . and labor pains, and babies, and these smiles we have for each other, and the strength with which we are fighting this robot that's at our throats. You want to see the Goddess?" It was all very clear to her. "Look at the woman next to you."

They looked, and some of them embraced, shyly.

Someone asked Gauri to tell the story of Mana and Snow Tiger. Someone led a dance. Very decorous, that first dance. With each new thing they did together they felt stronger, freer, cheekier, closer to each other. The full realization came slowly that there was, for this short time, no one to stop them doing whatever they could think of doing.

The dancing became wilder. When it was Eun's turn, she got them to take off all their clothes and dance naked "as we simply are," she said. Before they could dance, they had to giggle at one another's various sizes and shapes. They had seen one another naked innumerable times. But never in a gene lab. With the entire station planning how to defeat them, they looked at one another naked. At first, it did not increase their confidence.

Kumtacj said, "When I was a child, I never saw anyone like me. Look at these stretch marks, these breasts! Look at your belly!"

Six of them had pregnant bellies of various sizes. All had stretch marks. Their much-sucked breasts hung down, huge and ripe, or flat on their chests. Most had never lost the extra weight after each birth, and although no one else was quite as mountainous as Kumi, all of them were larger in one way or another than they had ever imagined possible. Gauri was the trimmest, because she had kept up her gymnastics in any way she could. They were all angry, but Gauri's anger was never at herself, always for Jiang and Sky and the society that made them. Some people's anger made them fat, but Gauri's made her lean. They told her that they envied her looks. She said, can you believe I have gray hair, and I'm only 29?

She told them of the goddess figurines that Mana had sculpted with massive hips and breasts, based on the ancient ones Osen kept in her room. When they finally danced unclothed, some of them felt elemental in a way they had never expected.

So they made it through the days of their captivity and rebellion. They came to feel, if not like goddesses, at least perhaps a little more like human beings. The sadness and joy grew
daily more acute. There were occasional negotiations with the
station authorities over a vidphone. They drew up a set of specific requests about the improvements needed for the breeder's
life. They had no hope that they would ever get out of there
alive. But every time their spirits drooped, they lay down in the
wheel, and someone suggested something to do together.

And now the days had turned into weeks, and it was Gauri's
turn again. She had had lots of ideas during the last few women's
turns, but suddenly the ideas had deserted her.

"I don't know," she said. "These days have been the best. I
feel so unexpectedly wonderful."

"Yes, Mother!" encouraged another.

"And not really scared."

"Kali is with us."

"These have been the very best days of my life."

"Of mine, too" came the echoes. "The best."

"But I can't think what to say or do now."

"Just relax. She has you in Her arms."

She remembered that first rolling round they had sung, and
the way it had turned abstract, and something she had said then.
Now she said it again. "Look at the woman next to you. Don't
you think, this time, we could make up our own rolling chant . . .
without getting all abstract? Shall we try?" She could feel the
agreement in the hands that held hers. She stared at the ceiling
of the gene lab. After a while she said, "Labor Pain Child."

Next to her, without a pause, Kumi grunted, "Pain Child
Grow."

"Child Grow Tall."

"Grow Tall Tales."

"Tall Tales Hurt." And it went on around the wheel: "Tales
Hurt No-one / Hurt No-one Kali / No-one Kali Lives / Kali Lives
Rock / Lives Rock Deep / Rock Deep Well / Deep Well Songs /
Well Songs Heal / Songs Heal Labor / Heal Labor Pain." They
had come back to the start.

There were tears. Kumi leaped to her feet and called for a
circle. "Throw off your clothes and sing it as loud as we can!
Wake the station!" Gauri looked at her and felt that if it hadn't
been for Kumi they would have given up long ago. They sang it

and danced. Their arms around their shoulders, they stomped the floor and healed one another.

Afterward, sweaty and glowing, they flopped down.

Gauri picked up the black and white top, and held it in her fist. "I keep thinking," she said, "I don't know why, of the peer I grew up with and loved."

And then the speaker that the authorities used came to life for the first time in days. "This is Govind from Terra Station and Karp. I want to talk privately with Gauri. Will you please come to the vidphone to talk with me? I repeat . . ."

"Govind!" Gauri leapt up and ran to the screen. He was there, trim and confident, an older face, just as she had imagined, but overcast by worry now, for her, of course. She wanted to embrace him. Together at last, again.

"What are you doing here?" he demanded.

"Here? Are you here on Sky?"

"I'm right outside your door. What are you doing?"

She wanted to throw the door open and hug him. It was agony to hold back for her sisters' sake. "Serving the Goddess!" she said. She heard the exultation in her voice, and saw the incomprehension it created in Govind's eyes.

For a moment she got a glimpse of what he saw: a crazed rebel. A wild, naked madwoman. The universe began to fissure and slide, reality inverted: am I mad? I am mad?

He asked coldly, "You are not part of the revolt, then? You are a hostage?"

Say yes? Say yes, I'm a hostage, and get taken care of, removed from here, be allowed to live? Because I have, truly, gone mad?

"I asked, are you a hostage?"

The world is spinning upside down on you and you've lost your gyro sense. Gauri heard her own small and distant voice from far in the past. Take six quick steps and somersault, the voice said, run down to the bottom point, don't be carried over and fall.

"You are naked," Govind said. "What have they done to you?"

The disgust in his voice turned her, against her will, screaming against her will, to run down inside the gyro of the world and back to right way up. It meant she had to cast him off on the way. But she knew which way was up. Her feet were firm on the planet, and he was upside-down looking at her through the glass panel of the door, as if someone had him hanging on a cable by the feet.

"They made me have five babies in seven years, Govind. They shot me full of drugs and they fed me to my fetuses. They made a machine of me, and then they took my babies away. The Goddess screamed in her labor and I rose to shoot the tiger. The tiger was in me and the roar was in Kumi. What else do you want to know?"

"You need medical care. What have they done to you? Are you sure you are not a hostage?"

"No, of course not. The revolt is the Goddess. Gaia has come. She is here. She was in my hand when I grabbed the nurse who was destroying this" — she held up the little black and white top. "Everything followed from that. Isn't it stupid? But Gaia is here, Govind. *She is here.*"

"You are naked."

"As Mana was when she was Goddess to you."

"You have bred five times?"

"Five babies from here." She instinctively put both hands to her lower belly, and he winced.

"Any with the Karp officers? Have you had sex with the Karp officers?"

"Yes," she said bitterly.

"Did one of them suggest this revolt to you?"

"Of course not. Do they know what it is to be a breeder? They made a mistake, Govind, they should never have asked for volunteers for this. They should have stuck to breeding a lesser kind of human who had no feelings."

"Are you claiming this was all your idea?"

"Not mine alone. Kumi's more. What's got into you? Aren't you happy to see me at all? I am the same Gauri, Govind. I still love you."

"How can you say you love and are filled with the Spirit when you have had sex with all comers and given birth and led a revolt? You're naked in the mud, Gauri. This isn't what we fought for."

"What's wrong with you? I was forced into it!"

"Yes, of course, I'm sorry. It's just seeing you naked and . . . The guards say you've been having sex in there, dancing naked. That's horrible."

"All acts of love and pleasure are Gaia's rituals!"

"And revolt? Is that Gaia's ritual? You killed a gene tech. This could set off revolts all over the Galaxy. Osen taught Gaia was for harmony, not killing."

"We had to kill him to be taken seriously. That's how we got the other techs to culture their disease viruses for us. Tell whoever sent you that we mean it: we will set the cultures free in the ventilation system and take the whole station to Kali with us. Kali devours all. Durga rides upon the lion to slay buffalo demon. We are the roar of Gaia!"

"Ha-a-a-r-r-rgh," Kumtacj roared. Kumi's bulk stood right behind her. She had come up as silently as a beast of the forest. Gauri suddenly felt her whole body begin to tremble beyond control, close to collapse. She leaned back into Kumi's arms and grabbed at her thigh with one hand to prevent herself from falling. Kumi held her upright.

Govind winced. He clearly found naked females disgusting.

"Don't let the wraith, the ghost in you take over, Vinny. Don't hate me. You're taking all my strength away."

"Bring this to an end, Gauri. Give up your bacteria and your hostages. I guarantee you that you will not be killed."

"Who are you to guarantee?" asked Kumi.

"I speak for Mqrisi, Space Marshal of Karp. You will be punished, but not killed. He guarantees it."

"What of our demands?" Kumi asked. "Limit of five children per breeder, two years between children, access to medical records, choice of sexual partner or none, new MAN programs for our needs . . . We have ten demands, Sri Govind."

"Just surrender, and we will see. Gauri, you must understand." He was trying desperately to talk with her alone. His eyes searched hers for connection. "This is a great opportunity for God's work. Don't you see? Mqrisi is with us! It's what we always dreamed of. The Center is ready to take us to its heart. I promised Mqrisi that you would help to bring this to a peaceful end. Now that you are actually in there, and you seem to be some kind of leader of this, you can do it! You can convince Mqrisi there is a better way than killing. He is a humane man. If we solve this together, we may win over Sky First Committee here. They will give better breeder conditions, if that's what you're worried about. And after them, Tarcuna First Committee. This is the time for catching trout, Gauri, not killing tigers.

Don't you have any feeling for strategy? Think: what would Osen do? Don't get confused by your hurts. It must have been hell for you. But see the bigger picture. It's your duty to Gaia."

"Mana followed her 'duty' when she came into space, and she's been half dead ever since. I'd rather kill tigers!"

"Mqrisi's men will kill you. I can save you."

"You said we'd be punished. Do you know what 'punishment' is for breeders? Brain peeling. They strip us of our identity, down to the level of a cow. Would Osen want that? Would Gaia?"

"Just for a moment think bigger than Gaia! She's a million light-years away. We live in Space. The Great Spirit of the Galaxy is greater than any one planet's Goddess. He can speak to you. But you are cut off from Him when you wallow in the flesh. Your lust almost killed you and me and all of Terra Station once. Now you're at it again!"

Kumi held her up bodily.

"All right," he said. "I'll talk to Mqrisi. We'll bring back the baby labs on Sky. No more breeders here at all. You won't be brain peeled, I promise you. You'll be retrained."

"The king," said Kumi. "What of the king? The king who killed the women of Osen's Cave."

"Who is this woman?"

"I am Kumtacj. I am the Goddess. You are the Goddess, Sri Govind, you don't have to look beyond yourself."

"Gauri, I want to talk with you alone."

"She is saying that you were born to save Earth from kings and war and Sky Gods. But you fear sex and birthing. What's the difference between you and the old kings and missile men who feared women and trod nature down?"

"What did they know of the Spirit of the Galaxy?"

"They did it in the *name* of that Spirit! *In God We Trust!* Don't you know the God and Goddess are not outside you? They are you. Be human. I know you were frightened when I almost died, but love me! Don't turn from me. Govind, I am your Shakti, your Kali — without me you will become a wraith. Or a king. Brahma, not Shiva."

"You are endangering all I worked for these seven years. I told Mqrisi you would be with the Spirit."

"You have made your Spirit in MAN's image. Can't you see that? A Spirit who plans and directs everything from outside. A

Spirit who despises ordinary people. You chose MAN's way, not Mana's."

"Mana is with me. She is here."

"I don't believe you. Let me see her. Let me talk to her."

"Think about my offer, Gauri. I have two days to persuade you. Then they will kill you."

"You didn't always want to rule, Govind. Those mad, horrible times of the crazes, you roared like Snow Tiger, you were Shiva: the people followed like sheep but a lot of the time you wanted just to *be*."

"Being isn't going to change anything, Gauri. There are thousands of us on Karp now, following the orders of the Spirit."

"Don't you remember when I spoke the truth to you in the labs and you said you wished I would be like that always? Who tells you the truth to you about yourself now?"

He glared at her.

"These disciplined followers on Karp? Do they call them followers of Govind, or . . . Govindis?" His eyes widened. "I'm right, aren't I? That's not spirituality, that's hierarchy. That's making your vision rule. Don't you remember that day in the gene labs when we made love? I had criticized you for manipulating everyone, and you took it from me? You said it was scary, remember? Scary to hear a slim girl tell you you were using your great power harmfully. But I got sick and then you . . ." she said the next three words really slowly ". . . just ran away."

His lips were pressed tight together. But he was listening. There was still hope for him "What were you afraid of, Vinny? Was it really disease? Accidents? Death? Social collapse? Or did you use all those real fears as an excuse to get away from me? You were secretly happy when you thought you were leaving me on Earth Station, weren't you! And you never shed a tear when I was kidnapped to be a breeder. I'm right, aren't I?"

"I did cry for you. I wept."

"For yourself, too, I hope! Because I was your last chance! You last chance to become a man who could use his great power to empower others, not manipulate them!" His eyes flickered. "Or have there been others who challenged you too?" His eyes dropped. "Well, go back to her and beg her forgiveness, Govind, because you have lost me. You threw me away. I am done with you." She didn't know it was true until she said it.

He was breathing heavily. She felt she could get in one

more arrow before she lost him. "Think about this, Govind. If you went back to Osen's king you would try to convert him, wouldn't you, like you're doing with this Karp general? You'd give him your vision and your Spirit of the Universe which countenances the punishing of breeders and calls Gaia a little unimportant goddess, and he would kill the priestesses of Gaia and enslave the world in your Spirit's name!"

He turned and walked away. She shouted, "Set us free and we will wake the Goddess on Sky! She is here. Just remove Her shackles. She is in you! You've become a wraith. Be a man!"

He was gone. Soldiers appeared on the screen with their weapons up, and she saw fear and contempt in their eyes. Soldiers from Karp no doubt. She switched off the screen and leaned back exhausted into Kumi's arms.

A familiar voice suddenly came through on the speaker. "Gauri, let me in! Open the door."

It was Mana.

Gauri switched on the screen. It was Mana indeed, right outside the door to the gene labs, standing in the midst of the Karp soldiers. "They're going to let you in?"

"I'm just an old woman. They don't care if you grab me."

"You aren't booby trapped?"

"Gauri, that is unworthy of you! I am the same Mana you always knew!"

"Tell the soldiers to stand back. Again. Farther," Gauri ordered. Then she opened the door, and pulled Mana in. For a moment they sized each other up, and then she was in Mana's arms.

"Dear Gauri."

They hugged a long time. Then Gauri stood back, new energy running through her.

"This is Kumi." The two women looked at each other and their smiles said they liked what they saw.

"You aren't with him, Mana, like he said, are you?" Gauri asked.

"He has done wonders, Gauri. It would make all the difference if you accepted his terms. He had to do a miracle with Mqrisi to get such terms. I heard your whole conversation with him. I know he talks of the Great Spirit. I don't know what that means — but I can tell you he's done more than was humanly possible."

"You always were on the fence. I never, never saw you, except in the briefest flashes, as the woman who killed Snow Tiger."

"Gauri!"

Mana looked so hurt, Gauri could feel herself back as a child, taking the bewildered Mana's hand and comforting her. That Gauri would have backtracked to save Mana's feelings. But she had been a breeder now for seven years and certain things were clearer, and there were truths to say.

"I was cut off," Mana said. "From Gaia, from everything solid."

"You cut yourself off. Why didn't you smash the gene tanks on Terra Station? That would have got everyone having babies! All you did was confessions and discussions. You never even had sex. Where was your anger? Your love? Why did you only hug me that once, when you first saw me in the nursery?"

"I . . . I . . . was lost."

"The one thing you did that grabbed Govind was when you became the Goddess to him. She took you over and he came into you and wanted whatever that was. But instead of giving it to him, you taught him to start a religion!"

"But that's what Osen taught me."

"That's what Osen and José taught you. What about *you?* Osen chose *you.*"

"But I didn't know how to feel it. I was out of touch. Nothing worked for me. I couldn't feel!"

"I'm sorry, Mana, I'm sorry. I know how it was for you. It was like that for me until this happened. You should go back out there to him. I can't help him now. If I hadn't got sick that time, or if José hadn't come to take us off, or if Rocco hadn't split us up, it would all have been different. He's trying his best, in a way. But he's too powerful. He needs you. You can restrain him, a little."

"You found the Goddess. Here. You're different. Grounded."

"Yes. She is here. Stay with us awhile before you go. She isn't a spirit, Mana, I don't think She is or ever was. Not in the sense of something separate from us. She is us and all life. If I've learned one thing . . . Don't you think you made up Her spirit form because that was the only thing you could visualize to help you? It's all right — anyone would do the same. But now Govind has made up his MAN-god to help him. It gets further from reality every time. He's beyond grounding."

"He needs ten years in Mana's Caves," Kumi said. "That would ground him."

"Osen was a great visionary," Mana said. "I have only tried to live her vision."

"Maybe she chose you because you were not her, because you were an antidote to visions. Did you have visions or voices telling you to kill Snow Tiger?"

"I was whole then."

"You have always been whole. We are whole now. Join us for a while. Mana," Gauri hugged the older woman fiercely, "I love you so much."

"But without faith in Gaia outside of you, how can you go on? You need faith."

"We have faith. But doesn't it take *more* faith to go on when you haven't formed an image of some person outside of yourself to have faith in? It's ourselves, it's all of life, it's the rock out there and the waves . . ."

"I don't know. I don't know."

"Nor do we," said Kumtacj, leading Mana away from the door and into the room.

When the wheel re-formed, there were not twelve but thirteen women lying on their backs on the floor.

# Five

Passarin seated himself conspicuously in the Sky 'Seaview Room' as arranged for the Starlight agent to find him. Outside, under a violet-pink sky, great waves crashed onto bare rock outcroppings and onto the little beach between them. The waves were green, the rocks black. There was no green on the land. The Seaview Room had high walls of triple glass, a glass ceiling to reveal the stars — the only place in the habitat where you could see them properly — and a speaker system to bring in the rhythmic thunder of the waves. It was hard to hear himself think, or even to remember the passwords.

He felt that he was awake for the first time in seven years or more. No more passive observer. There were women to rescue, and one of them he had connected with momentarily — a moment of wakefulness in that seven years — and she was still large in his mind; and an old man to get to Starlight, an old man he certainly loved though they had barely spoken for ages; and an unbelievably stubborn Terran woman to get onto the Starlight ship with them, against her own will if need be, whom he thought he might love as much as he loved his own mother.

It was as bad as he could have imagined. Gauri and her friends had imprisoned themselves in the gene labs. Govind had talked to her, and come back looking like the grim reaper.

Mana had gone in there, stayed for hours, and come out with a strange look on her. Mqrisi's men had run her through a portable detox as soon as she came out. Now she was saying she wasn't going to go to Starlight after all. They had had a big talk in the visitors' dorm. José had a gadget from the MAN labs that he said would scramble any listening devices. Passarin hoped to Space it had worked — voices had got pretty loud. Mana had said to José and himself, with that happy-sad look on her face, that she wished she could go to Kali with Gauri and Kumi and their friends. But she said she would stay and do her duty by Govind. Gauri would not die in vain. Mana would have to be Goddess for Govind somehow or other. She told José he should go to Starlight, because what did she want with sending him off to the long sleep on Madlarki? Of course, he refused to go without her.

So what was Passarin to say to the Starlight agent who was due here any minute? Starlight was expecting to take off him and Mana, and if they didn't get what they wanted, how could he persuade them to do what he wanted, which was to rescue Gauri and her friends.

It had turned into a big row with Mana. "I must do my duty to the Goddess!" Those were Mana's words, which really made him see red.

"There is no Goddess outside of you!" he objected.

"That's what Gauri said."

"Tell me everything she said," he had insisted. She had done so.

And then, stupid fool, he'd gone into a diatribe that had alienated Mana totally. "Of course, Gauri's right about the gods," he had said. "They're only metaphors that we make up for the unknowable — and most of the metaphor is our wishes and fears. You thought you killed the Goddess Herself, but it was only an old sick snow tiger. You thought the Goddess told you to leap on the space ferry to take you to Terra Station, but it was only your own guilt, or idealism; if it was Osen's voice, then it was only telepathy. And when you were Goddess to Govind, you were just telling him in the only language he could understand that you were a beautiful, passionate woman once, and that awoke him to a fact he must have known in his subconscious a long, long time: that he had rejected you and your message all these years out of childish incomprehension — he thought your stubbornness killed Osen. And maybe it did. But that was no reason for him to reject you, when Osen died to get you to him. It wasn't the Goddess in you which pulled him back onto Osen's path — it was the you in you."

"Well, then," Mana said bitterly, "you and Gauri would get on famously. A shame she's going to be killed."

"I'm sorry. I know your belief means everything to you . . ."

"I have *experienced* the Goddess — it's not belief. She lives. It is my own fault that I get confused and cut off from Her. I know perfectly well that was an old sick tiger, but I did kill Her in Snow Tiger too, even so. Why else would I have been punished all these years, living in these sterile lands?"

"No, please, you don't believe that," he said. "If you believe that you're punishing yourself. I didn't mean when I said you 'only' killed snow tiger that it was not a glorious thing. A seventeen-year-old girl? It was incredible. It makes it all the *more* wonderful that you did these things yourself, that it wasn't the Goddess doing them. It was your humanity."

"Without Gaia I am nothing."

He turned to José. "Can't you persuade her? You want her to come with you to Starlight, don't you?" The old man nodded. He looked miserable and truly old, diminished in a way Passarin had not seen before. "You won't abandon José, Mana, surely not for Govind?"

"José makes his own choice," Mana said. "Govind is the task my life has given me. He says he is coming next to Madlarki. If I am there, I may influence him yet."

"It's martyrdom," he yelled at her. "Your task was to warm the Earth, not to run after Govind. And Starlight could probably warm the Earth just as easily as Tarcuna — and they'd be a lot easier to persuade." Now that was the line he should have started with. That brought the first flicker of interest to Mana's eyes.

"Would they?" she asked.

"Well, I don't know for sure but . . . I'll ask the Starlight agent. She will know."

He had come within a hair of driving Mana away and endangering Gauri's rescue — what a child! What a stupid, reactive adolescent! Here was Gauri bearing children and the weight of oppression and rebellion, and he couldn't hold his tongue enough to make a deal happen. Starlight wanted him and Mana — the least he could do would be to deliver both in return for their taking Gauri and her rebels. Time to grow up, boy. Time to do some real work.

There was an emergency airlock from the Seaview Room to the outside. He wished he could run out of it to stand before those mighty waves in the spray and the thunder and make his promise to the cosmos to save her life. But the airlock was covered in warning signs: TOXIC ATMOSPHERE: EXIT ONLY WITH RESPIRA-TORS — CLEARANCE REQUIRED FROM EXTERIOR SERVICES TO OPEN AIRLOCK — EMERGENCY MANUAL OVERRIDE OPENS AIRLOCK FOR 30 SECONDS AT A TIME. It was another planet awaiting terraforming. Why would they ever warm the Earth for Mana's people? It didn't make sense. They had too many worlds of their own in worse condition than Earth.

The woman who came up to him had the Maintenance Services logo on her fatigues.

"The Galaxy is in good hands."

This was it! "Kuan-yin gives suck to all Her creation." He had remembered the response.

"Great. I love it," the young woman talked softly, with laughter lines around her eyes. He liked her immediately. "Head Scsuzz has a sense of humor. Kuan-yin's my name at home, but it's not an approved name here. My name here is Hideki. Remember that. Hideki. Glad to find you so easily. Talk low like this. I scrambled the bugs here a long time ago, and the sea noise drowned them out anyway, which is why they didn't pay attention to them, but it's always worth being cautious. Are you all prepared? These will be my only instructions to you. We have a ship standing by in this system. It will put down a small lander on this beach the night after tomorrow at 0300. The station is quietest then. Don't worry about it — our wraiths are highly skilled. They can spot it down twelve feet above the sand — that's below the scanners. Sky will never know. We do this a lot, don't worry. Its own motors will take it down the rest of the way, dead quiet. It will not be detected. You and Mana will meet me here at 0245. I will provide the respirators and have the airlock open. All you will have to do is run to the ship. Any questions?"

"I am not going. Mana is not going."

"What do you mean? Is this a joke?"

"The people you should take out are the rebel breeders. They will be brain-peeled or killed if you don't."

"Believe me, I suggested it to Head Scsuzz already. But orders are that's unacceptable interference. My brief is you and Mana."

"Then, Starlight doesn't understand what's at stake. First, it would be an incredible blow to Mqrisi. He is fighting for his command right now, with the Tarcunan dynasts. He needs to be seen to deal with this revolt firmly. He's one of the main bastions of the old system." Passarin wasn't entirely sure if that was true, but it was probably close enough. "And second, I can tell you, if you got the breeders out it would take the wind out of the sails of a religious cult that looks set fair to revive the whole MAN system in another form for another thousand years. The Govindi cult will revive the Karp military too, and Starlight won't like that. You'll be a hero on Starlight if you rescue those women. It'll make Mrqisi and Govind look prime fools. They'll be singing songs about you down on Foundation Square for a hundred years."

Muffled by the thunder of the waves, talking in an intense whisper, Passarin told her the entire tale. He could see it was the "hero on Starlight" pitch that hooked her interest, not just the fate of the breeders. Soon he saw it was the logistics of the operation that excited her the most, the snatching away of thirteen heroic women from under the noses of fanatical religious soldiers. She was a woman of action — perhaps this might even work!

"How would we get them out of the gene labs?" she asked. "They're heavily guarded."

"Bring your wraiths down here. Wraith them out."

"What?"

"If they can set a ship from orbit down to twelve feet above the sand, they could whip thirteen women all holding onto one another out of the gene labs into this room."

"You don't know what you're asking. If they misplace them a few feet too low, in a chair or in the floor, they'll explode — probably kill us all."

"Tell them you think they can't do it. If I know Starlight wraiths, that'll be enough. They have pride in their craft. They can place them five feet off the floor, right here. I'll get the furniture out of the way. You provide thirteen masks and open the airlock."

"All right, I'll ask them. On one condition."

Passarin raised his eyebrows.

"That you and Mana come with them."

"That's two conditions. I can't answer for Mana."

"It's three conditions, in fact, and you have to answer for all three. One: Mana comes. Two: you come. Three: you agree to return to your home planet. That's why we're running this whole caper. Your planet wants you back. I can't think why. You're a cold fish."

Passarin turned and stalked toward the door.

"What are you afraid of," she ran after him, "that's worth the death of thirteen breeders?"

He stopped. He turned. "You'll really do it?"

"If the wraiths will do it, I'll take responsibility with Starlight."

"All right. You persuade the wraiths. I'll persuade Mana."

"So you'll both come."

"We'll both come, though there's one more person. Mana's lover, José. If she comes, he comes."

"Holy crapola! Last thing: You'll return to your home planet?"

He took a deep breath. "I'll return to my home planet."

"Well, cheer up. It isn't the end of the world."

"It's the end of the only world I've ever felt at home in. But tell me one more thing. I need to know. To persuade Mana. Would Starlight warm the Earth? If Mana went, could she get them to do it? All it needs probably is a good load of the right chemicals dumped in the upper atmosphere, and soot or something spread over the ice. I've studied the question."

"Depends. If Mana's story catches the people's interest, I suppose so. You know Starlight. There's no government — we negotiate among the webs and tangles. I think there was an Earth Project once, years and years ago, that had some contact and found them too primitive. Mana would have to convince a lot of people to divert resources away from their current concerns. There are so many projects on Starlight that people are enthusiastic about already — but Earth has a natural sentimental appeal. It's possible."

"Thanks! That's enough!"

But it wasn't. "It's no more certain than getting Tarcuna to do it," Mana said when he got back to her. "And it was no part of Osen's plan. I'm better off sticking to what she wanted me to do. I have to have faith."

"Can you be doing the right thing if you're not happy?" asked José gently.

"Dearest friend, I have been so happy these years with you." She stroked José's face. "You have given me my only happiness since Earth . . . and what did I achieve? A few piles of leaves. Now it's time to return to the task Osen chose me for. But you must go to Starlight." She drew him slowly into her arms, and Passarin looked away as the tears on their cheeks mingled.

He wondered if he would be up to kidnapping her at the last minute, to fulfill his promise to Hideki.

But later that night, without Passarin, Mana's thoughts turned to just what it was she was taking on in trying to influence the new Govind.

"José, where did I go wrong? He's going to let her be killed. I saw it in his eyes." The surf thundered and José shaded his old eyes against the light. Passarin had told them where they could talk. "She's so stubborn — she's in the Goddess and she won't compromise, and she's right, damn it. Was Osen's planning and scheming all wrong? I was so happy when Govind told me all he had done. I never thought he could turn against Gaia — but he hates sex, he hates birthing. He thinks lust and passion and anger must be suppressed if love and fellowship and spirit are to flower."

"Did you know that 'lust' in Old German meant 'religious joy'? They turned it around when their Spirit God told them sex was bad," said José. "Just like 'man' in Old Hindi meant 'mother' and in Old Norse 'woman'? The Norse had another name for male person, which was 'wer,' as in 'werewolf.' When the sky gods took over people's minds on earth, they turned the old language around. 'Man' was such a powerful word they made it mean person and then only male person. All this has happened before — this turning upside down of things. It's not new. It's quite understandable."

"My dear, I don't need antique wordsmithing. I need help. Be Osen to me?"

"All right. If you want. I'm old enough."

"Osen," Mana said. "I failed you. It didn't work. Govind isn't Christ. He isn't Buddha. You said you wanted a son to show them what a man could be. You said it would be more shocking to them if the one who brought love was a man. Well, this man chose wrong. He's another hierarch. I taught him wrong."

"No, you taught him what was in my Chronicles," Osen-José said.

"But Gauri says he's become a Sky God, and it's true."

"The Sky Gods weren't all wrong."

"They taught control — of nature, of women, of self."

"Was that so wrong? People were tired of being at nature's mercy."

"So they almost destroyed the world!"

"But the fact is, the power exists now to make and unmake worlds. We can't wish it away. We can't return to being a helpless part of nature. We have to use that power. If we don't, worse people than us will. Misuse of the power was just a step on the road to learning right use of it."

"If it was just the desire to use power responsibly, that might be all right. But with Govind it's fear. He pretends otherwise; I'm sure he doesn't even know it himself. But it's fear."

"Of what?"

"Fear of death. Of broken space stations spinning in the void. Of the real nature of life. Of the fact that we're never ultimately in control, terraformers or not. Desire for abstract perfection and transcendence. I don't know. Sometimes I've thought, these last twenty-four hours, that Govind somehow can't stand life. He can't stand Kali in her ferocious form, hung with death's heads, so he rejects Her in Her lustful form and as Mother too. He's going for nirvana. Nothingness. An end of suffering. Maybe he is Buddha. But not Christ. Christ loved women . . . didn't he?"

"My motherline lived always to make a synthesis," said Osen-José. "The live-within-nature people lost before to the defeat-nature people. They will lose again. They always will. As long as nature lets humans survive. Unless we become a third type, a synthesis that accepts our godlike power to change nature, but doesn't hate and fear her, so we use our power with humility: call it the work-with-nature option."

"Is that just fancy words to rationalize what you really wanted Govind to do: to get the big guns of the Collectivity to defeat your king and his warriors?"

"You have to live in the real world. I don't want to see the kings run mad again."

"You want a middle road. I know that. But in balancing the lover and the schemer, Govind's gone too far the wrong way. Why didn't you write about that in your Chronicles? All your advice was how to scheme."

"Balance is hard to achieve, especially in one life."

"You mean, Govind goes too far to the schemer, the next person will go toward the lover?"

"Look at you — with your songs on Earth, your plants and animals on Madlarki. You're not a planner. That's why I chose you."

"Is it? I thought you wanted me to become a planner. My mistake was to come to space at all, wasn't it? I acted on a sense of duty, an abstract idea, instead of love."

"You loved me. And I manipulated you."

"But I chose. I did it. If only I had listened to my father. Be my father now, José. Oh Daddy, I'm no connection woman. I knew — you knew — I was meant to sing the Deep Fire sagas!"

"No one knows what might have happened if you had." José's voice and manner changed toward the quietly philosophical, away from the passionately committed. "You might have spent your life in regret at not helping Osen: it was a single chance, and you took it. An instant's choice, a window made for you alone by the long-term and the short-term causes." That was pure José, but Mana knew her father Rudradaman would have understood it. "You jumped through, and so you spend the rest of your life working out the consequences. And you know, you've made some good connections. I'm proud of you."

"Will it come right, Daddy? Osen? — will Earth be warmed?"

"Is that your definition of 'things coming right'?"

"She has turned away from the Spirit, sir. Believe me, this is not what I expected. Her circle of naked women is not what I am advocating. She glories in the flesh. I am afraid to have to report that she has become part of the debauchery of Sky."

"You give up?"

"No, sir. Please let her think about it, at least for twenty-four hours."

"You think she will cooperate?"

"Honestly, sir, no."

"I will bring the rest of the riot squad down, then, with their equipment. It may take them your twenty-four hours to seal the gene labs' air system. I am sorry, my boy, very sorry. I know you had hopes for this woman. And love for her, too, am I not right?" Mqrisi put a fatherly hand on Govind's arm. "It will be a quick, clean end. Gas and ultra sound together — they will never know."

"They will be with the Spirit."

"It will be out of our hands then. They will be judged by another and greater power, as you say. It is a comfort."

"Will you pray for them with me?"

"Yes, of course. And while you're in that other land of yours, do you think you could talk to those wraiths of mine on the space station up there? I don't trust anyone on this damn planet. Tell them to send the riot squad ship down, will you? Then no one will know what we're up to, at least until they arrive."

"Yes, sir, I'll try."

"Then, young man, let us pray. You lead. I don't know how."

Passarin found José and Mana in the Seaview Room. "Well," he asked, "have you thought anymore about what you'll do?"

"I have to stay," Mana said. "I started all this with Govind. I must see it through to the end. There is a lot of good in him. He's powerful. We need to work with him. It's not what I hoped, but as Osen said, you can't get it right in any one generation."

"Come on, Mana. Think of your own needs for once. Don't you want to step out into the sunshine in a field of ripe dusty wheat and poppies? How about scuffing up the leaves in a fall forest, with the scent of wood smoke calling you home to tea? No respirator. No walls to bump into when you run through the trees. No hologram. Real acorns, squirrels, cawing crows, mushrooms, pine sap sticky on your fingers."

"Don't! My duty is hard enough as it is."

"There's something up, young man," said José. "Why this obsession about getting Mana to Starlight? You weren't so keen on its beauties back on Madlarki. Almost sounds like you're planning to go yourself."

"I am."

They both narrowed their eyes, peering at him as if they could see through his words to his meaning.

"Your duty may be here. I don't know," Passarin said. "Mine is there."

"You don't look like a man who is grimly following his duty," said José. "You look more like someone who has just begun an adventure."

"The glittering eyes," noted Mana.

"The limbs eager to run, jump . . . kiss?"

"Don't joke about it. She's facing death!"

"I'm beginning to wonder. You've got something up your sleeve."

"Will you at least come and say good-bye to me? The Seaview Room at 0230 hours, two nights from now."

"I think we could do that," said José.

"Dear Passarin, I'm glad you're going. For more reasons than one. I can guess you're cooking a plan to save her. I won't ask. But if there's anything we can do to help — apart from go with you. And listen, I'll miss our tea and talks. Of course, we'll be there."

He had to make do with that small victory. If he had told them they wouldn't take Gauri without having Mana, then they might not have shown up at all. Would the Starlight agent have a stun gun? Or would he have to knock her out himself? Could he get a respirator on Mana when she was unconscious and carry her out to the ship? Would José cooperate in kidnapping his lover?

The demon Goddess pinned Passarin to the ground and began to engulf him in the devouring pink folds of her monstrous yoni. He writhed and struggled . . . and woke. There was a hand on his wrist.

"Ssssh," said a tense voice that was trying to sound soothing. He raised himself on an elbow and peered into the darkness of the dormitory. "It's me, Hideki. Come into the washroom." And she faded away.

He lay back and breathed deeply, the devouring pink folds still more vivid to him than the ghost who had come and gone. He started awake again. Panic gripped him. Hideki! He slid out of bed and tiptoed through the dorm full of sleeping Skyers.

She drew him to the oval of toilets and indicated to him to sit down. If anyone came in, it was a chance encounter of two weak bladders.

"We've got to bring it forward," she said in an admirable impersonation of a sleepy grumble about nocturnal necessities. Passarin could hardly believe that the dozing bureaucracy listened in to toilet talk, but there was a rebellion on, so perhaps they might. He did his best to copy the tone of voice.

"When?"

"Tomorrow night, same time," she mumbled into her hand. "My friends heard your former friend talking to his team upstairs. They're moving in tonight. Probably here already," she yawned. "Well, get some sleep. G'night."

He went back to bed and lay awake staring at the dark until the lights came on.

The first thing was to tell Mana and José.

# Six

"Passarin? Where are you?"

Mana's voice. Thank you, cosmos.

"Here." It was shadowy dark in the Seaview Room. A single broad spotlight from the ceiling dramatically illuminated a wide starview map on a sloping table at chest height, for those who wanted to identify their night sky. But that only threw the rest of the room into deeper gloom, particularly for anyone first walking in from the brightly lit corridors. The night outside was blacker still. The stars were sparse here, away from the Galactic Center, as sparse as at Terra Station. Their needle points glittered but did not illuminate. Sky had no moons. Passarin strained to catch the occasional glint of phosphorescence on the breaking waves, or the first reflecting glint from a spaceship hull.

"There are soldiers all around the gene labs," Mana whispered. "We couldn't come that way."

"Are there?" Fear in his guts. He had come the other way. "Did they see you?" José was behind her. He came up and touched Passarin's shoulder in greeting.

"No," Mana whispered. "I'm a hunter. Remember?"

"Help me move the chairs. We have to make a big space in the middle of the room."

"Oh? Why?"

"You promised you wouldn't ask." They cleared the space.

Passarin jumped as another figure loomed up.

It was Hideki.

"Good. Is this Mana?" Hideki asked. Even she was whispering under the roar of the waves.

"Is it still safe to talk here?" he asked her.

"Yes. Just nerves."

Introductions were made. Mana asked about the soldiers.

"They arrived last night. Came down on this beach, and in through this airlock — like we're doing, and for the same reason: it's isolated."

"Damn. Will they find us here tonight? Who are they?"

"Mqrisi's riot squad. Our wraiths caught a crudely broad-cast telepathic sending from that Govind of yours asking for the riot ship to come down and enter secretly, giving directions. Mqrisi has the whole area around the gene labs sealed off, even from Sky Security. His men went in and have been sealing the labs physically, making them gas-proof, I reckon, ever since. I think they're trying to keep it secret as far as they can even from Sky First Committee."

"How do you know?"

"There have been rows between Mqrisi's men and the First Committee. And we maintenance folk get everywhere — they needed our help to seal the labs. They're obviously going to go in there and hope to contain the virus. I doubt if it can be done, myself. Thank heaven we're leaving. Where's that damn ship?"

"Will we be in time to rescue them?"

"I don't know. I think they're still sealing the place up. The riot squad hasn't gone in yet."

At that moment in a corridor a little distance from the gene labs, a distraught saint knelt in humble prayer for the souls of those about to die. His prayer encompassed not just the unsuspecting thirteen breeders but the whole habitat, humbly beseeching that the virus would not take them all down together. To be on the safe side, the saint, like Mqrisi and all his men, wore full virus protection suit and helmet. There were none for the rest of the Sky population — they would have to take their chances. The saint prayed that those who died would go straight to paradise. He begged the Great Spirit to forgive the rebel breeders their sins and take them to heaven straight away.

A few paces away from him, the space marshal ordered the ultra-sound and gas teams to ready their weapons to instantly para-lyze and kill the thirteen rebels at his signal.

A pin-prick hole had been secretly lasered in the gene lab wall, a needle-thin scope inserted and sealed in place, to give a view of the disgusting rebel women inside. It was dark in the gene labs during the night, but Mqrisi's excellent nightscope technology worked like a charm. The screen in front of Mqrisi focused on the breeder who held the dish of disease virus by the ventilation outtake. The squad had managed to seal the vent thoroughly — or so his men promised. All Mqrisi needed now was for the woman to put down the dish for just a second on the counter beside her. Just put that thing down, he breathed, just for a second or two, and I can give the signal. Just so you don't drop it when you get ultra-ed. That'll save a hell of a cleanup. Mqrisi was ready to wait an hour or so. The log showed they did put it down occasionally.

The team with the portable airlock stood by in their pressurized suits to clamp onto the gene lab's door and rush in, meter the air for virus, and, if clean, get the hostages out. They might be revivable from the gas, and the ultrasound was not headed their way.

"They're here," whispered Hideki.

Passarin couldn't see a thing.

But Hideki was certain, for she moved straight to the airlock. She waited less than a minute and then opened it. The weirdest bunch of people came in. Party hats and magicians' robes, wands and face paints and, under one joker's arm, a large and apparently real ginger cat dressed in a suit. There were eight of them.

While Passarin, Mana, and José watched open-mouthed, the clowns — for so they appeared — took out big, colored crayons and started drawing little patterns on the floor. Soon the patterns started to join up. Within five minutes, one huge, intricate, multicolored mandala took up half the cleared space on the floor.

"They must be wraiths!" whispered Mana. "Starlight wraiths."

Hideki stepped into the center of the pattern and placed a tiny projector on the floor. She touched it and stood back. A hologram of this end of Sky Colony sprang out from it. She had colored the Seaview Room green and the gene labs blue. The wraiths studied it and looked at the Seaview Room around them, apparently judging scale.

Hideki came over. "They say someone's got to go in," she said. "Best be you, Passarin. The wraiths will whip you in there, above the floor, of course, and hold you there a minute or so while you get the women in a circle, all holding onto one another and you. Understood? Then you shout 'Go!' and they whip you and everyone who's hanging onto you back out here, five feet up, and you all drop to the floor in a heap. Got it?"

"What do I say to them?" Passarin's stomach had fallen a mile, his skin cold and clammy. How the hell . . .

"You'll have to work that out. You know them. I don't."

A sudden dream memory sparked a crazy idea. One of the wraiths was dressed in a wide, white, floor-length magician's robe dotted with moons and suns. "Can I borrow your robe?" Passarin asked him.

"Good idea. You'll show up better. Have you done this be-fore?" asked the wraith. His voice was surprisingly thin for so flamboyant a character.

"You must be joking."

"It would be even better if you were up above us, or in a bright light. Then we can see and hold you better. Kuan-yin," he asked Hideki, forgetting her Sky name, "are there lights here, apart from that one. . . ?" The wraith was looking at the spot-light that came down on the star map. "Here, put my robe on," he said to Passarin. The wraith pulled it off over his head and revealed a pair of blue-starred long johns. Passarin ducked into the robe. "Quick," said the wraith. "Get up on there."

Mana and the wraith helped Passarin climb up onto the slop-ing star map table. He looked down at himself, a brilliant white figure in the light, dotted with moons and suns.

"Perfect," said the wraith. He went to join his friends, who had sat down upon their crayoned pattern in a tight circle around the hologram of the building, leaving one space for him. Each sat in lotus, with their arms around one another's shoulders. They began to hum and their upper bodies to sway.

Govind prayed. He prayed for himself as well as for Gauri. "Great Spirit, with this death of the whore after whom I lusted, let all my lust die. Let her be forgiven and purified in heaven, and let us meet one day chaste, made absolutely pure by the fires of your cosmic love . . ."

Mqrisi beamed inwardly at the smoothness of the operation, the way he had sidestepped any Tarcunan or Skyer interference by swift and autonomous action.

He looked down at his screen, where his excellent nightscope technology cut through the dark of the gene labs to the fat, sleepy woman by the ventilation outtake.

Kumi felt the stiffness in her right arm, and switched the petri dish to her other hand. She rubbed her eyes with her right hand and yawned.

Mqrisi cursed inwardly.

The wraith circle in their crazy costumes swayed and sang in a growing frenzy. Soon they seemed less a motley crew of jesters than a single writhing entity unlike anything human that Passarin had ever seen. Their song became more of an animal scream, an angelic vibration, a metallic feedback loop . . . There was a promise of extraordinary power in them — either that, or they were going to melt or explode as they shimmered beyond what would seem physically and mentally supportable. For the first time he could believe it was people like this that made the space-ships go.

He balanced on the star map, his cloak spread out around him, and closed his eyes. He tried to think only of Gauri — would he recognize her? — and of his instructions to her. He tried not to think of appearing in the middle of a wall or of some gene-lab equipment. Perhaps in a person — in Gauri herself? Hideki had said there would be a massive explosion. At least I'll take Govind with me, he thought — along with everyone else on Sky, once the explosion loosed the virus. He tried not to think of it. He opened his eyes, to watch the writhing wraith-being.

Its frenzy climaxed. For a moment the wraith-creature hung suspended on its own energy, and then their heads and shoulders drooped, separated.

Hell, thought Passarin, it didn't work.

I'm still here.

Oh Mary, our Mother, how can I go through that again?

Oh Gauri . . . wait for me.

Then he saw that the hologram in their midst had changed. It showed now a dark, shadowed area, perhaps . . .

"It's all right, Passarin," said Hideki, beside him. "They sent the projector in to take a snapshot — make sure they had the positioning right. They'll adjust now, and do you." Hideki looked remarkably cheerful.

"God, you might have told me!"

The wraiths patted one another's backs and started a slow hum again.

Govind prayed for Gauri to enter paradise, and for the success of the Govindi revolution across all three central planets.

Mqrisi gave himself another forty minutes of waiting before he would go in anyway.

Kumtacj slapped herself on the cheek to wake up. How many more weeks was this going to go on?

The wraith circle's frenzy climaxed for a second time. Mana saw the unified being freeze at climax, a single creature in time suspension, their torsos stretched up, taut, their heads together, unbearable tension. This time they stayed that way. She tore her eyes away from them. Passarin was gone.

Light flashed as brilliant as an explosion in the gene labs.

Mqrisi yelped as his screen went white. He blinked to try and see.

Kumi fell back against the counter. Stars and spirals zigzagged across her eyes.

The women woke with the afterimage of the flash half blinding them.

Mqrisi readjusted the nightscope controls.

Mqrisi and the women saw a vertical shaft of light. A man hovered within, dark-haired and golden in the light. His cloak dazzled their eyes.

"Don't be afraid!" he said. "I come from Gaia. Quickly, gather around me. I come to take you away. Do as I say and you will be safe. Gather in a circle around me, and hold tight to one another and to me. Be quick. Get up! NOW!"

"He is the Goddess," said Kumi as the stars spiraled through her brain. Still miraculously holding the petri dish in one hand, she stumbled over to the women and started dragging them to their feet with her other hand. "Do as he says!"

Mqrisi's mouth had dropped open.

"No!" shouted Gauri. "The Goddess is us. She is within us. She is not a spirit to send angels. This is a trick. This is a Sky God hologram!"

Passarin hung in midair. A swirl of tingling force wrapped him around and dazed him. He felt that if he put out his hands he could zap the frightened hostages, the awestruck women, with fantastic energy. I am an angel, he thought. Or am I a hologram? He pinched himself on the arm.

"Feel me! Gauri, come here and feel me. It's me. Don't you recognize me?" He saw the little top on the floor where she lay cowering. "I gave you that top!"

"Is it you?"

"Get around me in a circle: the wraiths can only hold me a few seconds more. A circle, holding onto me and one another."

"Yes, Kumi, do it!" Gauri leapt up. "Everyone, a circle."

They did it, painfully slowly, taking seconds.

"All ready?"

"No! Kumi, put the damn virus down!"

She knelt to put it down on the floor. Gauri kept a grip on her fatigues shirt.

"Now!" Mqrisi shouted to the ultrasound and gas teams.

"Now!" yelled Passarin to the wraiths.

Govind dug his nails into his palms and sweat burst from his brow.

The ultrasound and gas fired.

In a blinding flash of light, the women dropped five feet from nowhere onto the hard floor beside the wraith circle.

Mana, José and Hideki took their hands from their eyes and rushed forward to help them up.

The wraiths collapsed backward from their circle until each lay separate, alone and immobile on their patterned floor.

Passarin had been five feet off the floor in the labs already, and so he had fallen ten feet. But the tingle of light energy had still been in him, and he landed easily, on his toes. There were screams and groans around him. He tried to help everyone up.

Heads had banged and pregnant bellies had been badly bruised. They were all aching and completely disoriented. Kumi had landed on her broad butt and she was the second breeder to stand on her own power. The first had been Gauri, whose tumbling instincts had fired as soon as she felt the floor disappear from beneath her. Most of them finally found they were mobile, though there were three sprained ankles. Only one could not rise at all. She was very pregnant. Mana and Passarin tried to hoist her up even as Hideki hustled the others to the airlock, fitting respirators onto them as they went. José and Gauri helped get the respirators on. The sprained ones hobbled with arms around the shoulders of the fit. Kumi led the first five of the dazed throng out the airlock onto the beach. Only six people could go through the airlock at a time.

Gauri and José went back to where Mana and Passarin had the heavily pregnant woman almost onto her feet. "Let her lie down," Gauri said to Mana and Passarin. "She could miscarry. This is Nitaj. These are my friends from long ago, Nitaj. Haven't you got a stretcher? Where are we going?"

"Starship out on the beach," said Passarin. "To Starlight.

Hideki!" He shouted as she entered the airlock with the rest of the women. "Stretcher!"

"I'll get one from the ship!" she shouted. "Get the wraiths going!" She led the women out and in the darkness they could see her running ahead.

"Is it really you?" Gauri reached up and kissed him. She embraced Mana and José. "Thank you, all three."

"It's nothing to do with me," Mana replied. "I'm not coming."

"Nor me," said José.

"But Starlight's like Earth. Passarin told me about it. You'll love it!"

"Govind needs me." Mana shrugged. "Without you — he needs me."

"Don't blame it on me!" Gauri warned.

"Come on! The wraiths need help," said Passarin.

He went over to the circle of apparently unconscious bodies, and started to try to wake them. The others followed. As she shook awake a man with an orange fright wig, Gauri said, "So it's desire versus duty, is it, Mana?"

Mana gritted her teeth as she helped a wraith to his feet. Don't question me, her eyes said.

"Just answer me this: which one is it that holds the universe together?" Gauri asked as she put a wraith's arm around her shoulder and moved off to the airlock with him. All of them were stumbling to their feet now.

The airlock's inner door opened and Hideki came in out of breath, ripping off her respirator. She had a stretcher from the ship. "They're on board already," she said. "Get a move on."

Mana and Gauri lifted Nitaj onto the stretcher while Hideki ran to the door that led to the rest of the station, to listen. "Nothing yet," she came back. "I disconnected the airlock alarm for half an hour — that's all I'm able to do for routine maintenance. We've got eight minutes left before it goes off." She ran to the airlock as the wraiths grouped around it, strangely forlorn now in their party gear. They put on the respirators they had dropped by the airlock on the way in, and Hideki yanked the manual lever to let them out, six at a time. They staggered off in two groups into the darkness of the beach, toward the faintly visible grey shape of the ship.

Gauri and Passarin came up with the stretcher. "She's having contractions," Gauri said.

"Shit! It's only a hundred meters to the ship. They'll take care of her. Here, put a respirator on her. One for you, Passarin, one for Gauri. One for Mana — I'm sorry, I don't seem to have one for you — you must be the lover, what's your name?

"José."

Mana took the respirator from Hideki's hand and offered it to José. "Please," she said.

José stepped back, rigid and immovable.

Mana placed the respirator on the stretcher.

"Good-bye, Mana," said Passarin.

"She's not coming?" Hideki asked in alarm. "But she's got to. That was the condition."

"Condition?" Mana raised her eyebrows at Passarin. She saw Hideki transfer the respirator in her right hand to her left and slide the right hand into her fatigues pocket. She stepped briskly up to her and hugged her fiercely. "Thank you, Hideki, for all you've done," she said. "Don't spoil it by drawing a gun on me." Her hug had pinned Hideki's arms to her sides.

Mana looked over Hideki's shoulder at Gauri. "She's got something in her right pocket. Take it out for me." Hideki struggled. But Mana was surprisingly strong. Gauri lowered her end of the stretcher, forcing Passarin to do the same, and set it down on the floor. She got her hand over Hideki's inside her fatigues pocket, and the Starlight woman gave up. Gauri pulled out a hand-sized stun gun.

She offered it to Mana.

"No, I can't keep this. What if they find it on me? It's time we got out of here anyway. Good-bye, Gauri dear. Keep this woman covered while I leave." Gauri did as she asked. Mana let go of Hideki and stepped back. "Passarin . . . you did well. For an academic observer." She smiled, but kept her distance from him. She walked smartly away. José nodded to them and followed.

Gauri's eyes had a desperate sadness in them when they met Passarin's. "That's Mana," she whispered. "She'll never change. I couldn't force her."

He sighed. "No. You were right." He turned to Hideki.

"Well, what happens now? Is it all off? Do you bring them all back here again?"

"Don't be stupid." Hideki was furious. "We're almost out of time. Put on your respirators."

\*      \*      \*

In the corridor outside the Seaview Room, Mana and José waited for the closing click of the airlock. Then they stole back into the empty room, and made their way to the windows to catch a last glimpse. The spotlight still shone down on the star map, the night outside was still as dark, but their eyes were more adjusted now. They could make out the dark shapes of stretcher bearers and stretcher as they made their way carefully over the rough terrain, not daring a light. Behind them came a slighter figure.

"Gauri's holding the gun on them," Mana whispered. "I wish she hadn't taken my side. Then you'd be on board."

"And you would have a clear conscience about abandoning Govind, to go and run in a forest. You would have been forced at gunpoint to do what your heart desires."

They couldn't see the ship. The figures disappeared into the darkness. There was a long silence.

"I'm a fool," said Mana.

"Yes. You are."

"I'm a stupid, idiotic fool."

"This is true."

There was a further silence.

"So are you."

"I know. What shall we do about it?"

"Run."

"No respirators. I'm too old to run a hundred meters holding my breath."

"I'll take you on my back."

"You're a crazy woman. Can you do it?"

"Let's go."

They walked swiftly to the airlock. José grabbed the manual lever.

"So you're leaving us."

They turned. It was Govind.

"The Spirit hinted to me that you might be leaving by the same way our soldiers came in," he said. His walk across the room toward them contradicted the cool ease in his voice. Mana could see in every muscle the man's tense fury.

"We are not leaving. We just came here to look at the stars. We couldn't sleep. What soldiers?"

"These soldiers." Govind indicated the dozen uniformed men who were coming down the corridor and into the room.

"Come with us to Starlight, Govind!" Mana pleaded.

José swung down on the airlock handle. The door opened and an alarm blared out. Hideki's alarm-free half hour had ended.

The first thing Gauri said as the ship's airlock filled with air and she ripped off her respirator was, "What did you say to try to persuade her to come? Did you argue that Starlight could warm the Earth?"

Passarin, still holding the stretcher, could only nod.

The inner airlock door opened, and they entered the ship. It was tiny. Bruised women and exhausted wraiths were crammed up against one another, moaning and shifting against uncomfortable equipment, trying to obey the flashing sign which read: GET COMFORTABLE FAST — TAKEOFF IN TWO MINUTES. There seemed to be only one crew member, with the Starlight insignia stuck onto a dazzlingly striped green-and-purple shirt.

"Can't they do it?" Gauri would not let go. "Put Nitaj down. Can't they warm the Earth?"

Passarin put the stretcher down in the small area left for them. The crew member and Hideki pushed him away as they knelt to check on Nitaj. He pulled off his respirator. "Hideki said there used to be an Earth Project on Starlight, but it died. People don't care enough about somewhere so far away."

"Of course, there's an Earth Project," said the crew member as she read information from an instrument she'd touched to Nitaj's temple. "She's all right for takeoff. Let's go."

"What did you say?" Passarin and Gauri grabbed the woman simultaneously.

"My auntie has an old friend from dolphin camp who runs Earth Project. Formidable lady. Get a place to sit. Captain's ready to go."

"I've got to tell her," said Passarin wildly.

"Tell who?" asked the crew member.

"Mana," explained Hideki. "The other woman we were meant to pick up."

"You mean she isn't here?" The crew member was shocked. "It's Earth Project who requested her. Didn't you know that?" she accused Hideki.

"No one told me. I thought Earth Project was dead."

"Friggin mix-up. Where is she?" asked the crew woman.

"Anywhere on station by now."

"Didn't you see her?" asked Passarin. "They crept back in to watch us go. It'll take three minutes. I'll go. Open the airlock for me." He was pulling his respirator back on.

"No," said Hideki. "You're not going to give me the slip now. If anyone goes, I go."

"I can persuade her if anyone can. You can't. I know her. And don't worry. I'll leave my heart as guarantee, with Gauri. Will you take it?"

Gauri looked with shock and surprise into his intense eyes. They had been so gentle seven years ago, and now they were burning. But not like Govind's. The corners of his mouth were quivering with amusement. She could almost believe that he could persuade Mana in a mood like this.

"Oh well, if it's like that," said Hideki. "Why didn't you tell me before? Didn't know if she'd have you? No one tells me anything."

"I'll keep it," Gauri said to Passarin. "At least 'til you get back." Her smile was the most beautiful he had ever seen.

"Here, take two respirators for Mana and her friend," said Hideki. "I took all the ones from the airlock earlier to slow down pursuers. If there's the slightest sign of other activity, come straight back. I want that woman, but it's not worth endangering the ship. Understand? At worst, I'll leave without you. Now, run."

For a moment Mana thought Govind might agree. He put his hand on her arm as the soldiers came running across the wide room. They were shouting and leveling small hand weapons of some kind. José had the airlock open. She looked into Govind's eyes. He was angry. He was frightened. If only she had time!

She kissed him hard on the mouth, ripped her arm from his grasp, put both hands square on his chest and pushed him toward the yelling soldiers. He staggered back, knocking over two soldiers as they came. She leapt into the airlock and pulled the door to. Burn marks smeared into the side of the heavy frame as the door swung into it.

"Breathe deep!" José instructed. She took one great breath, and he pulled the exit lever. The alarm rose from a blare to a scream. Red lights flashed inside and out. They ran out into the toxic wasteland, leaving the airlock door open. It closed at once. In the red flashes they could see the squat gray metal ship on the beach. It was so small!

After ten paces José breathed and let out a hoarse scream. Mana stopped and turned to face him. She raised his arm, ducked her shoulder down into his waist, and rose with him slung over her shoulder. He was so light! Then she started to run again, still holding her breath.

Another ten paces and she knew she would never make it. She looked at the ship in desperation, and saw a door open in its side and a figure leaping to the ground. She staggered on, holding her breath.

When they were thirty paces apart, she could tell it was Passarin. He carried respirators. It would be all right.

Then it all went wrong. In one red flash of the airlock emergency light, Passarin was running toward her. In the next he was rolling on the ground. The next, he was lying, clutching his leg. She couldn't look back. She could hardly think as the pressure in her lungs and head mounted to the unbearable. Now Passarin was kneeling. Only fifteen paces. He was throwing something.

She staggered two more paces and fell toward the thing he had thrown. José rolled off her shoulder. She found the feel of rubber, pressed it into her face, and breathed. There was a foul odor and searing pain in her lungs. It was only half on. She fitted it more snugly, not bothering with the straps, and lay still, gasping in sweet oxygen.

She turned back to look. The soldiers were tumbling back into the airlock. They didn't have respirators, either! One of them took a shot. It seemed to be just a little handgun, probably a visual-aim thing or close-quarters heatseek — otherwise she and Passarin would be dead. The riot squad had not been expecting a fight. She watched the last one get back into the airlock. They must have thought they had hit her. Had they hit José on her back? She crawled over to him, took a deep breath, and pressed her respirator to his mouth. He was unconscious. I'm sorry, dearest, I'm sorry. Sitala and the forest buffalo — now you, my fault again.

But Sitala had lived.

She took back the respirator for several deep breaths, then quickly strapped it onto José's face and head. She stood, hauled his light, old body onto her shoulder and ran to Passarin. She set José down, put on the respirator Passarin handed her, and breathed again.

Passarin pointed to the building's airlock. The soldiers were coming out again. Where in blazes were the Starlight people?

Passarin stood, hopped on one leg, and fell in agony. They'd hit him again. Mana hauled José onto her shoulder again, steadied him with one hand, grabbed Passarin's fatigues at the shoulder with the other, and pulled him upright. He fainted and fell against her. With a strength that later she could never begin to duplicate, she got a grip with one arm around his body, and started dragging him toward the ship.

For long moments there was nothing but rough rock and red flashes and her breath rasping in her ears.

Then hands grabbed Passarin, and she looked up into Gauri's eyes. They were ten yards from the ship. I've done this before, she thought, as she saw the metal ladder and ran with José on her shoulder. She pounded her feet up the ladder and fell into the airlock. A moment later Gauri and Passarin fell on top of her. As the door slammed to and air flooded the chamber, the ship lurched upward.

Gauri pulled off her respirator, and gasped against the G forces pressing her down, "Now I believe."

As the inner airlock door opened, Mana dragged her respirator off and asked, "In Gaia's plan?"

Hideki and the Starlight crew woman brought oxygen and first aid to José and Passarin where they lay. Passarin gasped, "Him first. I'm only shot."

Mana did not know when the wraiths on the Starlight mother ship up in Sky orbit grabbed the little lander in their minds' eye and whipped it into space. But the G forces were suddenly less. Hideki and her crew woman worked for José.

"Will he make it?" Mana asked.

"He's been hit twice," said the crewman. "But it's the stuff in his lungs that might kill him. Good thing you got that respirator on him when you did. I think he'll make it. His heart's strong."

Passarin's eyes were open, and his hands were clasped in Gauri's. He had had nothing yet for his pain, but he looked blissfully happy. Mana smiled at them. "Gaia's plan works in funny ways, but it works. In spite of people like me. I'm glad you believe."

"To hell with supernatural plans," Gauri said. "What I believe is that you killed Snow Tiger."